THE PLAYBOY BILLIONAIRE

AN OPPOSITES ATTRACT ROMANCE

THE FRAZER FAMILY
BOOK TWO

ZOE DOD

Edited by
V STRAW

MILKY DOWN PUBLISHING

Copyright © 2024 by Zoe Dod

All rights reserved.

No part of this book may be reproduced in any form or by any electronic or mechanical means, including information storage and retrieval systems, without written permission from the author, except for the use of brief quotations in a book review.

This is a work of fiction. Names, characters, places, incidents and dialogues are products of the author's imagination or are used fictitiously. Any resemblance to actual people, living or dead, or events is entirely coincidental.

The Playboy Billionaire is written in British English.

ISBN ebook: 978-1-917413-02-2

ISBN paperback: 978-1-917413-03-9

Editor: Victoria Straw

Cover Design by ChristineCoverDesigns

To Lolly
I'm so proud of you.
Love Mum xxx

CHAPTER 1

CALEB

"Evening, Mr Frazer. Welcome back."

I pause as the doorman opens the door and thank him as I pass.

The hotel lobby is a hive of activity, with guests checking in, others milling around, and some sitting on the vast sofas, drinking and chatting. Everything I've grown up to expect from a Frazer hotel. A grand chandelier that lights the foyer, reflecting off the marble walls and floors. Dark artwork is positioned to add contrast and depth. The private seating areas are welcoming and practical, opposite the reception desk.

I inhale and smile, the signature scent of the Frazer Hotels surrounding me. The zesty and vibrant bouquet transports me home. It's the same scent my mother introduced years ago, and it's still used worldwide. Hats off to Kat, my big sister, for the opulence and elegance—she knows what she's doing.

"Evening, Mr Frazer. Can I get you anything?" the concierge asks me as I move to collect my key card.

"No, thank you, Annie," I say.

It's getting late. Jet lag may no longer be an issue, having been here for two weeks, but Jaxson wants to get the latest plans finalised and submitted as soon as possible, which means another early start.

Soft piano music drifts out of the bar area, drawing my attention. I collect my card and move towards the sound. Our dinner lasted longer than we expected, but we made progress. It's also what happens when friends get together. And Jaxson has become that over the years. A friend. My brain is buzzing with the ideas we've thrown around tonight. Tomorrow's meetings will be intense. One drink—better in company.

I've never been one to enjoy drinking alone, preferring my whiskey surrounded by others.

After taking my usual seat in the corner, the waitress brings me my order.

"Are you waiting for someone, Mr Frazer?" she asks, her interest clear.

"Not tonight," I tell her honestly. "A drink before bed."

I don't miss the unspoken invitation she sends me as she places my drink on the table. I watch as she turns, the sway of her hips intentional as she walks away. I've never been shy when it comes to the opposite sex. A beautiful woman should be savoured like a fine wine. I look away, knowing I won't be taking her up on her offer of company. Kat will have my balls in a vice if I mess around with any of her staff. It's her one stipulation to all of us, but Kat always looks at me when she presses home that point.

A flash of blond catches my eye. Endless toned legs, killer red heels, and a black dress that accentuates every curve. My attention is fixed as I watch her navigate her way to the middle of the bar. I nurse my whiskey and watch her over the top of my glass. I guess she is a model by the graceful way she moves, but then again, how she's pulling and tugging at her dress? No, definitely not a model. I smile and take a drink, enjoying the burn, but my attention is still focused on the newcomer. It appears she'd be more comfortable in leggings or jeans than in her current attire.

She takes a seat.

Before I know what I'm doing, I walk across the room to the bar, stopping beside her. She pauses, letting me know she's aware of my presence, but makes no outward acknowledgement. The bartender delivers her order.

"Add it to my tab."

"No… thank you." Her tone is sharp as she turns towards me. My breath catches as deep blue eyes lock on mine, her gaze narrowing as she glares at me.

"Ah, a fellow Brit?" I say, ignoring her obvious annoyance, instead dropping onto the stool beside hers.

She raises one eyebrow and shoots me a glacial stare before returning her gaze to the bartender.

"Please tell the gentleman I'm not interested."

He shoots me a look of panic, and I grin. He knows who I am, but it appears the little firecracker next to me doesn't. This will be interesting.

Her pale cheeks develop a rosy glow when she takes in his expression.

"Never mind," she says, swivelling her stool to face me. "Can I help you?"

I bite the inside of my mouth to stop myself from smirking. Her eyes flash fire, yet there is still no recognition.

She doesn't know who I am.

I relax, and she folds her arms over her chest.

"I saw—" I don't get any further before she rolls her eyes.

"Oh, please. You saw me across the room and just *had* to come across and introduce yourself?"

"Well…" For the first time ever, I'm at a loss for words.

She raises an eyebrow and rolls her hand as if urging me to say something.

"Go on then. What's your best line?"

I cough, making her smirk.

The bartender drops his head, concentrating on the glass he's been polishing repeatedly. When I look over, he moves to the far end of the bar.

I smile. "I don't need lines." Or at least I haven't until now. Usually, my face and name do the talking for me.

She looks me up and down before shaking her head, her lips tilting at the corners.

"Why doesn't that surprise me? I just bet you have all the women falling at your feet."

I stare at the woman beside me, my heart rate picking up. I haven't felt this excited about meeting someone in a while.

"So if I were to try a chat up line on a stranger in a bar, where should I start?" I ask, turning my stool to face her before leaning an elbow against the bar.

She purses her lips and lets out a breath. "Now that would be telling," she says.

"How about I start with, hi, I'm Cal," I say, holding out my hand.

She glances down, her head inclining.

"April," she says, placing her small, delicate hand in mine, giving my hand a single shake before letting go.

I lean forward before whispering so only she can hear. "Well, April, I'm pleased to meet you because I'm sure you'll be invading my dreams. As a wine connoisseur, which I can assure you I am, I can only imagine you taste like a *fine* wine…"

Her eyes widen at my words, her lips twisting as she tries hard to suppress her smile.

"Nothing about how I look?" she says, quirking one eyebrow.

"Now… I could say you look *beautiful* in that dress, but that's not very original. I think I'll go with your smile as my absolute favourite."

Confusion crosses her brow, and I grin.

Realisation dawns, and I see her lips twitch at the corners.

"I knew it would be."

I watch her eyes sparkle as she battles to contain the smile that threatens.

"Impossible," she says, rolling her eyes before finally giving in. "Are you always this forward?"

Her smile steals my breath.

"Only when I'm in the company of a beautiful woman," I tell her truthfully.

This earns me a groan.

"Too much?" I ask.

"Definitely."

Only this time, her smile remains, her eyes twinkling.

My intrigue grows.

Who is this woman?

It's been a long time since I spoke to anyone who isn't in awe of my last name. Is it possible, or could this be an act?

"Are you drinking alone?"

"I'm waiting for friends," she explains, as her phone pings on the bar in front of her.

The name Samuel flashes up on the device, and I'm surprised when my ribs grow tight.

"Damn you, Samuel," she says, picking up her phone and reading the message she's received.

"Is everything all right?"

She turns, her shoulders dropping. "My friends got held up. They're going to be late."

"Well, I'm happy to keep a fellow Brit company. Until they arrive."

"It's fine," she says.

I shrug and move to stand. "No worries, have a pleasant evening."

I go to turn but freeze when her hand lands on my arm.

"I'm sorry, that was rude. Please finish your drink. I'd like the company while I wait."

I turn my head away and smile, sitting back beside her.

"Business or pleasure?"

"Pardon?" she asks.

"Are you in New York on business or for pleasure?"

Her smile illuminates her face, and my breath catches.

"Pleasure. I'm here visiting a friend. He's been touring with the London cast of Mischief. Tonight is their last night in New York. We're going out to celebrate. How about you?"

"Business, with some pleasure on the side."

I shoot her another grin.

She shakes her head… tough crowd.

"How long are you here for?"

I wonder if I can see her again after tonight.

"I leave tomorrow," she says, her gaze returning to her drink. "Then it's back to reality."

"What is reality?"

"I'm a dancer," she says.

Well, that explains the toned legs and arms. My body hardens as I imagine those thighs wrapped around my waist or, more interestingly, around my head. My body temperature rises, although I clamp down on it.

"Classically trained?" I ask, and she smiles.

"Yes, although I mainly teach now."

"Have you visited the David H. Koch Theatre and seen the ballet while you've been here?" I ask, suddenly wanting to know more about her.

She shakes her head. "No. Sadly, there hasn't been time. I'm here in a supportive role. I have, however, been to see

THE PLAYBOY BILLIONAIRE

Mischief twice. And if you ever get to see it in the future, I can highly recommend it."

Her smile remains, but it's impossible to miss the longing look in her eyes when I mentioned the ballet.

"Favourite ballet?" I ask, wanting to see her sparkle return.

She grins. "Now that one is easy. And you may think it's unoriginal, but it has to be Swan Lake. The music, the choreography…"

She trails off before straightening her spine and staring me in the eyes.

"What about you? Are you a patron of the arts?"

My mind wanders to the actresses, pop stars, and dancers I've dated. I can be accused of being an avid supporter of *the arts*, but I don't think that's quite what she means.

"I'm not averse to the ballet, although my favourite is Don Quixote."

"Ahh, that makes sense. One must genuinely live their life passionately, despite what other people think," she says, narrating the story's message.

I nod. "Although I must admit, I prefer Formula One and fast cars."

She rolls her eyes and laughs. "I should have guessed."

I grin, and her shoulders relax.

"I also saw Mischief in London before it left on tour," I admit, earning myself a quirked brow.

"A man of diverse tastes. I'm impressed," she says, holding her drink and clinking it against mine.

"Are you going to the Grand Prix while you're here? It's in Vegas this weekend, isn't it?" she asks.

I nod.

"I'm flying out on Sunday with some friends. My business and pleasure," I tell her, widening her smile.

She really has the most expressive face.

"Once your pleasure is over. What will you be returning to?" April asks.

"I'm in property development," I tell her, watching for recognition.

Still nothing.

"So, you're good with your hands?" she asks, the twinkle evident in her eyes, making my breath catch.

"Among other things."

* * *

APRIL'S LAUGH IS NATURAL, and it's a breath of fresh air to talk to someone who isn't fawning all over me because of the Frazer family name. Tonight, I'm enjoying being Cal, not Caleb Frazer.

My eyes are drawn to her almost white blond hair and pale complexion, strikingly contrasting my olive skin and dark eyes. A rush of desire floods south as I imagine her pale skin stretched out against my darker complexion.

She looks over my shoulder and gasps. Her expression lights up as she jumps to her feet. Before I know it, a man appears at my side, pulling her into a bear hug.

"I'm sorry," he says, his accent also British. "The producer wanted a word with us all before they packed up. We have a few days off before we open in Philadelphia, and he wanted to read us the riot act."

April grips his arms, and my stomach drops.

"Don't worry," she says, looking up at him.

It's then he seems to realise she's not alone. Pulling back, he turns to face me, his eyes widening before grinning.

"Samuel," he says, holding out his hand. "And you are?"

"Cal."

I smile.

Samuel takes my hand in his and shakes it. "Pleased to meet you, Cal."

His gaze returns to April, his head tilting. I hold my breath and wait.

Have I been made?

"Cal has been keeping me company while I was waiting for you," she says, sliding her arm through his.

His grin widens, and I exhale. Maybe my secret is safe for another couple of hours. "Wonderful. Thanks for looking after my girl. We're about to head out to a club. Would you like to join us?" Samuel asks.

I flinch at his use of the term *my girl*.

Are these two an item?

I see him grimace, his eyes flying to April. I bite my lip when I notice her hand on his waist, her knuckles white as her fingers dig into his side.

"I'm sure Cal has better things to do," she says, her tone firm.

"No, nothing," I say, turning my attention back to her friend. "I'd love to join you. Where are you heading?"

Samuel's enthusiasm is genuine.

"That's great." He grins as April outright glares at him. "The rest of the gang are meeting us at Odyssey," Samuel adds, ignoring April's obvious annoyance.

I stifle my smirk.

"Give me a moment." I get up and move away, pulling out my phone before turning back and asking. "How many?"

"Ten."

I turn away only to hear Samuel stage whisper to April. "Wow, baby girl, where did that bundle of hotness pop up from? I can't leave you alone for a minute."

His tone has no aggravation, so maybe they aren't together.

My phone connects, so I don't get to hear her reply.

"Devlin. Caleb Frazer. Can I get entrance for eleven?"

"Sounds like quite a party. I'll have the champagne chilling."

My friend laughs.

I wait as I hear him tap on his keyboard.

"It's done. I take it I'll be seeing you in Vegas this weekend?"

"Need you ask?" I say. "Thanks, Dev, I owe you one. I'll catch you at the race."

CHAPTER 2

APRIL

"It's not what you think. Cal came over when I entered the bar. We were talking. Why the hell did you invite him to join us?"

Samuel looks over, his face serious for the first time since he entered the bar.

"Because, baby girl, when I walked in here, I saw your face. It was animated, and you were smiling, I mean really smiling. I don't see that look often and want to see it more."

His eyes wander over to where Cal is on the phone, and he inhales deeply.

"Have you looked at tall, dark, and stunning over there? If he wasn't as straight as a rod, I'd be stealing him out from under you. Or over you."

Before I can say anything else, Cal returns.

"We have access," he says, putting his phone away.

I recognise the look in Samuel's eyes and pinch the bridge of my nose.

I say nothing. Instead, I follow them out of the hotel, listening as they chat like old friends.

Who am I to complain? This whole trip is courtesy of my bestie.

A flight to New York is a little out of my current budget, with all my money pumped into my dance school.

The doorman calls us a taxi. Cal helps me into the cab before giving the address of the club.

When we pull up, the queue is around the block. Like a gentleman, Cal climbs out and extends his hand, which I accept. My fitted dress and killer heels may look the part, but they make it hard to manoeuvre with any finesse. He grips my hand, interlinking our fingers, before guiding us towards the doorman. Samuel motions to his group of friends, who all step forward, their excitement palpable.

Cal murmurs something to the doorman, who smiles before nodding and stepping aside, allowing us to pass.

The music is thumping inside the club, and the dance floor is alive with movement. We find ourselves ushered towards the VIP section and a reserved table.

"O. M. G. Who have you pulled?" Samuel says close to my ear.

I hiss at him as Cal pulls me further into the area.

"Champagne?" Cal asks, his breath tickling my ear, sending butterflies loose in my stomach.

"Yes, please," I reply, my breath hitching.

As I turn my head, our lips are millimetres apart. I refrain from running my tongue over my lips as his eyes sparkle.

Oh hell. Who is this man, and what has happened to my restraint?

I weigh up what I know. Cal exudes power and confidence, and he clearly has influence. He gets us entrance to this club with one phone call when the queue is around the block. I watch him ordering our drinks. He looks away for a second and motions to one of the waitresses working in the area, pointing to the group and giving her our order. She smiles, and her cheeks flush. I'm clearly not the only one affected by this man's presence, although I'm a little unnerved when his attention immediately returns to me. He exudes charisma and charm, a lethal combination. I doubt he's ever been turned down in his life.

I find myself smiling at him. Something is intriguing about him, aside from his drop-dead good looks.

The man is hot, and he likes musicals, ballet and F1.

Maybe it's the romance of New York. My last night before reality takes over. My work-imposed dry spell. For some reason, my usual rationale sounds weak. I must be losing my mind. I return my gaze to Cal, only to find myself drowning in his dark eyes.

Oh hell, I'm done for.

I'm here with the most gorgeous, attentive man I have met in a long time. We may be surrounded by beautiful people, but his eyes haven't strayed once.

I look over at Samuel, who is sporting an enormous grin. He shoots me a wink and blows me a kiss. This is our last night together for another three months. I'll miss him, but I also want my bestie to have the best night.

A hand touches my arm, warmth spreading from where it connects with my skin.

"Do you want to dance?" his voice says close to my ear.

I turn to face him, our faces close. "I'd love to."

* * *

THE ELEVATOR DOORS CLOSE, and Cal has me backed up against the wall before I can think. His mouth crashes down on mine, my lips parting, allowing him access. From the moment his lips touch mine in the club, I've known where the evening will end. My body is hot, my clothes are too tight. I don't think I've ever felt this desired or turned on.

His tongue tangles with mine, his hand sliding down my thigh, lifting it against his hip. He rocks into me, leaving me in no doubt of his desire.

I moan at the sensation.

When the door pings, Cal pulls away, his eyes never leaving mine as he clasps my hand in his and leads me across the hall and towards a door. His keycard is already in his hand. The light flashes green as he pulls me into the room, the lights coming on. Illuminating the space.

My jaw drops as I take in our surroundings.

Before I can say anything, Cal is in front of me, his hands cupping my cheeks, drawing my attention back to him.

"Now," he says.

His mouth drops to mine, and his tongue teases the seam of my lips, which I'm happy to give. He moans into my mouth, pulling me closer, his kiss becoming more desperate and demanding. I jump, wrapping my legs around his waist, as he walks us into another room, kicking the door closed behind us.

"Now, little dancer, the fun begins."

He lowers me to the floor, and I feel the zip on the back of my dress give. His lips find my throat, his mouth working its magic as a thousand butterflies take flight low in my stomach. Strong fingers tease the straps on my shoulders until my small breasts spring free as he lowers it, my nipples tightening in the cold air.

He lifts his head, his gaze connecting with mine as he teases the sensitive points with his thumbs. Dark eyes lock on mine as they harden further at this touch. He bends, drawing one of my nipples into his mouth, sucking and lavishing it with his hot tongue. The warmth is a sharp contrast to the air-conditioned room. I clench my thighs as a wave of pleasure shoots south, and I let out a low moan.

Cal recaptures my lips with his, nipping and teasing. He walks me backwards until my legs hit the edge of the bed.

He steps back and drops to his knees, sliding my dress down my thighs, letting it pool at my feet, leaving me in nothing but my lacy panties.

"Beautiful," he says, gazing up at me.

The look in his eyes makes me believe him. This is one night. What harm is there in allowing myself to go with the fantasy? Being swept off my feet by a handsome stranger.

He stands up and drops his mouth to mine. He gently pushes me backwards until I find myself lying across the bed. The back of his finger traces a line from between my breasts to my stomach. My muscles contract at his touch.

"A fine wine," he says, making me giggle. A sound alien to my ears.

I wrap my hand around his neck, my fingers grazing the soft, short hair at the nape. Cal moves over me and deepens the kiss. I pull him down on top of me, loving the hard feel of his body against mine. My naked skin against his clothes. I can't believe I'm here doing this. Not that I have a sex issue. I like it. I don't go for one-night stands, choosing some connection to none. But in a few brief hours, Cal has breached my barriers.

I drop my head back as he works his way down my neck, finding every sensitive spot until I am squirming beneath him.

I clasp his head in my hands as his mouth once again finds my nipple, his hands snaking lower.

Cal pulls my panties to one side, his fingers trailing through the evidence of my desire.

"So wet," he murmurs against my skin. "Do you like this? Are you wanting to ride my cock?"

My hips undulate beneath his fingers, and I let out a groan.

"I take it that's a yes," he says, sliding first one, then a second finger into me, pumping in and out, stretching me before curling against my g-spot and almost making me come on the spot.

"Ahhh," I manage before Cal's lips crash onto mine again.

"Clothes off," I say, breathlessly against his mouth.

I feel him grin as he pulls back.

"If you want them off, then you need to take them off," he says, standing at the foot of the bed.

I rise onto my knees, catching my bottom lip between my teeth as I move forward before resting my hands against his chest.

My fingers move to the buttons, relishing the firm muscles I'm about to uncover, feel pressed against me. The shirt parts under my hands, and I smooth it away from Cal's shoulders, loving the expanse of toned olive flesh.

This is a man who clearly takes care of himself.

I push it down over his shoulders, surprised to uncover a tribal tattoo circling his left bicep. I let my fingers trail over the black-and-white design.

Cal grips my chin in his fingers, tilting my head up before recapturing my mouth, stealing my breath again. His hands drop, and it's only then I realise he's dropped his trousers.

I press a hand against his chest and tilt my head, my tongue moistening my lips.

His boxers stretch as the tip of his hard, swollen cock almost pops out of the top, revealing a damp patch of pre-cum.

"Like what you see?" Cal asks as I raise my eyes to his.

I lick my lips at his words. I don't think I have ever wanted to taste another person as much as I do the man standing before me.

I drop my hands to the elastic, never moving my eyes

from his. I push them down, and our gazes lock as my hand travels up and encircles him.

Holding his gaze, I climb off the bed and drop down onto my knees, letting my tongue lap at his tip before stretching my mouth over the end.

"Fuck," he hisses before letting out a deep groan.

His hands sink into my hair. His fingers lock against my scalp but allow me free rein to savour and tease. I look up. His eyes are almost black, his cheeks darkening with my ministrations. I swallow around him, eliciting another groan, before I find myself back on the bed and flat on my back, his body covering mine, his hard cock, still wet with my saliva, nestled between my thighs, its impressive length pressing against my most sensitive place. I tilt my hips, rubbing myself against him, coating him with my desire.

"Do you know how easy it would be to slide my cock into you right now?" he says breathlessly, pressing himself against me. "You're dripping for me."

"What are you doing to me?"

I moan, my hips undulating against his. I've never been this carefree and easy with anyone. It's like he's cast a spell. My body is no longer my own. It's a slave to passion, to everything this man is making me feel. His words make me reckless. I spread my legs wider, sliding myself up and down his rigid dick.

Cal moans, his hips pressing against mine. Taking his cock in his hand, he torments my clit with his tip, sending sparks of desire through my body, a telltale pressure building low in my pelvis.

"God, Cal... please," I hear myself beg, making him chuckle.

He moves to one side, and I hear foil tearing before he's back.

"I need to taste you first," he says against my mouth.

His lips slide down my neck and body before he positions himself between my thighs.

He presses an open mouth kiss to my pussy. His tongue laps from my entrance to my clit. He drinks me down. His lips, tongue, and teeth send my body soaring higher and higher. My hands fist the sheets as my body spirals towards the edge as Cal teases my entrance with the tip of first one, then a second finger.

"Cal," I yell.

One hand fists in his hair as he uses his tongue and fingers to drive me higher. He presses in and curls his fingers against my g-spot, the burn of his invasion skyrocketing me higher.

"Relax, beautiful," he says against me, gently easing his fingers in and out, twisting and stretching me, heightening my desire.

I drop my head back, biting down on my arm, the pressure of my orgasm rising.

"I'm going to…" Cal removes his fingers before I can finish my sentence, and I growl in frustration.

"Oh no, when you come, I want you strangling my cock. Not my fingers," Cal says, his lips finding the space below my ear that has me squirming beneath him. "I want your tight little pussy wrapped around me. Is this what you want?" His deep voice whispers next to my ear as he presses the tip of his cock to my opening. I spread my legs wider.

God, yes, this is what I need.

My hands slide around the back of his head, pulling his mouth back to mine. My eyes widen at the taste of my own desire on his lips.

He presses forward, the swollen head of his cock breaching my entrance. The size of him burns and my muscles clench. I now understand why he used his fingers to prepare me. He was big in my mouth, but… I moan as he presses forward, my body stretching to accommodate him. My desire makes it easy for him to slide into me, but still. It's been a while. With work and my lack of funds, socialising and sex have been low down on my priority list.

I moan at the sensation. My arms wrap around Cal's back as my fingers dig into his shoulders.

"Breathe, baby. Take a deep breath in," Cal whispers against my lips, allowing my body to adjust to his presence. "That's it, relax for me."

As soon as he feels me relax, he presses forward until he's fully seated.

"Little dancer," he murmurs, gently nipping my lower lip.

"Cal," I whisper, pulling his lip between mine and sucking.

I wrap one hand around his head, the other sliding down to his tight ass. My fingers dig into the hard muscle. I groan as he moves, my fingers tightening.

"You're so tight," he whispers, burying his head in my neck.

"It's been a while," I admit, wrapping my legs around his hips.

He sinks deeper.

I whimper at the invasion, my senses in overload. Cal kisses my nose, eyes, and cheeks until my body relaxes, a distinct pressure building. One that has me moving.

"Such a good girl," he whispers against me. "Feel how you're hugging my cock. I can't wait to feel you coming all over it."

I moan at his words, not usually turned on by dirty talk but his husky voice and the way his dark eyes are drinking me in. I would do anything for this man at this moment.

Cal slides his hands under my ass and flips us. My legs bent on either side of his body, his cock buried so deep within me, I'm surprised I can't feel him in my throat.

"Oh... wow," I moan, grinding down on his cock when he chuckles.

He lets out a long and deep groan before he draws me up, allowing me to move against him.

"I need to come on your cock. Make me scream, Cal," I shock myself by saying.

"That's my girl," Cal says, his hands gripping my ass.

I draw up, my hands behind me for balance, as he once again thrusts home. We move, creating our own dance, his cock finding sensitive places I didn't know existed until now. When he finds my clit and pinches, my body explodes. My back arches and I throw my head back, letting out a scream as my body contracts and pulses around his. My hands fist the sheets as stars flash behind my eyes. He growls and continues to pump in and out of me, drawing out my orgasm.

"That's it, little dancer. Ride me."

I move my hips, sliding up and down Cal's rock-hard cock. He picks up the pace, grabbing my hips and driving in and out. Pressure begins to build again, and as if sensing my needs, Cal shifts position slightly, finding that perfect spot deep inside and sending us both over the edge. He freezes, his cock jerking as my muscles once again contract around him. He buries his head in my neck as he pants, his body stretches taut, his muscles twitching. I wrap my legs around his back and hold him close as I run my hands up and down his back.

He pulls back, his eyes staring into mine.

I smile at him shyly.

"That was..." A frown forms between his brows, both of us panting. "Amazing," he says eventually.

I lift, letting him pop from my swollen pussy.

His cock stands proud between us, the condom full of his release.

Cal tilts his head and gives me a panty-melting smile.

"Let me get rid of this," he says.

I uncurl myself from his lap, moving next to him as he gets up and moves to what I assume is the ensuite.

He returns naked, without the condom. His eyes sparkle, and he takes me in, lying used and dishevelled on the bed, my muscles still quivering.

"Hmm, now what should I do?" he moves back to the bed, dropping next to me, his hands trailing down my stomach, causing my muscles to jump and contract. He lowers his head, his mouth following, kissing and suckling. No one has ever worshipped my body like this man is right now.

He finally reaches the apex of my thighs, his fingers touching my engorged and swollen flesh. "So... Perfect."

His fingers slide over my sensitive skin, my hips jumping.

"Cal, I can't..." I pant.

"There is no such word as I can't."

I watch as Cal lowers his head, his hands spreading my thighs as his mouth once again finds my core, his tongue lapping at my clit and then my entrance, spearing me with his tongue.

"Now I need another orgasm from you, only this time you will be quivering on my tongue," he says before setting his mouth to work.

Who am I to complain? This is one night.

CHAPTER 3

CALEB

My hand goes to my eyes, my fingers rubbing over my eyelids to try to open them. Wow, last night. Snippets of the evening come back to me. My cock hardens as I'm flooded with the memories of the previous evening. A hot, tight body. Screams of pleasure echoing around the suite. Soft, demanding lips. *Coming* harder than I ever have before.

My ears tune in to the sounds around me. It's far too quiet. My hand snakes out, only to find cold, empty sheets. I listen for the sound of the shower, nothing.

I sit up. The sheet covering me drops to my waist. Suddenly awake, my eyes struggle to focus on the darkness. The heavy blackout curtains doing their job. I flip on the bedside light and look around. My clothes litter the floor, where they were abandoned in our speed to get to each other's bodies. But it's only mine. My little dancer's clothes are gone.

I drop back and fling my arm over my eyes.

"Fuck."

I throw back the covers and dive out of bed. Breathing a sigh of relief when I find my wallet in my jeans, untouched.

Dragging them on, I walk barefoot into the main area. The family suite is extensive. They are in all the family hotels. Fully catered and set up to allow the family to stay with minimal disruption. My grandfather started it, and my dad and sister continued the tradition. I can't complain. With the amount of travelling I do, it's nice to have a home from home.

I scan the room, checking for any sign of the woman who joined me last night. When I find nothing, I run a hand through my hair, frustration blooming in the pit of my stomach.

Did she sneak out?

Nothing seems to be missing. She must have simply got up and left when I finally fell asleep.

I look at the clock.

Seven-thirty.

We got back to the room at three. There was not much sleeping as we enjoyed each other's bodies.

I pull on a jumper and head downstairs, hammering on security's door.

A man in uniform opens the door, his face not hiding his shock at finding me there. "Mr Frazer. Um... Can I help you?"

"I came back with a woman last night." I'm not really thinking how that sounds until after the words leave my mouth. "Bert," I say, reading his name tag before giving him one of my most dazzling smiles.

He looks at me, his expression blank.

"I want to know who she is and where she went."

He steps back and lets me into the room. A wall of screens monitors different parts of the hotel, from the lobby to the dining room. Even the bar area.

"Was your visitor a guest of the hotel?" he asks, taking a seat at his desk, his fingers poised over his keyboard.

I grimace.

Maybe this wasn't such a good idea. I'm about to admit to a member of Kat's staff that I spent the night with a stranger I brought back to the family hotel and know next to nothing about.

She's going to kill me!

"April. Her name is April," I say, praying he doesn't ask me for a surname.

He types into his terminal.

"Not a guest," he says, turning his head to look at me. Nothing but professionalism showing on his face.

"We came back at around three AM," I say, pulling up a chair and dropping into it next to him.

He pulls up the lobby feed, finding the time I gave him and letting the feed run. Sure enough April and I appear. We're laughing, my arm around her, her hand resting on my chest, as she looks up at me. My stomach clenches at the sight of us.

"That's her," I say, watching as we disappear off-screen.

It was two minutes after this, we were in the lift. Me pressing April against the wall, our hands roaming freely. We barely reached the suite before tearing each other's clothes off.

Shit! I scan the monitors, letting out a sigh of relief. No lift cameras.

Kat really would kill me!

Bert skips the feed until April reappears. He lets the feed run, and I stare at the woman who has left me sleeping upstairs. Her clothes are in place, her hair scraped back, her face clear of any makeup. She walks confidently out of the front door without a backward glance.

I check the time stamp. Five AM.

My heart sinks. April is long gone.

"Is everything all right, sir?" Bert asks. "Did the lady steal anything? If she did, I can call the police."

I give him a weak smile. "No, April didn't steal anything," I tell him.

My eyes move back to the screen, and the picture Bert has frozen. I stare at April's image.

Not anything you can see that is…

CHAPTER 4

APRIL

My hand shakes as I re-read the letter.

This can't be right.

I heard about the development, but our building is occupied, with several businesses running out of it. I look at the date.

Shit!

This is dated over a week ago. The bloody post office.

I glance at the clock. I have half an hour before my first students are due to arrive. Pulling on my jacket, I head out of the front door and into Mable's Cafe next door. Several ladies are already there, drinking tea and eating cake. They look over and grin.

"Morning, Ms April. Oh, dear ladies, it looks like we've been caught," Alice says, grinning.

She's a white-haired lady in her early eighties and one of my regulars.

"Don't worry, Alice. I've seen nothing," I say, plastering a smile and going to the back.

I knock on the kitchen door. "Hi, Don, Betty."

I step through and into their tiny yet immaculate kitchen.

"April," Betty says, rushing forward and pulling me in for a hug. "What can we get you? Don't you have a class?"

I pause, absorbing Betty's hug, letting it sink into my weary bones. She pulls back, gripping my upper arms, her brow wrinkling.

"What's up?" she asks, her tone motherly.

Two years ago, they were the ones who first greeted me when I moved in. Their little cafe and my dance studio have thrived together. My dancers fill their tables before and after class.

I pull the letter out of my back pocket and watch resignation and understanding flash across her face.

"I wondered whether you'd received one too," she says, pulling me further into the kitchen and manoeuvring me onto a stool.

"Don. Customers," she says over her shoulder to her husband, who is listening, while wiping down and clearing away from the sandwiches he's been preparing.

"On it, dear," he says, gently squeezing my shoulder as he passes.

"I don't... what..." I stumble, not sure what I'm trying to say.

Betty sighs and leans against the counter.

"I don't know what to say, either," she says. "Apparently, the landlord is within his rights, even with a contract, to sell up."

"But—"

"You need to get a solicitor, April. Find out where you stand."

My heart sinks. More money, I don't have. As for a contract...

Betty continues.

"For Don and I, it's different. It's time we retired. I know Jerry feels the same way about his garage. He said it was time to put down his wrench and spend time with his grandkids. This is the push we all need."

I drop my chin to my chest. I know this. Crime on the rise in the area has just made everything harder. I can't blame them. I've chased off several lowlifes from outside the studio, trying to deal drugs to my kids. I've even installed dummy cameras as a deterrent. They don't need the stress at their age, so I can't blame them.

Betty grips my shoulders and squeezes. "You've invested a lot of time and money into your business. It's different for you."

Betty goes over to a drawer and pulls out a business card.

"We've used this man in the past. He's reasonable. He will look at your contract and tell you whether you have a case."

I take the card and pop it into my jacket pocket.

"Thanks, Betty, I'll call him," I say, giving her a hug. "I'd better get back, or Alice and her gang will be rioting."

Betty smiles and hugs me back.

"Take care. Don and I are here if you need us."

I hug Don quickly as I leave, my ladies following me out.

Time to dance away my blues.

* * *

I stare at the phone, my heart sinking.

My tenancy agreement is ending. The fixed period is up. According to Betty's solicitor friend, I don't have a leg to stand on. He apologised he couldn't be of more help. The landlord's word that I could have the property for as long as I like means nothing. Now he's selling. The developer has no obligation towards me or any of the previous tenants.

I sink to the floor and lean against the mirror that lines the wall. I look at the space that I call home. A space regularly filled with members of the community, my community.

Members of all ages, ranging from four to eighty-four. Since I opened the dance studio two years ago, they've come.

"Hey."

Samuel comes in and drops down next to me, pulling me into his side. I drop my head on his shoulder when he wraps his arm around me.

"We can fight this," he says, squeezing my shoulder.

"No, according to the solicitor, we can't." I sigh, sitting up and hugging my knees. "It's all lost."

The sprung dance flooring, the custom-made mirrors and bars. The sound system. I completely remodelled the place when I moved in. My stomach churns as I consider the investment I've made into this building. An investment that is worthless once the developer comes in and tears it down. "We cannot move the flooring, and the mirrors are too big to store. The cost alone of storage would be enormous. All my hard work and effort gone," I sigh.

"Since when did you become such a pessimist? This isn't the April Wilson I know." He mimics my position, resting his chin on his knees as he stares at me. "Have you tried speaking to the developer?"

I drop my head back against the wall and close my eyes. "I've been sending emails every day this week. All I get is a holding message telling me someone will be in touch."

"Hey, this isn't you. You're not someone who rolls over and gives up. You're a fighter."

I open my eyes and stare at my best friend. "Samuel, big developers aren't interested in the little people like us. I'm inconsequential in their eyes. I must face it. My landlord has screwed me over, but that isn't their problem. Frazer Development is a big business. They're interested in lining their pockets and appeasing their shareholders and board members. They want their fancy apartments and boutique shops. Not some second-rate dance studio with a—"

"Stop. There is nothing second-rate about your dance studio or your teaching. You're a first-class dancer," Samuel says.

I look away, unable to meet his optimistic gaze. That may be the case, but I'm obviously not a businesswoman. The worst part is, it's my fault. After discovering the building, I acted impulsively without considering the outcome. Instead of giving me a five-year lease, my landlord talked me into accepting a rolling contract. Renewing last year went smoothly, so I didn't give it much thought. I understand more and more local businesses have closed over the past two years, but my business is growing.

I swipe my cheek as the first tear falls. Samuel pulls me back into his arms and rocks me as I give in, and the floodgates open.

When I finally stop, he turns me to face him, his thumbs rubbing away the tear tracks. "Well, if they aren't answering your emails, we take the argument to them. How many students do you have?"

"And families, probably two hundred now," I say, my voice catching as I think of the fact a lot of the kids and teenagers use my studio as somewhere to go, keeping them off the streets. I offer a range of classes, from traditional ballet to street dance.

"Then we arrange a protest. Let's create banners to make this development company aware of the community's stake in this area. Make them listen."

"I don't know."

If I'm honest, I'm unsure whether the families and kids will want to be involved.

"Well, if you don't ask, beautiful, you don't get. Ask them. See what they think. Do you think these developers really want to piss off the locals?"

I stare into my friend's eyes before resting my forehead against his chest. Absorbing his strength.

"You've worked too hard to just let this go," he says, his voice vibrating through his chest wall.

"I know. You're right." I say, wrapping my arms around his waist and holding on tight as I absorb his strength. "I didn't give up four years of my life and my dignity to work as an exotic dancer, only to have my asshole landlord destroy all I've worked for. That is not who I am."

"That's my girl," Samuel says, giving me a squeeze.

He's right. I fought hard for this place. I don't have rich parents to fall back on. Being a foster kid, I've been financially independent since I turned eighteen, although I was luckier than most. My foster mum is a dance teacher. She has taught me everything I know. She is and always has been my greatest supporter, even when I was officially no longer her responsibility, and for that, I will be forever grateful.

"Okay. I'll ask."

He drops a kiss on my head and gives me a squeeze.

"We've got this," he says. "You're not on your own."

"I'm so glad you're home," I say, not sure what I'd do if he was still travelling. But he's right. It's time to stand up and fight—for my studio, these kids, my community. Not let some big shot developer walk in here and destroy all I've built.

CHAPTER 5

CALEB

The restaurant is bustling for a Wednesday night, but it only takes me a second to spot our table. Xander and Tristan are already here, their laughter echoing through the air. I make my way towards them. Our weekly get-together is the highlight of most weeks. It's something we've done since we all returned from university. That and socialising. But this is our time... boys' night.

"Caleb," Xander says, getting up and slapping me on the shoulder. "Thought you weren't coming."

"Ha, ha. I'm not that late," I say, grabbing the chair next to him. "I'm also not the last one here. Where are Marcus, Quentin?"

"Marcus is pussy whipped. Probably doing the laundry or something before he's allowed out." Tristan says, laughing.

"As for Quentin, he's probably lost track of the time shagging his latest secretary," Xander adds before pointing to the door where Marcus and Quentin have just entered. "Speak of the devil and his sidekick."

The guys walk over and sit down. Our waitress appears and takes our order.

"Sorry we're late. Lucy asked me to drop her off at a friend. Girls' night."

"Ahh, the joys of married life," Tristan sighs dramatically.

"Don't knock what you haven't tried," Marcus shoots back with a wink. Our friend is the first among us to take the plunge. His eyes move to Quentin, and whatever he sees has him flinching.

Quentin was due to fall first until his fiancée left him standing at the alter—literally.

"Well, I'm pledged to bachelorhood," Quentin says, raising his glass before taking a long swallow. "To those of us left in the Kingland Players."

The rest of us grimaces at the name we were given in college.

Our group of five became known as the playboys of Kingland College. A reputation we enjoyed and nurtured in our late teens and early twenties. But although life may have moved on, the name and our reputations have remained. A blessing and a curse, at least for most of us.

"How is your new secretary?" Tristan asks, rolling his eyes. "Happy and satisfied?"

"Completely," he laughs, but I notice it doesn't reach his eyes. It never does these days. I lean forward only to receive a glare that stops me in my tracks.

Tristan shoots me a look before changing the subject. "Has your new motor been delivered?"

"It has. I'm heading down this weekend to take it for a spin if anyone wants to join me. I've booked time at the track."

"I'm in," Xander says.

To my relief, Quentin nods. Getting away will do him good. They both share my love of fast cars.

"How many is that now?" Tristan asks.

"Twenty-five," I tell him.

Tristan shakes his head with a smile.

"I know, I know," I say with a shrug.

Some might say my car collection is getting a little out of control. But with a racetrack near my mother's.

What can I say? I love driving.

Each car has its own unique features and performance. It's also not something I get to enjoy on a daily basis living in the city.

"Fine. I'm in," Tristan says, grinning.

"I'll let Mum know to expect us."

I know my mother will be over the moon to have us all for the weekend.

A group of women enter the restaurant and take a seat at a table near ours, looking over and smiling. Xander and Tristan exchange a look, and I can already guess where this evening is heading. I sit back, leaving my friends to it. It isn't long ago I would have been a part of it. But since New York...

Marcus shakes his head. "Don't you guys want to find someone you connect with? What about you, Caleb?" he asks.

Quentin ruffles Marcus's hair hard. "Why would our super stud want to settle down? Last year, it was best friends in Monaco. He's constantly photographed with a string of models, not to mention that supermodel last week. He gets to play hard and party hard."

God, my friend makes me sound like a complete womaniser.

Last week, someone photographed me talking to a supermodel whose name I can't even remember. It was a ten-minute conversation, but the guys and the newspapers assumed she ended up in my bed. The truth is, I dropped her home at the end of the night when she couldn't get a taxi. I suppose that's the thing with reputations. Once they're established, they're hard to shift.

And the older I get...

Maybe Gabriel's settling down has rubbed off on me.

Identical twin juju.

Then again, who am I kidding? Love is a fairy story told to children, but like every story, it's a dream, an illusion.

"I'll leave the happily ever after to my brother," I say, ignoring the heaviness that's taken up residence in the pit of my stomach since New York. Her laughter, that smile, and not forgetting her body and those legs. I can't shake the memory. Not that I would ever admit that to the boys. April is my secret.

"To the continued dodging of social climbers and their mothers," Xander says, clinking his glass to each of ours. Xander fell prey at my mother's birthday party/fundraiser last summer, especially when everyone discovered my brother Gabriel was no longer available.

"You are all just cynical," Marcus says. "There will be a woman for each of you, mark my words. She'll sneak up on you when you are least expecting it."

The others groan at his words.

I am cynical. An excessive number of people pursue the Frazer name for their own gain, and I refuse to be used. I won't be one of those people who plays at love and marriage. I will not compromise and, therefore, have no intention of settling down.

We spend the rest of the evening chatting and catching up. The women from the other table come over, and we leave as a group, making our way to one of Tristan's bars. My best friend is making a name for himself. Has opened several wine bars across the city and is looking to expand into other major cities across the country.

Marcus makes a speedy escape as we move on, and I don't blame him.

One lady tries to sit on my knee, her hand trailing into

the short hair at the back of my neck. She leans in, the scent of her perfume triggering memories of another woman. A woman who vanished in a puff of smoke. If not for the smell of her perfume on my sheets, I may have assumed I dreamt her.

I tracked her friend Samuel's dance company to Philadelphia, but he was a bust.

SAMUEL SHRUGS. *"If she left leaving no forwarding information, then..." He doesn't need to finish his statement. I know he's right. She saw us as a one-night stand. I should be grateful. No awkward morning after conversation, no pretending to swap details you're never going to use.*

"I just wanted to check she was okay." I sound lame even to myself.

"She's fine. Got back to the UK in one piece," he says, the conversation getting awkward.

"No problem, that's all I wanted to know." I turn to leave.

"Hey, Cal," I stop as he calls my name. "Thanks. I haven't seen April smile like that in ages."

I nod. "Good luck with the show."

I leave.

Samuel is right. If she wanted me to have her details, she would have left them. I could have used Elijah to track her down, but that was stalkerish. Maybe I misread the whole night. If she wanted something more, she would have stayed instead of disappearing like a thief in the night.

"WANT TO COME BACK TO MINE?" the woman mutters, nipping my earlobe with her teeth.

I turn and stare at her, snapping myself back into the

present. "I really need to get going," I say, standing up quickly. Suddenly desperate for the peace and quiet of my apartment.

CHAPTER 6

APRIL

The number of people filling the dance studio surprises me. Samuel comes up and wraps an arm around my shoulders, giving me a squeeze.

"Don't look so shocked. You've done a lot for this community. They appreciate it."

I look up into his face. "I just hope it gets their attention," I say, annoyed I still haven't received an email from the company.

"Well, I've called the local radio and television stations, got the head office address. Hopefully, our little protest can get some traction. Make Frazer Development sit up and listen."

I don't know what I would have done if it wasn't for Samuel taking on all the organisation of today. I've been trying hard to keep it *business as usual,* which doesn't leave much time for anything else.

I give myself a shake. I need to think positively. Only, I've seen this so many times before. We are the small fish, and the sharks just gobble us up.

"We've got this, Ms April," Tyler, one of my teenage

dancers says, coming up and standing next to me. Placard in hand.

SAVE OUR DANCE SCHOOL

I smile. "Thank you, Tyler."

I look around and find most of the dancers and their parents, even my older ladies, all standing around the room with placards in their hands. The pressure in my chest lifts a little as they all raise them in the air and begin chanting.

Samuel turns to the rest of the troop. "Let's do this. We want to make the developers realise what this place means to us."

I swing to face him, and he looks over but continues addressing the crowd.

"We want to save your dance school and Ms April's business. We may be dancers and not singers, but we have the best voices out there. Let's make sure Frazer Development hears us."

He turns and winks at me. If it does the job, who am I to complain?

* * *

We ride the tube to Frazer Development's head office. It's mid-morning, so the pavements are clear. We form a circle outside the front of their offices and begin to chant, the mood positive. A few passersby stop and stare. Some even get their phones out. A light-hearted feeling spreads through my chest. Maybe, just maybe, this will work.

Samuel moves to one side, speaking on his phone, his

hand covering his other ear. I watch as his face freezes, and a frown appears.

I move to his side, allowing the kids and their parents to continue to march up and down.

"What's wrong?" I ask.

"The press, television. They're not coming." His shoulders sag. "Apparently, we're not big enough to warrant airtime. It seems Frazer Development are city heroes. No one wants to say anything negative."

I give him an empty smile. It's as I suspected. There's no getting around the bigwigs in this city. The fat cats stick together.

Who am I?

A small-time dance teacher whose tenancy agreement has expired. My life savings and livelihood may be tied up in the building they are about to purchase, but that will mean little or nothing to them. Why should it? Pain resonates through my chest, and I rub it with the heel of my palm.

A burly man comes up to stand next to us. "Excuse me, Miss?"

"Yes," I say, turning towards him.

"The lad over there pointed you out." He turns and points to Tyler, who is frowning in our direction. "Are you the organiser?"

"Yes," I repeat, taking in the Frazer Development logo on his jacket.

"You need to move on," he says. "You can't protest outside these offices, blocking the pavement."

"We can. That's the whole point of a protest," Samuel jumps in. "Freedom of speech."

"Well, I'm warning you. Management will call the police if you don't leave," he says, shrugging.

I square my shoulders. Damn Frazer management.

"We want to speak to management," I say, unsure where my sudden backbone has come from.

"Mr Frazer and his team are on an off-site. He's not here today."

"Is he really? How convenient," I say.

The guard sighs. "Look, I'm sure you don't want any trouble. I wanted to give you a heads-up. You have kids and older women here."

"We're not going anywhere," Samuel says, folding his arms over his chest.

"Have it your way. You've got ten minutes before my boss calls the police," he says, turning and leaving.

I watch him go. My heart is pounding.

"What do you want to do?" Samuel asks.

I drop onto the wall and look at the group in front of me, circling and chanting. Their smiles and togetherness warm my insides.

We tried.

"We go home." I sigh. "I'm not risking any of these kids. This is my battle."

When he goes to open his mouth, I hold up my hand. "Our neighbourhood—the police don't need any excuses. I won't be part of these guys getting hauled into a police station. This is a peaceful protest. We've all seen on the news how things can escalate."

Samuel pulls me in for a hug before moving off towards the group.

Tyler appears with his friends beside me. "Is everything okay, Ms April?"

"Everything is fine." I give him a bright smile.

"Is what Samuel says true? Are we really leaving?"

I nod. "We are. Apparently, management isn't here today. We are wasting our time."

I want to get them out of here as quickly as possible.

Tyler and his friends already have some minor misdemeanours from their time before me.

"But—"

"No buts, Ty. We are heading home. Round up the gang." I rest my hand on his shoulder, giving it a gentle squeeze. "This is phase one. Next week, phase two. We have to be clever."

I pray the boys listen and heed my warning. I don't want them getting into trouble on my account.

"If you're sure, Ms April."

"I'm sure. Let's go home. Betty and Don promised cake and coffee when we return."

Tyler and his friends whoop before returning to the group. Word spreads quickly. No one turns down Betty and Don's cake.

"So what next? Please tell me you're not giving up," Samuel says, returning to my side.

"No, but dragging these people into my battle is not something I'm prepared to do. This is my fight." I turn towards the offices. "This is not over. I will find another way, and if I can't, then I'll need to work on a backup plan. But one that only affects me."

Samuel nods, although my mind is already elsewhere. I don't have a legal leg to stand on. But despite what the landlord and my solicitor say, I see my dance school's impact on the community and these kids. I just need to make this Mr Frazer and his team see it too. There's nowhere else for these kids to go. I used every tool in my arsenal at the beginning to pull them together. I found them dancing on street corners, hanging out in the park, decorating the outside of local buildings! Now they have a purpose, somewhere to go. Whether Frazer Development likes it or not, these kids will be part of their new neighbourhood.

I follow behind as everyone makes their way to the tube

station. The sense of camaraderie is strong among the old and the young. I watch them laugh and joke together. Tyler and his friends carrying Alice and her friends' banners. Helping them. Maybe, just maybe, even if I can't save my studio, I can make Frazer Development listen to the needs of the community.

The battle begins.

CHAPTER 7

APRIL

"Ms April."

I look up to see Alice come into the studio as my current students file out.

"Alice. I wasn't expecting to see you today."

She smiles. "No, but this can't wait." She holds out a letter.

I take it.

"Looks like Frazer Development is holding a town planning meeting tomorrow morning. I wanted to check you knew."

I scan the details.

It's a letter inviting all local residents to a meeting to discuss the new development plans.

Damn mail.

"I didn't. Thanks, Alice."

My heart begins to pound. This may be the opportunity I've been waiting for. It says the development team will be present to answer any questions.

Alice pats my arm. "Well, now you do. The ladies and I have already spread the word. We'll be there, along with anyone else who isn't either at work or school. It's time to get yourself heard."

I stare at the woman before me, surprised at the stubborn set of her jaw. "You are going to stand up tomorrow, and you're going to put your case forward, and we are going to back you. This is the chance you need. A place to be heard."

I purse my lips before breaking into a grin.

"How can I say no to that?"

Alice grins back, her warm eyes sparkling. She's been with me since the beginning and at eighty-two, is one of the fittest and most put together OAPs I've ever met. Also, the feistiest.

"You can't. Take it from this old lady. Some things are worth fighting for. This is one of them. The community is not going to let this place go without a fight. The last two years." She pauses. "The last two years, you've made a difference, young lady. More than you know."

I watch her eyes fill before she blinks away the moisture.

"Anyway, I have places to be. See you tomorrow."

Before I can say anything else, she turns and leaves.

I stare at the letter in my hand, pick up my phone, and fire a quick message to Samuel. If I'm going to do this, I'll need all the support I can get.

* * *

SAMUEL PLACES a hand on my knee, stilling the bouncing.

I look around, surprised at the turnout. There are a lot more people in attendance than I thought. As promised, Alice and her friends and several of my student's parents are scattered around. Betty and Don are also here. After Alice called in, I checked my mail. Nothing, so I went to see them. We did not receive letters, but I suppose we no longer exist as far as Frazer Development is concerned.

"Stop worrying, you've got this," Samuel whispers.

I take another sip of water, my mouth drier than the Sahara Desert.

"Easy for you to say," I hiss, making him chuckle, my stomach in my throat.

We sit and listen as the men and women at the front sell the new development to our community. I must admit, on paper, what they're selling is impressive. New businesses and jobs, restoration and repurposing of rundown, empty buildings. Cleaning up of the streets. A new park for the children.

"Any other business?"

Samuel gives my knee a squeeze before removing his hand. The butterflies flap around in my stomach, upping their tempo as I stand, and I swallow past the lump in my throat.

"Hi," I say, coughing, needing to clear my throat and nerves. "Sorry. Hi. I'm April Wilson. I currently own a dance school on the proposed development site."

Two of the team at the front look at each other, their brows furrowed.

"Hi, April. How can we help?" The gentleman at the front says.

"I'm being forced out of my business with your development, as are several fellow associates. It seems like Frazer Development doesn't care that businesses that are part of our community are being destroyed by your proposal."

They shoot a look at my landlord who is sitting with the panel. He is openly glaring at me.

"We have purchased the property as vacant possession, Ms Wilson," a grey-haired gentleman on the end states.

"You may have, but not all the properties are empty, sir."

"Excuse me?" The grey-haired man turns to the man who was my landlord, whose face is now puce.

"Your tenancy agreement is up, April. I'm well within my

rights to sell and not renew your agreement," he says, standing up, pointing his finger in my direction.

"You promised me a minimum of five years," I say, facing off against the man who is selling up and destroying my business, happy to line his own pockets. "What about all the money I invested in the building in good faith?"

"I made no such promise. You chose to invest that money." He looks at the men next to him. "You won't find five years anywhere in writing," he says, pushing his shoulders back before sitting down, shooting a smirk in my direction.

Snake!

"My mistake. I thought I was dealing with a gentleman."

The grey-haired man looks at the landlord and back to me.

"Ms Wilson. Once the development is complete, we offer all current tenants priority in applying for one of the new units at cut price rates."

"Sadly, sir, that will be of no use. The sprung dance floor, floor-to-ceiling mirrors, and bars I installed are all fixed. I can't simply up and move them. I'll have no business left after the redevelopment."

I stare at the man, who is now looking increasingly flustered.

Samuel squeezes my hand.

"Not to mention Ms April keeps our kids and teenagers off the streets. They love her classes. Where are they going to go when you kick her out?" A voice chimes up from the back.

"You fat cats just want to gentrify the area and drive out our community." Another voice yells, followed by a lot of other voices agreeing with them.

There's movement at the side of the room as someone moves forward, coming to a halt in front of the table.

I inhale sharply as the new arrival turns and faces me.

"Mr Frazer," the grey-haired man says, standing up and shaking the newcomer's hand. "We were just discussing…"

"I heard." Cal's voice sends sparks of recognition firing through my body, settling low. Memories swirl thick and fast.

"Ms Wilson," he says, turning to face me. His eyes spark with recognition, although his expression remains purely professional. "I've just heard what you said. I'd like to invite you to our offices to discuss this with me and my team. See what we can do to resolve this issue."

He turns and shoots my landlord a look that would freeze hell.

"I can assure you, this is not how Frazer Development does business."

CHAPTER 8

APRIL

Immobilised, I feel a knot form in my chest, making it difficult to move or breathe. The firm grip of Samuel's hand grounds me. He squeezes gently as a gesture of support. I nod at what? I'm not sure, but I retake my seat. I try to catch my breath by looking away from the man standing before me. A man I last saw sprawled naked and sleeping peacefully as I crept out of his hotel room. Another person stands and gives their point of view.

When I eventually lift my gaze, his intense gaze locks onto mine, stalling my breath. The tension in my chest remains under the weight of his stare.

"I need to get out of here," I whisper. Samuel takes in my features as if weighing up what I'm saying. "Now," I say, getting up and navigating my way down the seated row and to the door.

I don't look back as I walk out onto the street, needing to put as much distance between myself and Cal, or should I say, Caleb Frazer.

Shit. Why does my life have to be this complicated?

"Holy shit—Was that Cal?" Samuel asks from the doorway behind me.

I continue walking.

"April, stop. Aren't you going to wait? Speak to him?" He calls after me.

"I can't. Not now."

Samuel catches me, grabbing hold of my forearm and pulling me to a stop.

"Why not? You heard the man. He wants to arrange an appointment to discuss this, try and sort it out. Are you just going to walk away? What happened to *fighting* this? Are you really going to give up on everything you've worked so hard for?"

"Don't push me," I say through gritted teeth. My best friend doesn't realise how close to a knife's edge I'm currently walking. "Men like Caleb Frazer say one thing and do another. You know that. Asking for a meeting was all for show. His perfect company getting called out embarrassed him."

Leaning against the building next to us, he takes my hand in his. His hulking frame towers over me.

"Okay, but I think you're making a mistake."

"Duly noted." I sigh, running a hand down my face. "Look, I have a class to get back for."

I pull my hand from his and continue down the road. This time, Samuel lets me go. My mind is in turmoil.

Oh god, you couldn't make it up.

My one-night stand is *bloody* Caleb Frazer.

Seeing him standing there was a shock. The man exudes wealth and power, not forgetting bucket loads of sex appeal! I'm the first to admit that night was incredible, but that was supposed to be it. One night! I left, got on a plane, and returned home with memories that would blow one's mind.

Memories you're supposed to reminisce about when you're old and grey and sat in a rocking chair.

Instead, it's just my luck. That perfect memory is now linked to the man about to destroy my future and everything I've worked for.

"He came looking for you, you know," Samuel calls out, stopping me in my tracks.

I turn to face him. "What do you mean?"

"He came to Philly, to the theatre. Asked how to find you. I tried to call, but I couldn't get through. I assumed if you wanted him to have your number, you'd have given it to him."

What the hell!

I look at the floor. I can't process this information right now.

"You're right. There was no point. It was one night of great sex."

The best.

"Men like Cal and women like me, we don't mix. Look at us. Our lives are polar opposites."

"Not usually, but he made you laugh that night. I don't think I've ever seen you look so relaxed, carefree."

He comes towards me and cups my cheek.

I shake my head, needing to deny his words. They aren't helping. I made a choice.

"I was on holiday. A last fling before coming back to reality. This is my reality, and Caleb Frazer is my nemesis. He wants to destroy everything I've worked for. He and his damn company. Don't let him fool you. They don't care about me or the community. Whatever their company line states. I'm the underdog. If I was so important, someone would have come to see me or at least replied to one of my emails." I stop and sigh. "Yes, he'll pretend to give me a bone, and what then? We both know I'll never be able to afford their rent or to refurbish another studio. It's over, Samuel. There's nothing left. It took me four years of dancing for those…" I run a hand through my hair, not wanting to bring up the past. "Living on air to save up for what I have."

I bite my lip and sigh.

"I just want to go home. I really do have a class in an hour."

Samuel pulls me in for a hug, dropping a kiss on the top of my head.

"Don't give up. Promise me," he says.

Although I'm not sure Samuel knows what he's asking. All my life, I've held a belief that things will get better, that something will change. But that belief is waning as time goes on.

CHAPTER 9

CALEB

"Can someone please explain to me what the *hell* is going on?" I ask.

Most of those who attended the meeting have left. There are only a few stragglers left talking to members of my team.

Wes comes up, his phone pressed to his ear.

"I don't care, Caleb wants answers." There's a pause. "And so do I," Wes says, disconnecting.

"Where's Finnigan?" I ask, looking around. If anyone can answer the question, the bloody landlord can.

"He's gone. Left as soon as the meeting ended," Jeff, the man who chaired the meeting says, coming up to stand next to me.

"Get him on the phone," I say. "I want a meeting with him, in my office, either later today or first thing tomorrow morning. I do not like being blind-sided, gentlemen."

I feel the glances passing between the men surrounding me but damn it. This is not how I do business.

Wes steps forward. "Her name is April Wilson. She owns a dance school on Sunny Down. It's on the edge of the development site."

"Wes, I'm aware of Sunny Down's position. I know the bloody site inside and out. I've been staring at development plans and schematics for over a year. What I want to know is how the hell we've missed this?"

I run a hand through my hair. I want to yell at someone but know it will achieve nothing. Bloody hell, this is not what I need today. And seeing her again, hearing her voice—this is not how I wanted us to reconnect.

Shit! All this time and she was right under my nose.

Wes stops and looks at me strangely.

"Sorry." I take a deep breath. "Go on."

"Doug just informed me that the building was locked up the week we reviewed the area. The landlord claimed she was moving out, and it wouldn't be an issue. Told him she had new premises."

"Did no one check with her?" I ask.

"They couldn't. As I said, the premises were locked up, and the tenant was absent. The landlord got a key from the neighbour to enable us to view it. Doug has just said he was surprised because the building was in good repair inside, but the landlord's story was plausible."

"Well, clearly, that is not the case," I say, knowing I'm stating the obvious. "Did no one follow up when she got back?"

"Caleb, it's one woman," Wes says, a frown marring his brow. "If her tenancy agreement is up, then we've done nothing wrong. We've purchased all the property as vacant possession. It's a landlord issue."

I stare at the man who's been by my side since the beginning. "That's not how we do business, or have you forgotten?"

Wes steps back as if I've struck him, and I know I'm being unreasonable. But seeing her again has left me flustered. She talked about her business, what it meant to her, how hard she worked to get it off the ground, and now here I am about to destroy it…albeit unknowingly.

"Were they the protestors?" I ask.

"It looks like it," Wes says, sighing.

He knows this will be one of those scenarios where I don't let go.

"The landlord is within his rights not to renew her contract. I understand that. However, listening to Ms Wilson and then other members of the local area, I see that this dance school is part of this community. It needs looking into." I hold Wes's gaze. "We're doing this to assist and improve communities. We don't destroy businesses. It's the company's bloody ethos. It's *my* damn ethos!"

"Can we not just buy her out? Compensate her?" One of the newer members of the team says as they approach.

"Community—look it up," I snap, walking away before I say something that I'll regret.

I'm known for my even temper, but this afternoon, I'm on the verge of exploding.

Wes appears at my shoulder. "Where are you going?" he asks.

"I'm going to track her down."

Wes grabs my arm, stopping me in my tracks. "Do you think that's such a good idea? You should speak to our lawyers. Find out our position."

My eyes drop to the hand clasping my arm, and he lets go instantly.

"It's the best fucking idea," I say. "And tell Doug to do his job. I want every ounce of information we can find on Ms Wilson's Dance School. I'm going to fix this mess before the press gets hold of it."

The furrow between Wes's eyes deepens, but he knows when to stay silent, and a brief nod is the only acknowledgement I receive.

I turn and walk back to my car.

Mason gets out and holds the door.

"Where to, Boss?" he asks.

He's driven me since the beginning, a driver making it easier to visit sites than find somewhere to park in this city.

"Sunny Down. There's a dance school there."

He nods and closes the door.

I run a hand down my face.

"Fuck!" I hiss, pinching the bridge of my nose.

Mason gets into the car, and I sit back, staring out of the window.

It's time to find April Wilson.

CHAPTER 10

APRIL

I unlock the door and storm into the dance studio, making my way to my office at the back. That's where my living accommodation is. Samuel is hot on my heels.

I tear off my top and throw it on the bed, followed by my bra, before reaching for my dance clothes. I pull my workout bra on as Samuel stands, arms folded in the doorway. It's not anything he hasn't seen before. He was my roommate for years, and breasts aren't his thing.

I pull off my trousers and yank on a pair of leggings. Stopping only to hang them up. They're my only good pair, and I hate ironing.

"Are you going to speak to me?" he asks as I scrape my hair up, knotting it in a bun.

"What's there to say?" I say, securing the knot in place with some hair clips.

"Stop for one second," he says, running a hand down his face. "What are you going to do next? The man you slept with in New York has bought the building in which your business is housed. He wants to have a meeting. I'm not sure you pulling a Houdini act will deter him. I'd say there's quite a lot to discuss."

I spin on my friend and glare at him.

"Do not bring up New York. That was a mistake." I turn and throw my blouse into my washing basket. "One I blame you for entirely. You're the one who invited him to join us."

He smirks, and my blood pressure rises. "And you're the one who snuck out of his room in the middle of the night."

How the hell does he know that? Oh, of course, Cal went to find him... went all the way to Philly to track me down?

We had a one-night stand. Who does that?

I cross my arms over my chest.

Moving into the room, he clasps my shoulders, making me look up at him.

"Would it hurt to talk to him, baby girl? He might surprise you."

I drop my chin to my chest.

"We were in the presidential suite," I mutter.

"What?" Samuel tilts my chin up, but I pull away, putting some distance between us.

"The reason I left... I woke up and realised we were in the presidential suite." I run a hand down my face, my eyes going to Samuel's, his gaze questioning. "I panicked, okay. I didn't want to see *that* look in his eyes when he woke up. Or listen to the *last night was fun but* speech, as he ushered me out of the door. The walk of shame through the hotel lobby was a lot easier at five than it would have been later."

I pause and smack my hand against my forehead. "Oh shit." I shake my head as two and two become four. "It's his family's hotel. It was a Frazer Hotel. No wonder."

"Didn't you question him when you first arrived? You must have noticed the room."

I raise an eyebrow.

He smirks.

"A little distracted, were you?" he asks.

"Shut up," I say, lobbing a cushion across the room at him.

Distracted isn't the word for it. Of course, I noticed the opulence. But it was all we could do to wait until we got back to the room and not get arrested for indecent behaviour in the back of a cab.

"It was just sex," I say.

"Keep telling yourself that, baby girl," Samuel says as the door to the studio bangs, announcing my class arrivals.

"Look, none of this matters. Cal is Caleb Frazer, and he owns this building and half of the city. I'm me, a little nobody. Men like him don't look twice at women like me, unless we're taking our clothes off. Certainly not in the cold light of day. My one night with him is all there will ever be, all there was ever *supposed* to be."

"I don't believe that," Samuel says. "Caleb Frazer is not like the men who frequented the club." I walk past him, knowing there's no point in continuing this conversation.

I'd like to think he's right, but experience tells me otherwise.

Samuel is a romantic. He loves a Cinderella story. I hate to break it to him, but fairy tales are just that… tales and tall ones. Billionaires from upper-class families don't fall for foster kids, especially ones who've worked as strippers in the past.

CHAPTER 11

CALEB

Mason parks on the road outside the building. The area requires a lot of work to regenerate it, but it's the challenge I love. Once we've finished with it. This place will become another thriving community.

I step into the reception area. It's small and compact but well-maintained. It makes my blood boil even more that we didn't feel the need to question the legitimacy of the landlord's statement.

I hear the thump of the base coming from inside the studio and recognise April's voice as it echoes around the room and through the door.

"Stretch up to the ceiling. Give yourselves a round of applause, ladies and gentleman," she says before I hear clapping followed by a masculine whoop. I find myself smiling, the energy coming from inside positive, energised.

I start to push open the door, only to stop at the sound of voices.

"This morning's meeting was exciting," a lady says. I can't see her, but I can make out her voice.

The voices have moved away from the door, and I wonder if they surround April.

"You did good," the same voice continues. "Standing up to Frazer Development. These companies can't get away with just coming in and taking over."

I flinch at her words. Is that what they think we're doing? Coming in and displacing them. Nothing could be further from the truth. That's not our company ethos.

"Thank you, Alice. The same goes for all of you. It's been amazing to have your support."

I recognise April's voice immediately and inhale sharply.

The door jerks under my hand, and swings open, exposing my position.

A dozen faces turn to face me.

My gaze moves to April's face, her eyes widening as she takes me in.

"Ooh wow, he may be a shark, but I can understand why he's won the Most Eligible Bachelor," another lady whispers loudly, only to be elbowed by one of the others.

My lips twitch, but I refrain from smiling. I get the impression that it would not sit well with these ladies, who are currently scowling at me.

My eyes find April's, the colour rising in her cheeks.

Samuel steps up behind her, resting a hand on her shoulder.

"Come on, ladies, Betty and Don are calling. They have coffee cake this afternoon." The woman whose voice I heard before says, ushering everyone from the room.

The leader of the pack, a grey-haired, perfectly made-up older woman, presses a finger into my chest as she passes. "Be nice to Ms April. We'll be watching you," she says through squinting eyes.

I smile down at her. "I have no intention of upsetting Ms April. I promise you."

She glares at me as she ushers the other women out of the door, each shooting me their fiercest look. Before leaving, the leader turns, giving April an exaggerated wink. I watch April stifle a groan, as she knows I saw it all in the mirror.

"April, Samuel," I say, stepping further into the room and allowing the door to shut behind me. My eyes take in April in her dance attire, memories of her body and how she felt pressed against me flooding my senses.

April turns without acknowledging me and walks to the back of the dance studio, grabbing a grey sweatshirt from one of the benches and pulling it on in silence. Samuel stands still, his arms crossed over his chest while his gaze burns holes into me.

I remain silent, watching as April makes her way to the front of the class and picks up her drink bottle. She unscrews the lid before taking a long swig of whatever it contains. I stop myself licking my lips as I watch her throat bob as she swallows, having no idea of the effect seeing her again would have on me.

Eventually, she turns, her gaze locking on my face.

"What do you want, Mr Frazer?" she asks.

"April. I—"

A movement stops me, and I watch Samuel grab his sweatshirt.

"I'm going to leave you to it," he says. "Coffee cake is my favourite."

April looks like she's about to commit murder as her best friend heads to the door. Samuel shoots me *a don't mess with her* look as he passes.

We both flinch as the door slams shut.

I take a step towards April but freeze when she glares at me.

"You left," I say.

Unsure if I'm talking about her leaving today's meeting or

that she disappeared into the night without so much as a *goodbye* note.

"I had a class," she says sharply.

"I'm not talking about now. I'm talking about New York," I say.

Sudden clarity. It's the answer I've wanted since I woke up in an empty bed five months ago.

Her body tenses at my question, and she turns away. She picks up some papers before returning them to the almost exact spot.

"No point in drawing out the inevitable," she says with her back to me, her shoulders shrugging. "No one wants the awkward morning-after conversation. You should be thanking me."

I frown.

She inhales, her eyes locking with mine in the wall-to-ceiling mirror in front of her. "What do you want, Mr Frazer? I have things to do."

It's my turn to inhale, and I run a hand through my hair.

"I didn't know about your business. This morning was the first time I knew the business was here."

April harrumphs, turning to face me once more.

"It's the truth. We were told you were leaving," I say, holding out my hands.

"So much for due diligence," April says, her expression disbelieving.

"The information we were given was false."

The words sound weak even to me. This is her livelihood, the business she talked about with such passion the night we met.

I take a step forward and stop.

"So, no one came to see the property before you purchased it?" she asks.

"Of course they did," I say, knowing I sound exasperated.

"I wouldn't invest this kind of money in something we hadn't viewed."

"So you just didn't care enough to ask? Speak to the current business owners?" she says, her voice incredulous. "You cared or didn't care that much?"

I run a hand down my face. April's eyes spark, reminding me of when I first approached her.

"Five months ago, my team came and scouted the property. The property was locked up throughout the entire week they were around. We were told you were moving out."

"I'm always open. Someone on your team lied. I'm never closed. I even run classes through the holidays."

She freezes, and her shoulders slump.

"The bastard." She hisses. "New York. I let the landlord know the building would be closed in case of any issues."

"And he invited the team to review the buildings that week," I say, realising how we've been duped. "According to my team, he got the keys from your neighbours."

"Yes, Don and Betty. They mentioned he'd been in when I got back. He told them he needed to carry out some maintenance work. They gave him the keys so he could let himself in."

April drops onto one of the benches positioned around the perimeter of the room. "Not that it matters. My tenancy agreement is about to expire. He's refused to renew it."

I move across the room and lower myself onto the bench next to her. I watch her lips twitch as she takes in the awkward angle of my legs and knees.

April turns to face me. Memories of our time together spring to the surface as the scent of her shampoo and her perfume invade my senses. But that's not why I'm here.

"I meant what I said at the meeting," I say quietly. "I want you to come into the office. See if we can come to an arrangement. When I said Frazer Development does not look at kicking out local businesses, I meant it. Especially ones that offer a service to the community."

"Look, Mr Frazer," she says, raising my hackles. I want to hear her using my name. Not my bloody title.

"Mr Frazer was my dad," I say, plastering a fake smile.

"Fine, Cal or Caleb, or whoever you are—"

I almost sigh as the words leave her mouth.

"I'm Caleb to most people, but I liked the way you screamed, Cal," I add, my tone lowering.

"Don't even say it, that night was…" she snaps, and I instantly regret my words when she gets up and puts some distance between us. This woman does strange things to my body and sends my mind into turmoil.

"Amazing? Unforgettable?" I say before I can stop myself.

"I was going to say *regrettable*. And nothing to do with our current situation."

Her eyes once again flash fire, shooting sparks of desire south.

I lean back against the mirror, stretching out my legs. And watch as April's fists clench by her sides.

"Let's be honest about New York, Cal. I won't give you a cliched response and say it wasn't me or that I'm not that kind of girl. I slept with you," she says, although the fact she hadn't done it for a while tells me she's not being entirely truthful.

"There wasn't much sleeping as far as I recall," I say, finding I want to get a reaction out of her. I want her angry enough that she doesn't roll over and walk away.

She grits her teeth, and I bite back a smile.

"I had sex with you—whatever. But that was it, one night, two strangers, working off their sexual frustrations in a different city," she says, shaking her head. "Look, Cal, you're

Mr Big Business. We're from different worlds. I'm just a dance teacher, you're a CEO of the biggest property development firm in the city. Our worlds are poles apart." She shakes her head and looks at me. "In terms of why you walked through that door. You and your company have all the power here. Whatever I say to you is meaningless. Your business is about your bottom line. Every business is. Hell, my business is."

"That's why I'm inviting you to a meeting. I mean it, April. I want to find a solution."

I push up off the bench and move towards her.

She steps back, but then something makes her stop and hold her ground.

"You forget, Cal. I've just been to *your* meeting. Seen your plans. My dance school doesn't exist."

Shit, she's right. That must have been hard to swallow.

This space has been carved up into smaller retail units.

"That's fair enough. Until today, I didn't know you were here. That there is an issue. Agree to a meeting, April. Give me a chance to put this right."

Her eyes widen as she looks at me.

She remains silent, and my head begins to spin with possibilities.

"Look, I think we've got off on the wrong foot. Can we start again?"

I hold out my hand, but drop it when she doesn't even look at it.

"Meeting again was a shock—for both of us. But, April, I want to find a solution. Come to my offices. Discuss your business and its future. Something that should have happened five months ago if Finnigan hadn't tried to con us both."

She looks taken aback, but remains silent, so I try again.

"How about this Thursday or Friday?"

"I..." she says, her arms wrapping around her waist. April defeated is not something I want.

I sigh and pinch the bridge of my nose.

When I drop my hand, I find her watching me.

"Why? Why, Cal? Why do you want to help me all of a sudden? What about all the emails I've sent? Not one person from your team has taken the time to respond to any of them, except for acknowledging that my issue will be *looked into*."

I stare at her, my stomach hardening. A picture is beginning to form. One I know I'm not going to like.

"Emails?"

"Yes. Ten now. All ignored. We even came to your offices, some of the community members and me. We were told, if we didn't leave, *management* would be calling the police." she says, her words suddenly making sense of her hostility. "So, *please, Cal,* maybe you can understand why I'm a little cynical about your offer."

"I promise you," I say, taking a step forward only to draw up short at the look she sends me. "I haven't seen any emails, but I promise I'll look into it as soon as I get back to the office." I make her meet my gaze. She nods at whatever she sees there, and I exhale slowly. "As for the protest. My team and I weren't even in the office that day. We were on an offsite. I didn't hear about it until I got back, and then all we could do was set up today's meeting." I move to stand in front of her. "Give me a chance, April. Please. Let me try to make this right."

"Fine. Two o'clock, Thursday," she says, stepping back.

"Done. I'd like to invite you to dinner," I say.

April raises an eyebrow and I grin.

"But I'm getting the distinct impression you might poison my food," I say, earning myself a harrumph.

"Don't flatter yourself. You're not worth going to jail for."

I smirk at her scowl.

"I'll see you Thursday, April," I say, deciding it's time to leave while I'm ahead.

"Thursday," she replies as I make my way to the door.

I step out through the door and head towards Mason, my heart suddenly feels lighter than it has in months.

CHAPTER 12

CALEB

I slam into my office, Trish, my PA, trailing after me, her tablet and list in hand.

"Caleb," she says, drawing up short when she takes in my expression. "I'll come back when you're ready."

She leaves before I can say anything, so I sink into my chair and rest my hands on the desk.

Fuck, how did everything go so wrong?

This was not how I wanted to see April again. The woman who has plagued my dreams for the last five months. Has made every woman since appear dull in comparison. Oh, how my friends would laugh if they found out about my little dancer, a woman who made such an impression in only one night that I've been celibate ever since, and not the raging womaniser they think me to be.

There's a knock on my office door.

"Come in," I say.

Wes pops his head in. "How did it go?" he asks, entering and closing the door behind him, taking a seat in front of my desk.

"She's coming here at two on Thursday," I say, bringing up my calendar. I fire a note to Trish telling her to rearrange my two o'clock on Thursday and replace it with April.

"I've got the team working on a proposal. Reimbursement for her fixtures and fittings. Unnecessary but a goodwill gesture," he adds flippantly, and I smart at his words.

"No," I say, his gaze snapping to mine.

"What do you mean, no?"

"It's a functioning, successful business. It's part of the wider community. It's not something we can throw money at and hope it disappears."

"We can, and we do. What's got into you? We have plans for that space. Planning has been approved. Anyone who wants to stay gets first dibs on the new units and a fifty per cent reduction in rent. It's how we work. It's a model you designed."

I run a hand through my hair and down my face, clasping my lips as I exhale. "Maybe so, but this time, we need to work out an alternative."

Wes drops back hard in his chair, so much so it rocks. "What's going on? You're rattled, and you're never rattled."

"I've just had my ear chewed off by a bunch of OAPs telling me how much Ms April and her studio mean to them. We've fucked up Wes, and we need to fix it. We can get Jaxson to revise the plans."

"The board will never go for it. They won't accept any more delays," he says.

"I don't give a fuck what the board will and will not go for," I hiss.

Wes shakes his head at my outburst. "I don't understand. It's a dance school. You're not thinking straight." He looks at me confused until a dawning crashes over him. "Oh. My. God. You want to get in her pants." He laughs, making my hackles rise, and I dislike my right-hand man for the first time in forever. "What are you doing? Slumming it? Although I must say—a dancer. I bet she's flexible—"

"Be careful, Wes," I say through gritted teeth, my fist clenching.

I've known Wes since school. When his father went bankrupt, I offered him a job, and he's been with me ever since.

He gets up, wiping the tears from his eyes, totally oblivious to my anger. Is this how I'm perceived? I know my reputation and have, over the years, nurtured it to serve a purpose. I have no time or interest in social climbers, of tying myself to someone who is only interested in my name or bank balance. The models and actresses I'm photographed with, are there for our mutual benefit, often never in one place long enough to form a deep and meaningful relationship. They like to be able to call and know what they're getting.

"Fine. I'll talk to the team. See what we can come up with. But Caleb, think with your head and not with your dick," he says, still chuckling as he makes his way to the door.

I stand up and lean forward, my hands resting on my desk. I keep my voice low and cold. "I am not thinking with *my dick*, as you so eloquently put it. And if you ever say anything like that to me again." I leave the unspoken threat hanging. "For your information, I met Ms Wilson in New York, and while I was having *dinner* with her and some friends, her landlord was busy screwing her over. In my absence, the man I left in charge of Frazer Development was letting him."

His eyes harden, knowing that person was him. He makes his way to the door, and I let him go without another word, too angry to say anything else.

Damn it! The woman has me tied up in knots.

April has more class than any of the women I've met recently or maybe ever. She also has the ability to make me laugh. In my company, she was oblivious to who I am. She knew me as Cal, not Caleb Frazer. Even when we returned to my suite that night, her eyes were on me, not the luxury surrounding us.

I pick up the phone and dial.

"Caleb?" Elijah, my older brother and head of Frazer Security, comes onto the line. "What can I do for you, little brother?"

"I need a favour," I say, knowing what I'm about to ask is totally unethical.

"As family, we don't do favours. What do you need?"

"April Wilson. Owner of Wilson's Dance Studio, Sunny Down. I need you to tell me all you can about her."

I hear him typing. "I'll see what I can dig up."

"And."

"It's between you and me. No one else will be involved. I'll get back to you as soon as I find something," he says.

"Thank you," I say, my hand gripping the phone.

Elijah cuts off the line. Whether I should involve him, I don't know. He's been erratic lately, his mood swings are getting worse.

I stare at the phone as I replace it. Two days, and then I'll see her again. I hope I can find a solution to assist April and the community. I pull up the plans on my screen. Running a swift calculation, I glance at the clock and pick up the phone.

"Caleb?"

"Jaxson. I need to talk to you about the plans for Sunny Down."

There's a groan at the end of the phone. "What's happened?"

"April," I say.

There's a long pause. Jaxson is the only person I've ever spoken to about that night. My meeting with him the following morning was a disaster, my mind otherwise occupied. After three disastrous hours, Jax had demanded to know *what the fuck was wrong with me,* and I'd ended up spilling my guts.

"You better start at the beginning. Let me make a coffee…"

CHAPTER 13

APRIL

The thousand butterflies that have taken residence in my stomach and chest have gone into overdrive. Frazer Development's building looms in front of me. I pinch my nose against the impending headache that's been brewing all morning... well, for the past couple of days. Days have merged into one since a certain Caleb Frazer reappeared in my life. Even Samuel hasn't been able to pull me out of my funk.

I walk across the street, inhaling before exhaling slowly and deeply, my head and thoughts spinning. *What the hell am I doing here?* I know I should turn around and go home. This is pointless. Caleb Frazer won't listen to me. What game is he playing? Is it merely to placate me? Keep me quiet? Look to be the good guy, helping out the poor dance teacher. Not that I have any sway. I'm a dance teacher. The press didn't even bother to turn up to our little protest. I'm sure when he hears that, he'll be turning me away.

As for the kids, how can I help them? They come to my dance school, and it provides them with somewhere to go, but that's all. Yes, I listen to their problems, but that doesn't make me an expert. I'm not a social worker.

I stop and look up at the sky, my breathing becoming more and more erratic. My heart races in my chest.

I bend over, resting my hands on my knees. Breathe in, breathe out.

I've got this. What's the worst that can happen?

Cal and his team do nothing. In that case, I'm no better or worse off. As of next week my tenancy agreement has ended. My business is gone. I accept that. I just need to decide my next steps. I've advertised the flooring and mirrors on Dancer's Marketplace, to see if anyone wants them. I may get some money back. Nothing like I spent, but beggars can't be choosers. I may get enough to scrape together a deposit for a studio room somewhere.

I step up to the office building. It's more impressive than I remember. I wasn't paying attention the last time we were here. I wanted to make a point. Now I can appreciate the glass and the large double-height foyer.

A man appears and opens the door as I approach. Smiling in greeting.

"Afternoon, Ms," he says.

"Thank you."

I step past him and make my way towards the main reception desk. A young woman with perfect hair and perfect makeup smiles up at me from behind the desk.

"Afternoon, Welcome to Frazer Development. How may I help you?"

The warmth of her greeting surprises me, and I find the muscles in my shoulders loosening a little.

"I'm here to see Caleb Frazer?" The words sound awkward as they leave my mouth.

"You must be Ms Wilson," she says, catching me off guard. She hands me a visitor's badge already bearing my name. "If you'd like to take a seat, I'll let Mr Frazer know you've arrived."

I'm early, unsure how long it would take me to make it across town. I walk over to the beautiful white leather sofas and take a seat. Glossy magazines and newspapers are neatly placed on the glass table in front of me. No expense spared.

There's a knock on the window next to me. I see Tyler grinning through the glass. What the? I look around and see several other members of the dance studio milling around. Tyler winks. He's one of my best students—was one of my first students. At fifteen, he's been dancing with me for two years and is a natural. He initially thought it uncool, but when I demonstrated that dance was not only ballet, he was hooked. He's a natural hip-hop dancer.

But why isn't he at school?

"You brought your fan club, I see," a voice behind me says, making me jump.

I turn to find Cal stood next to the sofa, staring out onto the street.

"I…"

Music starts up outside, and two of my dancers come into view. Their movements coordinated with a dance we've been working on. More dancers appear. Several people have their phones up, recording the kids as they dance. I grin as Alice and some of her fellow keep-fit ladies join. Their movements are not as smooth as Tyler and his peers, but their grins tell me how much they're enjoying themselves.

Before I know what I'm doing, I move to the door and step out onto the pavement. It's then I spot Samuel, camera in hand. What has my friend done?

"Ms April," Tyler shouts, beckoning me over as they dance.

"Go on. You know you want to," Cal says next to my ear, the feel of his breath raising every hair on my body.

Tyler and Alex run forward and pull me into the mix. My feet take over before I can stop myself. This is what I need, what I've always needed. To lose myself in the dance. My heart rate slows. The butterflies settle as I let my body join those of my students.

When the music finally stops, everyone crowds around. The audience that has formed around us claps enthusiastically.

"They wanted to give you some moral support," Samuel says, coming to stand next to me.

My eyes well with unshed tears.

What have I done to deserve this?

I turn to Cal, who is still standing in the doorway of the building. Some of his staff are next to him.

Oh hell.

I should be in a meeting with him, not dancing on the street. He's busy, and I've got him waiting. But then, if this is the end, what a way to go. This is a memory I'll never forget.

I turn back to the building, extracting myself from the group.

Cal steps forward—the look he gives me—one I can't decipher. Moving past me, he walks towards the crowd.

"Refreshments and snacks are available in the canteen for anyone interested. Sign in, and Sara will take you through," he says, motioning to the *perfect* receptionist I spoke to earlier, who is now smiling broadly.

"Samuel?" I say.

"I've got this. I'll stay with them," he says, squeezing my shoulder. "You concentrate on keeping your business."

"Thank you," I say, squeezing his arm as Cal returns to my side.

"Are you ready?" he says, holding out a hand, motioning for me to lead the way.

I nod before entering the lion's den.

CHAPTER 14

CALEB

I hold open the door to my corner office, allowing us both to enter. April has been silent since we left her band of loyal followers and Samuel downstairs.

She moves to the chair opposite my desk, but instead, I point to the sofa and chairs by the window.

"Can I get you a drink?" I ask.

"Water, thank you."

I watch as she takes a seat, her hands rubbing up and down her trouser leg, her knee bouncing.

I move to my desk and press the intercom.

"Hi Trish, can I get a water for Ms Wilson and my usual."

"Of course, Caleb, I'll bring them straight in."

I grab the folder and the new architectural plans Jaxson sent through this morning off my desk and make my way towards April. Her rigid posture and lack of eye contact tell me this may not be as smooth sailing as I hoped.

"That was quite an entrance," I say, taking a seat in the chair next to hers, watching her move her leg away from me.

"I'm sorry it delayed our meeting. I did not know they were going to do that," she says awkwardly.

I hide my smile. April clearly has no idea how much her community thinks of her, or the letters we've received to protest against the current plans.

"No harm done," I tell her. "You arrived early, so we're still on time."

Her shoulders relax a little at my words, although her back remains ramrod straight.

"I know you're busy. Shall we get down to business?" she says, her eyes finally rising to my face.

Okay, no small talk.

There's a knock on my door, and Trish enters carrying our drinks.

"Here you go. Is there anything else I can get you?" she asks, smiling over at April as she places our drinks down on the table next to us.

April returns her smile, and my heart skips a beat.

I'm still waiting for Elijah's intel. I know I'm overstepping, but there's something about this woman. I want to know what makes her tick.

"Thanks, Trish," I say, wanting her to leave.

She nods with another smile for April.

When the door shuts, April turns her attention to me, all signs of the smile gone, her expression focused.

"I've read your emails," I say, opening the folder. "I can only apologise for not getting back to you."

I was furious when I finally received the messages. The team in charge of incoming communications won't be making the same mistake again.

April nods, her gaze moving to her hands.

She remains silent, and I sit back in my chair and watch her. As I suspect, she takes a few moments to realise I've stopped talking. She looks at me, her eyes wide, but there's a spark of annoyance in their depths.

"Why have you called me here?" she asks.

Ah, there she is, the firecracker I met in the bar.

I tilt my head and stare at her for a moment.

"I want you to forget what has been," I say. "Imagine we're meeting for the first time five months ago. We've come to your studio with the landlord. What would you be asking of me and my company?"

"Isn't that a moot point and a waste of both of our time? We can't turn back the clock."

"You're right," I add.

We both sit in silence.

April drops her chin to her chest and inhales. "Sorry. It's been a long couple of weeks."

I can only imagine.

I know the affect seeing her again has had on me, with the added stress of losing her business…

"We can't change the past, but we can look at moving forward," I say and watch her nod.

She takes a deep breath. The shuddering exhale lets me know exactly how tense she is.

"I'd be asking to renew my lease," she says, sitting up and holding her shoulders back. "But I've seen Frazer Development's plans for the building. It's been redesigned as small industrial and retail units with apartments above. There's no space for my dance studio. You have a new swanky gym and fitness centre for that."

I grimace. She's right, of course. All our developments include a fitness centre, gym, and pool. We aim to offer all the residents and community a place close to home where they can go to exercise in the city. That and eat and buy groceries. It's why our waiting list for apartments continues to grow daily. It's become so big we're struggling to keep up with the demand. The apartments for our last development sold out within a day of going on sale.

"Would you be interested in space within the gym

complex?" I ask. It's not something I had given much credence to.

Her laughter shocks me. "Can you really see Tyler and his mates wandering into a swanky gym with a membership policy, alongside all the new DINKies that have moved into the area? My teenagers and OAPs are not part of that world —not when their families are on minimum wage or benefits."

My mind wanders back to the OAPs who had just finished her class. Who were willing to fight for the woman in front of me. Of the kids currently downstairs, who have skipped school to support her today.

"Okay, but just so you're aware. Our development includes family apartments and social housing. Yes, there will be young couples, but in fact, the development will contain a range of apartments, from one-bedroom studios to four-bedroom apartments."

I keep my tone neutral, but I want her to understand what we're trying to do for her community.

"You might be interested in this."

I pull a piece of paper out of the file and hand it to her.

She sits forward and takes it before dropping back in the seat as she stares at the numbers.

"I don't understand," she says, glancing up at me.

"The left column is your old rent. The figures we got from your landlord. The figures on the right are what you would be paying Frazer Development Management Company."

"But?"

"The figures are lower than what you're currently paying. Add in all the additional factors and improvements that make the building more energy-efficient and cost-effective. You should see a dramatic drop in your overheads."

"There is still the issue. My dance school is now retail outlets."

I roll out the reworked set of architectural plans Jax sent over this morning and lay them out on the table. The board have yet to approve them, but that's my problem. I just need to get April on board.

I say nothing, patiently waiting for her to engage.

Jax has come through. In the new plans, he's repurposed the proposed retail outlets and reinstated the dance school, moving it from the centre of the building to the end. He's increased the space and allowed for additional rooms, including a coffee shop next door after I mentioned how popular the current one was with the kids and ladies. When I mentioned the Frazer Foundation was thinking of employing a counsellor, he included space for additional meeting rooms. The retail and industrial space is vastly reduced, but the community will gain what it needs.

April stares at the plans but remains quiet.

"What are the kids and I supposed to do in the meantime, or can we stay in situ?"

I shake my head. "Unfortunately, that's not possible. The redevelopment is taking the building back to bare brick and rebuilding the inside using modern eco methods."

She throws up her hands and gets to her feet. "Then what the hell is all this about, Cal? This will take months. I won't have a business."

"Please, April, sit down."

Shit.

In my desire to see her again, I have not thought this through. This is not like me. I never go into a business proposition unprepared.

Since she reappeared, my head has been in a tailspin.

I almost sigh in relief when April sits and decides to close our deal instead.

"I haven't ironed out all the details yet, but as you can see.

I've made progress," I tell her. "I need you to trust me. Give me time to iron out all the kinks, talk to my board."

She gives a little snort, but when her eyes meet mine, I see a flicker of hope.

"Okay, I can give you time, Cal. It's not like I have any alternatives. But at the end of the day. *Actions* speak louder than words, and trust needs to be earned where I come from."

My heart skips a beat, and I find myself wanting to punch the air. She's giving me a chance and I will fix this.

She's right, and now I have to earn her trust. If Wes and the board don't like it, *fuck 'em*, I'll bloody cover the cost myself if I have to. April is not losing her business.

"I understand. I get it—just let me prove you can trust me."

"Why?" Her question comes out of the blue. "Why are you doing this? You don't owe me or the kids anything. You would earn more money with the industrial and retail units."

Taking a deep breath, I lean forward, hoping she believes what I'm about to say. "That might be true. I'm a developer." I shrug. "But I aim to redevelop rundown areas, improve them for everyone concerned. The old and new residents. Create sustainable communities that can continue to grow on their own. Displacing the old, simply doesn't work. In the long run we will earn more money with a thriving community."

I couldn't be more surprised when she nods.

I stand up, and she follows. I hold out my hand, which she stares at for a moment before placing hers in mine.

"I'll be in touch after the weekend when I have some more information," I say, clasping her hand in mine. The memory of her hands and mouth on other parts of my body, sends a sharp ache through my chest. She pulls away, her hand fisting at her side.

Before I can stop myself, I add, "Work with me and my team to help your community."

"What? Why?" she asks, her blue eyes clashing with mine.

"Why? You know the community better than anyone. The support they showed you at the meeting and today. You can help us bridge the gap, help us understand what they need. Your dance school can be that bridge between old and new."

The more I speak, the more I can see this isn't the crazy idea I first thought it to be. She will also be near, and I want her nearby.

"I don't know."

I see her wavering but decide not to push.

"Think about it. Talk to Samuel," I say, although his name sticks on my tongue. I hate the familiarity he has around April, the way he's always touching her. I know he's gay, but still. She relies on him.

"Okay. Thank you for taking the time to see me today, Mr Frazer."

I quirk a brow in her direction. "Back to Mr Frazer again?"

"Yes, Mr Frazer. This is a professional working relationship."

I laugh then, a true belly laugh, and she looks at me like I've lost the plot.

"Oh—not even the cleaning staff call me Mr Frazer. I'm Caleb to everyone here and Cal to you," I say.

"Fine, Caleb."

I bite my tongue to prevent the grin that threatens. I don't think me finding her comment amusing will go down well. I need to tread carefully. I hold open my office door, allowing her to step through, and walk her to the elevator.

"Until Monday, April. Have a lovely weekend."

I hold out my hand, which she shakes.

She says nothing, her eyes avoiding mine as the elevator

doors close. I make my way back into my office, my grin now on full display.

"What the hell is going on?" Wes slams into the office behind me. "We have a bunch of teenagers dancing in the canteen, and I've just had a new plan for Sunny Down delivered to my desk. Have you lost your fucking mind?"

The smile melts from my lips, my eyes hardening, making Wes stop. "Who the hell do you think you are coming in here and talking to me like that? I thought we had this discussion?" I say, my tone cold and hard.

"Me? What about you? Months of planning and money, up in smoke." He runs a hand through his hair. "All for what, a shag? You trying to get in her pants? Is she really that good?"

Before I can stop myself, I have Wes by the collar, his back slammed up against the door.

"Don't you fucking dare," I hiss, my eyes holding his. "Get out of my office and take this attitude with you. If I hear one word against Ms Wilson or the plan changes, you'll be sorry. Remember who you work for." I shove backwards. "Never question me again."

He pulls his shirt down and smoothes a hand down his front. "The board have called an emergency meeting in an hour."

I turn on him, my smile, all teeth. "I know, I called it." I tell him and watch as he deflates before my eyes.

"Get out."

He shoots me a look that tells me he thinks I've lost my mind. Maybe I have, but when he turns and slithers away like the snake he is, I let him go.

I move to my desk, dropping into my chair. Now I have another problem to solve. I promised April a solution, but I just need to convince the board that it's the right one.

CHAPTER 15

CALEB

I make my way into the boardroom.

"Thank you for coming on such short notice," I say, taking my seat at the head of the table.

"I take it, this has something to do with the new plans that have appeared on my desk this morning?" Donald says.

He's a friend of my father and one of the first people to come on board when I set up Frazer Development.

"And the fact the canteen is currently full of teenagers and OAPs."

Elana smiles. I saw her outside watching the flash mob.

"A proposed change to the current plans for Sunny Down," I say. "As for the latter," I shoot Elana a smile. "We are trying to win over a community. This was the perfect opportunity to show them we are on their side."

Everyone opens the packs Trish prepared this morning before my meeting with April.

"As you can see," I say. "The changes to the plans will involve a time delay and additional costings."

"Is all this really necessary?" Donald asks. "Can't we just

move the dance school into the proposed gym facilities? Kill two birds with one stone?"

My mind drifts to April's reaction to the same proposition.

"A dance school is very specific. Whichever option we take, it will require a change to the current plans." I pause and let my words sink in. "Jeff, you were at the town planning meeting. Would you care to give your view on the meeting?"

Jeff looks up. "We've been royally stitched up by the landlord," he says in his matter-of-fact way, and I bite my lip to prevent myself from smiling.

"What do you mean? Does this have anything to do with the demonstrations or today's flash mob outside?" Donald asks.

"Unfortunately, it's come to light the landlord wasn't entirely honest with us. We're not sure why, but anyway. The community are in uproar over what they see as the forced closure of one of their businesses."

Donald sits back and crosses his arms. "Can't we just compensate this business?"

It's my turn to step in.

"No. The business in question offers a place to go for the younger generation. It has been heavily involved in keeping the kids off the streets. We have been inundated with letters and emails complaining about our supposed treatment."

"But that's not our ethos," Elana sits forward.

"Exactly," I say. "We build up and improve communities. It's been our motto from day one. When we get the community onside, we have somewhere like Copper Town."

Murmurs go around the room.

"You're saying Sunny Down could be another Copper Town?"

"I think it can be bigger and better. We learned a lot the first time around."

"But Caleb, the cost increase. Budgets are put in place for a reason. This project is already flying close to the wind."

"I understand. If you look at page three, I'm proposing we take funds from the proposed Spencer Lane development."

"It's a big risk. It could have a knock-on effect," Elana says, looking at the document in front of her.

"True, but it's a risk I'm willing to take. It's the right thing to do, for the good of the community and our company," I tell them. "I need you to trust me. When have I let you down?"

A few heads around the table nod.

It's Donald who speaks first. "The time delay, Caleb? Can we really afford to push this project back any further? We're already six months behind, courtesy of the landlord."

"I think I can pull it back in," I say, meeting his steely gaze. If there's anyone I have to win over, it will be Donald. At sixty, he's seen and done it all.

"I'm speaking to the contractors and our onsite team at the start of next week. I did, however, want to update you all on the changes I am proposing."

"And we appreciate being kept in the loop, Caleb." It's Jameson who steps up, the head of communications and public relations. "If I can add. I think we all need to take these figures away and think about what this means. I tend to agree with Caleb. This community are not going to sit quietly by on this. There are already stirrings. I've had reporters on the telephone, sniffing for a story. Today's flash mob got people's attention. We don't need to damage our reputation when we have a proposed fix."

It was a member of Jameson's team who sat on April's emails.

"I called the planning office and spoke to Mo. The retail

outlets proposed for development can easily be repurposed with a change in planning application. As the business has already been present, there should be no issues," I say.

"Fine, then I suggest we all take the weekend to process what is going on. Have another meeting once Caleb has spoken to the developers."

"You are taking a great deal of interest in this project," Donald says, staring me down.

"It's my reputation. I did not set this firm up and work this hard to have miscommunications and false truths derail us."

"I'm happy to reconvene next week and see what you come back with. But you need to fix this, Caleb, ASAP. We can't afford for our reputation to be damaged any further. No more protests or flash mobs."

"Just give me your approval next week, and I promise you, all this will go away," I tell him.

CHAPTER 16

APRIL

I hang up for the fourth time this morning.

Who would have thought one small flash mob would go viral?

Social media is lapping it up, especially since Samuel leaked the story behind it.

The City's Golden Boy Meets His Match

Although I'm not sure that is the case.

The first reporter I talked to was, without a doubt, *Camp Caleb*. She wanted to disprove everything I said. When I mentioned my tenancy had expired, she couldn't get off the phone fast enough. Not that it stopped the red top papers. But then again, they're always looking for salacious gossip. They want some sordid love triangle between me and Caleb's latest supermodel. I wonder what they'd think if they knew he's already been there. Fortunately, being in New York meant there was no video footage or at least none that anyone would think to search for.

I groan when my phone rings again. I need to be getting ready for class. At this rate, I'll be switching the damn thing off. I look down and see Di's name flash up on the screen.

Why's my foster mum calling me? It's not our usual day.

I answer in a heartbeat.

"Di?" I say.

"Morning April. How are you?" Her calm voice instantly soothes me.

I lived with Di and her husband, Julian, from age twelve. They were foster parent set number four. My previous family, decided it was not for them after only six months. The two before that I lived with for three years a piece, but they had reached retirement age and wanted to travel.

Who could blame them?

I did.

By the time I landed on Di's doorstep, I was an angry preteen with a large chip on my shoulder.

"I'm." I pause. I learned a long time ago not to lie to Di. "I could be better," I sigh.

"I thought as much. I saw the video. One of my students recognised you and showed me before class."

I inwardly groan. "Of course they did."

"You looked good. So did the kids and your older ladies. That was quite a routine you put together."

Shortly after moving in with Di and Julian, I ran away. The police found me trying to check into one of the local shelters. Instead of ostracising me, Di sat me down and told me about the danger I put myself in. After that, she made me join her every evening at her dance studio after school. Initially, I did my homework, but as time went on, I found myself watching. One evening, Di invited me to join in. By age fifteen, I was competing in dance competitions alongside her other students. When I left school, I picked up A-levels in Dance and Performing Arts and began to turn my life around.

"The flash mob was mainly Samuel, although he used my

routine. I was there for a meeting. They surprised me as a show of support."

I force down the lump that has formed in my throat.

"So what's happening? Why are you having meetings with the city's leading property developer?"

I drop down onto the floor and lean back against my bed.

"I screwed up," I say.

"Oh, honey. What's happened? Is there anything Julian and I can do?"

"It's fine, I'll sort it out. Unfortunately, my landlord turned out to be a snake. His offer of yearly renewals was not for my benefit but more because he knew he was going to sell."

I finally understood it after a long chat with Betty and Don. They thought I knew. Were surprised when they saw how much money I was investing in the property.

"Anyway, my lease is up. The future of the dance studio is at the mercy of Frazer Development... *shit*," I say, trying to keep a tight hold on my emotions.

"What about all the money you've invested?" Di asks, her concern evident.

Pinching the bridge of my nose, I answer, "Unless I can work out an agreement with Frazer Development, it's lost. I've tried advertising, but no one is interested in a second-hand floor or mirrors. It's expensive to move and the cost of relaying. It's cheaper for them to get a warranty and buy new."

There was one inquiry since I advertised, but when they looked into the cost, they came back and pulled out.

"Maybe this Caleb Frazer can find a solution? I've done some research. His family runs a scholarship program and foundation for underprivileged kids. For a family with money, they do a lot to help those less fortunate. So much so,

I'm going to get a couple of my students to apply. It offers them a partial or full ride."

Just what I need. Di fan-girling over Cal.

"His offices and car show his success, Di. They're all modern and swanky. He even invited the flash mob in and provided food and drink for them all while he and I were in a meeting." I say, and Di laughs. "Quickest way to shut everyone up, get them off the street."

"Or a kind gesture because they showed you their support," Di adds, never one to look on the dark side. It's what makes her such an amazing foster parent. "Remember, there are always two ways of looking at things."

"I know, I know. It's what you taught me. Never judge a book by its cover. He tells me he wants to help, but…"

"But you're struggling to trust what he says?" Di fills in.

"Exactly. I can't help it. How can someone like him even begin to understand someone like me and our community? He's a good-looking playboy who was born with a silver spoon in his mouth. He doesn't know what it means to struggle, to fight for everything you have. He doesn't live pay cheque to pay cheque, or have to wonder where his next meal comes from. Life comes easy to him. Do I trust he'll follow through and not roll over when his board says no? I don't know."

"Oh honey, I understand. You're having to put your faith in a stranger. But look at it this way. There are good people in this world. Caleb Frazer might surprise you." I rub my temples, trying to alleviate the headache that is forming. Di doesn't know Cal is not quite the stranger she thinks he is.

"Why don't you look Mr Frazer and his company up? See all the good he's done for this city? The areas he's redeveloped and the improvements he's made. He works with a top eco architect. Their buildings are innovative. He tries to work with communities to rebuild them, improve them…"

That is what Cal told me, but I took it as a company line. Trust Di to be the voice of reason. With everything that's happening, I feel like I'm losing perspective.

"He wants to work with me for the good of the community," I admit.

"Then why aren't you grasping this opportunity with both hands?"

I hear her sigh and drop my head back against the mattress.

Di continues. "I remember the angry young woman dropped off at our door. Her clothes and belongings were in a bin liner." I hate it when she reminds me of where we started, but I know she wants to make a point, and I owe her that. "You were so angry, so scared. You had created a fortress around yourself. No one was coming in. But then, month after month, we got glimpses of the girl underneath. One that has a heart of gold. Sometimes, we need to look beneath the surface when faced with new people and things. I know you find it hard to trust… and I don't blame you. But don't look a gift horse in the mouth. Not when you can make a difference. It sounds like you're being offered a chance to help the kids you love so much. Are you really going to turn him away before you've given him a chance?"

Is that what I'm doing? If New York had never happened, would I feel differently?

"But…"

"No *buts*, you'll never know unless you try."

"What would I have done if you hadn't come into my life?" I say, emotion crushing my chest.

"You'd have found a way. You're a survivor, April, and don't you forget it." Her own voice choked.

"Thanks, *Mum*," I say, and she laughs.

"How are you doing?" I switch our conversation.

"I'm doing okay," she sighs.

"Still no news on your operation?"

"No, it's now a waiting game."

My heart sinks. Here is someone who has done so much for her community, but she is left waiting.

I hear the door bang to the studio.

"I've got to go. I've got a class. I'll call you tomorrow."

"Only if you have time," she says. "Take care, April, and remember what I said."

"I will."

"We miss you," she says, and once again, I force away the lump in my throat. Di and Julian were the first people to give me a real chance. To prove the existence of individuals who were willing to support me, that I wasn't just a pay cheque, and for that, I will be eternally grateful. "Just think about what I've said. We love you, April, and are here for you."

With that, she ends the call.

"I love you too," I say, smiling.

CHAPTER 17

CALEB

The door opens before I knock. My brother's wife, Leah, is grinning back at me.

"Hey, stranger," she says, stepping to one side.

"How's my favourite girl?" I ask, pulling her in for a hug and swinging her around.

"Hands off Casanova, she's mine. Find your own woman," Gabriel says, coming up and pulling me in for a hug.

"Where have you been?" he asks, slapping me on the back.

The change in him since Leah came into his life has been enormous. My twin was my polar opposite, a hermit to my party animal. He still hates the limelight, but with Leah by his side, he's embraced the outside world instead of hiding from it.

"Don't tell me you've missed me?" I say, stepping into the apartment. "Love what you've done with the place, Leah."

"Hey, who said it's all Leah?" Gabriel asks, making Leah laugh as she walks ahead of us.

"Because, brother dearest, everything was black, white, or stainless steel before Leah moved in. Now there's colour. The sofa has cushions and throws. The walls have artwork. Even your dining chairs have been upholstered. It looks like a home."

Gabriel grunts, but I can see he's pleased with my observation.

Gabriel's penthouse is one of the first Jax and I designed and built together. Its views over the Thames are spectacular. Gabriel and I own several apartments in the building we rent out. The other side of my property business is my rentals.

"How are you, little momma?" I ask Leah.

"I'm good. Callum is doing well. He's sleeping. I'll take you in for a peek in a moment, but first..."

She hands me her phone and the latest photos of my nephew. Something inside me wrenches.

"When did he get so big?" I ask, unable to take my eyes off the pictures, itching to get my hands on the little man. "I need cuddles."

Leah laughs. "Don't worry, you can give him his bottle when he wakes up."

Gabriel huffs.

"Don't worry. You can do the two AM feed so you don't feel left out."

I laugh at my brother's face. "Hopefully, Callum will be able to tell us apart, like his mother."

I can't keep the grin from my face. "If not, I can be the cool daddy, and you can be the boring old fart."

Gabriel picks up one of the colourful pillows and throws it at me. Leah rolls her eyes at us both. She's known me for almost as long as my brother, having worked for him for many years. Yanking Gabriel's chain has always been enjoyable, especially when it comes to Leah. Now I have Callum to add to the list.

"Dinner is ready," Leah says.

Gabriel and I grab the pots from her hands before she can carry them to the table.

We sit down and tuck in. Leah is an amazing cook. For my brother, the way to his heart was through his stomach, although I cannot imagine anyone more perfect for my twin.

"Any updates on the new development? There are all sorts of things on social media," Gabriel says, refilling my wine glass.

I take the wine, followed by a large swig. It's only been twenty-four hours since I saw her, but the woman is invading my every thought. I've spent half the day on the phone trying to solve the planning issues to get the board off my back.

"It's nothing," I say.

Gabriel looks at me over the top of his glass. "It doesn't look like nothing. Protests outside your office, a flash mob. Looks to me like someone wants to be heard."

"They do—she does," I say, sighing, sick of trying to explain myself. "Her landlord, the seller, has sold her business out from under her. A business she's invested a lot into. She and the community are rightly aggrieved."

Gabriel frowns. "Can you compensate her?"

I run a hand through my hair.

"It's more complicated. She's a large part of the community. The flash mob. Those were her students. Kids whose lives she's turned around. Got off the streets, given a purpose to."

Leah leans forward. "Can you incorporate her business into the new development?"

I stare across at Leah, my shoulders sagging. "I'm trying. I've got Jaxson reworking the building plans, and I called a board meeting earlier. I've asked her to trust me, but she told me *actions speak louder than words.*"

I scowl at the smirk that appears on my brother's face.

"What?" I say, snapping at him.

"Sorry, but it appears this woman is the first person in

history to resist your smooth-talking charms. Sounds like she's asking you to put your money where your mouth is, brother."

"Excuse me." Leah coughs with a chuckle, looking at my brother. I watch in fascination as his hand snakes out and captures hers, raising it to his lips.

"Second woman. Maybe you've met your match." He smirks in my direction. "Or you're losing your charm in your old age."

Leah gets up and begins clearing away our dinner. The baby monitor goes off, and a squawk comes out loud and clear.

"Someone's awake and hungry," Leah says, shooting us both a glance.

"On it," I say before Gabriel can do anything.

I take off up the stairs and head to my nephew's bedroom. The night light is on, and I make my way over to his crib.

"Hey, little buddy," I say, looking down into eyes so like my own.

Callum's face screws up, his arms and feet kicking at his covers.

"Okay, no need to get cross."

I scoop him up and hold him to my chest, his little head nestling into my neck.

"There we go," I say, his mouth latching onto my skin.

"You might want to stop him," a voice comes from the door. Gabriel steps into the room, pulling back his t-shirt exposing what looks to be a large love bite. "Quite the suction on him," he says.

I move Callum, only for him to let out another yell.

"Here you go. Leah sent me up with this."

He hands me a bottle and I make my way over to the feeding chair, making myself comfortable. Eyes blink up at me as he latches onto the bottle.

"You are hungry, little buddy," I say, watching his eyes close as he guzzles down the bottle.

Gabriel watches me with his son.

"You're a natural."

"Brotherly instincts. Also, I want as many cuddles as I can get."

I missed his birth three months ago. He came early. One of my many trips to and from the US.

Gabriel pulls up a chair.

"So, this woman?"

I sigh. "April is pricklier than a porcupine and has more edges than…"

My brother leans forward, running his finger down his son's cheek, his face a picture of contentment. "I get the message. She hasn't rolled over. Has Elijah run a background check to ensure she's legitimate?"

I nod. "I'm still waiting for his response, but from what I can tell, April's genuine. The locals all seem to love her. You should have seen and heard them coming to her defence at the town hall meeting."

Gabriel stares at me for a moment. I hate it when my brother starts to psychoanalyse me. As my identical twin, it's like he's in my head.

"There's more. Spill."

I laugh and bite my lip. "You've always been good at reading me. What gave it away?"

"I'm your twin. I know you, and there is definitely more to this than you're letting on. You care too much."

"New York. I met her in New York."

"Ah, the reason you were so evasive about your trip. A woman. That makes sense. I wondered if something had happened."

Gabriel studies me over his wine glass. I want to snatch it out of his hand. His smug expression starting to wind me up.

Callum finishes his bottle, and I put him over my shoulder to wind him, the way Leah showed me.

"Well, April happened. Then she left before I woke up. Left without a word," I say, knowing it sounds petty, but then I've never had sex and just upped and vanished. Not that I could, even if I wanted to. People recognise my face. That's why I was surprised April hadn't, especially since she came from London.

Gabriel chokes on his wine, and I know straight to where his mind has gone.

"Let me remind you of Monaco. I haven't *lost* it before you say anything."

"Please, don't remind me. I'm still trying to get over that night."

"Dramatic much!"

Facing my brother and his communications officer the following morning was embarrassing. The two women were anything but quiet, but it was one hell of a weekend.

"April is complicated. As I said, she has trust issues the size of Greater London."

"So what are you proposing to do? Can you leave her in situ?" Gabriel asks.

"Unfortunately, no. The development means taking the building back to brick. It would not be safe to leave anyone inside while construction is underway."

"What's your next move?"

I inhale before shaking my head. "That's my dilemma. I need to sell something to the board. Something they will go with, within budget and limited time constraints. But will also appease the community. The board want no more bad press."

"It sounds like you've got your work cut out," he says. "But what about April herself?"

Callum takes that moment to let out an enormous belch, milk leaking out of his mouth and onto my shirt.

"Is that better, little man?" I say as my brother laughs.

"Nothing like baby vomit to attract the women."

Gabriel takes Callum and hands me a packet of baby wipes along with his wine glass.

I watch as my once-distant brother coos at the baby in his arms. I use the wipes to clean myself up and think about what Gabriel has just said.

"What are your plans for the weekend?" he asks, distracting me.

"I think I'll go home. A few spins around the track should help to clear my head and finish these proposals."

Or at least I'm hoping it will. My new car needs another outing, and I need to get a certain little dancer out of my system.

CHAPTER 18

APRIL

Campfires, roasted marshmallows, and sitting in front of Di and Julian's log fire. The memories invade my dreams, shooting me from one to the next. The warmth and glow of the fire. I'll never forget the first time they took me camping. I'd been about fourteen and been such a nightmare, sure I'd hate it. But I hadn't. I'd loved it, and it had cemented our bond.

I cough, drawing in a choking breath. The thick, clogging air makes me cough again. Rolling onto my side, I pull the covers up over my shoulders, but the need to cough again is overwhelming. Still lost in my dreams and memories, I sit up, coughing again. This time, I struggle to get enough air into my lungs, and my brain comes around in a panic. I prise my eyes open but see nothing. Flicking on my bedside light, nothing.

Damn, the electrics must have gone off. I pick up my phone and use the torch feature. The surrounding air illuminates. But it's not just illuminated. It's a smoky haze. Smoke drifts up and onto the ceiling.

What the hell?

I cough again, realising I'm choking on smoke. My office-come-bedroom is smokey. I pull my pyjama top over my mouth and get out of bed, making my way to the door. Tendrils of smoke snake through the gaps between the door and its frame. I reach for the handle but leap back as it scalds my hand.

Shit!

I grab my towel, still damp from last night's shower, rolling it into a tube. I stuff it against the bottom of the door, thinking back to my fire safety course. The window, high above my bed, is small and compact, but big enough for me to squeeze through. I know I can open it. Once Samuel realised I was both living and working here, he made it his top priority to ensure I was safe. The windows and doors being number one.

He fitted a lock but also ensured it opened. He spent hours oiling the hinges.

"You can never be too safe," he said when I asked him why he was bothering.

I'll be giving him the biggest hug when I next see him.

The smoke begins to form its own eery cloud on the ceiling, descending towards the window. I grab what is left of my water by the bed and empty it onto my t-shirt, pressing it to my nose and mouth, the relief almost instant. I watch as the smoke begins to curl slowly past the towel. My heart rate picks up, and my breathing stalls. There's no one around this area at this time of night.

I check my phone.

Damn it, no signal!

No one to raise the alarm. I begin to cough again, the air thickening. I press my t-shirt more firmly against my mouth. I need to get out fast.

I move to the bed, pulling on last night's jeans, which are lying at the base. There's a drop on the other side of the window. I just hope someone hasn't moved the bins. I pull on my trainers before climbing onto the bed.

Crap, my handbag.

I'll need my cards. I look around and spot it through the haze. It's sitting on the chair near the door.

I jump down, the toxic smell searing my nose and throat, even through the material of my top. Grabbing my bag, I spot Mr Ted in the corner. I swipe him up as I head back to the window, stuffing him under my t-shirt.

I push the window outwards and inhale deeply, my lungs crying out for a gulp of fresher air. The smoke still clogs the air, but not as much. I throw my bag out through the open gap, hoisting myself up towards the ledge, thanking my dancer's flexibility and strength. My fingers grip the edge as I take my weight on my arms before swinging my leg around. The first time, I miss so I use my trainers to help walk up the wall, pulling myself up onto the small, narrow ledge. The window bangs down on my back, making me suck in a breath, but at least it's semi-fresh air I'm now drawing into my lungs. I wriggle sideways, manoeuvring myself through the thin gap. I can hear shouts from outside.

"Miss?" I wriggle around to see a fireman standing beneath the window. He places a ladder against the wall and climbs.

"Miss, if you can move yourself around."

With his help, I get my feet onto the top rung of the ladder.

"Thank you," I say breathlessly.

"Is there anyone else inside?" he asks.

"No, just me," I say, coughing as my lungs try to clear themselves.

"Are you sure?"

"Positive. There's only me. At least in the dance studio," I say as he leads me away from the building.

He moves me to one of the fire engines and grabs a foil blanket, wrapping it around my shoulders. He motions to one of the paramedics. I stare at the building that has been my home. Black smoke billowing from newly broken windows. An orange glow is visible on the inside.

The medic hands me some water, and I think they tell me to drink it, but I can't move my gaze away from the sight before me. They're dousing the building with jets of water. The hiss and squeal are audible as the fire resists them, devouring the old wooden timbers and connecting walls.

What the hell happened?

There's a shout, and I watch the firefighters draw back. An enormous crack fills the air before the roof caves in. The orange flames now dancing high into the night sky.

There's a certain beauty to the organised chaos that follows. Men and women work in tandem, like a dance troop, as they battle the blaze. Another two fire engines appear. More men and women jumping out. The main coordinator fires orders at the different teams. The sign outside Betty and Don's is black. The paint has bubbled and melted in the heat. Flames lick under the doors. Everyone's businesses in Sunny Down have gone.

My heart drops, a deep chill spreading out from the centre of my body.

Thursday's meeting.

All the things Caleb asked me to trust him on.

I sit and watch it burn.

There's no business left, nothing left for him to save. It's all gone. Their diggers can move in, their designs can remain the same.

The only question will be, what happened?

But that's irrelevant to me. My insurance provides minimal coverage for the building's contents. I needed to secure liability insurance in case of injury, and when I had to choose between the two options. The second had won out.

"Miss?"

I snap out of my haze and look up.

"Miss?" he says again.

"Yes, sorry," I say, trying to stand until he holds out his hand in protest. I drop back onto the edge of the vehicle.

"Do you have any idea what happened?"

I shake my head. "No, I woke up, and the room was full of smoke."

"You were sleeping here?"

"I own the dance school. I must have nodded off. I was doing paperwork," I say. "It's been a long week."

My rental agreement was a commercial one, but I wasn't bringing in enough money to pay for a separate room, especially in the beginning. When the showers were installed, adding a sofa bed to the office seemed like the perfect solution. I was onsite for security to ensure no one tried to break in.

He doesn't argue.

A heavy feeling settles in my stomach. Did someone break in, and I didn't hear them? How did the fire start?

"Any ideas about how the fire started?" I ask as he goes to move away.

"Not yet, but there will be a *full* investigation," he says.

I'm unsure whether it's just me, but his tone is accusing. Not surprising. A building burns, and I'm the only human around.

A police officer appears behind him.

"Hi, Miss?" he asks.

"April Wilson," I say.

"Flash mob lady?"

I give him a weak smile. "That would be my students, yes."

He nods before pulling out his notebook. "If I can just take some details…"

CHAPTER 19

CALEB

The exquisite sensation of my cock being engulfed by warm and skilful lips.

A talented tongue expertly teases and explores the sensitive underside, before moving to my slit.

I moan, lowering my hands and gripping hair as my hips thrust off the mattress.

An incessant buzzing pulls me out of the moment and from my dream.

Is that my phone?

It stops only to start again a second later.

I prise open my eyes to stare at a room, not my own. Although I recognise it, which is a positive.

Tristan's spare room.

I throw my legs over the side of the bed and stand up, my head spinning.

How much did I have to drink last night?

I search for my clothes. My jeans lie on the floor in a heap. The night before comes creeping back as the endorphins of my morning wake-up wear off. I pinch the top of my nose to stem the headache that is threatening to split my skull in two.

My phone rings off again as I pull it from my jeans.

I stare at the screen.

06:30

Shit, I need to get ready for the office.

There are twenty missed calls from Wes. Bloody hell, is this the apocalypse?

Please tell me he's not grovelling after Friday's ambush.

I run a hand through my hair. The fact I slept through that number of calls indicates it must have been a good night, although the details are a little hazy. It's then I notice someone has switched it to silent.

There is a knock on the door, and Tristan enters carrying a steaming cup of coffee before grimacing at my naked form.

"God... put some clothes on," he huffs, shielding his eyes with his free hand. "I thought you might need this," he says, indicating the coffee and the two painkillers he has placed on the side.

"My phone?" I ask, grabbing my jeans and pulling them on.

He grimaces.

"Sorry about that. You were out for the count," he says. "When I couldn't wake you... You really went for it last night."

I groan, snippets of the night before coming back to me. I'd come back from the track yesterday. I'd been right. Racing at high speed had worked as a distraction, or at least I thought it had. Tristan called and asked me to join him at a club he's looking at purchasing.

"Thanks," I say, memories of my dream fading fast, being replaced by those from the night before. I'd gone to Tristan's for a few drinks and to catch up with my friend. It had clearly been a long night.

Tristan leaves me to finish getting ready.

I grab my t-shirt and coffee before dialling Wes's number.

"Where the fuck have you been?" he yells down the phone.

I flinch as his voice shoots through my tender head.

"Remember who you're talking to," I say calmly. "What has you screaming at six thirty in the morning?" I ask.

"There's been a major fire."

His words get my attention, a sinking feeling taking root in the pit of my stomach.

"Where?"

"Sunny Down. The entire building has gone up. The roof collapsed. Firefighters have been working all night to get the blaze under control, trying to stop it from spreading to the surrounding buildings."

"I'm on my way," I say.

Tristan appears at his bedroom door.

"Thanks for last night," I tell my friend. "There's been an incident at the development site. I've got to go."

"Anytime. You've put me up enough," Tristan says. "I hope everything is okay."

I smile.

Ain't that the truth.

"Oh, and Caleb, whoever she is…"

My eyes clash with my friend's. He knows me well enough to know that drinking my issues away is *not* me.

He laughs. "Don't panic, you haven't said anything. All I'm saying… if you need to talk… I'm here."

I nod and turn to the door.

What the fuck?

I've never discussed April. They've always fished, known, or at least suspected something happened in New York, but I've never confirmed or denied.

I turn and leave, hailing a cab as soon as I hit the street. It will be faster than waiting for Mason to arrive. Instead, I shoot him a message telling him to meet me at Sunny Down.

"Sunny Down," I say as I get into the back.

"Mate, I'm not sure how close you'll get. There's a major fire. They've diverted all of us."

"It's my building, so as close as you can make it," I say before sitting back.

My phone buzzes again. This time, I answer it almost immediately.

"I'm on my way," I say.

"Prepare yourself. It's a wreck," Wes says.

Not one to exaggerate, I hate to think about what I'm going to find.

"It's a miracle that no one was injured. Thank God, it was during the night. According to the fire officer, there was only one woman in residence. She escaped by climbing through one of the back windows."

"Who?"

An icy dread shoots up my spine.

There's a mumbling on the other end of the phone.

"Your new bestie, April Wilson."

My chest constricts.

"Is she…"

"She's fine. She gave a statement and left. She was working late and fell asleep at her desk, according to the statement she gave to the police. And Caleb, just so you're aware. They haven't ruled out arson."

Wes's attitude towards April is grating on my nerves. He's treading on dangerous ground. Although I have to admit, why was she on site so late? Especially on a Sunday night.

The taxi makes it in record time. Dropping me around the corner. I approach the burnt-out shell of the building that once housed the dance school, a cafe, and a garage. The smouldering building still sending toxic fumes into the air.

"Excuse me."

A man approaches.

"I'm Caleb Frazer," I say, holding out a hand. "I own the building."

"Ah, Mr Frazer, your colleague is over here. We're still trying to find out what caused the fire," he says.

"Thank you. I look forward to hearing your findings."

I make my way over to Wes.

He looks up from his phone.

"You look like hell. A good night?" he asks, smirking.

"It was okay. I met Tristan at his latest venture. He's looking at opening a club," I say, regretting the words as soon as they leave my mouth.

Wes's mouth twists at my words. "Always had the Midas touch, that one. All your Kingland Playboy Posse do."

He smiles, but there's no hiding the bitterness in his tone.

I decide to change the subject. He is, after all, my right-hand man. His relationship with my friends, or lack of it, holds no sway here.

"So, what do we know?"

"Not much." His lips purse. "They think the fire started in the cafe, along the wall connecting it to the dance studio. They will need to carry out further investigations to confirm.

"Where is April Wilson now?" I ask.

"Don't know. The police took her statement, and she left." Wes shrugs.

I want to grab him by the shoulders and shake him, but refrain.

"Do we have an address?" I say, trying hard to keep my cool.

"No," he replies.

I grit my teeth.

"I'm going to head into the office," I say. "There's nothing I can do here. Let me know if anything else comes up."

Wes nods, and I walk away, heading back to where the taxi dropped me.

I pick up my phone and dial.

April's phone goes straight to voicemail. I try again and again, but the same thing happens. I dial another number, which is picked up on the third ring.

"Caleb." Elijah's dulcet tones come down the phone.

"One of the buildings i'm buying burned down last night. I need all the information you've collated on April Wilson. She's the only one who was in the building."

"Shit. Is she okay?" he asks.

I'm surprised at my brother's concern.

"She got out, but I need an address."

I can hear him moving around on the other end of the phone.

"You're going to have a problem with that. From what my private investigator uncovered, her home was the dance studio. It looks like she's been living out of her office."

I stop in my tracks. "What?"

"The dance studio was her home. He made an appointment, pretended to want to enrol his daughter. Her office had a sofa bed and a storage box filled with clothes."

A pounding starts in my ears. "Why was he looking through her things?"

"He's a PI, Caleb. It's what he does," he says patiently. "He was following her, and when she never left. He was simply confirming his suspicions."

I must growl because Elijah hits back.

"Don't take that tone. You asked for her to be investigated."

I rub a hand over my face, my head pounding again.

"Sorry, it's just—"

"Look, the only place I can think she'd go is to see Samuel Lyon. She appears low on friends. She may return to her foster parents, but she left there at eighteen, and although they're close—"

"Foster parents?"

"What do you actually know about this woman?"

Relatively little, obviously.

When I don't answer, Elijah continues. "She was in the foster system from three. Look, I'll send you over what I have. It's too early to be sat here discussing some woman you have, well, whatever. Especially when I've only managed one coffee this morning."

I stare at my phone.

Foster system.

I squeeze my head at my temples as those two words spin around in my head. It explains her attachment to the kids in this neighbourhood, wanting to help them.

"Send it across. I'm going to head home. Forward me anything you have on Samuel. I've met him, so I can call him."

"Done. And Caleb—"

"What?"

"Never mind. Just take care," Elijah says, in an unlike Elijah way.

I stare at my phone.

What? No grumpy retorts.

I don't get my older brother sometimes.

CHAPTER 20

APRIL

I sit in almost a state of shock as they battle to bring the blaze under control. The building is now a derelict shell, the businesses little more than ash and rubble.

I grab my bag and open it. Sifting through the few items it contains.

Shit.

I check again and groan.

"Damn it," I say aloud.

My phone. It's gone. I was using it before I climbed through the window. I remember placing it on the window ledge to free up my hands before trying to climb out. Not once did I think to turn around and grab it. Staring at the smouldering mess that once housed my business and home, now it will be ash.

The sun has come up, dawn is finally breaking.

"Excuse me," I ask one of the firemen who has returned to the truck. "Do you know what the time is?"

He checks inside the vehicle. "Five-thirty," he says before moving off again.

Five-thirty, If I leave in thirty minutes. Samuel will be up, or at least waking up, by the time I reach his apartment, and, with luck, Daniel will have left for work.

I fold up the foil blanket and place it where I was sitting. I've handed over my details. All I can do now is wait.

My body aches as I make my way to the nearest tube station. The heaviness weighing my limbs is due to a lack of sleep and the smoke I've inhaled according to the paramedic who checked me over.

"It's perfectly normal when you've been involved in a fire," he tells me. "If your throat is sore or you're coughing, prop your head up on pillows, and cough drops can help with any irritation."

I smile at him. "Thank you."

"As I said, everything appears to be okay, but if anything changes or you're worried. Go to your doctor or get yourself to Accident and Emergency."

"I will, I promise. Luckily, I got out before it was too bad."

We both look over at the building, which the firefighters are still trying to save.

A dark, black cloud seems to have taken up residence above me. How has my life, in one night, gone to hell?

On the tube, people turn their noses up and move away. It's then I realise I must smell like a bonfire. I offer apologetic smiles, although it must be bad, as it's coming up to rush hour, and people want to get from A to B as quickly as possible. Dodging someone takes effort.

By the time I reach Samuel's place, I'm exhausted. Putting one foot in front of another is about all I can manage. I climb the steps to the front door. The Edwardian terraced townhouse has long since been divided into one-bedroom apartments. I press the buzzer for flat four and wait.

"Yes?" a voice, not Samuel's, comes over the intercom.

"Daniel, it's April…"

"He's not here," Daniel snaps.

We have never got on. Daniel sees me as a threat to his

relationship with Samuel. He hates the fact I've been in his life for longer than he has. Even though they've been together for four years. If he had his way, Samuel would never talk to me again. I know I've been the butt of many arguments between the two of them, and I wouldn't be here if I wasn't desperate. But they live together, and for all his arrogance and ignorance, my friend loves him, and I won't get between them.

"Do you know when he'll be back?" I know I sound desperate.

I'm holding on by a thread, but I'm not sure how much more I can take.

"No... he's at work. Leave him alone, April. You're a bloody leech. Protests and Flash mobs—he's trying to make something of himself, and you keep pulling him down."

He shouts over the intercom, making a couple walking past stare at me.

I raise a hand and grimace, noticing the black ash coating my fingers for the first time.

"Just one minute..." I say, feeling exhausted but unwilling to take the blame for all their disagreements.

"Leave," Daniel says. "Or I'll call the cops."

"Fine, but can you tell him I stopped by?"

There's no further comment, and I know he won't.

I lean back against the large door, my head dropping back against the wood with a bang. I look out onto the tree-lined street with its expensive parked cars. Samuel has come a long way from the mouldy bedsit we shared in the early days, and I will not be the one to ruin it for him. Daniel is older. He loves his younger toy boy, but Samuel's chosen career as a dancer does not thrill him. It doesn't quite fit the image he wants to portray, but I'm in no doubt he loves him, and that is the reason I'll leave. I'm not sure why I even bothered to come. It's not like I could stay.

I push off from the door and make my way back down the steps, looking up at Daniel's window to find him scowling down at me. I wave before turning and heading back to the tube station. This is the wrong side of town, with its tree-lined streets and fancy cars. I need to find somewhere to get washed up. This is not the place.

Stopping off at a cash point, I check my balance, flinching when I see how little is left in my account.

My bills have gone out, but the money I was expecting in will now not arrive. No business, no payments.

Shit, shit, shit.

A quick calculation. I have enough for two days in a cheap hotel, but then…

Thankful for my railcard, I make my way back across town.

I wander around until it is time for the local shops and businesses to open. My clothes reek of smoke, my head hurting from the smell, my lungs tight. A lady in the local charity shop unlocks the door, and I make my way over.

CHAPTER 21

APRIL

The lady turns back as I walk through the door.

"Oh, my dear," she says, wrinkling her nose as she steps closer.

"Sorry... I got caught in a fire," I say, my throat constricting around the words both from lack of use and emotion. My eyes fill.

"Oh heavens. You were there? Come in, my lovely. How can I help?" she says, wrapping her arm around my shoulder.

"Ms April?" Another lady appears from the back, her face a picture of horror and shock as she takes me in. I recognise her instantly. It's Jonah's Nan, one of my younger students. She brings him to class because his mum and dad work shifts.

"Hi, Dorrie," I say weakly.

"What on earth? Come in and sit down. Val, this is Ms April, Jonah's dance teacher. Oh lordy, the fire? Are you okay? I saw it on the news this morning."

I blink back tears, as I'm led to a chair near the back of the shop.

"Sit down, love," Val says, my movements delayed as my

brain tries to stay focused. Someone places a cup of steaming tea in my hand as the two women fuss around me.

"We've got you."

I sit and do as I'm told, no longer having the energy to argue as the events of the past few hours finally hit home.

"Let's get you sorted with some clothes," Dorrie says, ushering Val into the shop. They move through the rails, grabbing a few items. "I know. We had a new batch of clothes arrive yesterday. They've been through the washing machine. I was about to label them up," she says, disappearing.

I hug the mug of tea, taking small sips as I listen to her crashing and banging.

"Here you go," she says, coming back with some jeans and a couple of jumpers. Holding them up. They look brand new. "These should fit you," she says, winking. "Skinny person that you are."

She rubs a hand over her own generous midriff and laughs.

Val appears with a bag in which she is putting other bits and pieces.

"Some shampoo, conditioner, soap. Rejected Christmas pressies, everyone likes to donate. I've also put in some towels. One of the local factories has been giving us their seconds to sell. They're brand new and perfectly good, if you ask me."

She takes the clothes Dorrie is holding and folds them into the bag.

"Thank you," I say, my head struggling to make out what they are saying as exhaustion sets in.

"Oh, honey, you're in shock. You need to get showered. Is there somewhere you can go?" Val asks, kneeling in front of me, her hand gently squeezing my shoulder.

"Don't worry about me," I say, giving them both a weak smile.

I don't miss the look that passes between them. Most of the locals know I live on site. It was the worst-kept secret.

"Have you got somewhere to stay?" Val asks.

I give them a smile and nod. "Yes, my best friend. He's currently at work. I can stay at his place," I lie.

After a lot of convincing, the two women finally let me leave, although they refuse to let me pay for any of the items they've packed for me. "We are a charity, set up to help those in need. You, my love, need some charity and love today."

Their kindness floors me, and I tell them I'll repay them.

I make my way to the outskirts of the main shopping area and find myself outside the one place I hoped I'd never need to revisit. Somewhere, I've made countless donations since I opened the dance school. It was there for me once, and here's hoping it will be there for me again.

I ring the buzzer.

"Hello," a voice comes over the intercom.

"Hi, I need..." the door buzzes before I can say anymore.

I push it open as I hear the click and step inside. A familiar smell hits my nose, and I'm transported back to when I first arrived in the city at nineteen, with not much more than the bag on my back.

"April?"

Dawn, the manager, appears out of her office.

"Hi," I say, offering her a weak smile. "I need somewhere," I cough as I clear the lump from my throat. "I need somewhere to stay," I say, close to tears.

She nods once and beckons for me to follow her.

"You remember the routine?" she asks. "It's twenty a night."

She hands me a clipboard holding the relevant paperwork, which I fill out and pass back.

"Are those your belongings?"

She points to the bag I have over my shoulder. The one Val and Dorrie put together for me.

"Yes," I say.

She hands me a key. "This is for your locker. Items left lying around tend to walk. We added lockers to ensure the safety of each person's belongings."

She grabs a towel and hands it to me.

"Get showered before the rest of the rabble get back. You're in 2b. The other girls in there are nice. They've just left for work, so you'll have the day to yourself."

I don't ask what they do. This is little more than a shelter for those down on their luck.

"Thank you," I say, heading towards the door.

"I'm sorry, April," she says. "The fire, it's all over the news. If there's anything I can do," she says.

"Somewhere to lay my head. It's been a long night," I say before leaving her.

I can feel her eyes burning into me as I drag my weary body up the stairs.

I strip out of my clothes and place teddy on the sink. I step under the hot water, hissing as it hits my back. I turn around and catch sight of the welt-like bruises in the mirror. Remembering how the window hit me as I climbed through. Luckily, the shower room is empty, the water piping hot. The water runs through my hair and down my body until the pain subsides, and it washes away the grime and smoke of the previous evening. I close my eyes and let the water hide my misery. I gasp for breath, choking on the tears I can no longer contain. The sound of the water drowns out my sobs.

I grab the shampoo that Val put in my bag. Mango and apple. Adding a generous amount to my hand, I massage it into my scalp, washing away the smell of my burnt-out life. I rinse and repeat, before adding the conditioner. I almost cry again when I see a brand-new hairbrush set in the bag. It's amazing what people give away.

Wrapping my hair in a clean towel, I change into one of the sets of clothes the women provided. I pull on the clean jeans. They're a little baggy, but beggars can't be choosers, and you never look a gift horse in the mouth.

The dorm room is empty when I let myself in. I spend time towel drying and de-knotting my hair before pushing my bag up against the wall and lying down. I curl into a foetal position, hugging teddy and my knees into my chest. The tears come again, only this time silently, and I let them fall. Better out than in, as Di would say. I'll need to get a phone to let her know I'm okay, but at this moment, I'm too exhausted to think.

CHAPTER 22

CALEB

Nothing.
Where the hell is she?

I've been hoping April would turn up at the office, but nothing. The staff are on standby to call me should she appear. By four o'clock, I begin to realise she's disappeared, and thoughts of New York spring to mind.

I call Don and Betty. They're pretty shaken up but assured me their insurance will cover the damage. When I ask about April, they told me they haven't seen or heard from her.

Where are you, little dancer?

Her phone continues to go to voicemail. She's either switched it off, or… I think of the smouldering building and wonder if it's a melted pile of plastic and metal.

I reopen the file Elijah sent me earlier and extract Samuel's address.

I tried his phone earlier and it kept going to voicemail. If he's not answering his phone because April is with him, that's fine, but I need to know she's safe.

I ping Mason, telling him to meet me at the car.

I pass him the address before settling back into the seat. I try to concentrate on the influx of emails I have received, but I'm struggling to stay focused.

Damn you, woman, where are you?

We arrive outside the Edwardian Terrace. I walk up the steps and press the buzzer Elijah told me belongs to Samuel and his partner, Daniel Bishop.

"Hello?"

I recognise Samuel's voice from the few times we've spoken.

"Samuel, it's Caleb Frazer. Is April with you?"

My words come out in a rush. There's silence, and before I know it, Samuel is opening the door in front of me. He's wearing low-slung tracksuit pants and a t-shirt that looks like he's just tumbled out of bed.

"Why are you looking for April?" he asks, smoothing down his hair and t-shirt, as if just realising how he's answered the door.

I frown, and he shrugs.

"Sunny Down burned down last night,"

The colour drains from his face, and he puts out a hand to steady himself. "April?"

"She's okay. She got out, but she's missing. No one seems to know where she is. I take it she's not here?"

Damn, I thought this was where she would have come. Samuel is, after all, her closest friend. Even Betty confirmed that.

"Come in," Samuel says, stepping to one side. "I've been asleep this afternoon. We had an all-night rehearsal for the show I'm in. I didn't get back until around nine this morning."

He moves past me and takes the stairs two at a time. It's clear he wants to find his friend as much as I do.

He pushes the apartment door open, holding it for me so I can enter.

The apartment is small and neat. A living room faces the front of the building, and an open-plan kitchen is on one side. Large sash windows look out onto the tree-lined street, allowing copious amounts of light into the room. The developer in me appreciates how tastefully it's been decorated.

Samuel disappears into the room at the back, reappearing with his phone.

"Damn, nothing." He presses the phone to his ear and huffs when I assume it goes straight to voicemail. He does something else and then sinks down onto the sofa, staring at his phone with a look of *horror*.

"GPS last has her phone at Sunny Down. She clearly left it," he says, talking more to himself than to me. "Where are you, baby girl? Why didn't you come here?"

The front door opens behind me, and another man walks in.

"Samuel," he calls before spotting us.

He stares over at me, his expression hard. "Samuel?"

"Dan. Meet Caleb Frazer. He's here looking for April. She's missing,"

His voice catches. Something flickers across Dan's face before he masks it.

"Caleb Frazer? As in Frazer Development?" He steps forward and holds out a hand, which I shake.

"I'm looking for April Wilson," I say.

"What's she done now?" he asks, turning to Samuel, the contempt in his voice making my jaw clench.

Samuel looks up, and I wonder what he sees in this man. One who has so little affection for the one person he adores.

"Her dance studio burned down overnight." Samuel's voice catches.

"That was hers? I heard it on the news. I'm sure she's fine," he says, turning away but placing a hand on Samuel's shoulder, giving it a squeeze. His lack of eye contact. I see a flash of guilt cross his features. I'm good at reading people, and Dan clearly knows more than he's letting on.

"You haven't heard from her?" Samuel probes as if sensing his partner's distance.

"She called this morning." I'm surprised by his honesty. "It was before you got home. I was getting ready for work."

"Called?"

"Maybe not called. She turned up…" He rubs a hand down his face, guilt written all over his features.

"Why didn't you let her in?"

Dan raises his eyebrow at Samuel, and I watch as he schools his features, his nostrils flaring and his eyes cold.

"What the hell, Dan? Why the fuck didn't you let her in?" he asks again, and I'm amazed to see the older man squirm.

"How was I to know her building burned down?" he says, holding out his hands.

He turns to me as if for support, but whatever he sees on my face has him turning away. I grit my teeth, letting Samuel deal with this.

Samuel is now on his feet. He's half a head taller and looms over his partner.

"Did you even bother to ask why she was here so early in the morning?"

"No, I didn't really care. I was getting ready for work." The two men are now squaring off against one another. Dan looks shocked, so I'm not sure this has ever happened before.

"She's my best friend," Samuel hisses.

"No, she's not. She drags you down." Dan rests his hands on Samuel's chest, but he shoves him off. "You could be so much more. She holds you back. You've left that part of your life behind. Risen above it."

His tone is pacifying, but it's clear Samuel is past being pacified.

Instead, he spins on his lover. "What? Being homeless? Being alone in the world? Or is it my dancing? That is who I am... what I do. April was there for me when I had nothing. She supported me, helped me get back on my feet." He steps back from the man in his life. "I'm not changing Dan. You either accept me for who I am, or I leave. I'm fed up with your shit." Samuel's jaw flexes. "Do you know what? I'm going to leave before I say something I may regret. I'm going to go out and find the one person who accepts me for me. I spent too many years hiding who I am. I'm only with you because April helped me to accept myself. If not, I'd still be hiding at the back of that very dark and lonely closet. So when you throw dirt in her direction... oh, why do I bother?" He leaves us and slams into the bedroom, returning with a jacket.

"Samuel, stop. Look, I'm sorry—if I'd known," Dan says, stepping forward, his hand reaching out but dropping when he sidesteps.

"No, Dan, you're sorry you got caught. And before you say it. Even if you had known, I still think you'd have sent her away because I'm realising that's who you are. And it's not someone I like. However, now is not the time. I have to find April. She's my number one priority." Samuel throws a look in my direction. "Let's find our girl."

I walk past Dan without saying a word, not sure I can contain my anger. Who sends someone away without even checking they're okay? It's not like she lives in this part of town. To get here, she would have travelled at least two tubes.

"Samuel, please..."

"No." Samuel holds the door open while I walk through the corridor before slamming it shut.

The door opens behind us as we make it to the top of the stairs.

"If she comes back, I'll let her in. I'll call you. I'm sorry. I love you."

Samuel drops his gaze, some of the anger draining from his face. But he says nothing. Instead, he heads down the stairs.

We exit the building in silence. Mason holds the door for us both as we get into the car.

"Where have you looked?" Samuel asks.

"I've spoken to Betty and Don, but other than that, I'm at a loss."

"Why?"

"Why what?" I ask, unsure what he's asking.

"She wouldn't have done it if that's what you think. That business was her life, her new start. She worked hard to get the money together for it." He stops, and I wonder what he is going to say, but I don't push.

"I just want to know she's safe," I say, surprising both of us.

He nods and picks up his phone.

"Di."

I can't hear the other side of the conversation, but I can hear the panic tones.

"It's okay, I'm out looking for her… yes, she got out. She was fine. Her phone, not so much… No, I was at work… she didn't wait."

He looks at me. "I'm with Caleb Frazer. We're going to find her. I promise."

He listens for a few moments more. "I'll get her to call you as soon as we find her. Try not to worry… and Di, if she turns up at yours. Call me."

Samuel disconnects the call and drops back against the seat. "Her foster mum," he says. "The reason April is such a phenomenal dancer. April credits Di with turning her life around, giving her a purpose."

"Is she likely to be making her way there?" I ask.

"No. She got kicked out of the foster system at eighteen. Was told to stand on her own two feet. Di and Julian offered her a place to live, but April didn't want to take advantage of their kind nature. Not once her funding dried up. When she first left, she had her scholarship to a conservatoire…" Samuel stops as if realising he's shared too much. "Life isn't always easy when you're from the other side of the tracks. But April, she is one of the most amazing women."

I nod, unsure of what else to say.

My phone rings. Pulling it out of my pocket.

"Elijah."

"She's at one of our sponsored Hostels. Her name has flagged up."

"Flagged up?"

"After you called, I tagged it," he says unapologetically.

"Thank you. I owe you one."

Silence.

"I'm sending the address now."

He ends the call, and once again, my phone pings.

I open the screen between Mason and me.

"Change of plan. We need to go to…" I tell him the address.

Samuel looks at me but says nothing as Mason drives us to our destination.

CHAPTER 23

APRIL

A knock on the door brings me back to consciousness. I'm not sure how long I've been asleep, but I'm still exhausted.

"April?" a voice sounds through the barrier.

"Yes," I call out, pulling myself into sitting, catching my head on the upper bunk. "Ow," I rub at the sharp sting. Something I'll have to remember.

I stand up and make my way across to the door.

I scrub a hand over my face before opening it. I must look a fright, hair unkept from allowing it to free dry, tear-stained cheeks. The tightness of my skin gives that part away.

"Hi, April," Abigail says. "Sorry to wake you. There are two men downstairs asking after you. Dawn is talking to them. I wanted to give you a heads-up. I know you didn't say there was an issue with anyone, but we can never be too sure."

I smile at their thoughtfulness.

"Do you know who they are?"

Who would think of looking for me here? I haven't

spoken to Samuel or my foster mum. I doubt Daniel even told him I called by.

"One is Caleb Frazer," she says, trying unsuccessfully to suppress a giggle. "The other, I think he said his name was Samuel. That he's your best friend. Normally, we send people away, however, as you're here because your home burned down."

My heart constricts at the memory. I nod. What on earth is Caleb Frazer doing here? Does he want to accuse me of sabotaging his building now? Going to claim I burned it to the ground?

"I know them both," I sigh. "Let me just…"

"April? Are you here?" I hear Samuel's voice, and he sounds frantic.

"It's okay, I'm coming," I call, glad it's only early evening, and I'm not waking up any other residents. I can't believe I've slept the whole day.

I hear the hammering of feet on the stairs as Samuel's towering frame appears from around the corner.

"You can't go up there," Dawn's voice shouts after him.

"Hey, Baby Girl," he says, scooping me into his arms and squeezing me so tight it forces the air from my already bruised lungs in a whoosh.

"Samuel," I say, tapping his shoulder, sucking in a deep breath as he releases me, sending me into a coughing fit.

"Sorry," he rubs my back as I try to gasp for breath. Abigail reappears with a glass of water.

"Here," she says, placing it in my hand. "Sip it."

I do as I'm told. The dry feeling in my throat eases, along with the cough.

"You had me worried, baby girl," he says, grabbing my chin and inspecting my face. I'm not sure what he expects to see. "I'm sorry about Daniel. That man can be such a dick."

Ah, so he knows. I know my friend, and that will tear him in two.

"I'm fine," I say, pulling my face away, not wanting the scrutiny.

I look over his shoulder to find Cal standing behind him, his eyebrows drawn together. His eyes lock on me, and I squirm under his gaze. He opens his mouth as if to say something but closes it again.

When a couple of the other doors on the floor open and close, Dawn appears as if by magic.

"Gentleman, you're not supposed to be up here. This is the ladies' floor," she says sternly behind me.

I turn towards her. "Sorry, Dawn," I say. "We'll move downstairs."

"Lock up your things before you go," Abigail reminds me, patting my arm.

"Don't bother," Caleb interjects. "Grab your stuff. You're coming with us."

I freeze, not knowing what to do. If I leave now, I could lose my bed, and I don't want to risk that. After Daniel's reaction this morning, I don't want to cause issues for Samuel. Their apartment is one bedroom, and I'm not sure I could cope with the snide comments. I can't face being where I'm not wanted right now.

"I'm fine here," I say. "Just let me put my bag away, and maybe we can grab something to eat."

As if on demand, my stomach growls, echoing around the enclosed hallway.

To hide my embarrassment, I turn and re-enter my room, grabbing my bag off the bed, before moving towards the lockers in the corner.

"Come on." Caleb's hand lands on the handle, his skin touching mine. "You're coming home with me," he adds, his tone soft, as if trying not to spook me.

My head snaps up, and my eyes lock with his. He takes in my face, and I feel heat flood my cheeks. Heaven only knows what I must look like. While he's here, not a hair out of place, looking perfect as always.

"Why would I do that?" I ask.

"Because your home and business has just burned down, and you're homeless. I have an apartment with multiple spare rooms. I'm offering you one." He shrugs as if what he's telling me is no big deal. Why on earth would he offer me access to his space? It's not like he owes me anything, we had sex… Since meeting me again I've been nothing but a thorn in his side.

I shake my head, but I'm aware of movement in my peripheral.

"Please, April, don't be stubborn. Stay with Caleb. I'll feel much better knowing you're safe," Samuel pleads.

Cal tugs on the bag in my hand, and I let it go. I'm not standing and fighting with him. I'm too tired.

"I have a bed here," I say, looking between the two men.

"You can free it up for someone who doesn't have the option of their own room," Cal says.

He looks completely out of place here in his designer clothes and expensive shoes. Not that the hostel is shabby. It's relatively put together. A few scuff marks on the walls, but the bathrooms were clean and tidy. No mould or black sealant. No peeling paint. It's well-maintained. "This is a Frazer subsidised hostel. Think of my apartment as an… extension of this place." I want to laugh out loud. I can't even imagine the luxury a man like Caleb Frazer is used to. I'm surprised he's not squirming at being here. But then again, he's surprised me with the snippet of information he's just let slip.

I turn to Abigail and Dawn, who are standing by the door. Dawn nods. "The Frazer Foundation keeps us running.

It's why we always have a waiting list for beds come evening."

I squirm at her words. She's telling me outright that I shouldn't be selfish and should free up my bed.

"If I go, will my bed be taken?"

She looks embarrassed as if she realises what she's just said. "That's not what I meant," she adds.

"But it would?"

She nods, the colour in her cheeks highlighting her awkwardness.

"Fine," I say, turning to Cal, who is trying to keep his smug expression at bay. If I'm honest, I'm too tired to argue.

"Let's get out of here," Samuel says, wrapping an arm around my shoulders and walking me to the door.

I notice Mr Ted on the bed, half hidden in the sheets. I break free of his hold, snatching him up before stuffing him in my jumper, out of sight.

"Don't say a word," I say to both men as they go to open their mouths. Samuel wraps me in his arms and kisses the top of my head before leading me down the stairs and out of the door.

"Not saying a word," he says, giving me a squeeze. "But I'm glad Mr Ted survived."

His words bring tears to my eyes.

So am I.

CHAPTER 24

CALEB

Samuel leads April out of the hostel and towards my waiting car. I don't like the sight of her in his arms, but she looks like she needs it and at the moment... it's whatever she needs. I had no intention of inviting her to stay at my apartment when we arrived, but seeing her in ill-fitting clothes, her hair tangled, and her tear-stained cheeks seemed to have done something to me. A far cry from the woman who has been fighting me at every turn. The offer was automatic. I could lie to myself and say I'd have made the offer to anyone, but it's not true. There's something about April Wilson. She's got under my skin. *Something* happened the first night we met and it hasn't dissipated.

Mason holds open the door for Samuel and April before stepping forward and taking the bag from my hands.

"Sir?" he asks.

"Take us home," I say to him as he stows April's bag in the boot.

I think about the well-worn teddy bear she grabbed off the bed. It obviously survived the fire, something from her past that meant enough for her to save it, but what else did she lose last night?

The report Elijah sent me flashes through my brain. The findings shocked me. There will be hell to pay if she finds out I've investigated her. I'm going to have to tread very carefully.

We travel in silence, April's head resting on Samuel's shoulder, his arm wrapped around her. She's closed her eyes, but I can tell from her breathing she's awake.

When we finally pull into the parking garage under the apartments, Mason drives into my designated space. He opens the door and allows us out. April remains silent, and the way her shoulders slump suggests that the fight has almost drained out of her. I don't like it.

"Come on," I say, leading the way to the penthouse's exclusive elevator after grabbing her bag. "We can order some takeaway when we get upstairs."

I hear Samuel whisper something to April, the frequency too low for me to make out the words, but his tone is soothing.

The elevator arrives, and I use my card to access my floor.

I glance over at April, but she averts her eyes.

"Here we are," I say, allowing them both into my space. "The apartment covers two floors and has access to a private roof garden and pool."

My heart begins to race as I put April's bag down by the door and lead them into the main living area. This is my personal sanctuary, a space I have carved out for myself in the heart of this bustling city. Until today, only close friends and family have ventured inside.

"Holy shit," Samuel exclaims.

I turn to find him standing with his hands on April's shoulders, both mesmerised, as they stare out of the glass wall ahead.

"I've never seen a view like it," April mutters, making me smile.

"It's the view that sold this place to me," I tell her honestly. "There is nothing quite like it. Just wait until the sun goes down."

Her eyes lock on mine, her expression one of surprise.

"This isn't a Frazer Development?" she asks.

I shake my head. "I bought this place when I moved to the city seven years ago. Frazer Development was only just starting out. I fell in love with it, and there has been no reason for me to leave."

I watch as she tries to calculate my age. "I was twenty-three when I bought this place," I say. I don't and never will apologise for my wealth and all it has afforded me. In the early days, it came from a trust fund. Still, with strategic investments, courtesy of my twin and Frazer Development's successes, I have far exceeded even my wildest dreams. But then I work hard and play hard.

"What does everyone want to eat?" I say realising April must be starving.

I head into the kitchen and grab the menus I have stockpiled for when the boys come over. When I return, Samuel is sitting on the sofa, and April is still standing and staring out the window.

"Here," I say, placing them on the coffee table. "Choose what you want, and I'll get the food ordered. Most of these are local, so it shouldn't take more than half an hour."

April turns from the window. "I'm fine," she says, her arms wrapped around her waist.

"When did you last eat?" I ask.

She remains quiet, lost in thought.

"Samuel, choose something for her," I say. I'd do it myself, but I have no idea what she likes. The knowledge irks me.

Samuel tilts his head at April and shrugs, but I don't miss his grin.

"Do you have a preference?" Samuel asks me.

"No, they're all great restaurants. I'm happy to go with the consensus."

April snaps back into the present and joins Samuel on the sofa as he begins to look through the menus. She opens the menu for the Chinese restaurant situated downstairs in this building.

"Chicken with Cashew," she says after a moment.

"Samuel?" I ask.

"Sweet and sour chicken, please," Samuel adds.

I pull up the app each resident has access to. It contains all the local businesses and restaurants, allowing those living here to easily support their local community and businesses. Pen, Elijah's old uni friend, played a role in designing and developing it, and we have now incorporated it into every new development we open. As I live here, I got the building's management to have it installed. The local businesses and residents have loved it.

I send down their orders along with one of my own. I also order some crispy duck, spring rolls and a few vegetable side dishes and get an immediate confirmation.

"Twenty minutes," I say.

An awkward silence descends.

"Let me show you to your room," I say to April. "If you want to freshen up before the food arrives, you can."

I walk towards the enormous staircase against the back wall. I turn to find April following. The dark circles under her eyes become more apparent.

I grab her bag and head upstairs.

I move down the hallway. The end is open, and a large glass wall allows light to flood the space. On either side are several doors, each leading to a suite. There are six in total.

Over kill for a bachelor, but when the guys stay, it saves my sofa.

I make my way to the room that used to be Marcus's. Since he got married, he never stays. He's tormented mercilessly by the gang for being hen-pecked because he chooses to head home to his wife. Not that I blame him.

"Here you go," I say, stepping to one side to allow April to enter the room. Samuel has followed her up.

"Wow, this place." Samuel's eyes take in the room.

"There is an en suite through here." I open the door to the bathroom. "There are fresh towels in the wardrobe, along with a robe and slippers."

"Robe and slippers?" April says, turning to me.

I shrug. "A perk of the Frazer Hotel Group. When the boys stay over, I don't want their naked or boxer-covered asses walking around my apartment. They're all clean, I promise."

I watch as April bites the inside of her mouth. Whether to stop herself laughing or whether she just feels awkward, I don't know.

"Anyway, I'll leave you to it. Make yourself at home. I'll see you downstairs."

"This is only until I find somewhere," April says as I make my way to leave.

I shrug. "There's no rush. As you can see, the room is empty."

I don't wait for a reply. Instead, I turn around and walk away, leaving her and Samuel alone.

CHAPTER 25

APRIL

I watch as Caleb turns around and leaves, closing the door behind him. Samuel drops onto the bed.

"Wow, how the other half live," he says, unable to keep the grin off his face. "When he offered to let you stay, I bet you didn't envisage this?"

He throws himself back, allowing the spring of the bed to bounce him, his arms above his head. The bed must be a super king, as Samuel takes up no space despite his size. On top of that, the bed itself doesn't take up much space in a room this size. It reminds me of the room I woke in after my night with Caleb. The opulence of the room, with its own sitting area, dressing room, and en suite. The pale grey room has teal and dark grey soft furnishings. It makes for a very tranquil space. Whoever designed it has beautiful taste.

I smack Samuel's leg and head into the bathroom. A his-and-hers sink unit sits in a granite vanity top, with a ceiling-high mirror on the wall behind it. An enormous walk-in shower takes up the end of the bathroom. The wall is filled with more jets than anyone could need. An internal wall shields the toilet. I smile at the privacy angle.

I catch sight of myself in the bathroom mirror and groan. Samuel appears at the door in an instant.

"You okay?" he asks, his concern touching.

"I'm fine, apart from looking like someone dragged me through a hedge backwards, and I spent most of the afternoon crying about it."

The red blotchiness around my eyes is more apparent than the tear tracks down my cheeks.

"I shouldn't worry. I don't think Cal noticed," he says, leaning against the wall. "That man was about ready to turn the entire city upside down, trying to track you down. I think he's spent most of the day hunting for you."

"I doubt it," I say.

Although a certain warmth settles in my chest at the thought of him looking for me, caring enough.

What! Where did that come from?

"Damn, we need to call Di. She's beside herself," he says suddenly, pulling out his phone and hitting redial on her number.

"Hi Di, yes, she's safe. I'll pass you over."

He thrusts the phone into my hands before walking out of the room.

"Hi, Di," I say.

"Oh honey, are you okay? We've been worried sick. When Samuel said he couldn't find you..." her voice catches as she breaks off.

"I'm fine. Promise. I dropped my phone during my grand escape," I say, trying to make light of the situation, although the thought of having to eat into my meagre savings to replace it is a pain. Monday, I'll need to go to the job centre and sign on. See what I'm entitled to until I can get another job.

"Is everything gone?"

"Yes."

My throat closes over, forcing me to take a breath before I add, "I saved, Mr Ted."

I pull the old, dog-eared teddy bear from my pocket and hold it to my chest. It's one of the few possessions I have left from my childhood. I think losing Mr Ted might have broken me more than losing the business. The only item I have left from my birth mother.

"Well, as long as you and Mr Ted are safe, I'm happy. Do you need money? I can transfer you some if you do." Di says. "Julian and I, we are always here for you. It might not be much, but know we love you very much."

"I know, and I appreciate everything you've done and do for me. But I'm okay. I promise you. I have some money put aside," I say, although it's a lot less than I would wish for.

"If you're sure," Di says. The emotion in her voice lets me know how scared she's been.

"I promise to call if I need anything," I say. "Look, I better go. Cal has ordered takeaway, and it should arrive any minute now."

"Cal?" Di asks, her interest clearly peaked.

"Yes, Caleb Frazer, the property developer who bought my building."

"Really..." she says, the excitement in her voice makes me want to groan.

"Oh, I have to go. Our takeaway has arrived," I say, screwing up my face and holding my breath. I hate lying to Di, but I don't need her to get the wrong impression. Especially knowing he already has her seal of approval. She was the one who told me I should look him up after all.

I repent and sigh. "He's kindly offered me his spare room, and I'll be staying with him for a few days until I can get myself sorted. Please don't worry about me." Before she can say anything else or get the wrong idea, I continue. "Look, I better go. I'll call you as soon as I pick up a new phone. If you need me, call Samuel. He can get a message to me."

"Take care, April. Remember, we love you."

"I know. I love you too," I say.

Even after all these years, knowing they are there and care makes me feel a little less alone in the world.

I wash my face and put a brush through my tangled hair. Exiting the bathroom, I find Cal in the doorway and Samuel still sitting on the bed.

"Singing my praises?" Cal says, a smirk on his face.

"Did no one ever tell you it's rude to eavesdrop.?" I make a mental note never to use speaker phone again within Cal's hearing

"Nah, and if I thought you meant it—" he stops and shoots a look at Samuel. "The food's arrived. It's downstairs and waiting whenever you're ready."

Samuel is up and off the bed in a heartbeat, making his way downstairs. Cal holds his arm out, motioning for me to lead the way.

"Thank you," I say as I pass him.

"You're welcome," he replies, his smile genuine.

I don't understand this man. Everything about him is a contradiction. The things I've read about him, how he conducts his business, the humanitarian effort, his affordable and eco living and then there's...him. The man makes my head spin.

* * *

CONVERSATION OVER DINNER is a muted affair, everyone too hungry to speak. I wonder whether Samuel's assessment of Cal is true.

Has he really been out looking for me all day?

The thought does strange things to my insides.

When Samuel's phone rings for the fifth time, I growl at him.

"You can't ignore him," I say.

"I can and I will. Daniel needs to understand that what he did is unacceptable," he hisses.

"Maybe, but you know why he is the way he is. You ignoring him and being with me will not help the situation."

"If it hadn't been for Caleb, I wouldn't have known you were missing." He huffs before grabbing one of the spring rolls Caleb ordered.

"I wasn't missing. I was at a hostel. I would have called you tomorrow," I say. "I was just too tired earlier. It was a long night. The paramedic warned me I'd be tired from the smoke inhalation. Told me to sleep it off."

It's then I realise what Samuel said. I turn to Cal. "You went to Daniel's apartment?"

Cal nods but continues eating as if it's no big deal.

He tracked down my best friend to check on me.

I turn back to Samuel. His declaration is not something I can process right now.

"This is beyond Dan's control," I say. "He has issues. He's come a long way since you two first started dating."

I don't know why I'm sitting here defending him, probably because I know my bestie loves him, and I don't want to be the person who gets between them. Plus, someone else's problems are the perfect distraction for my own messed up life.

To say Daniel has issues with Samuel and my close relationship is an understatement. When Dan met Samuel, he'd gone through a messy divorce. Leaving him with multiple scars. Initially, he tried to smother him, not allowing him out, wanting to vet every friendship. Kudos to my bestie. He drew a line in the sand. But our friendship is still a bone of contention.

Samuel runs a hand down his face. When his phone rings again, he picks it up and leaves the table.

"Second door on the right," Cal says to him, pointing to a corridor that goes under the stairs to another part of the apartment.

This place is enormous. The explorer in me wants to seek out where each door leads. Be nosy, see what I can find out about this enigma of a man. As Samuel disappears, I turn towards Cal, only to find him watching me. The expression in his eyes is unreadable, but something in that look sets off butterflies low in my stomach and a flood of memories taking me back to that night.

CHAPTER 26

CALEB

Her eyes darken. Maybe my little firecracker isn't as immune to me as she likes to pretend. It's not surprising, just the memory of our night together in New York leaves me as hard as a rock, often at the most inopportune times.

"Why? Why are you doing this?" she asks, her back straightening.

"Doing what?" I ask innocently, taking a sip of my wine.

"You know very well what."

When I shrug, she sits back, crossing her arms over her chest. "I don't get it. You're free, Cal. Your company is free. No ties, no more responsibility. Everything I own went up in smoke. You can walk away."

Her voice catches on the last part, and I'm forced to school my features. This is not a time for sparring. This is her life. She drops her gaze for a split second but forces it back to mine. "No alternative dance studio. No dance studio, period. You can return to Sunny Down's original design."

I sit back and steeple my fingers, staring at her.

"Is that what you think?"

I'm not sure if I should take offence. I asked her to trust me, but trust is a strange thing. Something I've learned over the years. I've not done anything to cause her to distrust me, or at least I don't think I have, but have I really done anything to prove she can? However much I feel it's not true. We hardly know one another, although I intend to rectify that. Having her here is step one.

"I'm not free, April. There's still you and those kids you help. A community that relies on what you offer their children, their young people. You told me you've given them a purpose, somewhere to go. Kept them off the streets. As I said before, I develop communities. I don't want all your hard work to go to waste. The fire has destroyed the building, but all it means is we will need to rebuild it. Nothing changes."

She stares at me as if weighing up my words, looking for a lie.

In some ways, the fire has solved my problem with the board. Delays are now inevitable; their argument no longer carries any weight. I really do have a blank canvas on which to work.

April shakes her head, dropping it back and staring at the ceiling. "It's over," she says almost too quietly for me to hear.

"What's over?"

"There's nothing left for me here. I can't help you or them anymore."

When her eyes finally meet mine, I can't miss the sheen of tears. A sense of panic crushes my chest.

What does she mean?

I incline my head. Leaning forward, I take the hand she has placed on the table and bring her focus back to me.

"Has everything I've been saying to you over the past few

weeks gone in one ear and out of the other?" I ask. "Because I distinctly remember saying they do matter. That I want to ensure they have a place in the new development. You, April, are part of that. You are helping to bridge the gap. They trust you to be their spokesperson."

She stares at me for a moment before shaking her head.

"Have you failed to notice my home is gone, my business is gone? My foothold in their community has just gone up in flames. The only thing I have to my name is my handbag, some second-hand clothes the ladies in the charity shop put together for me, and an old stuffed teddy bear. My life is in tatters, Cal. You're delusional if you think I can help."

This time, I don't suppress my smile. "Maybe I am. I've been called worse. As for homeless, that's easily rectified. You can stay here—it's not like there isn't plenty of room. I'll employ you as a consultant. You can work with my team as a go-between."

"You're crazy. I can't stay here—with you," she says.

"Give me one good reason why not?"

"You don't know me." The jut of her jaw lets me know she's serious.

"Not entirely accurate. I know you *very* well." I watch as colour spreads up her neck.

She stares at me like I really have lost my mind.

"We don't even like one another."

It's my turn to frown.

"That's not true. I certainly like you."

Her cheeks darken further.

I think back to my dream. I know who I was dreaming about. The woman in front of me is tying me up in knots.

April is quiet for a moment.

"I still don't get it," she says.

"Get what?"

"Why do you think I can help you? Why do you want me to? I've done nothing but cause issues. The protests, the flash mob."

I smile. The issues she's raised have helped, not hindered, the process. It usually takes us months to get to the heart of a community and have them trust us. April has opened the door.

"You're their mouthpiece. You know how they work, who's who."

"I'm just a dance teacher."

April throws her hands in the air in frustration.

"Don't do that. Don't devalue yourself or what your community feels towards you. As for what you know, it's about being a point of contact," I say, having more faith in her than she does.

The sound she makes is like a grunt.

"Okay, so I can help with the community, but that doesn't explain you and why you're willing to let a stranger move into your home?"

"You're not exactly a *complete* stranger," I say, raising an eyebrow in her direction, watching in delight as more colour floods her cheeks.

"I won't sleep with you if that's what this is about," she says, crossing her arms once again over her chest.

I drop the teasing and school my features.

"Is that what you think? That I brought you here to sleep with you?" A tightness forms in my chest. "You really don't think very highly of me, do you? What's so wrong with letting someone help you?" I shake my head. "If you want to go back to the hostel, I can get Mason to drop you off."

"If I'm honest. I don't know what to think." Her gaze locks on mine. "We slept together in New York months ago. I never expected to see you again. Now, here you are. To say the past few weeks have been a whirlwind…" She uncrosses her arms and closes her eyes, rubbing her temples. When she opens them again, she shakes her head. "Cal, look at it from my point of view. You are buying the building I rent. Tonight, you ride in and rescue me like some knight in shining armour and tell me you want nothing from me apart from to be your mouthpiece in the community." She stops and sighs. "That's not usually how life works. People always want something in return. Forgive me for being cynical."

The colour remains in her cheeks, but her lips press together, her gaze ping-pongs, not quite connecting with mine.

"I promise you, that is not my aim."

"It's not the first time you've taken me back to yours," she says, raising an eyebrow. "So forgive me for thinking the worst."

"Believe me, I'd like nothing more than to take you upstairs and strip you naked, bury my cock deep in your pussy. However, that is not why I invited you here."

She gasps at my words, a dark flush spreading up her neck.

"I'll be honest with you. Yes, I want you, but I also know now is not the right time. I'll never lie to you. I'll never force my attention on you. When I told you, you could trust me, I meant it. I want to help you. That's why you're here."

Samuel returns at that exact moment, his gaze switching between us.

"What did I miss?" he asks.

"Nothing," April says. "Just Caleb being… Caleb."

April switches her attention to Samuel, and I smirk. There is clearly no comeback, or at least not one she wants her friend to hear.

"What did Daniel say?" she asks, ignoring our previous conversation.

He shrugs. "He apologised. "

She gets up and wraps her arms around her friend's waist, giving him a squeeze before looking up at him.

"You love him," she says. "You'll work it out."

April drops her head against his chest and holds him. Their bond is clear and strong.

When she eventually steps back, her hand comes up and rests against his chest.

"You need to speak to him," she says.

"But what about you?" he asks.

She turns to me before looking back at him.

"I'm fine. I've got Caleb here," she says. "He's already a notch on my bedpost, so you don't need to worry about me going there again. Once was enough."

"Ouch, man—that's got to sting." The mirth in Samuel's eyes gives away his thoughts.

I hold up my hands in defeat.

"Multiple orgasms in one night are clearly not enough for some people. What can I say?"

April lets out a snort, smacking her forehead with her hand while Samuel chuckles.

"If you're sure you're okay. I'll love you and leave you both. Just try not to kill one another when I'm gone."

"I'll get Mason to bring the car around. He can drop you home."

"It's no problem. I can get a taxi."

"This is no problem," I say. "Mason will be happy to do it. His mother lives near your place, and it's still early. He was telling me he wants to pop by and see her."

I send a message to Mason, who replies immediately.

"All sorted. He'll meet you in the garage, by the car."

Samuel nods, and I walk him to the elevator. He turns to me as it arrives.

"Look after our girl," he says, squeezing my shoulder.

"With my life," I say, knowing I mean it.

He gives me a small smile before looking over my shoulder and grinning.

"Behave," he says to April.

"Always," she returns with an expected amount of sass.

This is going to be fun.

CHAPTER 27

APRIL

I wake up with a start, the clock on the bedside table telling me it's ten already.

What? I never sleep this late. I'm usually an early bird.

The room is in total darkness. I hit the button next to the bed and watch as the blinds open, allowing the light of the day to stream in. No manual curtain pulling in this *penthouse*, no manual *anything* from what I can tell. This man has everything automated!

After Samuel left, Caleb gave me a tour of the apartment before telling me to make myself at home. I excused myself almost immediately, needing to put some space between us, especially after his revelation. I'm not sure what I'm supposed to make of that. Cal didn't say anything else, instead, he handed me one of his t-shirts and bade me goodnight.

I look down at the offending item. *Damn it!* Even the smell of his detergent brings back memories I thought were long forgotten. Memories that had me tossing and turning for hours despite my exhaustion. Last night, I grabbed a quick shower before I fell into bed, but the soothing smell surrounding me kept me awake for hours.

This morning, however, is the start of a new day. I throw back the covers and groan as I climb out of the most comfortable bed I've ever slept on. My chest still feels tight, but not as bad as yesterday.

I shower and get dressed in the second outfit Val and Dorrie gave me. I will need to purchase some new clothes. These are great for covering myself, but the trousers are just clinging onto my hips and will not suffice in the long run. Maybe shopping will be something I can do this afternoon.

I head downstairs and jump when I find a lady with blonde hair standing in the kitchen.

She turns and smiles. "Morning. You must be April. Caleb told me not to wake you. I hope I haven't been too loud?"

I shake my head, and she smiles at the look of confusion I send her way.

"Sorry," she says, stepping forward and holding out her hand. "I'm Paula. Caleb's housekeeper. I'm here every day. Let me know if there's anything you need."

"Pleased to meet you, Paula," I say. "Is Cal, sorry, Caleb around?"

"No, but he left you a note on the table."

Paula points to the table where we had eaten the night before.

"Thank you," I say, heading over to the note.

April

I hope you slept well.

I wanted to be around when you woke up, but after the fire, my attention is needed in the office so I'll see you tonight.

By now you will have met Paula, my housekeeper. If there's anything you need, don't hesitate to ask, she'll organise it.

The box contains a new phone for you. I'm aware yours was destroyed in the fire. I've already input mine, Trish's, my PA, and Samuel's number. I'll leave the rest to you.

The black keycard allows you access to the apartment and this floor. Concierge can let you up, if you forget it. They are aware you are staying with me.

Chloe is coming at 11:00. She'll be self-explanatory when she arrives.

Try to get some rest today, and I'll see you later.

Cal

WHO IS CHLOE? Clearly not his housekeeper, but who else?

Well, there's only half an hour until I find out.

I head into the kitchen just as Paula is leaving.

"I'll be down there," she says, pointing down the corridor with three doors heading off it.

"Okay," I say, not quite sure what to do or say.

She smiles warmly, and my shoulders relax. If I'm to stay here and she comes in every day, I better get used to it.

After our whirlwind tour, I know the first door is Caleb's home office. The second is a state-of-the-art home gym, and the third is a guest bathroom.

I shake my head, wishing I had my sports gear and could go for a run. My mind wanders to images of Caleb on a running machine, sweat dripping down his body, his olive skin glistening.

I lick my lips because my mouth is suddenly dry. I head into the kitchen and throw open the fridge, surprised to find it fully stocked.

"Oh, I forgot to say," Paula says, reappearing and making me jump. "Oh, sorry," she says, as I hold up a hand before clutching it to my chest, willing my breathing to return to normal. "I've stocked the fridge. If there's anything you need or want, let me know, and I can arrange for the concierge to have it delivered for you."

I stare at the woman open-mouthed before slamming it shut. "Er, thank you."

She smiles and makes a gesture to let me know she's leaving.

How the other half live. I don't even need to go to the supermarket to buy orange juice. I can make a call and have it delivered. This is surreal.

I pull out the carton of juice and hunt through the cupboards until I find a glass. I collapse onto one of the stools in the centre of the room, pouring myself a generous portion. The kitchen is a quarter of the size of my entire dance studio.

A buzzer sounds somewhere in the apartment.

I hear Paula answer, although I can't make out her words. She reappears at the door, but this time, I'm ready to give her what I'm sure is an awkward smile.

"Chloe is here. I've told them to send her up," Paula says. "If you need anything..."

"Thank you," I say again, unsure of what else to say. I don't even know who this Chloe is.

Paula greets someone, followed by a loud clattering and banging sound.

"Thank you, gents, that was really helpful," another voice says.

I step out of the kitchen, the sight in front of me taking my breath away.

A woman around my age stands in the living room. As if sensing my arrival, she turns with the most welcoming smile.

"Hi, I'm Chloe. You must be April," she says, stepping forward and holding out her hand. "Caleb sent me. He told me about your unfortunate circumstances. I'm so sorry. It must have been awful," she adds, her voice full of genuine sympathy. "I'm here to help replace some of the things you lost."

I stare wide-eyed at the woman in front of me.

"I think there's been some misunderstanding, Chloe," I say when I look at the store she's come from. Under no circumstances can I afford this shop or their brands.

"No misunderstanding," she says, leading me to the sofa. "Caleb left strict instructions. You are to have whatever you need. He's got it covered."

My phone beeps on the table, and I get up to retrieve it. I need to call Caleb anyway and ask him what the hell he's playing at.

I glance down at my phone.

Speak of the devil.

CALEB:

> I know Chloe has arrived. Let her sort out your clothes.

My head pops up, and I look around. Is he watching us? Does he have a nanny cam?

CALEB:

> No cameras. I checked with concierge I know she's arrived.

I can almost hear the smirk in his voice. He thinks he knows me *so* well.

ME:

> I don't need your charity. I can buy my own clothes.

Three dots appear and disappear, reappearing and disappearing as if he's trying to decide what to say.

The phone in my hand rings, and Samuel's name appears.

I answer and wait.

"Morning, baby girl," Samuel says.

I walk into the kitchen, wanting some privacy.

"Hey," I reply.

"What's happening?" he asks although I have a feeling he already knows.

"Has Caleb just called you?" I ask, suspicious of the timing and Caleb's lack of reply.

"Er…"

"Samuel, since when did the two of you become best buddies?"

"It's not like that," he says. "I'm… he's just trying to help you."

"I'm not *that* woman," I say, grimacing at the words as they come out of my mouth. "I've been taking care of myself since I turned eighteen."

"You have, and everyone else around you," Samuel says.

After a pause, he sighs. "Is it really so bad to let someone else take care of you for a change?"

I sit on one of the island stools, my elbows resting on the granite surface, phone against my ear.

"It's too much. I don't want him to think I'm taking advantage or worse. That he can buy me."

Does he think buying me some clothes will pave the way to his bed?

My stomach flutters at the thought.

"Ask yourself this. Why do you care?" Samuel asks quietly.

I drop my forehead into my hand and exhale into the phone.

"I'm not a charity case," I say eventually, not wanting to unpack Samuel's statement or examine it too closely.

"No, you're not. Caleb doesn't see you that way. He's simply trying to help. The same way you help all those who come to your dance studio. How many times have you sent one of the kids off with money to buy something at Betty's?"

"That's different," I say. I think back to Cal's declaration. He promised I was in control. I need to believe he means it. There's no way I'm going to end up back in his bed, however sexy he is.

"Why is it different? If you give all you can afford to help someone else, whether it's a pound, or two thousand pounds. Helping someone when it's within your means is an act of kindness. Are you saying because Caleb's wealthy, he's not allowed to help?"

I hate it when Samuel talks sense.

"It's different. I know those kids," I say, eventually.

Samuel laughs. "Baby girl, you exchanged bodily fluids with the man. Please don't tell me you don't know him or he you. He knows *you* in the biblical sense."

It's true, but it still weighs heavily in my stomach.

"If it was me offering to buy you things. What would you do?" Samuel asks suddenly.

"That's different."

"Why?" he says as my hackles rise.

"Because... because you and I have been friends for years, and when you needed it, I helped you out."

"Fine then, I'll give you the money," Samuel surprises me by saying.

What the hell is going on?

"You don't have that kind of money…" I say.

"I do. Caleb offered it to me last night after you'd gone to bed. He wanted me to buy you everything you need."

I pull the phone away from my ear and stare at it before putting it back. "Say that again."

"You heard me. I told him no. I told him that if he wanted to help you out, he should do it openly and honestly. It's funny how he knew you'd reject his offer. The man seems to know you better than you realise."

I'm not sure what to say. Caleb Frazer confuses me. My response to him confuses me. He ties me up in knots. But the more I learn about the man as an individual, the more I'm spiralling.

As if sensing my turmoil, Samuel speaks again. "You've always been the first to help others. Let someone who can afford to help you. Maybe you can repay him in other ways."

"I'm not prostituting myself out to him," I say sharply, as thoughts of having Caleb Frazer between my thighs sends an unexpected flood of moisture south.

"That's not what I meant. Why would you think that?" he says, sounding flummoxed.

Why indeed!

"Cook the man something nice to eat, get him a *thank you* gift. Hell, I don't know, buy him flowers or chocolates. I'm sure some form of acknowledgement would be welcome. Show him you're not taking him for granted. Agree to work for the man, help him, help the community—stop being stubborn."

I freeze. Samuel has never been short with me before, but I've pushed a button.

"Hey," I say

"Sorry," he lets out a huff down the phone. "Stop giving him a hard time."

"Since when did you become a Caleb Frazer fan?" I ask.

This entire conversation has surprised me.

"Since I watched the man tie himself in knots, turning a city upside down trying to find you."

My breath catches as my brain tries to absorb all Samuel has said. My head wants to rebel, but my heart tells me he's telling the truth.

"Okay, I'll accept his help. But I'll find a way to repay him."

Samuel chuckles. "I wouldn't expect anything less."

"Look, I need to go. Chloe is waiting patiently for me in the other room," I say, before adding, "And Samuel, thank you for always being there for me."

"Always, baby girl, always. I'm only repaying the favour."

We disconnect, and I stare at my phone. Should I be jealous? Few people impress Samuel. He's jaded. His past, like mine, has made him so. It's why we're two peas in a pod. But there's something about Cal that he admires. I can see it in his stance and how they are around one another. I get the impression the feeling is mutual. After all, Cal went to him to track me down.

I move back into the main area and look at Chloe, who is busy trying to occupy herself on her phone.

"Let's do this," I say, which earns me a great big smile.

"Perfect," she says, moving to the first rack. "We'll start with casual and move up. Just so you know. I also have a case full of dance and gym gear. Apparently, all the brands you like. Mr Frazer asked your friend which you preferred."

I roll my eyes. "I feel ganged up on. They've been colluding behind my back."

Chloe laughs. "They both clearly care about you," she says, and I decide against correcting her. I'm not going to try to guess what's going on in Caleb Frazer's head.

CHAPTER 28

CALEB

I make my way into the restaurant, where my friends are waiting.

"Is everything okay?" Xander says as I drop into my seat.

At eleven, when I finally checked my phone, I realised there were multiple messages from the guys and that I'd forgotten about our weekly poker night. I'd sent them an update, and we'd all agreed to meet for lunch.

"Yeah, sorry about that. It was quite a day."

"What's the latest?" Tristan asks.

"It looks like an electrical fire. Due to the age of the building, its completely gutted. Went up like a tinder box."

"Was anyone hurt? They said it was overnight, but the news was vague," Xander says.

I shake my head, although the vice-like grip that restricts my breathing every time I think about April being in the building is back. I can't think about what could have happened.

"What happens now?" Tristan asks. "Isn't that the building that housed the dance school? The one the protests and flash mob were about."

"It is, was." I run a hand through my hair. "I have back-to-back meetings with the planning and fire departments all afternoon, not to mention the council. The board is also chasing me."

"Sounds like you have your hands full," Quentin chips in. "What about the businesses? The dance teacher? The one who's been ruffling feathers."

Betty and Don's insurance will cover their losses. For April, after reading Elijah's file, she has nothing. Her business literally went up in smoke.

"That's what I was doing last night. April, who runs the dance school, was M.I.A. We knew she had got out, but was living there. I wanted to check she was okay."

"*Shit!*" Marcus says. "Is she okay?"

I don't miss the looks the boys shoot one another.

"She's fine. I tracked her down to the local hostel."

There's a pregnant pause.

"What?" I say as four sets of eyes lock on me.

"Nothing," Tristan says innocently, making the others laugh.

"So, what happened when you tracked her down?" he asks.

I inwardly groan, as this conversation is about to go downhill incredibly fast if I know my friends.

"I invited her to stay at mine," I admit, finding a speck of lint on the tablecloth and brushing it off.

I look up to find my friends staring at me, jaws slack.

"What?" I ask as if this is nothing special.

"You say, *what*? As if this is no big deal," Quentin says, when he finally recovers. "The man who has never taken a partner back to his apartment. Claims it's *his* space, *his* sanctuary. Now tells us he has invited a complete *stranger* into his home to *stay* with him."

"Unless she's not a stranger," Tristan chips in.

He shoots me a look that makes me wonder how much of my heart I spilled on Sunday night.

I look around the table to find my friends staring at me eyebrows raised.

I shrug. "She's down on her luck. What else was I supposed to do?"

"A hotel, one of your empty apartments?" Xander says. I grind my teeth. "There it is," he says pointing at my ticking jaw. "There is definitely more to this." He crosses his arms and stares at me. "I want to know why our best friend appears to be holding out on us."

April is the first woman I have never discussed with my friends. For some reason when I came back from New York it felt wrong. I didn't want to cheapen it. And the fact she disappeared.

In unison they sit back and cross their arms over their chests. If I didn't feel backed into a corner, it would be amusing.

"Fine," I huff. "I met April in New York."

"Ha," Marcus says, holding his palms out to the others.

"What the hell?" I mutter.

"Sorry man, I win," he says, as the others hand over a wad of cash.

"Win?"

"I told them you met someone special in New York," Marcus explains. "They didn't believe me."

I suck in a breath.

Is April special?

Hell, I know she's special. She's the first woman I have ever wanted to wake up next to, share a leisurely breakfast with. Instead, when I opened my eyes, she was gone.

When I don't say anything, my friends remain silent.

"She needs my help," I say quietly.

"Good for you," Tristan says, and once again, I wonder how much I spilled on Sunday. My friends shift in their seats.

I hear music and look up to find Quentin on his phone. I recognise the tune instantly and the background noise and groan.

"Really," I say, shooting my friend *that* look.

He simply shrugs as Xander and Tristan look over his shoulder. I know they're watching April as she dances outside my office.

"Wow, man, she's hot," Xander says. "And she can dance!"

It's Marcus who smacks him on the back of the head.

I don't like the look on my friend's face, it's too... interested.

What the hell?

I've never been protective of a woman before, especially with my friends. But April has been through enough. She doesn't need any of these *reprobates* messing with her.

"She's been through a lot," I say, feeling the need to defend my actions.

"Down, boy. No one's going to take or hit on your new toy," Xander chuckles.

"She's not a toy," I snap, only to be surrounded by their laughter, and I realise I've just walked straight into their trap.

"Sorry, Caleb, I'm only teasing." Xander squeezes my shoulder, and I realise my friends are now staring at me with added interest.

"Our friend is heading down a slippery slope. Marcus mark two." Quentin laughs.

"You're just jealous," Marcus says.

Quentin flinches, although he recovers quickly, adding, "Next time we visit, his bachelor pad will be filled with coloured pillows and fluffy throws."

I roll my eyes, and my mind wanders to Gabriel's apartment, which Leah has turned from a cold, sterile shell into something warm and inviting.

"He'll be ball and chained," Tristan adds.

Quentin lets out a fake sob, "Hearts are breaking all over the city tonight."

They continue their tirade until our lunch is delivered, and I let them.

My mind wanders to April, and I wonder how she got on with Chloe. She sent no more messages. Samuel must have convinced her to accept my support, or at least I hope he did. I take both of their silence as a good thing.

Lunch ends, and we say goodbye, with everyone heading back to their respective offices.

* * *

I FINALLY MAKE it home by seven-thirty. I met with the fire officer to discuss their initial findings. Antiquated electrics look to be the cause. The building was a death trap, a fire waiting to happen. The thought leaves me cold.

The leftover structure is unsafe and will need to be pulled down as soon as possible or made safe to ensure no one can get in. Wes and I have spent the past couple of hours talking to the planning officers and builders, ensuring they carry out the recommendations to make the remaining structure is secure. It might be late, and the fire only occurred yesterday, but the Frazer name makes people act.

I enter the apartment to the smell of food—home-cooked food. April is in the kitchen at the stove. I cringe when I catch sight of her wearing the inappropriate novelty apron, Xander bought me for Christmas. As if sensing me, she looks up. Her face is makeup free, and her hair tied up in a messy bun. When she looks up and smiles, my heart stops for a second.

"Hey," I say. "What are you doing?"

Her smile falters. "I hope you don't mind. I thought I'd make us dinner. Paula said she usually cooks for you and leaves it in the warming drawer. I said I'd do it as a thank you."

"Of course I don't mind." I step into the kitchen and throw my wallet and keys down on the side. "You're living here. I want you to make yourself at home."

Her cheeks take on a hint of colour.

The ribbing by the boys at lunch comes back to me, and I bite back a smile. I wonder how they'd react if the sofa is covered in throws and pillows the next time they come for a boys' evening. I'm half tempted to order my own just to see.

"Well, I've made roast beef and Yorkshire pudding. Paula said it's your favourite, but she struggles to do it because it's soggy by the time you get home."

I'm touched by her thoughtfulness.

"Let me get changed, and I'll come back down and help."

"No need. Everything is in hand. Should be ready in ten minutes," she says, stirring what looks to be gravy.

I go to leave.

"Er, Cal."

I turn at the sound of her voice.

"I'm sorry if I seemed ungrateful this morning." She runs a hand down her face and sighs. "I'm not used to people doing things for me. I've spent a lot of years looking after myself." She shifts awkwardly. "Thank you for the phone and the clothes. I'll repay you as soon as I can."

I pause in the doorway and exhale.

"I don't want repaying." When she goes to open her mouth, I hold up a hand. "I didn't do it to be repaid. I did it because I knew you needed clothes and a phone." I stop, wanting to change the subject, not get into an argument. "I'm sorry about what I said last night. I shouldn't have said anything. I don't want you to feel awkward while you're living here."

I watch the colour spread over her cheekbones and decide to change the subject.

"The fire department came by today. It looks like the fire was caused by an electrical fault. As the developer buying the building, I should have inspected it more thoroughly, especially when we found out businesses were still operating in it. Purchasing a few clothes is nothing."

April crosses her arms over her chest and stares at me. "I know that's not true," she tells me quietly. "My tenancy doesn't end until this week which means you don't officially own the building yet. I also have copies of all the safety certificates, gas and electrics. None of this is your fault, Cal. This is all on my landlord." She pauses, holding my gaze. "Thank you for the clothes and the phone. If I'm honest, I wasn't sure how I was going to manage, so for me, that is not *nothing*. I just want you to know that."

I stare at her for a second, before inclining my head. "I'll go and get changed," I say, when she doesn't say anything else. The last thing I want is for April to feel indebted. Damn Samuel, why didn't he just take the money I offered him for her.

I excuse myself before she can say anything else. April is correct, I purchased the property with vacant possession. The landlord is responsible, especially as completion hasn't taken place yet. But April won't see a penny from the landlord and as a company we won't be pulling out of the sale despite the fire, although the details are now with the solicitors.

I change into jeans and a jumper and return to the kitchen. April has placed all the food on the table.

"This is a small thank you for all you've done over the past twenty-four hours and what you're saying you're going to do for the community. You're not what I thought, Caleb Frazer. When I'm wrong, I admit I'm wrong."

"Thank you," I say, my heart racing at her words. I turn my attention to the food and take a seat. "This looks amazing."

April smiles, and my heart stops this time.

"Tuck in," she says.

And we do.

CHAPTER 29

APRIL

It's been several days since Caleb arranged for the personal shopper and I first cooked dinner for us.

On Friday, I accompany him to the office and meet the team. With the dance studio in ruins, there's little or nothing I can add. What is more concerning is there's now nowhere for the kids to go, while they rebuild, but that's not Frazer Development's problem. I just pray they don't get caught up in the very things I worked so hard to keep them away from.

By Friday night the tightness in my chest has all but disappeared and I'm finally feeling human again. The need to exercise overwhelming.

I head to Caleb's private gym, Chloe having delivered all my new clothes and a selection of beautiful sportswear.

I step onto the running machine and hit start, only for nothing to happen. Lights flash on the wall.

I follow the cable. Nope all plugged in. My confusion grows. I step onto the cross-trainer. The same. Nothing. I stand and stare at the equipment, perplexed.

"April?"

I hear Caleb call my name.

"Here," I say, coming out into the corridor and stepping into view.

His eyes skim my body, taking in my gym clothes, and my nipples harden under his scrutiny. I hate the impact this man's presence has on my body. Thank goodness for padded bra tops. Thinking I was alone, I'm in a sports bra and leggings.

"There you are." His voice sounds slightly husky.

Maybe I'm not the only one affected.

Why does that thought set butterflies off in my stomach?

"Here I am," I say, putting my hands on my hips. As a dancer, I know I look good in leggings.

"What were you doing?" he asks.

"I was about to do a workout, but I can't seem to get your machines to work."

Caleb steps around me and moves into the gym.

"Do you have your phone?" he asks, turning towards me.

I go over to the weight bench and retrieve it.

Unlocking it, I hand it over as he moves to a panel on the wall.

"What are you doing?"

Caleb looks over his shoulder before returning his attention to the flashing keypad.

"I'm synching your phone up. This is a smart gym."

"A what?"

"A smart gym. It takes the information you give it and it provides a personalised daily workout, depending on what other exercise you have done that day. I downloaded the app onto your phone, but forgot to go through it with you."

When his eyes drop to my wrist, I rub it self-consciously.

Caleb returns his attention to the wall, before turning and handing me back my phone.

"All set," he says. "Everything should work now. When you want to use the equipment, come in and hold your phone up to the screen. It will then use your vitals to ascertain what you need to do?"

"My vitals?"

"I'll get you a watch," he flashes his fitness watch at me. "It records my vitals. It already knows what I want, to keep me at optimal fitness. It then works out a routine for me."

I stare at him open-mouthed. This is equipment you only see in the most expensive and exclusive gyms, and he has it installed in his home. As if sensing my amazement he smiles.

"Pete," he says aloud. "April would like a workout routine."

"Okay, Caleb. Looking at April's profile." A voice appears through the speakers. "April as a dancer, I will prepare a routine that includes, cardio, as well as muscle toning and strength development."

I stare at the speaker as my phone lights up with the exercises it wants me to do.

"Er, who is Pete?"

"He's what I called the computer-generated voice. It seemed better to name him," Caleb says looking a little sheepish, making me chuckle. "You can go onto the app and tweak your details. Add in anything you want. If the equipment isn't in the gym, Pete will order it and have it delivered."

I stare at Caleb. "That is not necessary. I'm sure I can make do with whatever you have here," I say.

Caleb shakes his head. "You're my guest. If you want to get the most out of Pete, then you need to have the right equipment."

"But. I won't be here that long," I tell him.

He looks up sharply, his eyes clashing with mine. "Are you moving out?"

I feel my cheeks warm. "Um, I will be as soon as I can find somewhere I can afford."

Caleb's shoulders relax. "No rush. As you can see there is plenty of room here. It will be a while before the dance studio is rebuilt."

"This is very technically advanced for a home gym," I say.

Caleb smiles. "Maybe, but then I work long hours. When I'm in the gym, I want that time to be as effective as possible."

I think back to our night in New York and Caleb's body. My mouth goes dry. *Pete clearly works.*

"Okay, thank you," I say awkwardly, still unsure why Caleb is being so generous. The only thing I know is I can't stay here until the dance studio is rebuilt. That part of my life is over. I can't afford to refurbish and reopen it. That ship has sailed. But while I am here, I might as well make the most of what Caleb is willing to share. In the meantime, I will need to look for an alternative job and other accommodation.

* * *

THE NEXT DAY, Caleb presents me with my own Penelope Dawson fitness watch.

As a dancer, this has been a pipe dream of mine. An intelligent watch that monitors its wearer and ensures they stay at peak fitness. I thought I recognised Pete's app, but I've only ever seen it in adverts for posh gyms.

"I can't accept this," I tell Cal when he hands me the watch.

He looks at me a furrow forming between his eyes.

"Why not?"

"Because... this watch is worth about two and a half thousand pounds!" I squeak.

Caleb lets out a deep sigh. "Please just take it," he says.

My stomach clenches as if I'm being completely ungrateful.

When I look up, Cal is pinching the bridge of his nose as if trying to ward off a headache.

I clench my hand to stop myself reaching out to him, unsure why he is so bothered. Instead, I watch as he shakes his head. When he catches me looking at him, he smiles.

"What?" I ask, suddenly feeling defensive.

"It's you," he says, his grin widening. "You're refreshing."

When I shoot him a questioning look, he laughs.

My hands go to my hips, and I raise an eyebrow. "I don't understand."

"No, I don't suppose you do. You're different."

He makes it sound like a compliment, but I'm not sure. I can understand him buying a gift like this for a girlfriend, but I'm a nobody. Someone who has ended up down on her luck, living in his spare room.

Caleb runs his hand through his hair before adding, "I have bought the watch. Please, will you accept it as a gift?"

We stand and stare at one another, neither sure what to do.

My throat constricts, and I step forward, holding out my hand, suddenly feeling ungrateful.

Caleb smiles, our fingers brush as I take the box.

"Thank you. I will treasure it," I say quietly.

"You're welcome," he says before adding quickly, "It not only works in the gym but also works on a number of the appliances in the house. It controls the temperature, can set the coffee machine going—"

I spin to fully face him. "It what? Did I just hear correctly?" I say slowly, my mouth slack. "This watch can make me coffee?"

Caleb looks at me, his high cheekbones darkening. "Er yes," he says awkwardly.

"So, I can order a salted caramel latte?" I ask, trying not to laugh at his expression.

"Not right now, but if that is what you drink. I'll ask Paula to get some salted caramel syrup for you."

I stare at him, my mouth open. "Normal latte is fine," I tell him, shaking my head. "Tell me, what else can my magic watch do?"

Caleb grins and tells me all the appliances and integrated devices that are linked to Pete, his smart tech system. By the time he's finished my brain is in a spin. What happened to just pressing a button?

"Boys and their toys," I mutter, which Caleb seems to find incredibly funny.

CHAPTER 30

CALEB

"April?"

I enter the apartment but find it empty. Strange. When I spoke to her last night, she told me she was going to be home all day, going through some of the teams proposals.

I scour the downstairs, finding the gym empty.

"Pete, can you track April?" I ask.

Pete's voice comes through the speakers. "April is currently on the roof terrace."

I take the stairs two at a time, opening the door to the terrace.

I'm greeted by the sound of music pumping out of the speakers I have camouflaged in the plants.

I step around the trellis and freeze.

April has cleared a space on the patio and is lost in the moment. I watch as her body twists and turns. She locks her movement before drawing herself back in and changing direction, her arms and legs in perfect synergy. Her face is a mask of concentration, her eyes closed. Sweat covers her body, her dance clothes sticking like a second skin. It's clear she's been at this a while. I don't think I have ever seen anything as beautiful. April arches her back and my body hardens. I remember how she moved with me, how she arched off the bed as I drank down her orgasm.

"Cal?" her voice breaks through my fantasy. She has turned to face me, frozen on the spot. "Pete, stop the music… I didn't expect you home."

She grabs a hand towel and her water bottle from one of the sunbeds she's moved to the side, wiping her face and taking a quick drink.

"Sorry," she says, leaning forward, trying to steady her breathing. She looks around her and grimaces. "I promise to put everything back."

I smile, hoping she doesn't look down and catch the semi I'm currently sporting.

"No problem," I tell her. "It looks like a good dance space."

She grins and my body tightens further. "It's been great," she tells me. "And the weather."

She sighs and drops her head back, before closing her eyes. I watch her chest rise as she inhales deeply.

I move closer until I find myself standing in front of her.

"I want you to feel at home while you're here," I tell her truthfully, moving a piece of her hair that has come loose and stuck to her cheek.

Her head snaps up and her already glowing cheeks darken further, and her pupils dilate as they stare up into mine.

"Thank you," she says, her voice sounding even more breathless than when she finished the dance. As if snapping herself out of the trance, she looks away and moves backwards. She stumbles, and I reach out, grabbing her arm and pulling her against me.

"Cal," she whispers, our faces millimetres apart. Her tongue comes out and moistens her lips. "You're home early," she says, her eyes locked on mine. I could move forward, but I promised her and myself I would not force myself on her or take advantage. I don't want her back in my bed because she feels indebted.

The thought is like a bucket of cold water on my libido. I step back putting some distance between us.

"I came home, I have a surprise for you," I say, my voice sounding huskier than usual.

"You don't need to give me anything else," she tells me, inclining her head.

"This is not a gift. I need to take you somewhere. Grab a quick shower and meet me downstairs," I say, making a quick exit before I offer to join her in the shower, lick and wash the sweat from her delectable body.

"What should I wear?" she asks, making me pause.

I'd like to say nothing, but instead I pause. "Jeans, anything."

I don't miss April's frown as I turn away. "I'll see you downstairs."

I don't wait for a reply, instead I make my way to the kitchen and drink a large glass of ice-cold water as there is no time for the kind of shower I need right now.

April joins me in a tight-fitting pair of jeans and a crop top, exposing toned abs. I swallow hard and take another gulp of water.

"Where are we going, Cal?"

"It's a surprise."

She stares at me for a moment, then smiles. My breath catches in my throat.

"Intriguing."

I motion for her to lead the way as we leave the apartment, my eyes drawn to the fluid movement of her hips. I'm already playing with fire, and I must not go there. She's down on her luck. I will not take advantage of her. One night with April Wilson is not enough, but I'm not sure I'll survive another—not intact at least. This woman does things to me, makes me feel things. The more I get to know her, the worse it's getting, and she's only been here less than a week. My brain is full of her, so much so I'm struggling to even concentrate at work.

"So, are you going to tell me where we're going?" she asks, her interest piqued.

It's my turn to smile.

"What part of—*it's a surprise...*" I tell her, has her chuckling.

"You can't blame a girl for trying," she says as we make our way down in the lift to find Mason waiting for us by the car.

"Hi, Mason," she says, earning herself a smile from Mason.

I scowl at him which makes him smile even more.

"Do you ever drive yourself?" April asks when I finally join her on the back seat. "Can you even drive?"

I laugh.

"I can and do. Cars and driving are a hobby of mine," I tell her.

She looks at me, and I shrug.

"However, visiting building sites and potential sites, most of the older buildings don't have parking garages. Having to arrive thirty minutes to an hour early just to ensure I can find a parking space is not an economical use of my time. Having Mason drive me, saves me both time and money," I explain. "Plus, I'm not a great lover of talking while driving, especially in the city. Too many hazards… and people. This way, I can continue working while moving from A to B."

April nods. "That's logical."

We make small talk as we travel through the streets. It's not long before Mason is pulling up outside a large building.

April looks out of the window at the sign, before her eyes flying to mine.

"Why are we here?" she asks, her face a mask of confusion.

"This is your surprise."

"Er Cal, why are we at Scarlett Dupree's Dance and Choreography Studio?"

I can see the pulse throbbing in her neck, her heart is racing. Scarlett is one of the top choreographers in the world and a friend from school. She's also been involved in countless music videos, theatre, and film productions. She returned to the UK a couple of years ago, got married and set up this school after being based in the US for most of her career.

I say nothing. Instead, I get out and walk towards the entrance.

"Are you coming?" I say, turning around and waiting.

Clearly not wanting to be left behind, April jumps out of the car and follows me.

I hold open the door, and April steps around me. Her mouth drops but she quickly closes it. I must admit, Scarlett has done an amazing job. Even her reception area is stunning. The girl sitting behind the desk greets us.

"Hi," she says. "How can I help you?"

"Oh, hi Caleb. Scarlett said to send you straight through."

"Thanks, Kylie," I say, waiting for the door to buzz before pulling it open.

We enter a corridor with glass walls and doors along one side, allowing views of multiple dance studios. A class is taking place in the one ahead of us. The dancers are not much younger than April, their bodies moving in sync as they twist and spin. My mind goes back to her body twisting and turning on the terrace. April moves towards the class as if in a trance, unable to take her eyes off the dancers. Her love for her profession is clear, and I know I've done the right thing bringing her here.

"Caleb." Scarlett's voice draws my attention. "Kylie said you'd arrived."

I walk towards her, sweeping her into a bear hug.

"Good to see you, Scarlett," I say.

"You too, Romeo," she says, patting my cheek and making me scowl. Her laughter echoes down the hall.

"Hi," she says, turning to face April. "You must be April, I'm Scarlett."

She holds out her hand to April, who steps forward taking it in her own.

"Pleased to meet you," she says, although I can hear the nervousness in her tone.

Scarlett smiles warmly.

"I wanted to meet you," she says to April. "When I realised it was Caleb's building and the flash mob, I had to call."

"Oh. Oh!" she says as Scarlett's words sink in. "You called Cal?"

Scarlett turns her gaze to me, her eyes twinkling.

"I did," she says, returning her attention back to April. "Your routine impressed me."

April's cheeks darken at the compliment.

"Thank you," she says awkwardly.

I can see the confusion on April's face. She has no idea why she's here.

"Maybe you should tell April, why you wanted to speak to her," I say to Scarlett. "I haven't said anything. I thought I'd leave that to you." I tell my longtime friend.

"Perfect. Let's grab a drink."

Scarlett turns and leads us into a cafe. It sits at the end of the corridor, on the other side of the dance studios. Large glass windows overlook the car park.

"What can I get you?" she asks.

"Water for me, please," April says.

"Caleb?"

"Coffee, black, thanks, Scarlett."

Scarlett moves over to the counter and speaks to the girl behind it before returning and taking a seat.

"I have a proposition for you," Scarlett says, turning to April.

April stares at her wide-eyed, and I want to chuckle. It's fun watching her fangirl. "I heard what happened. Caleb told me. He also told me your dance school helps the kids in your neighbourhood. Gives them a focus."

April nods but stays silent.

"In the US, I did something similar, helped in local schools. Created somewhere for the kids to go." She touches her lips. "What I'm trying to say is I understand its importance."

"Thank you," April says again.

I smirk, this is probably the only time I've seen her lost for words.

"Let me cut to the chase. I'd like to offer you some space. Space to run your classes, at least until you can get your studio back up and running again."

I watch as April opens her mouth and closes it again.

"We're not currently at full capacity. I have four studios here. Some of my dancers are off-site as they're involved in various projects. If you want it. The space is yours."

"I don't know what to say," she says, shooting me a look, which I return with an encouraging smile. April's eyes lock on my lips, and I swallow.

"Think on it," Scarlett says, breaking the moment.

"It's amazing, and I thank you for the offer. But the kids I work with are miles from here. There's no way they could get across town. I wouldn't want them travelling this far, and there's the cost. My neighbourhood—it's a poor demographic. They don't have money to spare. A lot of the kids..." She doesn't add that some of them attended her classes for nothing more than the task of sweeping the floor at the end of the day or cleaning the showers as payment. Samuel filled me in on that little snippet of information. "They're streetwise, but..."

Scarlett looks at me and raises an eyebrow.

I turn to April and place my hands on the table. "Not an issue. We can transport the kids across in minibuses. The cost covered by Frazer Development. When I said we take the community seriously, I meant it. This benefits everyone. You wanted Action – this is me giving you action."

April stares at me before blinking slowly as if trying to absorb my words.

"We can arrange a schedule. Bring the kids over and ship them back."

April coughs, and I watch her eyes fill before she blinks the moisture away.

"Why?" she asks, her eyes darting between the two of us.

It's my turn to raise an eyebrow. "We've been over this."

She turns to Scarlett. "Why? Why would you offer this?"

"I may have money, but most of those I work with don't," Scarlett says, giving her a knowing smile and placing a hand over April's, squeezing. "Too many have battled their way out of poverty. It's about not missing the talent I know is out there. Some of your kids are good. I want to help you, help them." Scarlett's voice catches, surprising me. I watch these two bond over their love of dance. "Will you let me help you, April? I'm starting a dance program next year. A dance school to help kids like yours, those with talent, that can't afford the standard dance school fees needed."

"I'll need to talk to them. Spread the word. Some parents may have issues, especially where the younger children are concerned," April admits, but I can see the cogs turning in her head as she mulls over the possibilities.

"We can cater for parents. The purpose of setting up this cafe was to cater to student parents. Give them somewhere to meet and wait. I'm sure we can get large enough buses to transport parents who wish to accompany their children. If they don't want to attend, we have permission slips that will need to be signed," Scarlett adds, motioning to the surrounding space.

"I can arrange for the community centre to house another meeting," I say. "If you can spread the word and see who's willing to take us up on the offer."

"And if they're not interested?" April says.

I shrug.

"If they don't, then we'll find another way to help these kids. This is option one."

The determination in April's expression surprises me. She wants to make this work.

"Okay."

A slow smile forms on Scarlett's face as April says, "Let's do this."

Scarlett jumps up and wraps an arm around April's shoulder. "If you don't mind, I'll come to the meeting. Bring some of my dancers, give them people their own age to talk to."

April looks confused as if she's trying to grasp the logistics. She may have her work cut out selling this to the parents, but unless we try…

After we finish our drinks, Scarlett gives April a tour of the facilities. I leave them to it, telling April I need to make some calls and I'll meet her in the car when she's done.

"This is amazing," she says when she finally climbs in next to me.

I smile. "I told you I'd sort something out."

"You did," she says, grinning. "I'm sorry I doubted you. Now, all we have to do is convince the parents."

CHAPTER 31

APRIL

It's been several days since Cal took me to visit Scarlett. This morning, he called to say he's arranged for the community centre to hold our meeting.

Until today, I've stayed clear of Sunny Down. The sight of my dreams in literal ruins almost brings me to my knees. The entire roof has collapsed, and the outside is now boarded up with metal sheeting to keep the public safe. Graffiti artists have already moved in. Some common local tags are clearly recognisable.

I make my way to the high street. Val and Dorrie are in the charity shop as I walk past. After their kindness, I want to repay them.

"Look who it is," Dorrie says as soon as I walk through the door. She rushes forward and sweeps me into a bear hug. "Val, get your butt out here. Ms April's visiting."

"Hi Dorrie," I say, as she holds me by my upper arms, checking me from head to toe.

"Well, aren't you a sight for sore eyes? Looking a lot better than the last time we saw you? And you smell better."

I half grimace at the memory of my last visit. "I should

hope so." I chuckle. "I wanted to thank you for your kindness that day. I'm sorry it's taken me so long to come and see you."

Dorrie's hand comes up and pats my cheek. "Don't you be worrying. You've been through the wringer. Are things looking up? What's the latest? They boarded it all up. Worried about the *health and safety* of the building, I heard."

I follow her further into the shop. "The building has to come down. It's not structurally sound," I tell her as Val appears from the back. She obviously hasn't heard Dorrie because when she sees me, she drops what she's holding on the counter and rushes forward, barrelling Dorrie out of the way.

"April, so lovely to see you," she says, pulling me in for a hug.

The warmth of their affection doing things to my insides. I'm going to miss this community with its warmth and spirit when I move on.

"How are you doing, my lovely?" Val asks, sitting me down on the same chair she placed me on a couple of weeks ago.

"I'm good, Val. I popped in to thank you ladies for your kindness. For your generosity… and, of course, to pay you."

Val waves her hand at me. "No, you don't. It's what community and friends do. We've heard everything about you shouting about saving our community, standing up for the little people."

"Probably why that man in the fancy clothes came in," she says, pursing her lips. "He asked all about you and then left a hefty donation as a thank you."

"Dorrie," Val hisses. "You weren't supposed to say anything."

My eyes move between the two women, who have become very rosy-cheeked suddenly.

"Ladies, what's going on?" I ask, having my suspicions but not quite believing it.

"Er." Dorrie turns away.

"Dorrie, what's going on?" I ask again.

"I'm a silly old woman. Ignore me. I shouldn't have said anything. Confidentiality and all that. He asked us not to, and I opened my big mouth."

Val slaps her forehead in what I can assume is despair at her friend.

Dorrie slaps a hand over her mouth, and I can no longer contain my laughter.

"I'll let you keep his secret," I say as I watch the women become more and more flustered.

Their shoulders sag.

"Let's have a lovely cup of tea, and you can tell us what you've been up to," Val says, heading out of the back.

Dorrie comes up and looks at me. "Sexy man, dark hair, olive skin. He was the one who turned up late to the meeting that day," she says, winking. "He was asking after you."

She tells me in hushed tones before moving away as Val returns with three steaming mugs of tea.

Val shoots her friend a suspicious look, but Dorrie simply shrugs, winking at me when Val turns her back. I bite the inside of my lip to prevent myself from smiling.

"Thank you, Val, this is lovely."

They both pull up a seat, and we talk about what I've been doing. I leave out the part about moving in with said *sexy, dark-haired, olive-skinned developer*. The rumour mill will never survive the scandal. Instead, I tell them I'm staying with a friend.

"I need your help, ladies," I tell them eventually. "I have been given the opportunity to borrow some dance space at another studio. I want to know how many of those who attended my classes would be interested."

Val and Dorrie look eager. These two will spread the word. It's one reason I came to them. They are very much the heart of the local gossip mill.

"We will arrange transport, but we need to know the numbers. I'm wondering if you can help spread the word. I've arranged a meeting at the community centre to discuss options for next Wednesday night, at seven PM," I say.

Their chests puff out, and I know I've come to the right place.

"You leave it with us," Val says, patting me on the shoulder.

Dorrie already has the phone in her hand.

"Thank you," I say, once again overwhelmed at the kindness and support they've shown me. "You two are amazing."

"We know," Val says, winking, before leaning in. "And I know she told you."

I laugh and pull Val in for a hug.

Thirty minutes later, I finally make it out of the shop. Dorrie has already started the telephone tree, spreading the word as far and wide as possible. I'm in no doubt she will have the place filled to the rafters, or at least I hope she will. I want to show Caleb Frazer what our community really is.

CHAPTER 32

CALEB

I've received a message from April letting me know the Wednesday meeting is *a go*. The local telephone tree has started spreading the word.

Wes pulls a face and asks why I'm bothering, especially when the building is in ruins. When he uncovered her lack of insurance, he was all for cutting her loose. It's the reason I'm working around him. I'm tired of his shit, and I'm not sure how much more I can take. At least the board have come back in favour of Jaxson's changes. The fire turned out to be a game changer, although Elana warned me, they have their eyes on me. Donald is still concerned about a scandal derailing everything.

I let myself into the apartment. It's still early, as my last meeting was cancelled. I saw it as the perfect opportunity to escape, before Wes or any of the others could collar me.

I need to run. Not on my machine, but with the wind hitting my cheeks. Something I haven't managed in a while.

"Hey, you're home early."

I jump, glancing at my watch guiltily. It's just turned three. "So are you," I add, turning around as April appears behind me. The breath leaves my body in a whoosh as I take in her tight leggings and toned abs, fully visible under her sports bra. There are definite advantages to arriving home early.

"We really must stop meeting like this," I say, giving her the once over as she crosses her arms over her chest and scowls at me.

"Well, I was heading to the gym for a run," she says, making to move past me.

"I'm heading to the park for a run myself. Want to join me?" I say before adding. "If you think you can keep up."

April stops and spins on the spot, the gracefulness of the move reminding me of her job.

"I think it's likely to be the other way around, Mr Corporate," she sasses.

I bite the inside of my mouth to prevent the grin that threatens. I can't be successful because April raises an eyebrow, and her hands move to her hips.

She is not aware of how sporty or competitive my siblings and I are. Elijah set his sights on the Olympics before life threw him a curve ball. Gabriel swims miles daily. I run and swim. Kat runs marathons. Only Harper is a mystery. I know she exercises, but no one is sure what her poison is, and she holds it close to her chest.

"Let me get changed."

I pull off my suit jacket as I make my way upstairs. My bedroom is on the opposite side of the apartment to April's.

I switch out of my office clothes and pull on my training gear. My heart rate rises in anticipation of what's to come. I need to run. I always do when the politics overbear the corporate, and I need to clear my head. April is busy stretching when I make it downstairs. She holds out a bottle of water for me, keeping one for herself.

"Thanks," I say, taking it off her. "Ready?"

"You not stretching?" she asks, her brows furrowing.

"I'll stretch when we get there," I say.

She looks at me with an odd expression, and then clarity hits. "Please tell me you're not having Mason drive us to the park?" she says, her tone incredulous.

I find myself unable to hold her gaze. "Er."

"Stretch!" she says, continuing her own regime. I copy her moves, stretching out hamstrings, quads, glutes, calves. "Don't forget your groin," she says, stretching out her own. "I don't want to be carrying you home."

The word *home* on her lips sends an unexpected warmth through my body.

"You can tell Mason to stand down. We're running to the park. I've worked out the back route, so we won't be dodging pedestrians."

"Lead the way," I say, following her into the elevator, my eyes drawn to the smooth outline of her toned behind. The memory of how it felt to have her ass in my hands as I slammed into her, her moans echoing in my ear, comes storming back.

"Eyes up, Corporate," she says, and I feel myself blush.

This is where I'm pleased my shorts are loose, and she can't see the semi I'm now sporting.

We travel down in silence and make our way through reception. The staff greet both me and April. She's made quite an impression. There are no airs and graces, and I find being around her and not having her expect anything from me refreshing.

As it's still early, the pavements are quiet. April sets off, and I match her stride for stride. We run in silence, and before I know it, we hit the park.

We follow the trail, the greenery in contrast to the concrete of the rest of the city. We're fortunate that several spaces have been established and protected for the population.

"Do you want to use the equipment?" she asks as we approach one of the first sets of built-in gym equipment. Her voice is steady. It's like she's not just run for twenty minutes solid.

"You?" I say, my voice not quite as steady. Outdoor running is not the same as the treadmill. Something I need to remember. I need to get home and run around the family estate like I did growing up. The fresh air of the New Forest is vastly different from that of a city filled with traffic.

"Two reps," she says, grinning at me before making her way over to the body press.

I watch her sculpted muscles contract, my mouth becoming moist. She completes a set and gets up, making way for me. I sit down and take my turn before we switch again. This continues as we make our way around the park. Monkey bars, bench dips, bench presses. She matches me one-for-one. She teases and jests, making me laugh. It's clear she's in her element, and I love to see a more relaxed April. Another reminder of our night in New York, when she was carefree. I have not seen that part of her since, at least not until today.

She stops, and I narrowly avoid running into the back of her.

"Rain," she says as the first large drops hit. She throws back her head and smiles at the sky. "I love running in the rain."

I failed to notice the dark clouds coming in. Too distracted.

We continue running, the rain getting heavier and heavier, until we're splashing through groundwater, droplets firing up and into the air.

"Come on," she says, turning and grinning as she hits the street, leaving the park behind. Time to head home.

Lightning flashes overhead, followed by a rumble of thunder. People around us run for cover as the rain takes on another level of power. April's hair is flattened to her head. My t-shirt and shorts have become a second skin.

Another flash and an instant rumble goes off. Lightning hits one of the nearby buildings, the crack deafening. I grab April's wrist and pull her into an enclosed doorway.

"That's too close," I say, breathlessly.

She is also gasping for breath, but when she looks up, her eyes twinkle as large water droplets run down her nose. I don't think she's ever looked so beautiful.

Her eyes lock with mine, her chest heaving. I watch in fascination as her pupils dilate. A shiver runs through her, and I pull her into my arms, erasing the distance between us.

"What are you doing?"

"We're soaking wet. I'm sharing body heat," I say, looking down while manoeuvring her until her back is up against the wall.

Her lips part, drawing my eyes, a slight flush spreading over her skin.

"But we're both wet, not sure how effective it will be," she says, biting her bottom lip.

"I don't know," I say, pulling her closer, willing my body to behave itself but failing miserably. My fingers ache with the need to touch her. I have done for days. Having April Wilson in my space is torture.

I lower my head, my tongue snaking out, moistening my lips, water streaming down my face from my hair.

April lifts her chin, her breath quickening. I'm not sure who moves first as our mouths crash together. Her hands snake up behind my head, her fingers stroking the hair at the nape. I press myself against her, my desire obvious—and then she's gone.

She rips herself out of my arms and sets off in the direction of the apartment. I call after her, but the sound of the rain drowns me out. I drop back against the wall, my head tipped back.

"Shit," I say, knowing there's no way I can chase after her in my current state.

I bend forward and try to get my breathing and body under control. When I'm finally able, I set off. Taking a steady jog back home, not wanting to pull any of my now cold muscles.

When I enter the apartment, I can't see April, but I notice a pool of soaking clothes left inside the door on the tiles.

I groan. She stripped before heading upstairs, clearly wanting to protect my wooden floors. Who is this woman, and where has she been all my life? I'm not as conscientious, plus I don't need her catching me in my boxers. Instead, I stand outside her room, dripping all over the floor. I can hear the shower running inside. A low moan echoes through the door, and my body hardens. The thought of her naked, her hands running over her smooth skin. I turn and make my way to my room. Stripping off my clothes and leaving them in a heap on the bathroom floor.

I step into the spray, groaning as I take my stiff cock in my hand. One hand smashes against the wall as I lean forward, my head and shoulders under the spray, my fist working my dick with desperation. I close my eyes, imagining it's April's hand and mouth. It doesn't take long with those pictures in my mind before the telltale pressure builds. I throw back my head, moaning into the spray, hot cum spurting from my now tender dick. I shudder as my orgasm continues to rip through me, the water washing away the evidence.

I breathe deeply before washing myself off. I take my time, enjoying the warmth and post-orgasmic glow. When I finally make it downstairs, April is no longer in the apartment, her wet clothes are gone. A note telling me she has gone to see Samuel and that there's food in the fridge for me should I want it.

I take it out, disappointed. I've enjoyed our evening meals together. I'm just hoping our little doorway incident hasn't ruined it… that April isn't running scared.

CHAPTER 33

APRIL

Samuel is sitting at our usual table when I walk in. He looks up and grins when he sees me.

"Hey, baby girl," he says, standing up and pulling me in for a hug. A hug I return. When he finally lets go, he holds onto my upper arms, his eyes scanning my face as if checking me out. "You good?" he asks, his concern evident.

"I'm good," I tell him.

"That billionaire treating you right? He hasn't tried anything? Cause if he has, he's not too rich for me to kick his ass for you," he says, taking a seat, pulling me down next to him and calling over the barmaid.

"Hey, long time no see, April," Cassie, the barmaid, says.

"Hi, Cassie. I've been caught up in a few dramas."

"You could say that," she says. "I saw the fire on the news. You, okay?"

Her concern touches me.

"It's been tough, but I've arranged a town hall for Wednesday. Been offered a short-term dance space. I just need to see if the community wants it."

"Leave Bernie the details. He'll spread the word. You

know what he's like. He was so impressed with your flash mob. You *are taking on* the big wigs…"

A shout comes from behind the bar. "Is anyone working around here?"

Bernie pops his head up, and Cassie rolls her eyes. "I'll get your drinks," she says, grinning.

We watch her leave. "So, what's with the urgent call?" Samuel asks, picking up the drink he already ordered while waiting for me.

"What? Can't a friend call a friend?"

It's his turn to raise an eyebrow. "We spoke on the telephone yesterday—twice," he says.

I wrinkle my nose.

Busted.

"We kissed," I say, watching a smirk spread over his lips. "What?" I ask.

"I'm surprised is all," he says, sitting back and folding his arms.

I sigh, staring at the table. "I'm shocked at myself. Horrified, in fact. I don't know what I was thinking. We were in an enclosed space, and he was just there, and he smelled…" I look up from the table to find Samuel biting his lip as he tries unsuccessfully not to laugh.

"Why are you laughing?"

"I'm not," he says, wiping a tear from his cheek. "It's just you seem so surprised. You must be the only one who is. The electricity between you two is off the scale. I'm shocked you haven't ripped each other's clothes off yet. Especially with you staying under his roof."

I sit back in the chair and fold my arms, staring at him. Has he lost the plot?

"How can you say that?" I ask. "Caleb Frazer will be no different from the other men and women, who have grown up cocooned within a world of wealth and power. They are all used to getting what they want. I'm nothing more than a challenge."

"I think you're wrong," Samuel says, shrugging. "Caleb is nothing like the other arrogant pricks you met at the conservatoire or at Merryfellows. You shouldn't insult him by lumping him in with them," he admonishes me.

I stare at him, startled. "Maybe Cal is just better at hiding it?"

But as soon as the words leave my mouth, I know I'm wrong. I let the fight drain out of me. Our kiss has thrown me, knocked me off balance.

"I'm not going there," I tell my best friend, my voice sounding huffy.

He lets out a bark. "Why on earth not? It's not like you haven't been there before. From what you told me, it was *very enjoyable.*"

I smack his arm when he wiggles his eyebrows.

"Caleb seems like a nice guy."

"Are we talking about the same guy? He's cocky, arrogant, and far too charming for his own good. Not to mention the city's most prolific playboy! You're supposed to be on my side," I say, knowing the words are an excuse, and are not how I see Cal. Instead, he confuses me. The more time I spend with him, makes me question everything I thought I believed. He is not what I expected.

"I am, but *methinks you doth protest too much.* Why are you worried about kissing a guy you find attractive? Hell, *I* find him attractive," Samuel swoons.

He's never hidden the fact he finds Cal good-looking. I'm not sure many people would unless you aren't into tall, dark-haired men with a chiselled jaw, strong cheekbones, and dark eyes. Eyes that almost turn black when he's aroused.

Oh hell.

My mind flies back to that moment his lips descended,

and I wanted nothing more than to pull him close and devour him, have him devour me. My laboured breathing. My pebbled nipples pressed painfully against my soaking wet bra. I wanted him to warm me up, as I knew only he could, but not because of the rain.

Instead, I panicked and ran.

I was soaking wet, so I dropped my outer layers by the door, hoping Cal wasn't hot on my tail. Having felt his erection, I didn't think that was likely. I made it to my bedroom and locked myself in. I was so turned on, having watched Cal and his rippling muscles as he worked out, even our banter as we ran.

I'm doomed.

Even worse, I took the new vibrator Samuel had bought me into the shower. He gave it to me as a moving-in gift. Telling me I'd need it if I was going to live with all that Frazer hotness! I hate that he was right. I closed my eyes, imagining the water running down my body was Cal's mouth and hands. When I finally slipped the thing inside me, I came so damn hard I bruised my lip, biting down to stop the scream from escaping. I knew then I needed to get out of the apartment.

Cassie arrives with our drinks.

"Here you go," she says, putting them down and leaving again.

I take a sip, not sure what to say.

Samuel watches me over the top of his glass.

"He's professional, powerful, and sex-on-legs. He gets things done. Look at Sunny Down and what he's trying to do for the community? What he's done for you."

I take another large swallow of my drink. I know what he's saying is true.

Samuel sighs. "Yes, he has a love 'em and leave 'em reputation. But the man is in a different league from you and me.

All I'm saying is he's different from the man I've read about in the papers. The way he looks out for you. You need to cut him some slack." He leans forward and takes my hand. "The pair of you have some serious chemistry. You need to get that man out of your system. He's tying you up in knots."

I stare at Samuel open-mouthed and take another drink. At this rate, we'll be needing another round.

Is he right?

"So, what do you suggest?"

"I think the kiss will be just the start." He gives me a slow smile, and I shake my head. He knows me too well. "Think about it. Maybe you can have some fun with Caleb. Just be careful and protect your heart."

I don't need to fall for Caleb Frazer. That would be a disaster of epic proportions. But it's true, the man is invading my every waking and sleeping moment. Could we enjoy a sexual relationship but ensure it's just that—sex? We wouldn't need to exchange hearts, flowery words, or promises that can be broken, just simple orgasms. And experience knows the man can sure deliver those. Can we have a relationship built on mutual satisfaction?

My pussy contracts at the thought. My head and heart go into a tailspin. Just thinking about being with Caleb Frazer again, whether it's in bed, on the sofa, or in the pool, causes a throbbing sensation between my thighs that I can't ignore.

"How are things with Daniel?" I say, deciding it's time to change the subject.

CHAPTER 34

CALEB

April and I have spent the past twenty-four hours dodging one another. Not my usual M.O., but with her living in my apartment, I want her to feel at home, not threatened, or like I'm expecting something from her. The kiss was stupid. I promised myself I'd stay away from her, but then we laughed, and she teased me. The kiss felt so natural. Only it wasn't, and now we are being overly polite and awkward.

"This is quite a turnout," Scarlett says, appearing at my shoulder.

"She's loved by the community. I'm not sure even she realises how much," I reply, turning around and giving her a hug. "Thank you for suggesting this."

Scarlett looks at me and grins. "Oh, believe me, this is me being completely selfish. I want April on board. She's incredibly talented."

I smile at her and nod. I know she is. I'm just hoping other people telling her will help make April believe it.

It's not long before it's standing room only. Scarlett has moved towards April, and they are deep in conversation. She laughs at something Scarlett says, and I think back to our run. She was open and laughing with me that day. I would do anything to have that part of her again.

"Caleb," a voice appears behind me.

"Mum? What are you doing here?" I turn and face my mother. The matriarch of our family and a great parent, albeit a little meddlesome at times.

She pats my cheek. "I'm representing the Frazer Foundation, darling. Scarlett and I have been talking about sponsorships. We're looking at setting up drop-in centres. When Scarlett mentioned this project and her involvement, I thought this new development of yours could be our flagship. I've heard about the number of young people."

"Mother," I say. "A heads up would have been nice. You can't just turn up and—"

Ignoring me, she looks over towards Scarlett and April. "Ah, that must be April, the young lady I keep hearing so much about."

I freeze, a sense of unease settling in my stomach.

"What do you mean?" I ask slowly.

"Nothing, dear. She's quite the dancer. Scarlett was very complimentary. I'll go over and introduce myself."

She steps around me before I can stop her.

I'm going to string Scarlett up when I get my hands on her.

I watch her make her way across the room and groan. Can't she be satisfied with Gabriel being attached? He's made her a grandmother. The last thing I need is my matchmaking mother, around April.

Hold on... where did that thought come from?

I shove my hands in my pockets and draw in a breath. There's no reason for my mother to even think romantic thoughts where April is concerned. She doesn't know she's staying with me. No one does, apart from Samuel. Did April tell Scarlett? I know the boys wouldn't say anything. They know what my mother is like. She tries to fix them up every year at her birthday party.

I cringe as my mother makes it to her destination. Scarlett and April both smile at her as she's introduced. My mother is not like many of her peers when it comes to matching my siblings and me with potential partners. My parents had an arranged marriage but fell in love and raised a family. She and my father *became* a traditional love story. Their marriage may have begun its life built on what my father inherited, but they were a team. Their love and partnership thrived, as did everything they touched. They were still as much in love the day he died as they were when they first fell. His loss has been hard on her, but she's a survivor. I've never voiced it aloud, but their relationship is why I refuse to settle. I want what they had. I just have yet to find it, and if I don't, then that's the way it will be.

Someone claps their hands, bringing the crowd's attention to the front. My mother is still busy talking to Scarlett, but April has moved off. I exhale, quieting my racing heart.

"Welcome, everyone. I'm glad to see so many of you could make it this evening," April says. "Can everyone hear me at the back?"

Acknowledgements are heard from the rear of the room, and April smiles.

I listen as she discusses the fire, the issues, and how she's working with Scarlett and me to resolve them. I watch members of the crowd nod. Everyone focused on the woman standing at the front as she presents our proposal.

When she's finished, she opens the floor up for questions.

"I work. I can't travel all the way across town. It was hard enough when it was around the corner."

Scarlett steps in. "The centre has security measures. Once the children, especially the younger ones, exit the bus, the staff will escort them to the studios and provide continuous supervision. Once their lesson is over, they will be returned to the bus—like a school trip."

"Ms Dupree, you're a wealthy woman. Why are you doing this?" one woman asks.

"I have a great deal of respect for April. I know how much your children and young adults mean to her. What dancing means to her."

She looks over at April and the women share a smile. I see a friendship forming. One that will outlive mine and April's. My stomach hardens at the thought.

"I'm also setting up an independent dance school. Somewhere accessible for anyone with talent," she adds, making it obvious it won't be about the extortionate fees some places charge. "I'm working with the Frazer Foundation to set up realistic scholarships. That's why Mrs Francesca Frazer is here tonight."

I watch as my mum smiles and raises her hand in acknowledgement.

How the hell did this happen?

Somehow, I seem to be losing control here. The women in my life are taking over. All I can do is work on the development and get the studio back up and running.

"How long will this be for?" a man asks from the back of the room.

I watch April's face drop.

I step forward.

"I found out earlier today the council has granted us permission to begin work on the Sunny Down site immediately. Due to the fire and the current state of the building, they think it is in the best interest of the city and the community for the building to be demolished as soon as possible. Once the site has been cleared, the building team will move in." The man nods before sitting down. I keep my eyes on the crowd, although I can sense April's eyes drilling into me. This is all news to her. She's put distance between us tonight and used Scarlett as a shield, but I can feel her questions bubbling. I hide my grin as April is left speechless.

One of us fields the rest of the questions until April finally calls the meeting to a close. Parents line up to sign consent forms for their children. A couple ask if they can accompany the buses, act as chaperones. For those people, we get them to fill out security checks. Elijah has promised to fast-track them.

When I finally catch up with April, she's in deep conversation with my mother about the community centre and the councillors the foundation wants to put in place. This is a project close to my mother's heart. One she and my father began. I just hadn't realised how far along it had progressed.

"There you are," my mother says as I walk up to them both.

April smiles up at me. "Your mother was just telling me about her plans for the community centre. It's amazing. The foundation can do so much good."

The excitement in her voice is contagious, and I look at my mother, whose gaze moves between us with open interest.

I school my features.

"Mother, are you ready to go? I think Freddy is waiting for you," I say, pointing to the door where her driver is waiting patiently.

"I am," she grins, turning her attention to April and grasping one of her hands in both of hers. "It was lovely to meet you. I hope to see you again soon."

April smiles as we watch her walk away.

She turns to me, and I'm surprised to see a grin bunching up her cheeks. "It's okay, you're safe," she says. "I didn't tell her I'm currently living in your apartment."

I groan at her words, pinching the bridge of my nose to stem the headache that is threatening to hit. I know my mother, and I thought she was looking at April with far too much interest.

"Quite the matchmaker," she laughs, clearly enjoying my discomfort. "Spent a lot of this evening trying to sell me your virtues."

I close my eyes and pinch the bridge of my nose harder.

"Please ignore everything she said," I say.

What was my mother thinking!

"Are you sure? The things she was saying. Well, they were very flattering."

I do a double-take. April's laughter fills the air, and it does strange things to my chest. An unfamiliar warmth only she seems to ignite spreads out.

Unsure how to reply, I step forward.

"Are you ready to go?"

For the first time, finding myself... speechless. But also unsure if I want to listen to any more of my mother's *plus* points.

Scarlett and Samuel are deep in conversation when we finally approach them to say goodbye. I'm surprised to see Daniel, his partner, by his side. He looks more relaxed, they both do. They shake hands with Scarlett as we arrive before turning to us. He comes forward and kisses April's cheek.

"Well done, baby girl," he says, giving her a hug. I watch in anticipation as Daniel steps up and holds out his hand.

"Well done, April. I want to apologise for being such an asshole the other week." He looks at the floor. "I just…"

I'm as shocked as he is when April steps up and hugs him. He freezes for a second before relaxing into her hug, his arms coming up and around her.

"Thank you for coming this evening. I appreciate your support," she says, brushing over previous events.

"Thank you," Dan says quietly, standing there awkwardly until Samuel wraps an arm around his shoulder, giving him a squeeze. Dan looks up at him, an unspoken message passing between them.

"Come on. It's time to leave these good people and head home," Samuel says before wishing us all a pleasant evening.

My eyes follow them, and I watch Dan say something to Samuel, which has him taking his hand and bringing it to his lips. They're working on their issues. Seeing them together, I hope they sort it out.

"I'll see you tomorrow," Scarlett says to April. She pulls her in for a hug, bringing my attention back to the two women.

What is it with all the touchy-feely?

April seems to be happy to hug everyone but me, leaving a burning sensation in my chest.

"See you tomorrow," April says, returning the hug.

"What's happening tomorrow?" I ask.

Scarlett turns and laughs. "Nothing that concerns you."

She winks at April before making her way to the exit.

April looks at my face and grins before taking pity on me. "Scarlett wants to speak to me about maternity cover for one of her dance instructors."

I tip my head in acknowledgement before we make our way out of the building. The caretaker enters to lock up.

"Thank you," April says to the man as we pass.

I follow her onto the street, sensing she wants to ask me something but is holding off. She waves at a few stragglers who are still standing around outside.

"Tonight was a success," I say, hoping she feels the same way.

"I think it was. Thank you for helping to arrange it," she says, climbing into the car as Mason holds the door open. I watch as she shimmies across the seat, her trousers tight across her thighs.

I swallow before climbing into the car after her.

"You did all the hard work. You got the message out there," I say.

"Ah, the community grapevine." She grins. "It has its benefits and is perfect for things like this. Not so great for private and personal matters."

I wonder what private and personal matters they might be?

CHAPTER 35

APRIL

I follow Caleb into the apartment. Even after all these weeks of living here, it still takes my breath away. I've always loved the light, and Caleb's apartment is designed to allow optimal light into the space.

"A drink?" Caleb asks, moving towards the kitchen area.

I shouldn't, but one glass won't hurt.

I have a choreography session with Scarlett in the morning, followed by a meeting to discuss cover for one of her dance teachers. I nearly fell over when she asked if I was interested. Her logic is while I'm working out of her studio, it benefits both of us. I'm not hanging around and she has cover.

Caleb returns with two glasses of red. He's made note of my preference.

"Thank you." I take the glass from him, tingles of awareness darting through my fingers as they brush against his.

I turn away, not wanting him to see his effect on me or the colour I know has flooded my cheeks. Since our kiss, I've tried to stay away from him as much as possible. The man is temptation on legs, and having tasted that forbidden fruit, my body can't understand why my mind won't let it go there again.

Caleb moves past me to the sofa, dropping onto one of the seats. I follow, not knowing what else to do. After his bombshell this evening, I need to talk to him. It's time to put on the brakes.

We haven't discussed what happens next, it's not an area I have wanted to broach with him. All my fighting for my rights—I obtained exactly what I wanted. The plan had been perfect, but everything changed on the night of the fire. My business and dreams literally went up in smoke. I need to re-plan and rework my future.

Looking up, I find Caleb staring at me over the top of his wine glass. His expression is contemplative.

"What?" I ask, sounding defensive. I'm not sure what it is about this man that makes my hackles rise with simply a look.

He shrugs. "I was wondering why you haven't asked me about the dance studio plans?"

"There is no dance studio," I reply.

"Tonight, I said there is, or at least there will be. And relatively quickly. A new build is far quicker than a renovation," he says.

I sigh, needing to be honest. I can't be selfish or take his hospitality for granted any longer.

"About that," I say, putting my glass down on the coffee table between us. I can't bring myself to meet his gaze, so I stare at the floor. "I thought you understood. I can't afford the new dance studio."

The silence that descends has me meeting his gaze. "I told you before, I won't increase the rent. I'm not going back on our agreement."

I shake my head. "I know, and I appreciate it. However, our agreement was when we were using what I already had.

The flooring, the mirrors, my equipment. I lost all that in the fire." I take a deep breath. "I wasn't insured, Caleb. Stupid and naïve of me, I know. But the dance studio was a money pit. The liability insurance was the only one I could afford. That was the most important. The rest was a gamble that I lost."

Honesty is the best policy!

He's been a support. Not at all what I originally imagined. Caleb Frazer is an enigma, one I can't work out.

"I know," he surprises me by saying. "When you filled out all the paperwork, you told my team. So, what? You're simply going to walk away?" Caleb asks, his voice incredulous. "What are you going to do?"

My shoulders droop. "I'll continue to cover the classes at Scarlett's while you advertise for another dance school owner. A new building, in a new development. I doubt you'll have a problem finding someone to take it on."

I try to sound positive, but my heart breaks with every word. This is my area, my community. Someone else is going to come in and take over and reap the benefits because of faulty electrics.

"No."

It's one word, but it makes me stop.

"That's not an option," he goes on to say.

I shake my head. "You don't understand. It took me four years to raise the money to kit out the building. All my savings. There's nothing left. No bank is going to lend me the money, and I don't want to get into bed with a loan shark."

"It's you who doesn't seem to understand," Caleb says, leaning back and crossing his legs at his ankles. "I promised the community their dance studio and teacher. If you had no intention of continuing, what the hell was this evening all about? What was the point?"

I've been asking myself the same thing over and over,

hoping for a miracle or an epiphany. Burying my head in the sand, wanting a magic fix. But I'm not Cinderella. A fairy godmother will not appear, wave a magic wand, and make all my problems disappear.

"Do you want to walk away?" he asks quietly. "Is that what this is about? A way out?"

"No." I shake my head before dropping it into my hands. "The studio was a dream come true. Hard work, but it's my life's ambition since I met Di and learned to dance." My voice sounds wistful even to myself. I hadn't thought about it until that point.

"You're in luck," he suddenly states. "Our insurance policy includes coverage for fixtures and fittings. When the buildings were purchased, we took out a comprehensive insurance policy after exchanging contracts. All you need to do is let me know how much and it's covered."

My head snaps up, and I stare at Caleb. My throat closes over.

Is he about to become my fairy godmother?

"I simply need to know how much, April?"

"How much?" I choke out, and he knows he has my attention.

"You heard me correctly," he says, a small smile playing at the corner of his mouth.

I shake my head. "No."

When I look up, he's staring at me, his brow furrowed in obvious confusion. "What do you mean? No."

"What I said. It's never going to work. Sorry if you feel like I've wasted your time." I run a hand through my ponytail, the confused look on Cal's face telling me I need to explain.

"The studio was barely making enough to keep me afloat, and I was living on the premises. That won't be happening now. I'll need additional money for rent, bills, both for the studio and an apartment. The figures just don't add up. I'm sorry. I can't get myself in any deeper, with nothing to fall back on."

"But—"

"Thank you for the offer. It's incredibly generous, more than I ever dreamed of, but I must be realistic. You need to find someone else to take on the studio. Sadly, it won't, can't be me."

I get up and move away, heading for the stairs.

"Goodnight," I say, not waiting for a reply. The pain in my chest excruciating.

I make my way up to my room. Now, the truth is out there. I have no right to be squatting in Caleb's spare room. I should have left weeks ago. I've become too comfortable, too relaxed, and although I hate to admit it, I enjoy his company. Tomorrow, I'll see what I can do. Maybe one of Scarlett's dancers knows of a room for rent. It's time to get real.

CHAPTER 36

APRIL

I'm outside Scarlett's studio at the crack of dawn. Scarlett told me the previous evening that she had an early choreography session and would like me to attend. Of course, I jumped at the opportunity to see a master at work, although that was before I spent most of the night tossing and turning.

I let myself in. Scarlett supplied me with the code to get through from reception into the main studio area. The glass wall in front of me shows a group of dancers warming up. Scarlett, in the midst of it all, laughing at something a dancer says. As if sensing me, she looks up and smiles. If I'm honest, Scarlett Dupree is not what I expected. She's at the top of her field, but she is not stuck up or snobby. She's been nothing but warm and welcoming.

"April, come in," she says, throwing open the door and calling over to me.

Entering the room, there's a group of ten dancers busy stretching.

"Throw your stuff at the front. Get warmed up, and then I'll introduce you to the gang," she adds.

Too shell-shocked to say much, I go through my usual routine. Limbering up and warming each muscle group, pleased I've been using Caleb's gym to keep myself supple.

"Right, everyone," Scarlett shouts, grabbing everyone's attention. "Morning."

There are a few chuckles, mainly because the sun is barely up, and we're all standing in a dance studio, ready to go.

"I know it's early, but most of you have places to go and people to see. I'd like to introduce you to April. She'll be working with us for the foreseeable future. Please make her welcome."

The group turn towards me, each taking turns to introduce themselves. I'm a little surprised at their welcome as most dancers I've met, are highly competitive and, therefore, distant towards the new girl or guy. But that is clearly not something Scarlett puts up with.

"April, come and stand with me. Team, I want you to run through the routine. Show April what we have so far."

The group move as one, each taking up their position as I move to stand beside Scarlett. She turns to me and smiles.

"Watch. I want you to tell me what's wrong."

My face must relay my confusion because Scarlett chuckles.

"Pardon?" I say, choking on my surprise.

"There's something wrong with the routine. I want another set of eyes."

"But—"

I want to tell her she's made a mistake. I'm not an experienced choreographer, only ever having made up my own routines. Scarlett has got the wrong impression. What has Caleb told her about me? Whatever it is, I'm about to embarrass myself.

She looks over as if sensing my discomfort. "Don't think. Just watch and tell me what you see."

I nod, not sure what else to do.

When she starts the music, the dancers begin to move. The music is from a band I recognise, or at least I think I recognise the tones of the lead singer. My eyes track the dancers, listening to the lyrics and watching their moves.

The track ends, and I'm immersed.

"Again," Scarlett says, not asking me, almost as if she's aware I'm lost in the moment.

The music and dancers start up again. My brain breaks down the moves of each set. The hours I spent in Di's dance studio come back to me, dancing solo in front of the mirrors, choreographing routine after routine to my favourite songs. Then, my time at the conservatoire.

"Take a break," Scarlett says after they've run through the routine three more times.

I watch as they file out, heading to the canteen, the place I first sat with Caleb and Scarlett.

"What do you think?" Scarlett says, turning her attention to me.

"It's a great routine," I say.

She raises a brow. "Not what I want to hear," she adds. "Tell me honestly. Your body language gives you away."

I right myself. What body language? Of course, there are things I would have included, done differently, but that's only my opinion. The lyrics suggest something different to me—but this is Scarlett Dupree. She's today's master of choreography.

"Does it help if I tell you it's not my routine?" she adds, giving me a knowing smile.

My shoulders loosen up, and she chuckles. "Even if it was, I would still want you to be honest with me. That's my number one rule when people work with or for me. I'm not superwoman and even I can make the wrong decision. I'm not so arrogant that I can't take feedback."

"Why?" I turn to her fully. "What's this about?"

"I've watched your tapes, April. Spoken to your old teachers at the conservatoire."

I don't think I'd be more shocked if she struck me.

Scarlett shrugs. "Why did you drop out? According to your teachers, you had a promising future."

I shake my head and grab my bag. My past is my past. It needs to stay there.

"Why April?" Her voice is unapologetic, making me drop my bag and spin around to face her.

"Why?" I snap, unable to help myself. "Because I wasn't born with a silver spoon in my mouth. I had no one to pave my way. No support. From eighteen, I was alone. I was expected to stand on my own two feet according to the state."

There is no way she could understand.

I close my eyes and inhale deeply. When I open them again and exhale, I look at Scarlett. "Sorry, that was rude." She waves away my apology as if unnecessary, but I know I need to explain. "My student loan covered my tuition, but to live, I worked two jobs on top of studying, twenty hours a week in the evenings, just to get by."

I lower my voice. I hate discussing my past and what might have been.

"Then studying began to clash with work," I add more calmly. "One could not survive without the other. Believe me, I tried. In the end, I burnt out."

When I finally look at Scarlett, I see her arms folded over her chest. Her face gives nothing away after my outburst.

"Tell me what was wrong with the routine, April."

With nothing left to lose—that's exactly what I do.

CHAPTER 37

CALEB

April has been avoiding me again. She has worked with the team in the office, and I know she's been attending and teaching classes at Scarlett's. However, she may as well be a ghost where I'm concerned. I come home, and she's out or holed up in her room. I wouldn't know she was living with me if it wasn't for a single pair of shoes on the shoe rack by the door. We no longer eat together. Dinner is left conveniently in the warming drawer.

Tonight, I know she's out.

A message scrawled in her handwriting is waiting for me when I make it out of the gym. She's gone to the movies with one of the dancers from Scarlett's studio. The letter smells of her. Her floral scent clings to the paper. I'm becoming a sad sap, sniffing at a piece of paper, but I can't help myself. April Wilson has rankled me, making me behave like a lovesick teenager.

Not tonight, however. If she's out, then it's boys' night. I call the boys, and poker night is on, at mine. It's been weeks since I hosted—since my house guest arrived. Something the boys have mocked me for, relentlessly.

The doorbell goes. The guys have the key code to my floor. I've known them forever, and it makes life easier, especially when they stay over. Tristan, Quentin, and Xander walk in. Tristan carrying wine, Xander beer, and Quentin an enormous box of Chinese takeaway from our favourite restaurant.

The elevator pings behind them. My twin, Gabriel, steps out.

Gabriel has taken to joining us on boys' nights as Leah uses the time for her girlie evenings. He has tried to deny it, but I think he secretly enjoys getting out and reconnecting with the guys.

Tonight, the girls are invading Leah and Gabriel's apartment, which means Callum isn't here. For playboy men, my cool dude of a nephew certainly gets a lot of attention. When the girls go out, Gabriel brings him, or we go to his. Poker goes to hell on those nights, with five grown-ass men cooing and ahh-ing over the little man.

"How's Callum? Was it colic?" Quentin asks Gabriel.

What? Colic? How does Quentin know about Callum's colic?

I watch my brother's expression soften as he looks at our old school friend. I never thought I'd see the day my brother let down his walls.

"He's good. The colic seems to have passed. Great recommendation. Thank your old nanny." It's hard to believe my twin is a father. That he's found his soulmate. And that's no exaggeration. Leah is his other half. They've always complimented each other. It simply took them eight years to finally open their eyes to the fact.

Marcus slaps Gabriel on the back, and I nearly fall over when my brother smiles at him.

"It'll be teething next." It's Xander who chirps up.

"Then crawling. We'll all have to baby-proof our apartments," Marcus adds.

What's going on?

When did the bachelor brigade become interested in baby development?

In the months before Callum arrived, there was pregnancy chat and baby names. I watch in fascination as the boys all nod in agreement. Beam me up, Scotty. I've just entered the twilight zone.

"How about you?" Tristan slaps my back, shooting me forward, as I wasn't expecting it.

"What about me?" I ask.

"Don't play coy? How's your *not so* new housemate? Will she be joining us this evening?" Xander asks, waggling his eyebrows.

"Haha. I'm helping her out. And no, she's not here this evening. I wouldn't inflict you reprobates on her," I say, grabbing a beer as a distraction.

I ignore the looks that pass between the group, including my brother—traitor. I'm not in the mood for their teasing. I don't understand April. She's one of the most frustrating women I've ever met.

"Did you think about what I said?" Gabriel says, coming up to stand next to me.

I called Gabriel in frustration after April's outburst and refusal to think about taking on the studio once it was rebuilt.

It hadn't been Gabriel who came up with the solution, but Leah.

"Leah's suggestion," I say, shoulder-bumping him for trying to take the credit.

"Just remember, behind every successful man," my brother chuckles.

"In your case, most definitely," I tease.

Leah has, after all, worked for him for years.

I like this new relaxed twin. Not only because he doesn't blow me off every time, I try to see him. But he's just… more.

"I took Leah's advice, and I'm working on it," I say cryptically, not wanting the others to get into my business.

Gabriel nods before taking a plate and digging into the food that Quentin has laid out on the table. I follow suit, making small talk with my friends, finally letting my guard down for the first time in what seems like days.

After dinner, we sit down for our weekly poker game.

Gabriel wins. With his maths genius brain, I'm sure he's card counting, but it's impossible to prove. The guys all take it in their stride. It's become the group challenge—who will be the first to beat Gabe.

"So, Caleb, your house guest resisting your charms?" Tristan asks, throwing in yet another hand.

"That's got to be a first," Quentin chimes in. "Are you losing your touch, old man? You are thirty now."

"Shut up," I say, lobbing a cushion at him. "Plenty of years left yet."

"Just saying," Quentin shrugs, his grin splitting his face. "The proof is in the…." I threaten to throw another cushion, and he rocks backwards, laughing. He's only a couple of months younger than me, but now he seems to think of himself as a top-rate comedian.

"It's not like that. I'm helping her get back on her feet," I say, unsure why I need to defend my actions but doing so anyway.

"Sure you are," Xander nods. "How many apartments do you own in the city? Thirty? I know at least three are currently empty," he says, laughing. He would know, his company manage all mine and Gabriel's property portfolios. I shoot him a glare that would stop most people in their tracks. Instead of shutting up, however, he continues. "Instead, you're helping, by letting her stay in your apartment, under your roof. Don't play innocent with us. We know you."

"It's not like that…"

"I say he protests too much. He wants to get in her pants, and she's holding him at bay."

Quentin laughs.

There's a cough, and everyone spins around.

Oh shit!

My bloody friends and their big mouths!

April stands in the doorway, her cheeks flushed. This is where I want to murder all my friends and hide their bodies in the new foundations of her dance school.

"Hi, I'm April," she says, stepping into the room.

Quentin has the good grace to look sheepish, especially when Marcus smacks him around the back of his head. "Sorry, April. We were only jesting," he says, standing up and holding out his hand. I don't think I've ever seen my friend go so red.

"I wasn't expecting you home," I hear myself say.

April looks at me, her eyes sparking. Shit, she heard more than she should.

"Clearly," she says. "The movie was terrible. We gave up on it. Don't mind me, I'll leave you to your *boys* chat and head upstairs. Gentleman."

Shit! She did hear.

April turns to leave. Tristan, who is sitting to my right, nudges me hard in the ribs, gesturing wildly with his head.

"You're free to join us," I say, rubbing my bruised side.

April freezes before turning around. Making her way towards us.

"What are you playing?" she asks.

"Poker," Gabriel says, making space next to him, and allowing April to sit down.

April does a double-take before holding out her hand.

"You must be Gabriel," she says, her eyes flitting between the two of you. "Similar, but not quite the same."

Gabriel chuckles, and I know this is not the last I'll be hearing of this. Only a handful of people can tell us apart. It looks like April is one of them.

"That's what my wife says," he says, taking her hand in his. "Pleased to meet you April. Let me introduce you to the rest of these reprobates."

He introduces her to the other guys around the table, who are now on their best behaviour and incredibly apologetic.

It would be funny, if it wasn't so embarrassing.

April takes a seat.

"Can I get you some wine?" Tristan asks, jumping to his feet.

April smiles up at him and my muscles tense. "That would be lovely."

Tristan disappears into the kitchen and returns with a glass of wine. She thanks him with a dazzling smile, and my stomach hardens.

What's with all the gentlemanly behaviour?

"Are you going to deal?" I say to Tristan. My question sharper than I want it to be.

Tristan smirks before shuffling the deck and dealing.

Two hours later, April has a pile equalling Gabriel's. Who would have known my little dancer has a penchant for cards?

"Well gentleman. I'm going to call it a night. I have an early start in the morning."

My friends all nod like puppy dogs. When April goes out of sight, I scowl at them all, making Gabriel the only one unaffected, smirk. "For god's sake, put your tongues away. You're embarrassing yourselves," I snap.

The guys all turn at once before bursting out laughing.

"I don't think I've ever seen him jealous before," Tristan laughs.

"Nope, definitely got the hots for his lodger," Quentin adds, high-fiving Xander.

"Okay, enough. I think it's time to call it a night. You've had your fun."

"We're going," Xander says, "But make a move before you miss out," he says, clapping me on the shoulder.

They may now know we met in New York, but April, though, has made it clear she's not interested. While most women are falling over themselves for my wealth and status. It appears nothing could be more of a turnoff for my little dancer.

I shake my head and sigh at my friends. "You're all delusional."

"Keep telling yourself that," Tristan says as they file out of the apartment, leaving me alone with the mess of the evening and a frustrating lodger who refuses to accept my help in rebuilding her life.

CHAPTER 38

APRIL

I'm not sure what makes me head back downstairs once I know Caleb's friends have left. It could be the way they ribbed him all night at my expense or simply because I'm tired of trying to avoid him. I've missed him and our banter. I thought staying out of his way would lessen the desire. Instead, he's taken to invading my dreams, leaving me hot and wanton when I wake up.

"Scarlett wants to expand. She wants me to run the dance studio," I say, leaning against the wall, watching in fascination as his shoulder muscles shift under his t-shirt. I cross my arms over my chest to stop myself from reaching out and touching him.

Caleb turns to face me, giving me a half smile that doesn't quite reach his eyes. "I know. She called me this afternoon."

"Aren't you happy? You have a new potential owner," I ask.

Caleb shrugs.

"What's that supposed to mean?" I ask, annoyance bubbling in my chest.

"I don't know April. What *is it* supposed to mean? I've

tried to help you, enable you to keep your business, but you've thrown it back at me." He slams the takeaway containers into the bin before dragging open the dishwasher and loading the plates. Not sure why it's so sexy watching billionaire Caleb Frazer doing domestic chores, but it does something to my insides.

I pause. Is that what I'm doing? Throwing his generosity back at him?

"I can't be indebted to you," I say, wanting to explain, make him understand.

"Why would you be indebted? I'm offering to help you."

"I don't want to be beholden to anyone—I can't be bought." The words are out before I can stop them.

"Who said anything about buying you?" It's Cal's turn to look confused.

"I make my own way," I say, knowing to someone like Cal, it won't make sense. But help is one thing. It's when they want something in return, and men with money, they always want something in return. Endless promises were made and then broken when they got what they wanted. I saw it repeatedly in my past life. A life I'd rather forget. A life I have no intention of bringing up to the man in front of me.

Cal turns and leans his back against the kitchen unit. He folds his arms over his chest, his t-shirt stretching over his muscles, the sight making my mouth water.

What on earth possessed me to come downstairs?

"So I can't get involved in a business venture with you?"

"No," I say, shaking my head, even though I'm only half listening to his words.

His words penetrate my brain.

Business ventures?

What?

"I'm talking private investment," he says. "My own funds.

I'll invest my money, and you pay me back when you can. I'll be a silent partner."

I shake my head. No way. That would mean contact and contract. I need to put some distance between us, not tie myself to him. This playboy billionaire is playing havoc with my equilibrium.

"I said no," I snap.

"Why?"

"Because…"

"Would you have let Cal? The man you met in New York?" His expression takes my breath away.

"Cal didn't exist," I sigh.

"He does. He's me - only without your preconceived ideas."

I push off the wall and move towards him. "Why do you care so much?" I ask, finding myself getting closer and closer, as if drawn by an invisible string.

"Why are you so quick to judge me? Label me?" he asks, both our breathing become more laboured. His eyes drop to my lips, and I can't stop my tongue from snaking out, moistening them.

"I don't," I protest, but know I'm lying.

"You do," he counters.

I sigh, "I know all the good you and your family have done for this city."

"So why?" he asks, stepping back as if it's the only way he can maintain distance. Not the playboy image…

"Ah, there you go, labelling me again… playboy."

Shit, did I say the word aloud?

I must have, as the look on his face hardens.

"Playboy. That's what the press labels me." He leans forward, placing his hands on the kitchen side. "I won't apologise for enjoying my life. For living it the way I want to. As for the women I'm photographed with, they want the same things I do."

Cal turns to face me.

"Do you know what it's like to be raised in one of the wealthiest families in the country? What that means every time you meet someone new? Trying to figure out what they want. Do they want to be your friend or are they after something? Do you know how many people have tried to use me since I was a teenager? Social climbers who are only interested in my name. People who want to see what they can get out of me. My friends and I learned early on how to protect ourselves. I don't make empty promises. But I won't date or tie myself to someone who only sees my name and my wealth. Is that so wrong?"

I'm not sure how to reply. I never thought of life at the other end of the spectrum. For me, it has been a fight to ensure people don't gain enough power over me to force me into things I don't want to do. I never thought about people not being genuine, of using you, just in a different way. Maybe we aren't so different, both protecting our hearts.

Caleb stops and laughs. It's a hollow laugh as if he's chastising himself. I don't like it, especially when he says. "Do you know why I introduced myself as Cal when I met you in New York? When I realised you didn't recognise me, I could be me. You talked to Cal that night, not Caleb Frazer, billionaire. You laughed and joked with me. I hadn't felt that free and at ease in years. Then, the next morning, it was like I dreamt it. You were gone." Sad eyes clash with mine. "Why?"

"You want to know why?" I wrap my arms around my waist. "Because, when I woke up in the presidential suite of the hotel, you weren't plain, Cal. You were a somebody. I was out of my depth and so I left. I didn't want that awkward morning after chat. The one I assumed a billionaire would have."

"It wasn't the presidential suite. It's our family suite. We own the hotel," Cal says, and I laugh.

I shake my head and smile. Only he would say something like that.

"It was an amazing night," I say. His eyes snap to mine. "I didn't want to ruin it by having you realise in the light of the day, I wasn't anyone special. I wanted to preserve *the magic of the night.*"

We stare at each other. *What the hell possessed me to say that?* True or not, I just complicated things.

"I tried to find you," he surprises me by admitting. "I waited for Samuel and the show to reappear, but when they did…"

I smile. "Samuel said, *he told you to sling your hook.*" It's my turn to smirk, although the hollow feeling in my chest makes me wish he had told me Cal was looking for me. *What would I have done if I'd known?*

I'm playing with fire when the next words come out of my mouth. "What would you have done if he told you where to find me?"

A slow smile stretches Caleb's lips, sending waves of desire straight to my centre. Memories of what Cal did to me that night coming to the forefront of my mind.

"We'll never know," he says, shrugging. "We can't change the past."

Two can play at this game.

"Shame," I say, turning away and making my way to the kitchen door.

I don't make it two steps before a hand clamps around my wrist, spinning me around.

"But I will tell you this. That night you ruined me for all other women."

I have a split second to focus on the face in front of me before his lips crash down on mine.

CHAPTER 39

APRIL

I gasp as our lips collide, and my mouth opens, something Caleb takes quick advantage of. His tongue meets and duels mine, almost in a battle for supremacy. That seems to be the way with us... a power struggle. He wants to dominate, and I fight back.

My hands wind up over his shoulders and into the short hair at the nape. He moans into my mouth as I rake my fingers against his scalp, pulling him closer. There's no mistaking his desire as he presses his rock-hard cock against me.

I rip my mouth away, staring up at him. His pupils dilate, and his cheeks become flushed. Like mine, his breathing is uneven. I grin. We seem to bring out the lust in one another.

"This is just sex... clear the air, get us back on track," I tell him.

He looks down at me and smirks.

"I mean it, Cal. This is us scratching the itch that's been bubbling between us."

"So you think you can fuck me out of your system? Is that it?" he asks, a strange look passing over his features, making my breath catch. *Is that what I want?* I know the chemistry between us has been simmering in the background, but can I do this? Distance myself enough?

"You said you're straight with your partners," I add, trying to take back some semblance of control as I melt under his heated gaze. "This is me being straight with you. I'm horny, and I'm tired of fighting whatever this is."

I gesture between us and he captures my hand, pulling me towards his body.

"Sex it is then," he says as I collide with his solid chest, my nipples growing painfully hard as his mouth hovers above mine. "But what if I make you fall in love with me, little dancer?" he whispers against my lips.

"Never going to happen," I whisper back, dragging his lower lip between my teeth and sucking. He moans, his eyes closing. The way our breath mingles sends shivers down my spine.

"One night," I repeat before allowing my hands to sweep up and around his neck once more.

"Then I'd best make the most of it."

There's no warning before his mouth slams down on mine, stealing my breath. I open for him, his lips and tongue taking full advantage. He manoeuvres us backwards until I hit the side of the table where we spent the evening playing cards. Kissing him is like nothing I've ever felt before, at least not since New York. How did I have the strength to walk away from this man?

There's a sense of desperation, a need. We have spent weeks tiptoeing around one another, and now we are finally giving in to our desires... Kissing Caleb Frazer is like riding the fastest roller coaster in the fun park, all adrenaline, and nail-biting pleasure.

His hands slide down to my ass as he lifts me effortlessly, settling me onto the table. He moves between my legs, never once breaking our kiss. His hands slide up under my t-shirt, unclasping my bra and freeing my breasts into his hands. His thumbs brush against my pebbled nipples, eliciting another moan.

When my head drops back, his mouth moves to my neck, nipping and sucking, finding all those toe-curling spots that shoot darts of pleasure straight to my core. My pussy contracts sharply in delight and anticipation.

Before I can blink, my t-shirt is gone, my bra, history. Caleb's mouth locks onto my nipple, teasing me with his teeth and tongue. My hands lock in his hair, and I slide my hips forward, connecting with his cock, rubbing myself against him. His groan vibrates against my breast, and I undulate my hips.

"Keep up with that, and I will not last," he says, pressing himself against me.

I slide my hand under his t-shirt, pulling it over his head, exposing his broad shoulders and tight abs. He has a swimmer's body. I remember him mentioning he swam growing up but has taken to running more now. His body highlights how much care he takes of himself. That and the pool on the roof let me know he hasn't abandoned that hobby.

He watches as my hands explore the bare skin on his chest. Stopping when I reach his tribal tattoo on his bicep, tracing it with my nail. Goosebumps appear on his skin.

I lift my gaze to him, licking my lips as I stare at his swollen mouth.

His eyes never leave mine as he leans forward, drawing my bottom lip between his teeth. As if in unison, our hands move as one, both of us pulling at the other's remaining clothing. We only stop when they're in a pile at our feet, leaving our uneven breathing filling the air.

I reach for Caleb, his swollen cock standing proud against his stomach.

"No more waiting.... Now," I say.

My core throbbing, almost painfully, with a need to be filled.

"Impatient for my cock, little dancer?" he asks, and I growl.

His cock twitches at the sound. I'm not the only one desperate.

"Not until you're ready and begging," he adds.

The damn man is confident. He wags a finger at me, stepping out of reach. Using his hands to spread my legs. His eyes drop to the bare, glistening lips of my swollen pussy.

He trails a finger along my slit, humming in delight as he finds me wet and needy. His eyes clash with mine as he slides first one, then on the outward draw, a second finger into me, twisting and stretching my entrance before curling against that magic spot on my front wall. I moan as my hips dart off the table, my hands gripping his shoulders as I ride his hand. My muscles clench as his thumb strokes my clit, sending spikes of pleasure flooding through my body.

"Damn it, Cal," I moan, as he works my body.

His mouth drops to my neck, sucking on the sensitive skin beneath my ear, while his fingers and thumb play me like a finely tuned instrument.

Cal moans as the sound of his finger-fucking echoes around the room.

My desire leaks out onto my thighs as his fingers continue their assault. I bite down on my bottom lip.

Catching the move, Caleb moves his other hand to free the abused skin, running his thumb over my lip before I suck it into my mouth.

He steps closer, withdrawing his fingers and using them to explore my dripping pussy, his thumb deep in my mouth. I suck down hard on his digit, his eyes moving to mine. Our gazes lock as my body moves of its own accord, my hips rocking, wanting… desperate for more.

I drop a hand between us, capturing the warm, silky skin of his cock in my fingers. His eyes close for a second, his expression strained.

I spread my legs wider, bearing down as the telltale pressure grows between my legs.

"Caleb, please," I beg.

"What do you need?" he asks, his eyes once again on mine. "Is this it," He inserts one, then a second finger, pumping in and out.

"Ahh yes," I moan, my head dropping back when he adds a third, thick finger. My body explodes at the invasion. Pulling him in, my muscles milking his digits for all it can.

Caleb's mouth captures mine as I ride my orgasm, his fingers continuing to move until I pull his hand away, unable to take anymore.

He grins at me, and I scowl. Two can play that game.

"It's my turn, Mr Frazer."

Before he can stop me, I drop off the table and onto my knees, my eyes never leaving his. I clasp his cock in my hand, my tongue darting out to capture the pre-cum that has moistened the end.

His hands come off my head, sinking into my hair. His eyes closing briefly as I suck him down, running my tongue over the underside of his cock, a shudder racking his body.

He opens his eyes. The look I see there is one of pure desire… lust is a powerful thing.

Why can't we enjoy each other's bodies?

We're consenting adults. It doesn't need to be complicated. I draw him deep into my mouth, savouring the moan that echoes around us. Before I know what is happening, Caleb's hands are under my arms, and he's lifting me. Turning me around, spreading my hands on the table.

"Don't move," he says against my ear, his front pressing into my back, his cock nestled against my ass.

Before I can blink, he's gone, disappearing into the kitchen.

I hear a cupboard door slam before he returns a moment later. I haven't moved a muscle. It's only when I hear the tear of the packet, my body tenses. Caleb steps behind me, one hand resting on my hip while the other lines him up with my dripping centre.

I feel his cock as he rubs it up and down my slit, coating himself in my juices.

"Is this what you want, little dancer?" he asks, pressing the tip of his cock against my entrance.

I moan at the sensation of his tip stretching my body. Not much, but the sensitive muscles contract in anticipation of what's coming.

His next words come out near my ear. "I need to hear you say it."

I grit my teeth, pushing back against him, but he pulls his hips back out of the way. A chuckle escapes him.

I wiggle my ass, connecting with his cock, making him hiss.

"I still need your words," he says, teasing me once again, only this time pressing a little further in.

I moan at his teasing.

"Dammit, Caleb," I practically scream in frustration. "Please fuck me."

I don't need to ask again as he slides his cock through my silky folds and slams into me. My back arches as my body stretches to accommodate his size. Pleased he's already stretched me out earlier. I'd forgotten how impressive he is.

We both moan as he comes to a stop, his cock, balls deep in my pussy.

"You feel so good," he whispers close to my ear, turning my head to capture my mouth in an awkward kiss.

"Move," I say through gritted teeth.

"Your wish…."

It's all he manages before we begin our dance. Him sliding in and out, first leisurely, but then our pace becomes more frantic as our desire builds.

His hand snakes around the front, pulling me back against him. One hand on my clit, the other on my breast. His mouth latching onto my shoulder, suckling in a way I know is going to leave a mark.

The pressure builds in my lower body, and I press back against him. Meeting him stroke for stroke until finally, my body shatters. My vision darkens as stars explode behind my eyes, every muscle in my body tensing. Caleb grunts as my muscles contract hard around his cock.

"That's it little dancer," he pants close to my ear as he continues to thrust into me, his movements hard and frantic. He draws out my orgasm, before spiralling me straight into a second when his fingers find my clit.

I scream, as my knees buckle, my body quivering. He drives into me a couple more times, my muscles still contracting as he lets himself go. Cal moans and shudders, his body freezing, as his cock jerks deep inside me, pumping and filling the condom with his cum.

We collapse forward onto the table. The top cool against my naked breasts and stomach, a stark comparison to the raging heat and weight at my back.

After taking a few minutes to catch his breath, Caleb stands up. I feel him withdraw his still semi-hard cock, missing its warmth.

I push up off the table, trying to look as graceful as possible, even though my legs and arms feel like jelly.

Caleb has disappeared, probably to dispose of the condom.

"Goodnight then," I say, scooping up my scattered clothes.

"Not so fast," Caleb says, appearing in all his naked glory at the door of the kitchen. "I was promised one night… So where do you think you're going?"

My mouth waters at the sight of him. I lick my lips before I can stop myself. Caleb grins before taking a step towards me.

"That was only the beginning, little dancer."

CHAPTER 40

CALEB

To say last night was a shock is an understatement. I know the tension between us has been escalating, but April propositioning me...

"One night of sex," is what she said, and I made the most of it. Having her spread out on my bed for most of the night as I took her body in every position imaginable. We finally fell asleep at about four. My sheets still hold her scent. She was gone when my alarm went off, but then I know she has an early session with Scarlett. Her kids are also starting classes today, and I know she's worried about the logistics. The minibuses are all lined up to transport them, and Scarlett enlisted her team to help ensure all the children remain safe while under our care.

I'm not sure when it became *our* care, but it has. When Wes found out about it, he went nuclear. I'm growing weary of his constant arguing at every point. It's like he forgets who the boss is. I instructed him to bill me directly. April will never need to know. This project is too important to have Wes and his money-pinching derail it.

I stop by Gabriel's office on my way to mine. I can't help myself. It was good to see him last night.

He huffs as I make my way into his office. "Don't you have work?" he asks, sitting back and crossing his arms over his chest.

"Is that any way to greet your twin after I hosted last night?" I say, dropping into the chair opposite him.

Amanda his PA brings me a coffee, which I accept gracefully. Gabriel has a top of the range coffee machine in his staffroom. He likes his coffee like treacle, but the machine itself makes the best coffee around.

"You have remembered Leah is still off on maternity leave?" he adds as if that would be the only reason I called in.

"I haven't forgotten," I say, taking a sip of the rich, dark liquid.

I look up to find Gabriel watching me, a suspicious frown marring his brow.

"What?" I ask.

"There's something… oh my god—you got laid last night."

I spit the mouthful of coffee across his desk, making him frown even more.

Shit, when did Gabriel become so observant?

"Excuse me…"

"Don't play all coy with me. I'm your twin. That's why you're here."

He grins at me and I flinch. This is not what I'm used to where Gabriel is concerned. I expect this from the others, not him. He usually minds his own business.

"Leah was right," he continues. "That's a foot massage and a—"

"Stop," I say, holding up my hand, not wanting to know what my brother gets up to with his wife. Instead, I ask, "What the hell has Leah got to do with this?"

I've got a solid relationship with my brother's wife. We've known her for years. They only realised of their mutual feelings for each other last year. Now they're inseparable.

"She had a feeling there was more to your knight in shining armour routine."

I scowl across the desk at him.

"You can talk," I say. It had been his *knight-in-shining armour* routine that saw him get together with Leah.

"Exactly," he says, giving me an uncharacteristic grin. "Firsthand experience of Sir Frazer."

Shit, I walked into that one.

"So, are you telling me nothing happened after we left?"

"A gentleman never kisses and tells," I say, making my brother choke on his own coffee.

"Gentleman?" His mirth grates on my nerves.

"Fine, something happened, but it's a one off. A get-it-out-of-our-system." I say, knowing it's the only way to shut him up.

I don't like the way my brother is staring at me. It's only when he shrugs, I realise he's actually going to let it drop.

"When do you think you'll break ground?" His question comes out of left field, but I'm happy about the subject change.

"As soon as demolition finishes and the site is cleared," I say. "Planning and the board both signed off on Jaxson's plans, and with the building being deemed unsafe after the fire, they wanted something done about it."

"The fire was accidental, then?"

"There's going to be an independent investigation. They're looking into the landlord."

My thoughts go to April. Her vitality, her sassiness, her kindness. One selfish landlord, and I could have lost her. If she hadn't been able to get out. Thank God, Samuel had the foresight to ensure her office window opened, something April explained during dinner one night. A shiver runs down my spine when I think about what could have happened, if she hadn't woken up when she did. Smoke inhalation is worse than the fire itself.

"I better go," I say, not one hundred per cent sure why I even came here this morning.

Gabriel gets up and walks me to the elevator, not his usual MO.

"Caleb," he says, drawing my attention to him. "Don't overthink things. We've grown up protecting ourselves. We've had to. After Elijah. Remember, sometimes we risk missing what is right in front of us. Look at me."

I stare at my brother as he shrugs. "I'm not saying April is *the one* but having seen you around her. You've let your guard down." He turns towards me and places a hand on my shoulder. "You've never let anyone into your home, certainly not women."

It's my turn to shrug. I decide to stay silent. There's nothing I can say. Gabriel knows why I never invite women back to my home. The Penthouse is off limits. It's my space. Hookups and dates are for the hotels or their apartments. A safe space I can control. I wonder what April would think if she found out she's the first woman I've had sex with, in my bed?

"Caleb, you need to go with the flow. You can't force anything that isn't meant to be. You, of all people, know and understand that."

I huff, knowing that what he's saying is true. But after last night, it didn't come close to scratching the itch, or helping to get her out of my head. I hoped it would. Instead, it bloody fed it. I crave her. I want her wrapped around my cock, to lose myself in her sassy mouth or gorgeous pussy—preferably both. The fact I like her in my space, want her there. It's beginning to scare the crap out of me.

The elevator arrives, and I slap Gabriel on the back. "Give Leah and Callum my love."

My brother's eyes soften. They always do when anyone mentions Leah and their baby. The workaholic is a sap when it comes to his wife and child.

CHAPTER 41

APRIL

I'm not sure whether to be pleased or disappointed when I arrive at the apartment and find Caleb is MIA. No message or note. Just silence.

My mind is racing with possibilities.

Where is he?

Has he met up with one of his lady friends?

Is he doing to them what he did to me... only last night? It's not like we made each other any promises.

I want to scream as my mind torments me. I have no rights to Cal, I told him last night was a onetime thing. Me and my big mouth.

How could I have said such a thing?

The man is a sex god, and my pussy has been throbbing all day, wanting more.

The door clicks, and I step out of the kitchen.

Caleb looks up as I step into his line of sight. His eyes darken, if that is even possible.

"I went to see Tristan," he admits without prompting.

I take a step towards him and before I know it, my back is pressed up against the wall, Caleb's mouth devouring mine.

Hell, yes. I can taste the wine on his lips, and I suck his bottom lip into my mouth, eliciting a groan from the man whose body is pressing me into the wall.

His hands are everywhere, sending shards of desire straight to my needy core.

I strip his shirt from his shoulders, my mouth trailing down his neck. He tips his head, giving me access. His hands pulling and stripping my clothes. He makes light work of my top and bra, pressing his now naked chest against mine. Soft against hard. I bite down on his shoulder, as his hand makes its way into my trousers and discovers my dripping pussy.

The sound of delight that escapes Caleb doesn't go unnoticed, ratcheting up my desire. I feel his cock pressed against me. His stamina from last night, second to none. He was insatiable.

I spread my legs, giving him access. He pulls back and stares into my eyes as he spears me with first one, then a second finger. Pumping in and out. My pussy clamps down hard on the invasion, my juices dripping down onto his hand.

"That's it, beautiful. Relax and enjoy."

My head drops back against the wall, but my eyes stay locked on his. We are so close, our breath is mingling. He curls his fingers, hitting that magic spot inside and I inhale sharply, before letting loose the moan I've been trying to suppress. I ride his fingers, thrusting my hips as his thumb hits my clit. The sensation and my desperate need from the day send me shooting over the edge. I scream as my muscles clamp down on Caleb's fingers, milking them hard, as he continues to move them in and out as I ride my orgasm. My hips jerk, my vision darkens.

Before I can say anything, Caleb has reclaimed my mouth and has scooped me into his arms, as if I weigh nothing at all.

I know I'm not large, but he takes the stairs before shoulder barging his way into his bedroom.

We spent the whole of the previous evening here. His tongue, fingers, and cock sending my body to places it has never been or experienced before.

He places me on the bed, shedding the rest of his clothes, along with mine.

I watch as he stands before me before moving to his bedside drawer, pulling out the box of condoms we started the night before. His cock stands proud, twitching, as I watch him sheath himself.

I lick my lips.

I want a taste, but somehow, I don't think he's going to let me, not yet...

Later.

One time, be damned.

I'm taking as much of this man as I can.

Who turns down sex this good?

No one with any sense.

I reach for him, but he clasps my hand in his instead, taking it above my head and following me down to the bed. He clasps my other hand, raising it too. Locking them both in one of his.

"Now, little dancer," he says, his smoky voice sending shivers straight to my core.

He uses his other hand to rub his heated cock along my seam. Spreading my juices, tormenting my swollen flesh. Each bump against my clit has me spreading my legs wider and wider.

I refuse to beg.

He moves to my entrance, dipping the tip in. I bite my lip to stop myself from crying out.

"Is this what you want?" he asks, pressing forward slightly before withdrawing completely.

"You know it is," I say, lifting my hips to his.

"I thought last night was a onetime thing only," he replies.

I know I'm not the only one affected here, as I watch as tiny beads of sweat mar his brow.

"My mistake," I say, not too proud to admit.

I want this gorgeous man and his body. I want him more than I have ever wanted anything before. He's like a drug… not that I will let him become a habit. There's a shelf-life, an expiration date as I said last night. But who says I need to become addicted? Why can't I just indulge why I have the chance?

"Mistake?" he asks, clearly enjoying this. His cock now poised, once more, at my core.

"Yes, my mistake… I want…" Caleb thrusts into me in one swift movement.

Fully seating himself, we both groan. I bite down on Cal's shoulder before moving my mouth to his neck.

"Is this what you want, little dancer?" he asks, letting go of my hands before cupping my ass and thrusting in and out.

"Most definitely," I say breathlessly.

I gasp as he twists his hips, hitting spots I've only dreamed of or read about. No vibrator or partner I've known can do what this man does with his magic cock.

I let my hands explore his muscled body, my legs wrapping around his hips as I grip his ass kneading and moulding with my hands.

Caleb's mouth finds mine and we fall into a seductive kiss, one that goes with the slower rocking of our bodies. I slide a hand up and into his hair. We continue to move together, the sound of our passion, echoing around us.

He rolls us until I'm sitting astride him, our bodies still joined. This position moves him deeper, and I draw in a sharp breath. I don't think I've ever felt so full.

I look down to find him watching me. He links our hands

as I move on top of him. I take our hands and interlocked fingers, pressing them down next to his head, using my muscles to rock and ride the man beneath me, my clit rubbing against his body. I feel the pressure build again. Caleb swells inside me and I gasp.

"That's it, little dancer. Ride me…"

With his words spurring me on, I pick up the tempo, rocking, rising, and falling until we're both panting. Caleb jerks beneath me, shuddering, his muscles locking. His beautiful face is locked in pure ecstasy. The feel of his body coming tips me over the edge, and I follow rapidly behind him, milking his cock, heightening my own pleasure.

I drop forward, my forehead resting against his. Both of us working to catch our breath.

I pull up, letting Caleb flop forward against his stomach.

"Oh shit," I say, Caleb pressing up and almost head-butting me.

"The condom,"

The condom has split. Our vigorous pounding has taken its toll on the latex sheath.

Caleb's eyes widen.

"I'm clean," he says quickly. "I get tested regularly."

I don't want to delve too deeply into that statement.

"I am, too," I say.

I haven't been with anyone apart from Caleb for a couple of years. What with the dance studio and a lack of funds, my social life has been stagnant.

"Er…" Caleb looks at me questioningly.

"Don't panic. I'm on birth control. I have the coil fitted. Less of a problem with periods and dance classes."

I'd made the choice a while back when my periods had become a problem on my course. Leotards, leggings and heavy periods had not gone well together. One of my teachers had made the recommendation, and I hadn't looked back.

Caleb nods.

He should realise there's no way I'm risking a pregnancy. Foster kid here... the single parent game is not one I'm interested in.

I move off Caleb and watch as he grabs a tissue, removing the evidence, before dropping it into the bin.

Before I know what he's doing, he's scooped me up and is heading into his en suite. The room is opulence on steroids, with its claw bath, double sink unit and walk-in shower with more jets than I can count. The wall is all glass - one way, according to Caleb. We can look out over the city, the lights twinkling.

Caleb switches on the shower, stepping us into the water. His mouth captures mine, his lips soft and soothing. I sink into his kiss, my nipples hardening as he pulls me against him. This man is insatiable, but then who am I to talk? I'm already two orgasms in and I'm prepping for a third.

Grabbing the soap, Caleb worships my body. The only way I can describe it is he's taking care of me. I let him, savouring each sweep of his hands and lips.

It's my turn and I follow suit. Although I let my desire from earlier, rise to the forefront, now I drop to my knees and take him in my mouth, cleaning him until he's panting above me. His fingers flexing against the tiled walls.

I let him go with a pop.

"I don't go bareback," he says.

"I don't either," I tell him honestly. "As I said, my birth control is for other reasons."

We look at each other.

"It's too late for tonight," I say.

"It is," he says.

He scoops me up, the icy wall of tiles stealing my breath as I'm pressed up against it.

"Are you okay?" he asks.

"Please," my voice almost begging.

He thrusts forward, sinking his bare cock into my desperate pussy. The feeling is like nothing I've ever felt before.

"Holy…." Caleb lets out a deep sigh as he moves.

We take it slowly until neither one of us can take any more. I feel the jerk of his cock and the warmth as he fills me with his cum. My legs wrap tightly around his waist.

"That was…"

I place a finger over his lips. He nods, before setting the hand jet off and rinsing away the evidence that is running down my thighs. We dry off, making our way back into the bedroom.

I head for the door.

"Stay," he says.

"I don't think that's a good idea," I say honestly.

Sex is one thing. Cuddling… that's dangerous territory.

"I'm happy for more than one night," I tell him honestly.

He gives me a sly grin. "Good night, little dancer. Until next time."

I grab the handle and open the door.

"Until next time," I say, letting myself out.

CHAPTER 42

CALEB

Since boys' night when we gave into temptation, April and I have fallen into a routine. Every night we have dinner, followed by sex. Or sex followed by a more leisurely dinner, our appetite for one another insatiable. The guys are taking the piss. They know something is up as I've blown them off twice, but April is like a thirst I cannot quench, cannot explain. The taste of her, the way her body feels as she comes around my cock. But then it's not just the physical attraction, she tests my mind as well and when I'm around her, I find myself wanting more.

I'm like an addict and she's become my drug of choice.

It's why I've included Scarlett in my plan. Tonight, I intend on blowing my *little dancers* mind, and not only with orgasms. This time I'm going to try to employ other tricks from my toolbox to win her over.

I hear the front door go and make my way into the living room.

April jumps when she sees me. "Cal, I wasn't expecting you home," she says, her hand going to her chest, before a slow smile begins to spread.

My breath catches at her use of the word *home*.

"Ahh—no, but I was most definitely expecting you," I say, smirking, when she quirks a brow in my direction, her hands now going to her hips.

"And why would that be?" she asks.

"I have a surprise for you?"

"And let me guess, Scarlett is in on it?" she says, her lips twitching. "Their building maintenance excuse for closing at lunchtime, did seem a little... odd."

I asked Scarlett to allow April the afternoon off, and when I told her why, she was more than happy to find an excuse for sending her home.

"What is so special, that you are in cahoots with my boss, and have me walking in through the door at lunchtime?" she asks, stepping forward and wrapping her arms around my neck.

I drop my forehead to hers.

"Now if I tell you, it won't be a surprise."

I drop a chaste kiss on her pouting mouth, before pulling away when she tries to deepen it.

She draws back and shoots me a confused look.

I tap a finger on her nose.

"Patience. All will be revealed in good time. First things first."

I pull out my phone and send a call to the concierge. "Send them up," I say, watching a frown form between April's brows.

"Cal. What's going on?"

"Don't worry, you're going to love it, I promise," I say, pulling her in for a hug just as the buzzer on the apartment goes.

I move around her and open the door.

"Come in," I say, stepping back to allow our two visitors to enter.

"April, this is David, and Claire, his partner. They are here to help you get ready."

April spins towards me. "Get ready?"

"David is here to do your hair and Claire your makeup."

"A pamper session?"

"Not exactly." I turn to Claire and David. "You're set up in the room I showed you."

"Great," David says, smiling. "We'll see you upstairs, April."

With that they both leave.

When they are out of earshot, I turn back to April who is staring at me wide eyed. "I have something special planned for this evening. With everything you've been through recently, I thought I would make a day of it… or at least half a day," I say wondering if I've gone too far. I run a hand through my hair and step back. "If it's too much?"

April steps towards me and wraps her arms around my waist. "No, it's fine. It's just a surprise. I'm not used to people surprising me. Not on this scale."

I drop a kiss on her nose, making her smile. "We're going out tonight, and I thought you might enjoy being spoiled. I know my sisters usually do this for events like this."

April's eyebrows raise as she stares at me. I roll my lips to stop myself saying any more. April smirks.

I need to stop talking.

"Go," I say, turning her around and swatting her on her ass.

She giggles, a sound I'm beginning to recognise and love.

"I've set them up in Tristan's room."

I really need to think about renaming my rooms.

"Thank you," she says making her way to the stairs, before looking back and grinning.

She blows me a kiss before taking off up the stairs, two at a time.

CHAPTER 43

APRIL

I stare at myself wide-eyed in the mirror.
"Wow."

I look at the intricate and beautiful up-do David has masterminded. Soft curls framing my face.

Claire has painted my nails and done my makeup.

"Thank you, both. I…"

Claire steps forward and squeezes my shoulder. "You're welcome. It's been a pleasure."

We've spent the afternoon chatting. They are a husband-and-wife duo, who often work with the Frazer women for events, and know Caleb's sisters and mother.

"Now for your dress."

Claire takes a dress carrier out of the wardrobe.

It feels like they've been pampering me for hours.

Claire unzips the bag, and I gasp. It's one of the dresses I tried when Chloe came around. I had rejected it, citing I would never have anywhere to wear it.

Where the hell is Caleb taking me?

The man is full of surprises.

David leaves while Claire helps me get into my dress and heels.

My eyes fill when I catch sight of myself in the mirror. The scarlet mid-calf dress hugs my figure, flaring out at the bottom. It accentuates my figure perfectly, and the heels give my legs extra lift and shape.

"All set," Claire says, stepping back. "Here's your clutch. Although I've set your makeup, there's powder and a lip tint in there. This is a wrap in case it gets a little chilly later."

I take the small bag she holds out, and the silky wrap.

"Thank you," I say again. Unsure what else to say or do.

Claire smiles, "Have a wonderful evening."

I make my way downstairs, careful not to fall. Four-inch heels and stairs are a liability for someone who is used to dance shoes and trainers.

I pause when Cal steps into sight.

I freeze at the look on his face.

We stand staring at each other.

He is wearing a black tuxedo.

The man looks good in anything he wears, with his broad shoulders and trim waist, he steals my breath.

"April, you look—"

His words are breathy, and his eyes darken as he drinks me in.

I continue down the stairs, drawn towards him.

He meets me at the bottom.

"You look radiant," he whispers, his face inches from mine.

"You look incredibly sexy yourself," I say, the breathless sound of my voice surprising me. "So where are you taking me?"

He steps back and smiles.

"A surprise. Mason is here, ready and waiting."

He turns and holds out his arm, I slide my hand through the crook of his elbow.

"Lead the way," I say, excitement bubbling in my stomach.

Never before have I had anything like this. It is something that only happens in the movies or in books. Not to a broke dancer whose life is in chaos.

We meet Mason by the car.

"Evening Mason."

"Evening, Ms April," he says, smiling widely when he sees me.

Cal helps me into the car, before handing me my passport.

"You'll be needing this," he says, grinning.

"Cal—"

I stare at him, taking the passport he is holding. Luckily it was in my handbag when the fire happened, so escaped with me.

He says nothing, instead he takes one of my hands and raises it to his lips.

"To us, and this evening," he says, setting more butterflies loose in my stomach.

* * *

THE TRIP to the airport is quick. Mason drives us onto the runway, and we pull up alongside a private jet.

My eyes dart to Cal's, only to find him watching me with a strange expression on his face.

"This is our family jet," he explains. "It makes it easier to get from A to B."

Of course it does.

Although, who am I to complain?

Since walking in Caleb's front door, I've been lost for

words, and now I'm about to experience flying on a private jet.

Mason opens the door, and Cal helps me climb out. We are greeted at the steps by a beautiful woman in a uniform.

"April, this is Claudia. She flies with the family."

"Hi," I say.

"Evening, Ms Wilson. It's lovely to meet you. If there is anything you need, please don't hesitate to ask."

We enter the plane, and a combination of different seats is available. We take a seat at the table.

"Can I get you anything to drink?" Claudia asks.

Cal turns to me. "Champagne?"

"That would be lovely," I say smiling up at Claudia.

I'm beginning to feel like I'm caught in a dream. Is this how Cinderella felt when her fairy godmother turned up, and she found herself heading to the ball?

Claudia returns with two glasses of champagne.

Cal takes them both, passing one to me.

"To an evening to remember," he says, clinking his glass to mine.

I find myself drowning in his eyes.

"There is little to no doubt about it," I tell him honestly, taking a sip, savouring its sweet flavour.

When this dream finally comes to an end and we part company, I will forever have these memories to sustain me of my time with this man.

* * *

WE LAND in Paris and are met by a limousine. Cal has gone all out. He still refuses to tell me where we're going, and I've decided I'm happy to sit back and enjoy the ride. Simply spending time in this man's company is enough, and as

Samuel encouraged, I'm going to enjoy every moment while I can. No regrets.

We pull up outside a restaurant and once again, Cal takes my hand.

We're led to our table, where the maître d' pulls out my chair for me. Only when I sit down and look up do I realise the restaurant overlooks the Eiffel Tower in all its nighttime glory. It stretches high into the sky, its lights shining over Paris.

I clasp Cal's hand over the table as we finish our main course. I have never tasted food like this, and I doubt I will again.

"I don't know what to say," I tell him truthfully. "This whole day. It is not what I expected when I got up this morning."

"As long as you're enjoying yourself," he tells me. "I wanted us to get away, have an evening where we can be Cal and April again."

"Can we ever be those two people again?"

They were an illusion.

"I believe we can be what we choose," he tells me drawing my hand to his lips.

If only life is that simple.

I look into Cal's eyes and wonder what he would think if he knew how I raised the money for the dance studio. Will he look at me the same way?

I know he won't.

So, for now, I push it to one side and enjoy the sex and the time I am spending with this man. I'll protect myself because my past choices will come back and destroy my present, so the only thing I'm left with are the memories, like so many times in my past.

"Hey, a penny for your thoughts," Cal asks, his hand touching my cheek.

I give him a shy smile. "I'm just overwhelmed. This is…"

His face breaks into a grin. "Not the end—there is still one more surprise."

"Cal," I say, unsure my heart can take much more of his thoughtfulness. I quirk a brow instead. "And how are you going to top the most beautiful food, with the backdrop of the Eiffel Tower?"

He sits back, my fingers still intertwined with his.

"A beautiful woman once told me she always dreamed of watching Swan Lake."

My throat constricts as the words leave his mouth, my eyes welling. I blink rapidly as he sits forward, cupping my cheek in his warm palm.

He remembered?

"Tonight is the opening night of Swan Lake at The Palais Garnier."

I bite my lip to prevent the sob that threatens to escape, shaking my head.

Cal sends me an understanding smile.

"I wanted to do something for you."

He stands and I join him.

Then I pull him back and wrap my arms around his neck. My heels mean I don't have as far to reach, so I place my lips gently against his.

"I don't know what to say," I tell him when I draw back.

"Not a thing," he replies, capturing a tear I am unaware I have shed. "Come on, our seats await."

CHAPTER 44

CALEB

I look down at the woman asleep in my arms.

Tonight, we've laughed and openly discussed our likes and dislikes on everything from television shows to world events. I watched in awe as she was swept away by the emotion of the ballet. The music and choreography seeming to transport her. I wasn't interested in the dancers before me. Instead my gaze was locked on the woman I'm with. A woman who has turned my orderly life on its head. I cannot believe the difference she's made in such a short time.

"Hey, beautiful," I say, kissing her nose. Her body stiffens before she realises who's talking to her. "We've landed."

Her eyes flutter open, and I drop my lips to hers. I feel her smile where our mouths touch, her tongue darting out as she deepens our kiss.

I snake my hand behind her head, pulling her closer.

"Landed?" she says suddenly, pulling back, clearly having woken up.

I chuckle. "Yes, landed. It's time to go home."

I unbuckle my seat belt and get up, pulling her to her feet.

She comes with all the grace of the dancer she is, her arm

sliding through mine as we make our way to a waiting Mason on the tarmac.

When we're finally settled into the car, April turns to me, her eyes wide.

"Thank you. Thank you for these wonderful memories. I will treasure them."

She leans forward and presses herself against me.

In that moment I know I can't let her go. I will do everything in my power to keep my little dancer and make this one of many memories she can treasure. I just need to get her to trust me and see the real me, not the Caleb Frazer I have spent years presenting to the world.

CHAPTER 45

APRIL

I wake up with a heavy weight over my stomach and a rod of iron pressed up against my ass cheeks. Unable to prevent the smile that graces my lips, especially when lips tease my ear lobe, sending more shivers straight to my core. I groan, pressing back against the object of my desire. A hand disappears between my thighs, and a moan vibrates against my neck as he finds me wet and wanting.

"Morning, little dancer." The words fall from his lips as his fingers slide into me.

It's my turn to groan. I raise my top leg, my back still to Cal as he continues to nibble my neck, his fingers dancing between my entrance and my clit. I rest my foot on his calf, opening myself to him. When I can't take anymore, I grip his cock and line it up with my entrance. What a way to wake up. Orgasms before breakfast. A new one for me. I press down on him, and he sinks into my depths.

"Morning, Cal," I say a little more breathlessly than I intend.

I have already thanked him multiple times for last night. It's an experience I will take with me to the grave.

He groans against my ear as my body swallows him whole.

We roll our hips, his fingers now teasing and pinching my clit as we dance towards yet more orgasmic bliss. Sex with this man is like nothing I've ever experienced before, but then again, my previous partners were little more than boys. Cal is very much a man and the most unselfish lover I've ever had.

I give myself up to the moment, our movements becoming more and more frantic until we're once again flying over the precipice.

I extract myself and stand up. Needing to get ready for work.

Before I enter the bathroom, I turn towards the bed.

"Thank you for last night. I can't tell you what it means to me." I smile down at the god lying on his side, his head propped on his hand.

"I aim to please," Cal says, his gaze raking over my naked body.

I'm not shy. I lost my inhibitions years ago. I didn't have a choice.

"That's not what I mean, and you know it. But you did—please, that is," I say, laughing. I find myself laughing a lot these days. Cal seems to have that effect on me. He is also going to make me late. "But now I need to shower and get ready for work," I say, letting my own eyes rake over his naked chest.

His eyes darken, but I hold up a hand to stop him. "Alone."

He drops back on the bed with a dramatic sigh, making me chuckle, before sitting back up.

"Jaxson is arriving today. He's over from the US to discuss

the designs with the builders. One of those will be the dance studio."

My heart rate picks up. This is all becoming so real. Cal took me to the site the morning, the demolition crew started work, and something snapped inside me. I could not stop the tears that had been threatening. Watching them tear down the building I had called home for two years, regardless of its state, had caused me pain. More than I expected. Caleb was amazing. He held me and promised me the new building would meet all my dreams and more. His kindness unlocked something inside me... something that was now free-running.

"I'd love to meet him," I say. "What time? I have classes all afternoon. Scarlett's got me shadowing the lady I'll be covering for."

Cal gets out of my bed, as naked as the day he was born and even less abashed. We are standing chatting in our birthday suits as if it's the most normal thing. What surprises me is his next move. He makes the bed. Smoothing out the duvet, replacing the throw that landed on the floor at some point in the night, and repositions the scatter cushions.

"What?" he asks, clearly taking in my shocked expression.

I bite my lip and shake my head, unable to keep the smile from my lips.

He walks around and stands in front of me. "It's okay. I've invited him to have dinner with us this evening."

He grins as I look up at him. "I shall look forward to it," I say, turning away with sass.

He swats my ass and laughs as he walks towards the door. Heading back towards his own room. Last night, mine was closest.

"I'll see you later."

Before I can think better of it, I blow him a kiss before high-tailing it into the bathroom. More laughter follows me.

***

CALEB AND JAXSON are already home by the time I make my way into the apartment. Jaxson and Caleb get to their feet as soon as I enter. Their imposing maleness sucks the air out of the living area.

Caleb steps up to me, takes my arm, and drops a surprise kiss to my lips.

Not what I was expecting.

"April, I'd like to introduce you to Jaxson Lockwood."

Jaxson steps forward, holding out his hand.

What is it with the Frazer men and their friends? Were they all born with the gorgeous, sexy gene, or is that what money does to someone?

I take Jaxson's hand. He's as tall as Caleb, although his dark hair is short on the sides and longer on top, his temples speckled grey. He has a perfectly groomed beard that adorns his strong jawline. His skin has a tan, but it is not the natural olive of Cal's. Laughter lines deepen around his eyes as he smiles. Eyes that are an ocean blue, eyes a woman could drown in... if she wasn't partial to dark ones.

He is older than Caleb, but it's clear the two are close.

"Pleased to meet you," I say. "If you don't mind, I'll grab a shower before I join you."

I shoot Cal a look. I rushed home, not realising they'd already be here.

"No rush," Jaxson says.

"I'm ordering takeout," Caleb says as I move towards the stairs. "Your usual?"

I turn and smile, my gaze flipping to Jaxson, who is giving Caleb a look of interest.

"That would be perfect," I say, making a hasty retreat.

As I reach the top of the stairs, I hear Jaxson's amused tone saying, "Usual?"

"Shut up," Caleb says. "We live together. Of course, I know what she likes to eat."

"And that, my friend, says it all."

I make a hasty retreat, not needing or wanting to hear anymore. Nothing positive comes of eavesdropping.

I shower and change into jeans and a t-shirt, adding some makeup and making myself look a little more respectable.

"There you are," Caleb says when I return. "We've laid the plans out on the table if you want to have a look."

Jaxson is missing, although I spot him on the balcony, his phone pressed to his ear. His expression intense.

"Don't worry, he's on the phone to my sister, Kat," Caleb says, his arm wrapping around my waist as he pulls me back into him. His show of possession should annoy me, but instead, I relax in his arms, moving my head to one side as he kisses my neck. I bite my lip to stifle the moan that threatens to escape. Our one night has turned into so many, but I can't regret it.

"Sorry," Jaxson says, coming in. Caleb and I jump apart like naughty school kids, caught behind the bike shed. "I'm sorry, Caleb, but your sister is…"

He looks up and sees me standing there, the words pausing in his mouth. "Never mind," he says, putting his phone in his back pocket.

"Kat will come around," Caleb says, slapping him on the shoulder. "She's stubborn, but after all. You *are* the best, and Kat knows that."

He grunts but says nothing else. Instead, he turns to me and motions towards the plans.

"What do you think?" he asks.

"Er…"

I stare down at the lines and numbers that decorate the page.

Smiling, he moves in and explains what each line and

notation means. By the time he's finished, I'm in awe. Yes, the dimensions for the dance floor are the same, but the changes he's made will have this place running on a fraction of the previous overheads.

I turn to Caleb, my mouth open, only to have him grinning.

"He's the best—it's why I hire him."

I ask some questions, pointing out additional features.

"This?" I say, pointing to an additional part of the plan, something that had not been in the original building.

"An apartment," Jaxson says. "The ceiling height and additional windows have allowed for accommodation to be added above. A two-bedroom apartment, with kitchen and living space."

My eyes widen.

Shit.

Music travels. The last thing I'll need is complaints from an upstairs resident when classes go on late or start early in the morning.

"Um... how good will the soundproofing be? Only music from the studio is likely to travel," I say, pointing to the room. "Some classes may run late into the evening."

Jaxson gives me a confused look, which surprises me. An architect who hasn't thought about that.

It's Caleb who steps in. "Don't worry. Soundproofing won't be an issue. I promise. I don't want any complaints any more than you do."

My gaze moves to Caleb's, and he smiles reassuringly. "I'm trusting you. If I get a series of complaints—" I add, raising my eyebrows to let him know I'm not joking.

"Don't worry," he says, taking my hand and raising it to his lips.

Jaxson coughs for dramatic effect, and I can't hide my smile. Caleb is being attentive, and I like this side of him.

"This door is optional," Jaxson says, pointing to a door that leads from my reception area into the space next door. "This will be the community cafe. From which the Frazer Foundation will set up its counselling centre and support groups. It's up to you whether you want your students to be able to walk from your reception back and forth."

I think of the success of Scarlett's Cafe and all the parents who used to visit Betty and Don. Being able to go from one building to the other would make life easier, especially in the winter. Free up reception and allow parents and children to wait in a safe and welcoming environment.

"I like it," I say. "It would have made life easier for many of my students if they had easy access to next door. Especially with the younger students. Parents can wait there, and the students can be released to them via the door."

"We can add security to ensure people can't just move between the two, maybe key cards for teachers. But it's there as an option. As I said before. You have time to think about it."

He pulls out another roll of plans.

"This is the community centre. The cafe is here, and the upstairs will have offices and rooms. Speaking to the team, Francesca and her foundation are assembling. They're hoping to add family planning, a full-time counsellor, and career advisors."

I stare at the plans. This is not what I imagined the first time we headed to Caleb's office. Or when we protested outside, feeling a large corporate would run us out of our neighbourhood. I couldn't have been more wrong.

"What do you think?" Caleb asks, coming to stand next to my shoulder.

I look up and lose myself in his dark gaze. I could not have been more wrong about a human being if I tried.

"I'm speechless if I'm honest."

Jaxson moves to the other side of the table. "Have you not taken April to the Copper Town Development?"

Caleb looks across the table.

"What's Copper Town Development?" I ask.

The name sounds vaguely familiar, but it is not somewhere I can place.

"One of our first projects," Jaxson says, his eyes moving to me. "It highlights all the things we like to put into our developments, although I have improved many of the eco features since. We will upgrade them as we go. It showcases how an old and new community can work together." He looks at Caleb. "You need to take April. She's your spokesperson. I can't believe you haven't shown her Copper Town."

Caleb shrugs, and I know why. Maybe if I hadn't been a porcupine when we first met, he might have. Or after he kissed me when I ran for the hills. Until we fell into bed, we were ships passing in the night.

"We've been busy getting the dance school up and running at an alternative venue," I say, stepping in and defending Caleb. "But I'd like to see it," I add, turning to Cal, who smiles.

"Your wish is my command."

The doorbell goes. Our dinner has arrived. While Cal goes to the door to collect the food, Jaxson rolls up the diagrams. I make myself useful by grabbing plates and cutlery from the kitchen.

Dinner is a blast. Jaxson reveals that he's a close friend of Elijah, Caleb's older brother. He used to spend the summer holidays at the Frazer's house in Hampshire. How the house was never empty. Francesca and Robert opened their doors to whomever wanted a place to stay, and how Robert helped Jaxson get his first internship.

My heart twinges. It sounds amazing. No wonder Cal was

willing to open his home to me. His upbringing shaped him that way.

By the time Jaxson leaves, I've learned a lot about Caleb and his family. They are not what I expected. But Caleb and I have an undefined expiration date, but it's still there. As we make our way to bed, he takes my hand in his, an unspoken question in his eyes.

I nod.

What the hell.

I follow him into his bedroom. I might as well make the most of my time with him. I'll just have to protect my heart. Although I'm not sure anyone will ever replace this man.

CHAPTER 46

CALEB

*J*axson is waiting in my office when I finally make it in.

"Housemate, huh?" he says, laughing. Something you don't see much of with Jaxson Lockwood. The guy takes *serious* to a new level and is more buttoned up than my twin, or at least the old version of Gabriel.

"Housemate," I state firmly.

"Housemate with benefits?" he asks, a smirk gracing his lips.

"What is this?" I ask, turning to face him with my hands on my hips.

He shrugs. "Just wondering why you added an apartment to the dance studio but haven't told the woman it's being built for?"

I sigh and sink back against my desk. I knew he picked up on that detail the night before but let it drop.

Why hadn't I mentioned the apartment to April? The fact she's only just learned to trust me? Refuses to accept anything from me apart from a roof over her head? Even then, she keeps talking about paying me back—as if I have any need for more money, and particularly hers.

She's the most infuriatingly sexy, beautiful woman I've ever met, and she has me tied up in knots. My little dancer has turned the world of this reformed playboy upside down, and I've never been happier. However, I'm not about to jinx it by showing my hand, not before it's completed. Jaxson removed the internal stairs on the plans we showed April because when she realises the apartment is connected to the studio, she will know I designed it for her. She'll be mad, but it will be too late. She'll have her own space. But I can't explain all that to Jaxson.

"It's complicated," I say, earning myself a shake of his head.

"Complicated in that you don't want her to move out or something else?"

Jaxson's words stop me in my tracks.

It's true. I have got used to having April in my space. I'd imagined having someone always around would grate on my nerves. Instead, I enjoy coming home to someone there. Even in our attempts to avoid each other, her mere presence brought me solace. But that's not it. I know April needs to leave. Yes, the sex is amazing, and waking up next to her this past couple of days, her hot little body curled around mine. But as April continues to point out, we're scratching an itch that expires when she leaves.

"Complicated," I say, moving around the desk and switching on my computer. "April has an issue with me helping her, anyone helping her. I must tread carefully, otherwise, she's likely to run for the hills."

"Why haven't you shown her Copper Town?" he asks, clearly not going to let up about April.

I stand up, folding my arms over my chest. "What's with the thousand questions?"

"I'm trying to understand," he says, his shoulders rising and falling as he shrugs before dropping himself into the chair opposite my desk. "You've been telling me about this woman, who is pivotal to getting the community on board, yet you haven't shown her our flagship project. One that has been running for years and transformed a neighbourhood, much like hers, with unquestionable success."

I know his question is valid. It's true we can and will improve their community, but the community itself would have lost something greater had she walked away after the fire.

"After the fire, April had nothing to stay for. Everything she had worked for had gone up in flames. She is proud and stubborn and too independent for her own good. She's spent her whole life trying to be heard." I look at him and smile. "So I gave her a purpose, a reason. If she saw Frazer Development as the bad guys, she would have to stay and fight for the little guys. Just seeing her at that initial meeting with her community standing up for her. Seeing her with the kids. You and I both know that community is more than buildings and places to go. She's an enormous part of hers. She's placed herself at its heart. If she left…"

Jaxson looks at me, his expression contemplative.

"I get it," he says, taking me by surprise. "But now it's time to show her the bigger picture. Get her on board. It will be a win-win, I promise you."

Jaxson joins us when I collect April from Scarlett's.

"Wow. An escort," April says as she comes out of the changing room, showered and dressed.

"Thought we'd show you around Copper Town. Grab some dinner at one of the restaurants or diners," I say.

April tilts her head and purses her lips before smiling. "Dinner with two gentlemen. How can a woman turn that down?"

Jaxson's lips twitch, and I smack his arm. April sashays passed us and out towards the car.

Mason drops us off outside the main area. Like Sunny Down, we created Copper Town out of converted warehouses and run-down tower blocks. The residents have turned the once gangland paradise into a hive of activity and businesses. I want to show April that it's not only the residents who moved in but the community who already lived here who have thrived.

April gets out of the car, her eyes wide as she takes in the buildings and businesses. Jaxson steps forward.

He points out his eco features, explaining how they've made the buildings super-efficient and reduced their energy ratings. From electricity to water consumption, even gas. It's all as efficient as it can be. All down to his genius. On the outside, the old factory brickwork has been repointed and the windows replaced, making the apartment's bright living spaces.

"Where would you like to eat?" Knowing after a day of dancing, she's usually starving.

"Can we wander around for a bit?" she asks, turning to face me, her eyes wide, her expression intense.

"Of course," I say, motioning for her to lead the way.

April fires questions at us, which we take turns in answering. Several business owners pop out when they see us wandering around.

"Mrs Dale, lovely to see you," I say to the lady, who is just about to close her coffee shop.

"Well, if it isn't Caleb Frazer. It's been too long, young man," she says, dropping everything on the table and coming towards us. "And Mr Lockwood. You boys get finer looking every time I see you both." She winks at April, who smacks a hand over her face.

"I don't think these two need any more of an ego boost," she laughs.

"Probably not, but what they've done for this community, how they've helped us and... did I tell you?" She changes tack quickly. "Johnny has now completed his culinary school training. He's taken over Bobby's Bistro. Old Bobby retired last year, and Johnny stepped in."

I turn to April. "Johnny is Mrs Dale's grandson. He won a Frazer scholarship. He's been in culinary school this past three years."

"And it's all down to this man. My Johnny had nothing, was running with the wrong crowd. Caleb gave him a purpose."

Time to move on. Before April thinks I've set this up. What she is unaware of is that numerous comparable stories exist in this area. Where we've tried to help the community grow and prosper. As if sensing April's interest. "My Johnny isn't the only one. There have been schemes to help with business set-ups, reduced rents to employ local workers."

I step forward, knowing now might be the time to rescue April.

"We are looking for dinner. We'll head over to Johnny's and eat there," I say, earning myself the biggest, widest grin.

"God bless you both," Mrs Dale says to Jaxson and me. I'm not the only one whose cheeks are a little flushed as we say our goodbyes.

When we are out of sight, April turns, her eyes sparkling. "I assume you didn't plan that sales pitch," April says, her eyes sparkling.

"No," Jaxson says. "But she is one reason I suggested we bring you here. Caleb needs to show you what Sunny Down will look like once he refashions it. We want the current community to help build what will be there. Run the businesses, employ locals."

April turns to Jaxson. "If Sunny Down is anything like this. Wow."

We arrive outside Bobby's Bistro. Johnny has kept the name, and the place is buzzing. We enter, only to be rushed by one of the servers.

"Hi, I'm Wendy. If you could follow me," she says. "Mrs Dale just called. Johnny has set aside a table for you. He said he'll be out to see you shortly."

"Please tell him not to go to any trouble," I say, seeing how manic the restaurant is. I doubt he needs to take time playing nice with customers.

She gives me one of *those* smiles. The one that says, *yeah right.*

She hands us some menus and tells us she'll be back to take our orders.

April is busy looking around. "This is impressive," April says, looking down the menu.

I agree with her. It is impressive, and I feel a sense of pride swell in my chest at Johnny's achievements and how far he's come.

Wendy returns and takes our order, allowing us to make small talk in the meantime.

"Jaxson, how long will you be staying in the UK?" April asks, focusing her attention on my friend, my jaw muscles tensing as I watch on.

"I'll be travelling back and forth. I have some projects ongoing in the US, but this one is one of the larger ones, so I want to be on hand."

April nods, showing her understanding.

"You need to work on Kat. She knows you're the best. I'm not sure why my sister is being so stubborn," I add, watching Jaxson's jaw clench at the mention of my sister's name.

Am I missing something?

"Just drop it. It's up to her. I will not beg," he says, shooting me a look that tells me he means it.

His choice of phrase startles me, but before I can question him further, our food arrives, followed by Johnny.

"Mr Caleb," he says, approaching our table. I rise to my feet and hold out a hand in greeting. One he takes and shakes enthusiastically.

"I wanted to come and thank you personally. For making all this possible." My ears feel impossibly hot at his gushing words. This really isn't a setup, but I know April will think it is.

"You made the changes, Johnny. This isn't down to me. This is all you. I just offered you a way, another choice. You should be very proud of yourself."

He grins and nods, before turning to April. "This man, he got me out of a life that would land me in jail. Him and his family…" I watch as his voice catches.

I pat his shoulder. "You should be proud of all you've achieved."

"Not just me. You helped the entire gang."

When he says, *gang*. He's talking in a literal sense. Johnny ran with a group of lads who saw themselves as the Kings of Copper Town. When the police bust them for breaking and entering on the new site, I had a choice. Press charges or try rehabilitation. I went with the latter. At seventeen, they were smart lads. When given the choice and a firm talking to, they decided to better themselves.

"I heard. I've been keeping tabs. I hear Denny is working uptown," I say.

Denny wrote to me, thanking me for everything. Letting me know he had a new job, was changing his ways, and had encouraged his crew to do the same.

Johnny nods and smiles.

"I better get back to the kitchen," he says. "Let you enjoy your dinner. On the house."

I go to refuse, but April catches my attention, shaking her head.

"Thank you," I say to Johnny. "And congratulations."

"Thank you, Mr Caleb."

Johnny leaves, grinning, and I retake my seat.

"I can't let him give us our meal," I say to April.

"You can and you will. He wants to say thank you. This is one way he can. You've clearly impacted his life. It's what I'd want to do if someone did that for me."

Something in her tone catches me off guard. I look down at the table, knowing what she says is true.

She takes my hand, giving it a gentle squeeze until my eyes meet hers.

"It doesn't mean you can't leave a *very* generous tip," she says, smiling at me.

I grin back. "I knew I liked you for a reason," I say before I can stop myself.

My expression must give me away as Jaxson chokes on his wine, and April laughs.

"I'm glad I'm of use. Now shut up and eat. Our dinner is getting cold."

CHAPTER 47

CALEB

April shudders above me, her inner muscles clenching hard against my cock as she rides her orgasm. Her hands clenching at her breasts, squeezing her nipples.

I thrust into her, feeding the sensation, my fingers stimulating her swollen clit, driving her on.

I wait until she relaxes, my pace picking up, the pressure in my balls building until my muscles lock and my cock jerks, pumping my cum deep into her velvety pussy.

April's mouth locks on mine. Her tongue teasing and tangling, trying to win the battle.

I roll us, the daybed on my roof terrace, still warm from the day's sun. It was quite the surprise to find April sunning herself up here, her hair wet from using the pool. Her tiny bikini too tantalising to ignore. This is where I'm pleased I took the initiative to shelter the terrace from prying eyes from the neighbouring buildings.

"This is a pleasant surprise," I say, nestling April into my chest. I'm still amazed at how well we fit and how freely she allows me to do it. We've come a long way from sex with no snuggling until now.

"Hmm," she says, dropping a kiss against my chest, nestling deeper. "The pool was calling to me," she says sleepily. "The underground was hot and after a day of dancing."

"You know you're welcome to use it," I say.

"I know, thank you." She tilts her head up and drops a kiss onto my lips, but when she pulls back, there's a crease between her brows.

I run my thumb over it.

"Want to talk about it?"

"I don't know," April tells me honestly.

I run a hand down her body, loving how she shivers as my fingers glide over her skin.

"How did you start dancing?" I ask, as she rests her head on my chest, her hand drawing lazy circles on my stomach.

"My last foster mum, Di, runs a dance school." April pauses, and I let her. "I was twelve when I went to live with Di and Julian. My previous family decided they didn't want to foster anymore. Their own children left home, and they wanted to travel."

"I'm sorry," I say, smoothing a hand over her hair.

"It is what it is. I kind of got used to moving. Foster care isn't usually long term, so every three years I was moved." She looks up at the sky, her mind wandering, before giving a small smile. "I made Di and Julian's life hell for the first year. I was one angry pre-teen," she admits.

"You tried to push them away."

It's a statement more than a question. The more I get to know April, the more I understand her defensive measures.

April chuckles. "I did. Tested them to the brink. It was only after I ran away for the fourth time and the police returned me in a police car, Di decided enough was enough.

She made me join her at the dance studio every evening after school. All privileges revoked."

"That must have been tough."

I can't imagine an angry, pre-teen April taking too kindly to being told what to do.

"It was, but it was the best thing that ever happened to me. Di showed me there was another way. Initially, I went to do my homework, but then during the holidays I began to watch. Di caught me practising some steps at home. By the time of my thirteenth birthday, I was joining her classes. Found I had an aptitude for dancing, and Di used that to her advantage. Taught me everything I know and more. I owe her everything."

"She sounds like an amazing woman," I say, smiling and hoping I'll get to meet her one day.

"She is, they are," she says looking up at me. "But at eighteen I had to leave their care. My time in the foster system was officially over. They told me I could stay, but that would have been unfair. I couldn't take any more from them, they had already given me so much. Then I got my scholarship to the conservatoire, so I knew it was time to move on. Stand on my own two feet, so at eighteen, I moved out. I still speak to Di, at least once a week, if not more."

"That's young," I say, already knowing this much from the report Elijah has given me.

"It's the foster system," she says, her tone so matter of fact that my heart bleeds for her. At eighteen, I was still immature, too young to stand on my own two feet. I find it difficult to envision what life would have been like at that age without adult supervision or support.

I think back to the desperation in Di's voice when Samuel called her, when April was missing. This is a woman who clearly loves her foster daughter as if she was her own.

"She sounds like a special lady."

April smiles at me. "She is."

"And she still runs her dance school?" I ask.

April's smile begins to fade, and she sits up, clasping her knees to her chest. "Yes. Although she is being stubborn. She needs to have a hip replacement. Has been on the waiting list forever. Last time I saw her, she was using a stick to get around. She tried to hide her pain, but—"

April huffs, before turning her head to look at me, resting her cheek on her knees.

I go to open my mouth but stop. It's clear how much April loves her foster mum, but I'm also learning pride is a large part of her make-up, that and standing on her own two feet rather than accepting help from anyone. Instead, I change the subject.

"What about your birth parents?"

April flips over, resting her chin on her hands on my chest.

"According to what I've been told, my mum was young when she had me. I lived with her when I was little. Then, when I was three, I guess it got too much. I moved to foster care when she could no longer look after me."

"Have you seen her since?"

April shakes her head, and my heart gives a lurch. "I have some memories. But I'm not sure if they're dreams of a little girl or whether they were real. Whatever they were... I haven't seen or heard from her in a long time. I don't know where she is, or what she's doing."

I pick up on the loneliness in her tone and pull her tighter against me. April drops her mouth to my chest, kissing her way to my nipple before she takes it between her lips and rolls it between her teeth and tongue. I bite down to suppress the moan that wants to escape. Her hands move, beginning their own exploration. Her fingers trailing up and down my hardening cock. I know she's distracting me, and that's her choice.

I moan as her hand encases me, and I feel her smile as she follows her hand down with her mouth. Drawing me deep into her mouth, her tongue teases the underside of my swollen cock. I writhe beneath her, her hands massaging my balls, her mouth, tongue, and teeth tormenting me. Before she takes me over the edge, I scoop her up and run for the pool.

April squeals, her laughter filling the air as I jump into the water, submerging us both. We surface laughing, and April swims towards me, wrapping her arms around my neck. I manoeuvre us backwards until she's pressed up against the side.

"You have a naughty mouth, little dancer," I say, sucking down on her neck where I know she likes it. Her legs wrap around my waist, pressing her centre against my cock. I shift my hips so I rub against her, eliciting another moan of delight.

"You've got a greedy pussy, little dancer," I say, pulling her against me and continuing my leisurely movements before capturing her mouth with mine, devouring her lips.

We stay there, our bodies enjoying the feel of each other. Even in the water, I can feel how hot and ready she is. This is one area in which we're in sync.

April tilts her hips, and the tip of my cock finds her entrance before I pull back. Rubbing it along her slit. She growls against my mouth.

"Tell me what you want," I demand.

"You," she says, lifting herself up once more, hoping to ensnare me.

I tut and pull back.

"Use your words," I tell her.

"Ahhh," she squeals in frustration. "Fine," she moves her

mouth to my ear, capturing my lobe in her teeth and biting down. "I want you buried deep inside my weeping pussy. It's throbbing with need. It aches for your massive cock... does that answer your question?"

It's my turn to moan and I snake my hands under her ass and lower her onto my throbbing dick, sinking into her depths. When I bottom out, we both freeze, trying to capture our breath.

I cup April's jaw in my hand, making her look at me. "You drive me wild," I say, my words making her grin until I tilt my hips as I know she likes, hitting the spot inside her that leaves her quivering.

"The feeling's mutual," she pants, as I repeat the action. Her fingernails dig into my shoulders.

I sink us down until only our heads are above water. The pool offers a whole new dimension. The water feels pleasant, as the sun has been warming it all week.

I pull away and stare into April's eyes before thrusting into her. They flutter closed, her face caught up in the moment.

"Eyes on me," I say, watching as they reopen, her pupils dilated as they clash with mine.

April bites her lip as I begin a steady rhythm, my hands supporting her thighs, feeling her dancer's muscles contracting beneath them.

Her eyes remain locked on mine, her pupils darkening as her body begins its climb towards the abyss.

I tilt my hips further, knowing her clit is now rubbing against my pubic bone.

"Ahh, Cal..." April lets out a squeak, her body squeezing mine, and I know she's close. I can feel the tension building in her muscles. I up the speed, wanting to watch her as she breaks over my cock.

"Shit, Cal..."

I pound into her, clutching her closer. She meets me, move for move, until we are both flying over the precipice. Her muscles contract, and her eyes roll back into her head. I thrust twice more before letting my orgasm ride me. I feel my cum fill her up. I continue to move, not wanting this moment to end as we continue to watch each other. I know the look of satisfaction on her face matches my own.

I finally withdraw, the satisfied look on her face all I hoped it would be. She bites down on my shoulder. The aim was to remove all thoughts of the past and fill her with thoughts of a future. Our future. Thoughts that, until recently, I had thought an impossibility, but the more I get to know her, the more time I spend with her, I see a kindred spirit. April Wilson makes me a better person, she makes me want things I didn't think were possible. Things I've done my best to avoid, but now I find myself drawn towards them. This woman has changed my life since she slammed into it, and I'm not sure what I will do about it.

CHAPTER 48

CALEB

I walk in the door and April appears from the kitchen her mobile phone in hand. Her eyes wide, her face alight with delight.

"You look happy," I tell her, pulling her into my arms and dropping a kiss on her nose. She's practically vibrating. Her hands go up around my neck and she pulls me down for a proper kiss.

"That was Di. Apparently, she's been on the waiting list too long, and they are now going to do her hip operation privately. She is coming to London next week to see a specialist. I've just looked him up. He's the best."

I smile down at her. "That's great news."

April draws back, her hands moving to my shoulders. "Caleb Frazer, what did you do?"

"What do you mean?" I ask.

"Top specialist, two weeks after I told you about Di and her hip problem."

I shrug, saying nothing. I will not lie, but I don't have to confirm. This is about Di, not April. When I looked into her, she and her husband have helped hundreds of foster children over the years. With all the charity work my mother does with the foundation, she often talks about *life's angels*. It's clear Di is one of them.

I move away, unable to take the scrutiny of her gaze. "Caleb, did you have something to do with this?"

I turn to look at her. "I may have made a few phone calls."

She crosses her arms over her chest and stares at me.

"Why? What is Di to you?"

I step forward unable to believe the words she has just said.

"It is not what she *is* to me, but *who* and *what* she means to you. You're worried about her. I have more money than I can spend in a hundred lifetimes, why can't I help someone you care about?"

Silence descends.

"Were you going to tell me?"

"No," I tell her truthfully. I move towards her and tweak her nose. "But Di sounds to be a very deserving woman. She's fostered children for years. Sometimes the universe likes to give back."

I watch a tear track its way down her cheek.

"Hey," I say catching it with my thumb before wrapping my arms around her waist and pulling her towards me. "Why the tears?"

She shakes her head and offers me a watery smile. "Thank you." April goes up on her tip toes and wraps her arms around my neck. "Thank you for doing this for her."

"You're welcome."

CHAPTER 49

APRIL

When Caleb Frazer makes something happen, it happens. The following week, Di and Julian arrive to see her specialist. With her surgery scheduled the following week. Caleb tells me to invite them around for dinner but asks I don't tell Di about his involvement.

"Wow, this place is beautiful," Di says when I take her up onto the roof terrace and show her the view. Julian is inside talking to Caleb, allowing us some *girl-time*.

"He cares about you, you know," I glance over at her.

"Why would you say that?" Di gives me her knowing smile, one she always gave me when I tried to pull one over on her when I was growing up. "Paying for my operation, organising a top specialist. He didn't do that for me, April."

I stare at her open-mouthed. "How?"

"I'm getting old, not stupid." She laughs, wrapping an arm around my shoulders. "When I looked up the specialist I was assigned to, it didn't take a rocket scientist to work out someone intervened."

I shake my head, before resting it on her shoulder. "He doesn't want you to know," I tell her.

"That's his prerogative. But I was right in my initial analysis all those months ago. He is a good man."

"He is," I admit, making her smile.

"What happens next?"

I stand up and move to the railings, resting my elbows on the barrier. "I don't know. Things are good."

"Have you told him?"

I turn my head sharply and stare at Di. "Told him what?"

She tilts her head, her eyes filling with sympathy.

Horror dawns. "You know?" I whisper.

"I've always known," she says, a hint of sadness in her voice. "It was why I pushed for you to come home after you left the conservatoire."

I swallow against the lump that has formed in my throat. "But I wasn't your responsibility anymore."

"Oh, darling girl. You were never a responsibility, and our door will always be open to you. Julian and I, we love you like a daughter." Di wraps her arms around me and I sink into her embrace, the same way I did throughout my teenage years.

"I can't tell him," I admit into her neck as she rubs soothing circles on my back.

"Why not?"

"How does an ex-stripper fit into this world? Look around you. I'm here until the dance school is up and running, then I'll be on my own again."

"I think you're wrong," she tells me, pulling back and patting my cheek. "And you've never been on your own. We love you and are there for you. You just need to believe it. I think Caleb Frazer will surprise you."

I shake my head, "It's not telling Cal that scares me. It's more his life. His position makes us an impossibility once I do. The press will tear him apart if it comes out."

"And I think you are doing the man a great disservice.

The man I have met and read about, doesn't seem to give two hoots about what other people think. He's his own man."

"You read too many romance novels," I tell her, pulling back and wiping my cheeks, not wanting to burst her bubble. It's not just Cal. It's his friends and family.

"Nothing wrong with a bit of romance," she says, winking at me. "I think we better go back downstairs and rescue Caleb, before Julian talks his hind leg off about all his cars."

When we go downstairs, Caleb is in his element, promising Julian, he'll take him to the racetrack and let him take his cars for a spin. Di takes my hand and shoots me *a look*, that tells me she's going to prove me wrong.

CHAPTER 50

CALEB

"Another five children signed up this week," April tells me over breakfast.

"Really?" I say, looking up in amazement. Transporting the kids from Sunny Down to their classes has been a roaring success.

April laughs, a sound I'm becoming much more familiar with these days. "My business didn't go up in smoke, it's more like a phoenix rising from the ashes. With the new development, the community are really getting behind it." She leans forward and rests a hand against my cheek. "And it's all down to you."

"No, little dancer. This is all you. The community and its spirit were always there. I'm just making the wrapping more attractive."

"Don't undersell yourself. You're their hero."

It's not the community's hero I want to be. I've been bewitched by my little dancer, she is showing me a different way of looking at the world.

"I've got you something," she says, getting up and moving to the cupboard. She opens it. "A thank you, for all you've done for me, for Di. She went back to work this week, there's no keeping her down."

I chuckle. Getting to know Di, I now understand where April gets her steely determination. A case of nurture over nature. The woman is a force to be reckoned with but with a soft gooey inside when it comes to her foster daughter.

"You don't need to buy me things," I tell her honestly.

She shoots me a shy smile. "I haven't bought this exactly," she says, pulling out a decorated jar.

She returns to the table, carrying it in her hands, handing it to me.

"What's this?"

"I can't whisk you off to Paris or pay for hip operations. I can't buy you a new car. But this…" she covers her now glowing cheeks with her hands. "This is so silly; I don't know what I was thinking."

She leans forward and tries to take it out of my hands.

"Nope," I say, grinning as she tries to take it back. "Once a gift has been given, it can't be rescinded. Frazer house rules."

She leans forward again, but I stand up and hold it out of her reach.

She sits back in her seat with a huff and glares at me.

"Are you going to tell me what this gift is, the one you are so determined to take back?"

"It's a date night jar," she sighs, biting her lip.

"A date night jar?"

"Yes, each piece of paper inside holds personalised date night ideas," she explains.

I sit back down, my eyes going to the jar in my hand. I turn it around in my hands noting the label on the side.

Caleb and April's Date Night Jar.

I'm suddenly excited to discover the ideas she's come up with. Time we can spend together as a couple.

I look up to find her watching me, her cheeks rosy.

"It's silly, really," she says, leaning forward again.

"Can I open it and choose a date night?"

She sits back, the look of surprise on her face is priceless.

"Of course," she says quietly.

I place the jar on the table, and gently rock the lid until it pops free. Inside there are lots of multi-coloured pieces of paper, folded with care. I stick my fingers in and fish one out. I sit back in my chair, my elbows resting on the arms as I unfold the pale blue note.

Go for a moonlit walk along the river, followed by a leisurely massage.

Now this is a gift I can get behind. It makes me wonder what other ideas she's come up with for us to spend time together.

"I told you it was silly," she says.

I lean forward and take one of her hands in mine. "No April. It's not. I promise you; this is one of the most thoughtful and personal gifts I've ever received. I will cherish each one of our date nights."

I push back my chair and pull her forward and into my lap. "I mean it. Thank you."

She smiles shyly at me. "Are you sure? There is no comparison to the things you've done for me."

"I'm more than sure. I love it."

Like I love you, I want to say, realising I *am* and *have* fallen totally and utterly in love. Something I never thought possible.

* * *

THE PAST COUPLE of months have flown by. In between our date nights, I've been dealing with the new development, while April has been travelling to and from Scarlett's, where she's been working with Scarlett and her choreography team, when she is not working with her own kids. As a result, April is developing an air of confidence I've never seen before and it's amazing to watch her shed her shackles and come into herself. Even Samuel's noticed the difference.

"I have a surprise for you," I say.

It's Sunday morning, so neither of us is rushing out of the door.

Last night was one of our *date nights*.

Who would've thought, watching an old movie in the back row of the cinema, with a bag of traditional sweets and popcorn could have been so enjoyable. Holding hands and snuggling in the paired seats, like teenagers.

As it's Mason's day off, I grab the keys to the Porsche 911 Carrera four GTS Cabriolet, in ice grey metallic. My pride and joy. It's the only one of my cars, apart from the one Mason drives, I keep in the city.

The car's features are lost in city driving, but it's still smooth.

"Want to drive?" I say, holding out the keys to April.

I watch as her jaw drops. "Me? Drive your car?" she says, a slow grin appearing. "Your baby?"

I laugh at her words. "Yes," I say. "It's the least I can do after your wonderful gift this morning."

I've already spent hours showing her exactly how taken I am with my present.

I drop the keys into her outstretched palm and move to the passenger side. My heart rate picks up when she unlocks the door and gets in. This is, after all, my baby. All my cars are my babies. But April has always wanted to drive it, and I added her to the insurance months ago.

"Where to?" she asks, pressing the on button.

"Sunny Down."

April turns in her seat to look at me.

"You'll see," I tell her, as we set off.

By the time we arrive at Sunny Down, I know I must introduce April to the racetrack.

I'm about to say something, but stop when I turn to see April's jaw drop. "My goodness, Cal, it's...I'm speechless," she whispers, her face flashing to mine, her cheeks glowing.

It's been a couple of weeks since she was last here. The doors are now on, windows in place. Her studio still needs to be kitted out, but the holdup is due to the surprise I've brought her here for.

"I'm glad you like it. Come on," I say. "It gets better."

I get out before moving to her side and opening the door. Always the gentleman, my mother would say. I've trained April to let me as well. Told her my mother would have me in a headlock if I didn't.

We enter the building. The internal walls are in place. April moves to the door that will connect with the cafe next door. The security system wiring is already in place. One of Elijah's new designs.

The reception area is bigger than before, although not by much. More to allow for some seating and a desk. Changing rooms and shower rooms are off to the right. Before they were at the back, but new regulations and planning had us move them. Now, students can access these from the front of the building, no-longer disrupting the next class.

April pops her head into the rooms. The team has fitted the showers and is waiting to fit the hangers and lockers to the walls.

"I can't believe this," she says, a grin splitting her face. "This is going to mean the world to some of my students."

She's told me how some families are short of money and

hot water is a luxury. Jaxson's designs have meant these kids can shower here, but it won't be at any great expense to April.

"Come on," I say, taking her hand and leading her into the vast room that will become her dance studio.

"Oh Cal," she says, her voice catching.

She breaks free of my hold and moves to the centre of the room. The concrete flooring is not what she envisages, but I know she can see past that.

"The flooring and mirrors are being installed next week," I say, watching as she turns in a circle, almost trancelike.

"This is—"

Before I can stop her, she's running at me. I catch her as she wraps her legs around my waist, her lips crashing against mine. I drink her in. This reaction is everything I hoped for.

I've come to live for her smiles and making all her wishes come true.

"I still have the surprise." I pull back, lowering her, reluctantly to the floor. "Follow me."

I take her hand and lead her to a door situated at the back of the studio. I know she thinks it's to her office, but.

I open the door, exposing the stairs.

"What's this?" she asks, shooting me a look.

"Wait and see," I say, ushering her ahead of me.

We take the stairs in silence. At the top, there's another door.

"What's this?" April asks as I hand her the key.

I roll my eyes.

"Just open it," I say, trying hard to hide my grin.

April huffs but for once does what she's told. She pushes open the door and stops.

"Are you going to go in?" I ask.

She turns to look at me before stepping forward.

"What is this place?" she asks quietly.

"This is the flat Jaxson was telling you about," I say, not quite able to read her demeanour.

"But... I don't understand."

"The apartment belongs with the studio. When the roof caved in, we realised how cavernous the studio would be. Building this as a tag onto the studio made sense." I move next to her. "It's also included as part of the lease."

The studio is and never was residential. The apartment means April has somewhere to stay. Should she want it. The thought causes my chest to constrict, but it's not about me.

"I..." she walks away, exploring the open plan living area and kitchen before opening one of the three doors that lead off the main room.

"One is a bathroom, the other two are bedrooms. Although one can be your office," I say, "The master has an ensuite."

She turns to gaze at me, her eyes wide.

"I still don't..."

This is not the response I was expecting. Although April is a complex character.

I walk up behind her and wrap my arms around her waist.

"I want you to stay with me," I tell her honestly.

I've realised over the past couple of days that I don't want what we have to end. But that's me being selfish.

"But I want you to know you have somewhere for you. If you have late classes, we can stay here."

I turn her in my arms and lift her chin with my finger, making her meet my gaze. Her expression wrenches a hole in my heart.

"I want you to stay," I repeat. "I enjoy having you in my space, in my life. We designed this place before you and I—before our relationship developed."

I watch as her eyes scrunch, filling with tears.

"You did this while I was still being a *pain in your arse?*" she asks, giving a half laugh, half sob.

I wipe the tears that escape. My throat constricting.

"I told you I'd look after you, and I meant it. I know things have changed, but this space will always be here for you. It's yours."

April drops her head against my chest, her back shuddering as she tries to suppress the tears she can no longer contain.

"This was not supposed to make you sad," I say, pulling her into my arms, my chin resting on the top of her head.

"I'm not sad, I'm just…I don't know how to describe it. No one has done anything like this before. To say I misjudged you in the beginning. It doesn't come close to…"

I clasp her head in my hands, tilting it until I can kiss her lips.

"I'm falling in love with you, April Wilson. I don't know how, or when. It's not something I believed in until you appeared in my life. But you've hooked me. If you want to move out, I can't stop you once this place is complete, although I'd *prefer* to wake up every morning with you in my arms."

"You can't—I'm a nobody," she says, biting her lip, her eyes filling with confusion.

"To me, you're very much a somebody. You're kind, and caring. Everyone you meet loves you. I've never felt like this about anyone. As I said before. I didn't believe it was possible. I'm asking you to stay with me by choice, but know if you ever need to leave, you will always have somewhere to go."

I step back, giving her space. April turns and grabs my shirt, pulling me into her, slamming her mouth against mine. I don't want her to tell me she loves me. I know it's too soon. Her walls are thick, her moat wide, but she is slowly lowering her drawbridge and when she does, I'll be charging across and staking my claim. Loving her has scared the crap out of me, but I'm tired of fighting it. It's how I feel, so why not share it?

"I'll stay," she says.

Her words trigger an eruption of fireworks in my chest.

I can't contain the grin as my chest expands until I think it's going to explode.

"Thank you," I say.

When she shoots me a questioning look, I add, "For trusting me."

A strange look crosses her face as if she wants to say something but stops herself. Instead, she wraps her arms around my waist and rests her head against my chest.

"It's okay. You've only got to survive my family now," I tell her, and she groans.

"Don't say that, I'm already nervous. I can't believe your mum convinced me to get the children involved in the entertainment. Scarlett was no support either. She thought it was a fabulous idea."

I chuckle. "My mother is very good at getting what she wants."

She wants to know more about April and this is her perfect opportunity to snare her in her web. She knows we're dating, so she's used this opportunity to her advantage.

"Your Mum seems to think seeing some of the kids will have the donors dig a little deeper into their pockets, as they get a taste of what they are supporting. Her words, not mine. What if it all goes horribly wrong?"

"It won't," I tell her. "I know how hard you and Scarlett have worked with the kids. You've enjoyed choreographing and practising with the teenagers. Not to mention the younger children. Plus, it's time mum shook it up. She's been complaining for years, she's bored with it always being a band. She wants a flash mob and you're giving her that. You're her hero. With the older kids acting as waiters, she's got it all figured out. Don't worry. You've got this."

"No pressure then!" April says making me chuckle as I pull her closer.

CHAPTER 51

APRIL

Caleb and I arrive at his ancestral home early on Saturday morning. Today is for the family, and according to Caleb, I now fall into this category. He's determined to throw me in at the deep end, which involves a family dinner with his mother and siblings.

I know Gabriel and Leah and, of course, the gorgeous Callum. I have yet to meet Harper, his youngest sister, although I know her by reputation. Her press coverage and social media accounts outweigh the rest of the Frazer clan put together. Caleb has warned me about Elijah. His older brother can, by all accounts, be prickly, but I'm not to take it to heart.

His older sister, Kat, is known in the press as The Ice Queen. Ruthless in business and the boardroom. If she were a man, she'd be praised for her business acumen, instead, she's made out to be a cold, hard-nosed bitch.

According to Caleb, Jaxson is back in the country, so the big question is whether he will attend. I'm fascinated to meet the woman who has Jaxson Lockwood's jaw tensing at the mention of her name. The woman who has made her way to the top in a very male-dominated world.

I know Caleb's Playboy Posse will be in attendance. They've promised to look out for me if Caleb gets distracted. Caleb growled, and I mean *really* growled at his friends, causing them to fall about in raucous laughter. Not that it deterred Xander, Tristan, or Quentin. It only spurred them on. Only Marcus seemed to take pity on him.

"Hey."

Arms wrap around my waist from behind. I turn my head away from the window where I've been staring out at the vast gardens below. A team of people are erecting the marquee that will host the party guests. It seems like they've taken control of the entire downstairs as well. It's an all-out event with two hundred of the wealthiest citizens alongside beneficiaries of the charity. The success stories.

"You, okay? You've been quiet since we got here," he says.

I give him a weak smile. "Just feeling a little overwhelmed. I should be with Scarlett prepping the last-minute bits and pieces."

"No, you should be here with me. Scarlett is more than capable. It's what she does." He turns me to face him, his finger lifting my chin. "What's really wrong?"

I drop my head forward. My insecurities are my problem, not his. It's not fair to put this on him. Caleb adds pressure to his finger, making me look at him.

"My family is going to love you. My mum already does. As do Gabriel and Leah. Stop letting your thoughts overwhelm you."

I drown in his eyes. The sincerity is real, and I know this is on me.

"I know," I say. "It's just…"

I shake my head. I don't know how to articulate how out of my depth I feel.

"I've got you, and I'm not going anywhere. The guys and my family will also be here. You don't have to worry about anything. We'll be laughing about your nerves on Monday when everything has gone perfectly, I promise."

He drops a kiss on my nose, pulling me hard against his body, and I sink into him, allowing myself to absorb his strength. I don't know what I've done to deserve this man, and I desperately want to tell him I love him. I know he wants to hear those words, but I can't, not until he knows the truth.

"Come on," I say, taking his hand in mine before inhaling deeply. "I'm ready to face the lion's den—and I promise to be on my best behaviour."

"Oh, please don't. You'll make me look bad. I'm never on my best behaviour."

I'm chuckling as we leave the room, a strong arm wrapped around my shoulder.

* * *

THE HOUSE IS ENORMOUS. Its sweeping wooden staircase is like something out of *Gone with the Wind*. The hallway hosts an enormous fireplace with stone flooring. Everything seems super-sized. Caleb spends the time telling me all his favourite hiding places. I can imagine this was a child's paradise. I'm sure Francesca had a nightmare trying to keep track of her children. Caleb told me their mother raised them. There were no nannies, although they did have a houseful of staff to take the pressure off.

I envy Cal's childhood. It's clear it was filled with love and family. The fact Francesca and his late father, Robert, opened their home every holiday to their friends, tells me the type of home this was. Loving and inviting. I only hope they're as welcoming of me.

"April," Francesca says, rising to her feet as soon as we enter the room. She makes her way over to us, pulling me into a hug before she even acknowledges Caleb. He grunts but laughs.

"Charming, mother, my girlfriend gets the first hug," he says as his mother turns to him, tuts, and pulls him into a bear hug. My heart stutters at his words and I wonder if I'll ever get used to hearing it.

"You always were so needy," she says, laughing and patting his cheek, pulling him in for a another hug.

"Of course, we were the youngest, or at least we were until Harper came along."

Gabriel is ten minutes younger, and Caleb never lets him forget it.

"Now you're going to play that card?" Gabriel says, standing up and making his way over. His son Callum rests in his enormous arms. The genetics of these men take my breath away, especially when Francesca is so petite. How on earth did she produce such enormous sons?

"April, it's lovely to see you. I hope you're keeping my brother in check."

I smile at Gabriel, my eyes flitting to Callum, who is gazing up at his daddy.

"Hello, gorgeous boy," I say, running a finger down his cheek, earning myself a little grin.

"Here, my arms could do with a rest."

Before I can stop him, Gabriel has passed Callum over to me. I gaze down at the beautiful baby in my arms, and my chest tightens.

Cal moves behind me, his chin resting on my shoulder. "He looks good in your arms," he whispers close to my ear.

I turn my head and catch his gaze. "Don't go all broody on me," I reply, as his hands tighten around my waist, pulling me back against the semi he's now sporting.

What the?

The sight of a baby in my arms gives him a boner. Why does that send shivers of delight straight to my ovaries?

I need to get a grip. He still doesn't know. This could all be over in a matter of days.

"April, why don't you come and sit?" I look up to see Leah patting the seat next to her. "That boy of mine is getting heavy. We can have a girlie chat. Let the boys do something useful."

"I think they're dismissing us," Gabriel says, casting his wife a look of adoration.

"We are, now, scram. Your mother has given you a list of jobs to do."

Gabriel rolls his eyes. "And to think this time last year, we were sneaking off to the water tower," he mutters, causing Leah to blush and Cal to burst out laughing.

I'm clearly missing something.

"I'll explain," Leah says as I walk across the room.

It's Gabriel's turn to blush. I bite my lip to suppress my grin.

I carry the gurgling Callum over to his mother and take a seat, gently untangling my hair from his iron grip.

When I turn back, the boys have gone, leaving me alone with Leah.

"I thought I'd allow you five minutes to breathe," Leah says, giving me a gentle smile. "The boys forget how overwhelming this can be."

"It's spectacular," I say, finally getting the chance to look around the room we're in. Large sash windows flood the room with sunlight. A stone fireplace takes up space along the inside wall. There's a full-sized grand piano and multiple sofas.

"This is everyone's favourite room. We'll be in here

playing Monopoly later. It's a family tradition. Gabriel is, how can I put it, competitive?"

It's my turn to chuckle. "I've seen him at poker night," I say.

"So you get it," Leah adds, shooting me a telltale grin.

I gaze down at Callum and sigh. "He's so adorable." At five months old, he is starting to get big.

"He is, but then I'm biased. I wanted him for so long. I thought my time had passed, but then life changed direction, and here I am." Her wistful tone surprises me. "As for all this. The Frazers are the most down-to-earth family I've met. I won't lie, some people that will be here tomorrow have sticks lodged up their arses—*that* comes from Francesca, by the way. She asked me to warn you. But she said you're to ignore them. She does."

I wonder why Francesca sent the message through Leah rather than deliver it herself, but then Leah is like me... we're not of this social standing.

"You'll be fine."

"I will," I say, taking an exaggerated breath and making Leah laugh. "What's with the water tower?" I ask, wanting to change the subject.

It's from that moment on, I form a bond with Caleb's sister-in-law. We spend the rest of the afternoon laughing and getting to know one another. And that's how the boys find us.

CHAPTER 52

CALEB

April's eyes almost pop out of their sockets when she meets Elijah. My brother is a giant, towering over the rest of us. At six foot six, Leah describes him as a *man-mountain*. Unlike in previous years, however, my elder brother is acting like the perfect gentleman. If not strangely overprotective of our guest.

I take time watching as he interacts with Gabriel and Leah, holding baby Callum in his enormous arms, smiling down at the little man as he tries to grab his nose. There's no denying it's been a tough year for him. He and his wife, Darra, have finally decided to draw a line under their years of bickering and separate. I know they are in the process of divorcing, but as usual, he is holding all his cards close to his chest.

I'm pleased to see Lottie by his side, that Darra has let her attend. My niece is more relaxed than I've seen her in years. No longer being the filling in the sandwich between her warring parents has clearly had an impact.

Maybe I shouldn't be surprised she already knows April. She recently began attending Scarlett's dance school. Her face was a picture when I introduced them, and April smiled, telling me she'd been teaching my niece for a couple of months.

Since their separation, Darra has moved off the family estate and into the city. Lottie has gone with her, which has devastated my mother. But it means Elijah gets to see more of his daughter when he's working. What was weekends only is now half a week, and everyone seems to be happier. Darra, it appears, has realised the damage she's done, and although the battle between her and Elijah rages on, she's decided using their daughter as cannon fodder is out of line.

"You can't take your eyes off her, can you?" Kat's voice appears at my shoulder.

"No," I admit honestly, making her smile.

"She's the woman from New York," she adds, telling, not asking. I can't help but smile. This is so Kat, cut to the chase. "You should know. I know everything that happens in every one of the Frazer Hotels. Especially when one of my siblings makes a request for security footage."

I sigh.

"Oh, how the mighty have fallen," she chuckles. "I'm happy for you, little bro."

I look across, but she appears to be lost in thought.

"How is the hotel business?" I ask.

Kat was the one to take over the Frazer hotelier business after our father died. She'd been working alongside our father, learning the ropes until his untimely death.

Five years ago, when she was younger than me now, she was forced to confront the misogynistic board members, who argued a woman could not run a hotel empire. Kat has been proving the old fossils wrong ever since, expanding and growing the chain.

"How's the redevelopment going in Asia?"

Kat groans and wipes a hand over her face. "Don't ask.

The developer, who came highly recommended, is an eco-fraud."

I hide my grin, already aware of this fact. "You know I've told you before, Jaxson…"

The look my sister shoots me stops me dead in my tracks.

"Don't," she says. "Jaxson Lockwood is going nowhere near this project or my business."

"Wow, who rattled your cage?" I ask. I know I'm staring at her wide-eyed. Kat is hard to rattle, but the mere mention of Jaxson's name has her eyes flashing fire.

"I cannot work with that man, so don't even suggest it."

I hold up my hands in defeat and decide against telling her Jaxson will be attending tomorrow's party. Knowing my sister, she'll pack her bags and leave, or worse still, have a firing squad waiting for him. Kat on the warpath is not something anyone wants to encounter.

Before I can make any further comments, I notice Elijah is moving towards April. After last year's fiasco with Leah, I don't want to leave April unattended, so I make my way over.

April and Elijah are talking. Is that a smile I see threatening his lips? Wow!

"Hi, Eli," I say.

"Hi," he says, always the man of few words.

"Elijah was just telling me about the security features his firm will be adding to the new development. They sound amazing," April says, her smile genuine.

Who is this man standing before me, and what has he done with my prickly brother?

"We try," I say, raising a brow at Elijah when April turns to him. "It helps if they're integrated into the build, less chance of tampering. It keeps insurance premiums down for the businesses."

"We want the area to feel protected. They can sign up to our service, or monitor their own security, but it's there whichever way suits. With the dance studios, internal cameras will be under your control. Externals, you have the choice."

I'm surprised at Elijah's openness. He ran a security check on April. He knows her past, her present. Wouldn't surprise me if he knows her future, he has his fingers that far into the technical world. With Leah, he was defensive, with April, he's open. Has he learned his lesson? Or is there something more?

Harper appears and drags April off. Elijah and I watch them leave.

"Say nothing," Elijah huffs,

"What me?" I say, feigning innocence. "You just surprised me," I admit.

I couldn't be more shocked when Elijah says, "I like her."

I choke on my drink. "Like her? Wow, high praise coming from you."

"I give credit where credit is due," he says, staring me down. Which I always find quite unnerving. Elijah is intense, as our older brother, he's always been incredibly protective, something we have all baulked against as we got older.

Smiling at him, my eyes follow April. "I agree she's special. I just wish she saw it too."

"Her mother is looking for her," Elijah says quietly, and my eyes return to his in surprise. "I set up alerts," he adds, shrugging as if it's no big deal.

"What do you mean?" A coldness floods my system.

Elijah takes a deep breath, his gaze looking over at April. "What I said, her mother has approached several sites. She's searching for April. Wants to reconnect."

Shit, I wish he hadn't told me this.

How am I supposed to tell April I know this information? She's going to want to know how I found out. Saying my brother has run security checks and has dragged up all her past secrets. Secrets I know she is keeping from me, but I'm hoping she'll one day have the strength to trust me with. I'm not sure she'll understand why I have a report on her, on my computer. Something I regret and will always regret. I should have trusted her.

"I'll leave it with you. I've passed on the information. What you choose to do with it is up to you," Elijah says, shrugging his shoulders.

I stare at my brother for a moment. "How are you doing?" I ask.

His laugh is hollow. "Could be better, could be worse," he says. "At least it's nearly over."

"And Lottie?"

I know the reason he stayed in his disastrous marriage was due to Lottie. His love for his daughter is unbreakable.

"She's coping better than anyone," he says, his eyes searching out his teenage daughter, softening as they catch sight of her across the room talking to our mother. "I'm giving Darra everything," he says suddenly, shocking me into silence.

He looks at me, his gaze hard, as if daring me to argue. "Everything bar my company."

I take a breath.

"You do what you need to do. I know you'll have your reasons. I will not question them. But Eli." I move my head until he looks at me. "Just know, you're not alone. We're here for you. The secrets I know you keep. You don't need to protect us. We're grown-ass adults, well, maybe not Harper. She's a law unto herself." I know I'm waffling, but I want to make a point. "We want to help you. You and Lottie, even Darra if we must. But we want you to be okay. We'll do whatever it takes, but you need to let us in."

He stares at me. His gaze unwavering. If he wasn't my brother, I'd be terrified of him, his size and his stony expression. It's why I couldn't be more shocked when he says, "Thank you. I'll come and see you. There are a few things I'd like to discuss."

I hold his gaze and nod. "I'm holding you to that," I add, even more surprised when the edge of his lip curls up.

"I thought you might," he says, before looking down at his watch. "But that's enough of this mushy bullshit for now. It's time for Gabriel to kick our asses at Monopoly."

I laugh out aloud. "Our baby brother is a little competitive, but so is April. Gabriel may have met his match. I'm not taking bets this year."

This time, Elijah does grace me with a genuine smile, although it still misses his eyes. "I'll take your word for it. Let's go."

"Monopoly," I shout, garnering everyone's attention, a combination of whoops and groans all around.

CHAPTER 53

APRIL

I don't think I've ever laughed so loudly or as long as I do playing Monopoly with the Frazer siblings. Gabriel's competitive nature has no limits and is just as intense as his poker games against the boys, even with Leah reining him in. They play as a team. Kat's brothers tease her relentlessly, as she is the family hotelier. Harper plays with the devil on her shoulder, seemingly making purchases, with the sole purpose of winding up her brothers and sister. Caleb, the family joker, sits and enjoys the show. Since we've been partnered together, that leaves me as our strategist and, like Gabriel, I have a competitive streak. Elijah pairs up with his daughter and encourages her to stand up to her aunts and uncles, although I think it's a play. Making the others feel guilty against the youngest member so he can sweep in and win the game with her. Watching Francesca, she just appears to enjoy having her family all together.

It's gone midnight before we call it a night.

I fall into bed next to Caleb. It seems to have been a given that we're together. No-one questioned it, and no-one asked. I suppose his continued shows of affection, kissing my neck, pulling me against him are a bit of a giveaway. The greatest surprise of all is no-one seems to worry or care about the difference in our social standing. I'm not sure what I expected, but total acceptance wasn't it. Maybe Caleb always brings someone home and his family are used to it.

"Before you say anything, you're the first woman I have played family Monopoly with," he says, rolling onto his side to face me.

I roll and face him, placing my arm under my head, mirroring Caleb's position. I've already made it clear there will be no sex while we are under his mother's roof. Something he willingly agreed to.

I found out why, when he took me on a tour of the outbuildings to show me his car collection. He coaxed me into the back seat of one of his amazing motor cars, and we went on an entirely different ride to the one I was expecting. Thank God for flexibility.

Caleb's excuse—we weren't under his mother's roof.

"See, tonight wasn't too bad," he says, his thumb grazing my cheek.

I grin. "I had fun. Your family is amazing. Thank you for talking me into coming."

He gives me a satisfied grin. "You only have to survive tomorrow, which I know you will rock. Your kids are awesome, and Scarlett will be here to help."

"I know, and I'm so grateful for her. Tyler and Jonas are coming on in leaps and bounds. Scarlett wants me to encourage them to apply for the new scholarship."

"I think you should," he says, but then again, he's unaware of my fears. "You look unsure," he says, a furrow appearing between his eyes. I forget how good he is at reading me.

"I'm being silly," I say, knowing my own insecurities drive me.

"Nothing is silly, if it's how you feel. Talk to me." He

pushes himself up onto his elbow, his head resting on his hand. His eyes locked on me. I shirk at the intensity of his gaze.

I roll onto my back and stare at the ceiling. Not sure I want to see the pity, the sympathy.

"You know I went to the conservatoire?"

I sense him agree, refusing to meet his gaze.

"We had thirty hours of lessons a week. I was on a scholarship. It paid for my fees, however the rest, I needed to fund myself."

I turn to look at him, see if he gets the picture. "I had to finance my accommodation and my food. I took out a student loan, but it wasn't enough, so I got a job."

I have Cal's full attention.

"Initially, it was fine. I studied, I worked. Group work meant taking evenings off work. My boss understood in the beginning, but after a while he told me he wasn't a charity. In the end, I couldn't do it all. I wasn't sleeping, I wasn't eating properly. I knew I'd never survive another two years. I was running up more and more debt, with no guarantees in the end. Our teachers told us how competitive the industry is, that may be *one of us* might get lucky. With those odds, I left."

"What did you do?" he asks.

I pause. This is the ideal time to tell him, and I can almost hear Samuel shouting at me. But it's not fair, not while we're here, I made a promise to Francesca.

If I tell Caleb and he wants me gone...

I swallow the words that are on my tongue.

"I left and got a job, used the money I saved up to open the dance school. I gained some of the qualifications I needed while I was still living with Di, so I was already halfway there."

Caleb pulls me into his arms, my head resting on his chest, as he kisses my forehead.

"We'll speak to Mum and Scarlett. Make sure those on a scholarship have enough to live on. They won't have their dreams ripped away from them because it's been ill thought out." His arms tighten around me. "I want you to talk to my mother, to the Foundation Board."

I bite my lip, overcome with emotion. This man turns me into a wreck. His understanding and compassion. He's not the heartless love-em and leave-em type I thought he was.

My head rubs against his chest, acknowledging what he's saying. I wipe under my eyes.

"I'd like that," I whisper, hoping my voice doesn't give me away. It does, as Caleb's arm tightens around me, pulling me closer into him.

"We'll discuss it after the party tomorrow," he whispers, pressing his lips against my hair. "Sleep now."

I let my eyes drift shut, enjoying the warmth and comfort only Caleb can provide. I've never been into cuddles, never had the chance. Although I tell a lie, I recall a faint memory of a time when someone cuddled me. Cuddled and kissed, swung me around, tickled me. But those are distant memories and I'm not sure if they're the made-up fantasies of a foster kid lacking attention, or whether they were real. I want to believe they're real, that someone cared. I drift off, holding that thought close to my heart.

CHAPTER 54

APRIL

The next morning is crazy. Although they've hired people to cover every eventuality and every need, the family is all chipping in, with Francesca at the helm directing proceedings. They've banished Leah, baby Callum, and me to the drawing room where we spent the previous evening.

Caleb keeps popping in, demanding cuddles with his nephew. Telling Leah, he needs to know the difference between Daddy and Uncle Cal. Leah's good natured and hands him over. Gabriel, however, has other ideas when he comes in to find his brother slacking and stealing snuggles.

"Mum's after you," Gabriel says, taking his sleeping son from his twin.

I still can't get over how similar they are, the same, yet different. It's the differences that make me smile. Leah grins at the pair and rolls her eyes. It's clear she has a strong bond with both brothers, although the way she looks at Gabriel—is hot.

"Party pooper," Caleb says, handing the baby over to his brother, but not before he drops a kiss on his forehead. My ovaries do a little dance at the sight. Both these men, holding a tiny baby in their muscular arms, showing a soft and mushy side.

Be still my beating heart.

Gabriel turns to me. "Mum thought you'd want to know Scarlett has just turned up with the bus full of dancers. She's showing them to the library, where they can all get changed."

I jump up. "Thank you," I say, before rushing to the door and freezing. "Which way to the library?"

"Hold up, I'll go with you," Cal says.

I turn and watch as he runs a finger down Callum's cheek and grins before heading my way. The love he has for his nephew is immeasurable. Whether it's because genetically, Callum could not be any closer to him had he fathered him himself. His brother being his identical twin.

I wait until Caleb reaches me before we head off to the library. Scarlett's in there with the ten dancers we chose. They range from fourteen to seventeen. Their eyes are out on storks.

"Mr Frazer," they say when we enter the room.

"Hey, what about me?" I say, chuckling.

Cal has made quite an impression on these kids in the past couple of months, even discussed apprenticeships with his firm for anyone wanting to go into property development, or one of the related trades. The buzz and excitement has been extreme.

"Hey, Ms April," they say.

"That's better," I say, grinning at them all. "Are you ready?"

"We've got this," Amber says nervously.

She's one of my best dancers. Her natural ability and talent shouldn't be wasted.

"I know you have. I have every faith in you," I tell her honestly. I walk over and place a hand on her shoulder when

I notice her shaking. "I mean it. You guys are amazing and have worked so hard. I can't wait to show you off."

She gives me a shy smile as Alex walks over and fist-bumps her.

"Yeah, we've got this."

Scarlett and I hand them their costumes. Francesca got them suits from a local tailor. She said they can keep them once they're done. I won't even think how much they've set her back. But as she said, she wants the flash mob and for them to blend in. To do that, they need to look the part. Who am I to argue?

Caleb returns after making himself scarce while everyone gets changed. He sets about taking pictures of the kids so they can forward them to their parents.

"Okay, everyone, it's almost show time. If you'd like to follow me," Caleb tells them as he moves towards the door. He leads us to another part of the house and down some stairs.

"Are you taking us into the cellar to murder us?" Tyler asks.

Cal laughs. "No, Tyler, but I think this is somewhere you'll like."

He opens the door into a large games room. A full-sized pool table, pinball machines, a jukebox, and large sofas fill the room.

"Through there is a movie room. Help yourself, and we'll be back down when we need you."

The kids scatter to all four corners of the room.

"Thank you," I say. Looking around a teenager's paradise. This is magical.

"Mum is moving this stuff to the community centre next to the dance studio. It's sitting idle, and she felt they would benefit from it."

I bite my lip and nod, not trusting my words. I glance

around at the excited faces and know how well this will go down with the community. I'm not the only one Caleb Frazer is winning over.

* * *

THE KIDS ARE HAPPY, and even more so when it's time for their star moment. They enter the kitchen and grab the trays of drinks and canopies from the catering staff.

"Two hands," I squeal as I watch one tray wobble precariously on one of the teenager's arms. I don't want anyone spilling drinks down someone's three thousand pound or more dress.

Arms slide around my waist, and lips touch my ear. "Stop worrying. I'm off to speak to the DJ and make sure everything is ready."

I turn my head, only to have him drop a kiss on my lips as he takes his leave. Scarlett pops her head in and gives me the thumbs up. She looks amazing in her dress. Her husband, Seb, is standing behind her and waves. I raise a hand in return, although my stomach is churning.

What's the worst thing that can happen?

* * *

THE ANSWER to that is nothing. The group does us proud. They mingle and serve the canapés and drinks. Then, when the music starts, they dispose of their trays and dance. They dance as they were born to do. I watch the crowd as they stand back, their attention fixated on the group. Not one person continues their conversation. When it's over, the kids mingle with the guests, answering questions, while Francesca takes to the makeshift stage at the front of the marquee.

"Ladies and gentlemen, thank you for attending this

year's Frazer Foundation Fundraiser. I expect you all to dig deep into your pockets today. We've a lot of items at this year's auction. I'm sure there will be something to entice you. I'd like to thank the dancers from April Wilson's School of Dance. Come on up April."

Caleb pushes me forward and I move towards the stage, grimacing at Francesca, who is grinning at me.

"I'd like to introduce you to this special lady. Please welcome April, everyone."

Francesca claps, so everyone claps as I make it onto the stage. She hands me the mic, and I shudder.

"Hi," I say, the feedback buzz making everyone laugh. "Hi. I'll try that again." There's only my voice this time, so I smile at the crowd. "I'd like to thank the Frazer Foundation for having us. They're supporting our local community and the kids, and when Francesca asked, we were delighted to give something back. Scholarships for neighbourhoods like ours are a godsend, thank you. I hope you enjoy the rest of your afternoon."

I hand back the mic and move to follow the children out of the marquee.

"April," Leah's voice stops me, and I find myself pulled into one conversation after another.

When I finally make it back into the house, the kids have long gone, heading back to the playroom downstairs. I told them what Cal had said about the community centre, and they were all, "Cool! Wow!" Caleb and his mum have developed an even greater hero status.

"I almost didn't recognise you," a voice comes from behind me, and I freeze.

A sense of dread hits me in the chest.

I turn around to face the man who has followed me. There would be no other reason for him to be here. This part of the house has been closed off to guests. A wave of dizziness overwhelms me as I stare into the face of my past.

Sir Leonard Crawley stands in the centre of the empty hallway. His piggy eyes roam over my body, making me vomit a little in my mouth. This can't be happening, not today, not now.

"Sorry, do I know you?" I say, hoping if I play dumb, he might go for mistaken identity.

"Definitely you," he says with a smirk that sets my heart pounding. "At least with your clothes on." He takes a step closer, and I find myself frozen to the spot. "It's been a long time, Electra."

I attempt to suppress the shudder that wracks my body.

He steps forward and runs a finger down my arm. My body reacts, jerking away, slamming me into the cabinet that lines the corridor, shaking the pictures and ornaments on the top.

Sir Leonard tuts and smiles, his eyes twinkling with a twisted sense of delight.

"Careful now. You don't want to break anything. Franny has a strong attachment to her possessions."

I choke past the lump in my throat. "Can I help you?"

"Now Electra, is that any way to treat an old friend? We all missed you when you left."

I grimace at the use of my old stage name. A name I haven't heard in two and a half years. Adults always warn you that the decisions you make when you're young may come back to bite you.

I take a step back, my fight or flight finally kicking in, but before I can move, his hand grips my upper arm. I try to shake him off, but he's bigger and stronger than me.

"Take your hands off me." My jaw locks as I grind out the words. "I don't know who you think I am, but…"

"I know exactly who you are." His knowing smirk makes

me freeze. "But do they? Do the Frazers know who they've let into their home? Caleb Frazer was telling me all about his beautiful and talented girlfriend. All she's done for her community, he's quite the advocate, my dear. Imagine my surprise when he pointed you out."

I shake my arm once more, trying to dislodge his hand, but he just squeezes harder. So hard, I know I'm going to bruise.

"Let. Go," I say, through gritted teeth. When he doesn't, I decide to try another tack. "What do you want, Sir Leonard?"

He grins, his pearly whites flashing, reminding me of the wolf in little red riding hood. They're a contrast to the leathery skin of his face and the wobbling jowls of his jawline.

"Now, now. The Frazer boys need to be a little pickier. I was surprised when Gabriel chose his little secretary… beneath him. But at least she had a proper education, even if it wasn't obtained from a redbrick university. Elijah, well, he chose poorly, but at least Darra was from the right family. You, my dear…" He rambles on, loving the sound of his own voice, shaking his head almost in a fatherly fashion. "You'll never fit into this life."

His words hit almost as violently as a punch to the gut. I know this. I've just allowed Caleb to sweep me up in his dream.

"What do you want?" I ask again, only to see his smile widen. His thumb rubs lazy circles on my arm.

"A few choice words to the right people. That boyfriend of yours. His business…" he doesn't need to spell it out to me. He's threatening Caleb. But why?

I try to shake his hand off again, and this time, his face hardens, his smile gone.

"You always were an aloof little bitch."

That does it. "What? Because I wouldn't sleep with you

and your buddies? That you wanted more than I was willing to give? You're pathetic."

My anger rises. I will not let this man take any more from me than he already has.

It's not like pretending I don't know who he is, is working. So, I return to that place. A place where I wore a suit of metaphysical armour to work every day to protect both my body and mind. For four years, I took my clothes off and danced for these perverts. I'd smack away their wandering hands with a smile when I really wanted to smack them in the balls. At nineteen, when I started, I was young and naïve, but by the time I stopped at twenty-four, I was much more jaded towards men like the one standing before me. Wealth and power make them think they're invincible and can have anything they want.

Leonard Crawley was never one of my clients. I only danced for him once, and that was enough. He was a lecherous old perv, and I made it very clear to management and patrons that I was not into the other side of the business. I danced. Stripped for their entertainment, I took part in the shows, but that was where I drew the line. I didn't add extras. I didn't need to. I was earning enough taking my clothes off.

"The lady told you to take your hands off her, Crawley."

A voice comes from behind me.

I freeze, but so does Crawley, although his grip tightens almost as a warning.

"Ah, Elijah. Good to see you. How are you? Bad business, all that stuff with Darra."

I bite the inside of my mouth. Does Crawley have a death wish? The animosity swirling behind me is palpable.

"My business is my business, Crawley. I would advise you to stay out of it."

Elijah's tone is deadly. This is not the man I was speaking to earlier.

"Now, now." Crawley seems to have made a remarkable recovery. "Don't take it to heart. I'm just concerned for you, dear boy. I've been a friend of this family for many years." The smile he shoots Elijah is more like that of a tiger than a caring family friend. "And as for April here, I was just getting reacquainted with an old friend," he says, flashing those blinding teeth at Elijah.

His grip on my arm tightens further, telling me not to contradict him.

I sense Elijah come up behind me, his hand landing on Crawley's. "The lady asked you to remove your hand. From where I'm standing, you're still touching her."

I can sense the menace coming off Elijah in waves.

Crawley drops my arm, my other hand coming up to rub it. Elijah steps around me and gets into Sir Leonard's face. If my heart wasn't firmly in my mouth and my stomach doing somersaults, I may have found the situation amusing. Elijah towers over him. Sir Leonard is not small, but Elijah is a giant, at least a head and shoulders above the creep.

Elijah leans down, close to Crawley's ear. "Now I think you need to leave. I'll let Mother know that something came up and you were called away."

Crawley's eyes widen. It's then I see Elijah has his arm in the same hold Crawley had on mine.

"You're making a mistake, boy," Crawley spits, and I watch as Elijah pulls himself up to his full, imposing height.

"I haven't been a boy for a long time, Sir Leonard."

Crawley's shoulders sink before he peacocks out his chest.

"I'll leave, but you need to look more closely at who you let into your lives."

He shoots me a look that tells me this isn't over. "I'll be in touch, April."

He smirks again before turning and walking away.

"Sir Leonard," Elijah calls after him. "I'd think twice about that. And if I ever hear you threaten any of my family or the people we care about, I will destroy you." Elijah lets those words sink in before adding. "That's not a threat. That's a promise."

My eyes flit between the two men.

Sir Leonard Crawley's face loses a couple of shades of colour. I could almost say he turns a little green around his jowls.

"You're making a mistake, young Frazer," he splutters.

"No, Crawley. I don't think I am. I know where those skeletons are hidden. Threaten what is mine, and I will expose you. This is the only warning you'll get. Stay away from April and stay away from my family. Do I make myself clear?"

Sir Leonard Crawley doesn't say another word. Instead, he turns and leaves me alone with Caleb's big and incredibly scary brother.

He turns around, his face softening when he takes me in. "Are you okay?"

I stare at him, not sure what I should say or do. Instead, I nod vacantly.

"Give me your phone."

My eyes widen, but I'm too shocked to do anything but comply. The adrenaline of the past few moments is wearing off.

He holds it up to my face to unlock it before typing something in. "If that man ever contacts you again, or any of his cronies, you're to call me." His eyes locks with mine. "Nod, April, if you understand me."

I nod in response.

"If not for you, for my brother," he adds, having me nodding faster. His hand comes up and squeezes my shoulder before moving it away. "Leonard Crawley."

"There were always rumours about him, from some of the other girls. It's why I stayed as far away from him as I could," I say, before my brain can engage.

I cover my mouth, realising I've just admitted our connection. *Shit! What was I thinking?*

I drop my gaze, unable to look Elijah in the eyes. He must have heard my conversation with Crawley. I'm surprised he didn't ask me to leave at the same time.

"I should go," I say, stepping back.

"Don't," Elijah says, staying where he is. Almost as if he senses that by moving, I'll scamper away like a scared rabbit.

I raise my eyes to his, my heart rate finally calming enough to allow normal blood flow and brain function.

"I think we both know I need to leave," I say. "Thank you for stepping in. It's not something I'm used to. I've spent so much time fighting my own battles."

I glance up, only to find Elijah's intense eyes staring at me.

I sigh.

"This is not something that will go away. Crawley and his cronies. It's a decision I made a long time ago, when my back was against the wall."

"No one blames you," he says, and I give him a sad smile.

"It's funny, but I believe you. You're the opposite of what I always believed a family of your standing would be. But the problem is, where I danced, the men were from the upper class—your class. Crawley is one of many who saw me dance naked." I run a hand through my hair. "I'm not ashamed of what I did."

The bravado I'm trying to project, not quite ringing true. Exotic dancing is not on most girls wish lists, for their number one choice in career. At least it hadn't been on mine.

My eyes clash with Elijah's.

"I did it to survive, to build a future for myself. The

problem is, there will always be men like Crawley who think they can click their fingers and demand more. I can't do that to Caleb. Have him or any of you standing up for my virtue. I won't let my choices tarnish his or your family's reputation."

Elijah continues to stare at me but says nothing.

"I need to stay in my swim lane. Where I understand the rules. Community is where all this began. I just got swept away for a moment."

"Are you going to leave?" Elijah asks.

"I am. I'll speak to Caleb, I promise, just not now. Can you tell him something came up with one of the kids and that I needed to head back?" I ask.

"I won't lie to my brother for you," he says, his jaw tight.

"I'm not asking you to lie. I want to tell him the truth, but now is not the time. This is your mother's party. I don't want to cause a scene. Everyone has been so kind. Please Elijah, for them."

I know I'm begging and I watch his chin drop to his chest as he runs a hand down his face.

"He knows," he says suddenly, making me pause.

"Knows what?" My shoulders curl forward, and my stomach roils.

"He knows about your past, about Merryfellows," he says, his eyes never leaving mine.

My jaw drops and I flinch, "How?"

"I drew up a dossier on you." His voice offers no form of apology, no further explanation.

I drop my gaze and shake my head. It's no more than I expected. The thought of Caleb reading about my past and never saying anything however churns my stomach.

"I'm leaving," I say. "You can decide what you want to tell Caleb, but I need to go."

I turn and walk away, pausing when he adds, "He doesn't care you know."

I pause, but don't look back at the man who just rescued me. "He might not think he cares, but he will. Especially when his friends and business associates find out. And, even if he thinks he doesn't, I do. This is my worst nightmare. I've always worried my past would come back to haunt me from the moment I realised I could do more, be more. I've been stupid, and now this will not only destroy my relationship with Caleb, but potentially my business too. What parents will want their child taught by an ex-stripper?" I say, knowing I'm on the verge of a panic attack. I stop and inhale deeply, resting my hand on my stomach. When I finally get my breathing under control, I look up.

"Thank you again, Elijah."

"April. It doesn't have to. If Crawley contacts you, call me. I mean it."

I hold up my hand in acknowledgement but keep walking away. When I round the corner, I sag against the wall. What the hell just happened? I know, it's what I always feared. I'm not meant to be here, and the universe is telling me I was right.

When I reach the library, I'm greeted by silence. I pull out my phone. *Shit!* The bus has already left. Scarlett and I promised their parents we would have them home before dark. The bus and my only form of escape, thanks to Crawley, has left.

Making my way up to Caleb's bedroom, I grab my bag. I still need to leave. I need time to think. Samuel and Dan called to say they would not make it. Dan has the flu and my bestie is playing nurse.

I reach the door when I hear voices.

"Kat, listen. You're being ridiculous." It's a male voice. A voice I recognise as Jaxson's.

"Me?" comes the furious reply. My spider senses tingle. I

wasn't wrong, although I hate the fact I'm eavesdropping on their private argument.

"I'll leave," he says. "But this isn't over."

"Yes, it is," comes the sharp reply. "Get out and stay away. I don't need you, I never did."

Jaxson says something I can't quite hear, but the sound of heavy footsteps storming past my door lets me know he's left.

There's an annoyed shriek from one of the bedrooms, followed by a loud thump. I decide it's now or never.

Grabbing my bag, I head for the entrance. Jaxson is taking his keys from one of the valets.

"Jaxson," I call, making him stop and look over his shoulder.

"April?" He frowns.

"Can I grab a lift with you back to the city?" I ask, walking up to him.

He looks at the house behind me, and then his gaze locks with mine. "Throw your bag in the boot," he says, popping the trunk with his key fob. I do as he asks before climbing into the passenger seat next to me.

"I'm not going to be great company," he admits, his expression lost in thought.

"Don't worry, neither am I," I reply before turning to stare out of the window, my brain lost somewhere between deep thought and brain fog.

CHAPTER 55

CALEB

I spot Kat and head over to her.

"Have you seen April?"

"She's gone."

It's Elijah who steps up and gives me the news.

"What do you mean, she's gone?"

"She left. About an hour ago."

I stop. My brother knows more than I do and the confused look both Kat and I are giving him.

"Why would April leave?"

I look at my brother and see the guilt pass over his face. I step up to him, chest to chest. To outsiders, it may look funny as he has four inches on me, but I'm riled now, as my memory goes back to last year and the way he treated Leah.

"What did you do?" I hiss at him.

Kat places a hand on my arm, sensing I'm about to go nuclear.

"Nothing," he says.

I shove him in the chest. The surprise of the move, making him step back, more than my physical strength. My brother can bench press some ridiculous amount and is built like a tank.

"I'll ask again, what did you do?" I seethe.

April wouldn't just leave, not after everything went so well today. Something must have happened. If my brother has said something to her.

"She left with Jaxson," he says, and my heart stutters. Left with Jaxson?

"It's not like that," he adds, his monotone, minimal explanation beginning to wind me up.

"Elijah." It's Kat whose tone ushers our brother a warning.

Elijah steps back and looks me in the eye.

"Jaxson was leaving. He and Kat had words. April saw him as he was getting into his car and asked for a lift."

"And you know this how?"

I know it's a stupid question. Of course he knows. My bloody brother knows everything. That's the line of business he's in. Information is, after all, power.

I step back and take a deep breath, exhaling as I run a hand over my face.

"Let's start this again," I say, "Elijah, why has April left?" I relax my jaw so the words don't come out through gritted teeth.

Elijah holds the door open next to us and motions for Kat and me to step inside. I know from the look on his face, what he's about to tell me is not going to be good.

* * *

"I'LL KILL HIM," I spit, when Elijah fills me in on the conversation he came across in the hallway. "I've always thought he was a sleazy bastard. Not sure why our parents ever had anything to do with him."

Then again, I think back. Dad always made sure Kat and

Harper were with us and nowhere near Crawley, when he and his downtrodden ex-wife visited. I think Mum felt sorry for Mrs Crawley. I just always remember feeling a sense of unease in my stomach when he was around.

"You don't need to worry about that. I have it covered," Elijah says, and I can almost feel sorry for Crawley. Almost.

I turn to my brother. "Thank you. Thank you for looking out for her. I hate to think what would have happened."

"When I saw April leave and Crawley follow." He doesn't need to add anymore.

"Thank you," I say again, watching as Elijah tilts his head to acknowledge my words. "And I'm sorry I assumed the worst."

Elijah shrugs. "Not undeserved. Not after last year," he states.

"What I don't get is why she then left." Although I 'do' know. She's always questioned our relationship, felt I'm out of her league. Laughing that she was punching above her weight in more ways than one. She has it wrong, though. I'm the one punching above my weight. She might not have my bank balance, but her heart and generosity towards those around her. Her innate ability to bring people together. That is priceless.

"I tried to stop her, but she'd made up her mind. I even told her you knew about her past, and didn't care, but that didn't stop her," he admits.

I freeze. The bottom dropping out of my stomach at his words.

"You. Told. Her. About. The. Dossier?" I say slowly.

Elijah shrugs, not realising the bombshell he's dropped in the centre of my relationship. "Secrets are never good. Take it from someone who knows."

"But…" I glare at my brother. "That wasn't your information to share."

"Maybe not, but I'm the reason you had it. She also needed to know that hasn't stopped you from falling in love with her. Because you have, haven't you?" he says, his matter-of-fact tone conflicting with the topic.

"I have, but what's that got to do with anything?"

"She felt you couldn't be with her because of her past. All those people who had seen her. People of our social standing. Men like Crawley."

It's true. The gentlemen who frequented the club April had danced at were wealthy. They had to be to cover the exorbitant membership fees. The club only hires the most beautiful and talented individuals. It shows that even then, April was a talent that people noticed.

Clubs like these were always associated with rumours regarding additional services. When Elijah uncovered April's link, he investigated her further. Not that I asked him to. She was young, just nineteen when she started. Fresh out of the conservatoire. Elijah's investigator had uncovered nothing to suggest April sold herself alongside her dancing. Add-ons had not been part of her act. If they had. Would I feel differently? I'd be a hypocrite if I did. I've slept with more women for a lot less. Reading her dossier and knowing the desperate state she was in, alone and abandoned by the system. The fact she hadn't taken the easy option.

"Caleb, you need to go after her. If she means anything to you. You need to tell her, it's okay. It doesn't change the way you feel about her." It's Kat who breaks through my daze.

"Damn," I say, running a frustrated hand through my hair, as I drop into a chair, my head in my hands. "Any ideas how I convince her she's wrong?" I ask my sister.

The sofa sinks next to me. "Sorry, I'm not the best person to offer advice, especially of the romantic kind. My romance has been one fuck up after another." I hear the mirth in her voice, which surprises me. I know her relationship has ended, but she and Zack have been together for years.

I look up at Elijah, who holds up his hands and grimaces. "Definitely not the person to ask."

I look at him and realise my brother has been to hell and back this past year. All in the public eye. Before that, he'd been in a private hell.

Before I can say anything, he holds up a hand to stop me. "If you're mad about her, I'm with Kat. You need to talk to her. It will not be easy. She erected walls around her. Those will not be easy to breach."

I know what he's saying is true. I searched for an elusive drawbridge during the early part of our relationship, only to find it triple fortified. We'd made progress, but that asshole. Why the hell hadn't I let her know I knew about her past? I know why. I was hoping, always hoping, she'd trust me enough to tell me herself. Now it's too late. It's out in the open, and I'm going to have to coax the horse back into the stable, as it's way too late to close the gate.

The door opens and we both look up. Mother walks in and stares at the three of us before directing her attention to me.

"You need to go after her," she tells me. "Freddy will drive you."

"I can drive myself," I tell her. I certainly have enough cars in the garage, and I haven't been drinking.

"No. Freddy will drive you. And before you argue. Security have already removed all the keys from your key safe."

I stare at my mother, but she simply shrugs.

"I've seen you drive. April needs you in one piece."

I know there is little point in arguing. It will only hold me up. I make my way to the door but stop. Turning to my mother.

"How?" I say, wondering how she seems to have more information than I do.

She quirks a brow, before stepping closer. "This is my house. My guest of honour has left." She crosses her arms over her chest, her jaw locked. We know that stubborn look well. "I take it, Elijah, you will deal with the person responsible?"

What the... How does Mother know?

"Of course, Mother," my brother replies, trying to suppress his smirk.

"As for you," she says, turning her attention to me. "You need to tell April we don't care. And anyone who does will go through me and the rest of your siblings, capiche?"

I tilt my head. My mother only spits out my grandparents' native Italian when she means business. For the rest of us, our olive skin is the only sign of our European heritage.

"Of course, Mother," I grin, copying my brother's words.

"I'm glad you understand me," she says.

I make my way towards her, only to have her pull me down and into a hug. She's a lot stronger than her tiny frame lets on.

"Get your girl," she says, patting me on the cheek.

I kiss her on the cheek and shoot a final glance at my brother and sister. They tip their chins in an almost identical fashion, letting me know they've got mine and April's back. I love my family.

I make my way out of the door, my mother's voice following me. "Now, you two—"

I hear no more as Freddy steps in front of me.

"This way. I've brought the car around."

CHAPTER 56

APRIL

The penthouse is ominously quiet when I let myself in, despite the warmth of the sunlight bouncing off the floors and walls. I make my way upstairs and enter my room, my limbs feeling as heavy as my heart. Dragging open the case, I used over the weekend I pack my belongings. I look at the row of clothes Caleb bought me after the fire, and the ones I've treated myself to with the money Scarlett has paid me.

I sink to the floor next to my case, my hands dangling listlessly over my knees. My chin against my chest. I shouldn't have left the party. I'm a chicken. Cal deserves better. He always has, but I let myself believe in fairy tales. When will I ever learn? My throat thickens, my eyes growing wet. More tears, more despair. I need to wake up and smell the coffee. Get over this pity party. It's time to move on. Move back to my old life, my community. To what I know. Where the rules are ones I understand.

The door downstairs slams, and I jerk upright, rubbing my eyes.

"April!" I hear Caleb's frantic call.

I climb to my feet and make my way to the door, just as it flies open.

"April," he says, his voice filled with relief. He steps up to me, wrapping his arms around me, pulling me flush against his body. I want to sink into the security of his arms but know I can't. It's not fair to him.

It's because I have, I'm now in this predicament. If he and Elijah think they can do anything about Crawley and his cronies, they're mistaken. I've spent too much time around men like them. The club kept them in line, but now I'm fair game and I refuse to take this beautiful man down with me.

My arms hang limply by my side, until he moves back, taking my face in his hands. "I'm so sorry, little dancer. I'm so sorry. Elijah is dealing with Crawley. Mum is on the warpath. I promise you'll never have to worry about that man again."

I look into the dark eyes I've come to care for so much, my hands coming up to grip his wrists. I pull them away from my face. Holding them between us.

"I can't," I say, my voice thick. "I'm sorry, Cal. I can't let you do this. This is my reputation and therefore my battle. I will not drag your family's name into it with me. My choices, my problem."

"No, April. That's not how this works. When Crawley went after you. He went after all of us. You aren't alone. Not anymore. You don't have to stand up to him on your own."

"Crawley has nothing on your family. It's not you he wants, it's me. If it comes out, what will your board say when they find out I was a stripper. Think what the parents of my kids will say. Even Scarlett's business will be marred by a stripper teaching their kids." I bury my head in my hands. I knew it was all too good to be true.

Cal takes my hands and pulls them away from my face. When I finally look up all I can see is the beautiful man in front of me. "Everyone has been so kind, but this is *my* mess. If I walk away, hopefully he'll get bored. Realise there is no power in his words or threats."

"Ex-stripper," he says calmly. "And Elijah will see there is no story." The sincerity in his voice tears at my heart. If only I could believe him. He places a hand behind my head and pulls me towards him, our foreheads touching.

"We can get through this, April. I know about your dancing at Merryfellows. I've known from the beginning. I'm sorry I didn't tell you I knew. I honestly don't care about your past. It never mattered to me."

"Elijah told me about the dossier." I pull back and stare him in the eyes. "You know how screwed up that is, Cal?"

When he says nothing, I sink down to sit on the edge of the bed.

He drops to his knees in front of me, clasping my hands in his, his thumb rubbing soothing circles over my knuckles. "I love you, April. It's not something I ever thought possible. But you, little dancer have swept me off my feet, knocked me sideways."

I gasp at his words, the pressure in my chest building. I stare wide-eyed at Cal, his eyes radiating the honesty and belief he has in his words.

I shake my head before he cups it in his hands, making me stop and look at him. He inhales, bringing our foreheads together again.

"I'm not proud of what I did. But information in my world is power. You fascinated me from the moment I met you in New York. Then you disappeared, only to reappear. A scrap of a dancer with fire in her eyes who was taking me on. When the studio burned down and you disappeared again," he pauses. "I used Eli to track you down. I won't apologise, it brought you into my life."

"You can't love me," I whisper.

He pulls back, a frown marring his brow. "I can and I do. I don't expect you to feel the same way. Not yet. But know this. I love you April Wilson and nothing is going to change that. No bully like Leonard Crawley, is going to stop me. Nothing you have done in your past is going to stop me. We live in the here and now, and look only to the future. A future I want you to be a part of."

I let out a sob. Everything I have wanted to hear. Cal runs his thumbs over my cheeks, his eyes filled with love as he stares at me. "I've not exactly been a choir boy, and I hope you can find it in your heart to look past my misdemeanours."

I let out a choked sound at his words. He can't mean it.

I drop my forehead back to his.

"Sir Leonard won't give up. Even if he does, he'll be one of many. There'll be others, Cal," I bite my lip to prevent a sob escaping. "Every party we attend, there will be snide comments. They'll eat away at us. You think you love me now, but."

I can't end my sentence. My chest constricts at the thought of Cal one day looking at me with disgust in his eyes.

He pulls back, his eyes locked on mine. "I don't think. I know. I love you, April. I've never felt for anyone what I feel for you. It's like you're the air that I breathe, my world feels empty when you're not around." He shakes his head. "I thought I was going to suffocate when I found you'd left the party." The sincerity in his tone shocks me.

"But what if it's not enough?" I say, cupping his cheek, watching as he presses his head into it, closing his eyes. "I've survived many things, but the thought of watching the love you're showing me now, fade and die. I'm not sure I can survive that." My voice catches and despair engulfs me. "I've been alone so many times in my life. For the first time I feel like I've found somewhere, a home. Now after today... I won't be a burden."

When Cal's eyes open, the steeliness I see there shocks me. "My beautiful little dancer, you have no idea how powerful my family is. When I tell you, he will not bother you again, I mean it. Crawley's a creep. He won't get away with threatening you or my family."

My eyes must widen, because his face softens, and he smiles at me. "Unlike Crawley, we don't abuse our power. But we do protect ourselves and those we love." He takes my head in his hands. "I need you to trust me."

My mind wanders back to Elijah in the hallway. Crawley was scared. I assumed it was the man's towering presence that intimidated him, but now I'm beginning to wonder. Crawley hadn't expected his threats to be overheard.

"I will protect you. You just need to give me a chance. I want you to trust me, trust in us. Let me prove how much you mean to me."

I break eye contact, drawing in a deep breath.

"I'll trust you," I say, "But, Cal. All this, you and me. There are things you don't know."

He draws my hand up to his mouth, turning it over and placing a kiss against my palm. "I'll never hold your past against you," he says quietly. "We all have to do things to survive. You've nothing to be ashamed of. You're a survivor." He takes my chin in his hand and tilts it, so our eyes once again connect. "You should be proud of all you've done, all you've achieved."

His smile shoots arrows through my heart. Melting the surrounding ice.

"I know you used the money you earned from dancing to fund the studio. Why do you think I was so willing to bend over backwards to help you keep it? You deserve a break. All the good you've done, all the children you've helped. It was time someone helped you. Please don't give up on us, over some incorrect sense of self-preservation or before we've had a chance."

I grip the hand holding my chin, and squeeze. "I'm not giving up. I won't do that. But you can't deny we're intense."

He smirks at my words, and I raise an eyebrow. "The trip back in the car gave me time to think. Crawley opened the door to things I locked away. I'm on a rollercoaster, Caleb, and there's no way off. My life is charging ahead of me. I need space, time to think. I can't do that here."

"That sounds like a goodbye."

I glance down as he interlocks our fingers before meeting his gaze.

"Not goodbye. Space. We need to talk. I want to be transparent with you. About my life and my past." I sigh when he tilts his head. "I never sold my body. Stripping was one thing, but I couldn't…"

He pulls me into his arms. "I've not been a saint," he says. "You know that. I can't say I'm not glad you didn't have to do that. But I would not have held it against you. I've only read about your life. I can't imagine how scary it was living it, trying to survive on your own at such a young age."

"It's why Samuel is so important to me. He was always there. Like a big brother. We looked out for each other."

Cal moves to the bed next to me, his arms engulfing me as I drop my head against his chest. Letting the past drift away, at least for now. Choosing to trust the man who tells me I've stolen his heart. Knowing without a doubt, he's stolen mine.

"I can't stay here," I admit. "If I do, then I'll end up in your bed."

I feel his lips press against my hair.

"What I need is time to process, time to find myself. Ensure you're right. That there won't be any blow back on your family." I pull back and look up. I know it's the last thing he wants.

Cal drops his chin to his chest and closes his eyes. A silence descends.

When he raises his head, his lost expression breaks my already wounded heart. It's my turn to cup his face. I place my lips against his in a chaste kiss. "If we are going to survive, I need to do so from an even footing. I need to be able to stand on my own two feet."

"Is it so wrong I want to take away all your problems, protect you?" he asks quietly.

"No. But that would be the easy option for me. In the past few months, I've learned a lot about myself. What I want and who I want to be. As you've said yourself. I'm a survivor, but that's all I've ever done. Survived one crisis after another. What I want to do now is take charge, control my own destiny."

"And you can't do that with me by your side?"

The uncertainty on his face is surprising. My playboy, Caleb, looking insecure. I never thought I'd see the day.

My eyes widen, is that what he thinks.

"Oh Cal, I very much want you by my side. Please believe me when I say that. But us, what is going on between us. It has happened because we've been thrown together. You are my prince charming, my knight in shining armour. But life isn't a fairytale. I want us both to be sure, when we take the next step."

Cal's eyes scan my face as if trying to ascertain what I'm saying is true. Whatever he sees has him sighing.

"I'm not giving up," he tells me, his brow quirking, his expression smug.

"I should bloody well hope not," I reply, laughing. "I spoke to Scarlett. She rents out her old apartment as an Airbnb. It's currently empty. She says I can stay there until the studio apartment is complete."

"Okay," he says, his eyes locking with mine. "But promise me. If you need me, you'll call. You're not alone. I'm here for you and if not me, the other people in your life who love you. Di, Julian, Samuel, my family. They are all here for you."

I place a finger over his lips and smile. "That goes double for Elijah, apparently. If there are any issues, he's given me strict instructions to call him."

The look on Caleb's face shocks me, but then he gives a strange little smile.

"He made me promise. If Crawley or any of the others come, I'm to let him know. I won't try to handle it. And Cal, I promise not to run."

My words seem to hit home, and he smiles at me. Pulling me forward, pressing a kiss to my lips.

"I love you, April Wilson. Just remember that when you're curled up in your lonely bed at night. Your vibrator will be no substitute."

I bite my lip to prevent myself from laughing. He's right about one thing. My vibrator won't even come close. I'm not sure another man could replace Caleb Frazer, and that should scare me.

"I have you on speed dial. If Jeremy isn't up to the task," I say, winking at him before pushing myself off the bed and stepping towards the wardrobe and my half-packed case.

Caleb turns to face me. "Jeremy? You named your vibrator?" He shakes his head and laughs. "Fine. Just make sure you do," he says. "I'll arrange for Mason to come and pick us up. He can drop you at Scarlett's."

I nod before turning away, overcome with emotion. My chest is tight.

Caleb gets up before coming towards me, wrapping his

arms around my waist before dropping a kiss where my shoulder meets my neck.

"I'll give you the space you need, but just so you know. I'm not giving up on us," he says before letting me go and walking out of the room.

The hollow feeling spreads from my heart out, but not as it's done in the past. I know I'm doing the right thing in my head. I just need my heart to understand. I rub the centre of my chest, before continuing to fold the rest of my clothes into the case.

Cal returns as I'm zipping it up. Taking the handle from me, he wheels it out of the room. He takes my hand in his free one, bringing it to his lips.

"I'm going to work hard at convincing you to come home, but I understand this is what you need. Just don't be too proud to let me know when you're ready to come back."

I can't keep the smile from my lips, and his own eyes twinkle.

"Confident much?" I say.

"Totally," he says. "Love has to win out otherwise what's the point?"

Maybe he's right. But then, why do I always find myself alone?

CHAPTER 57

CALEB

I drop April off at Scarlett's apartment. I carry her case and help her with the shopping we bought en route. At least I know she can feed herself and has all she needs, although I'm not sure how I will manage. Having April around every dinner time has become a luxury I'm not sure I want to do without, although I know I will have to, at least until I convince her to come back.

My only saving grace is the kiss she gives me. It does not feel like she's saying goodbye. It's filled with the same passion she's always shown. Part of me hopes as I walk away, she'll ask me to turn around and come back, drop to her knees, and tell me she's made a dreadful mistake. I know that will not happen because then what? We kiss? She straddles me. It won't help with her insecurities. It's a simple fix of kicking the can down the road.

"I'll see you soon," she says, her hand holding the door.

"Count on it," I fire back, giving her my cheekiest, well-practised grin.

Now, I'm sitting here, in my apartment, with my back against the end of her bed, staring at the empty hanging space. Space where her clothes used to hang. She may be gone, but her perfume still lingers in the air.

I pick up my phone.

ME:

> I want Crawley destroyed. No one threatens us and gets away with it.

ELIJAH:

> I'm on it. This man has buried a lot of bodies.

ME:

> Make sure they're all uncovered.

ELIJAH:

> This is my speciality. Trust me. I've got her back.

ME:

> Thank you

I drag myself off the floor and turn to leave, noticing the book April borrowed from my library. I smile and move over to her bedside table. A pressed flower bookmark sticks out of the top, marking her page. No folded pages. Even the spine looks untouched. She has taken such care of the book. This is what I want to do for her. Take care of her. I need to work out how, without being a stalker.

Removing imminent threats is one way, but that's behind the scenes. I need to find a way to show her I'm in this for the long haul.

I place the book back on the side. As I make my way downstairs, my phone pings.

SAMUEL:

> Has something happened?

I smile at the message. Samuel, is messaging me to find

out what is going on. Even with him, her bestie, she has walls. Walls he wants gone as much as I do.

ME:

Sir Leonard Crawley.

That is all I type, wondering if Samuel has an inclination about what that man means to April.

SAMUEL:

Shit. Is she okay?

ME:

His name means something to you?

Three dots appear and disappear before my phone rings.

"He was bad news at the club—shit," Samuel says. It's then I realise he has no idea I know about April's exotic past.

"It's all right, I know all about Merryfellows."

I'm rewarded with a sigh.

"She told you?" Samuel asks.

"No, I've always known."

There's a longer pause.

"And you don't care?" Samuel pauses before adding, "Of course you don't." He laughs. "She was afraid to tell you. That you'd think less of her."

I drop my chin to my chest.

My heart hurts that she couldn't trust me with this, that she thought I'd think badly of her, but I'm starting to understand. She has spent so much of her life on her own, she can't seem to see when people are there for her, like Di and Julian, Samuel.

"Never," I say, and I hear him chuckle.

"I take it you told her that, and she clearly believes you, as she hasn't turned up on my doorstep—yet."

I run a hand through my hair, not wanting to tell him how close we'd come.

"It was touch and go," I admit.

"Ah, but she stayed, that my friend, is major progress."

"Not quite."

A strange tingling spreads through my chest.

"What do you mean?"

"She's moved into Scarlett's apartment. She hasn't kicked me out completely, but she needs to clear her head."

"Shit, that woman is stubborn."

I smile as Samuel is unaware of how much his words mean.

"She is. But I'm counting my blessings. She's still talking to me," I admit.

He laughs. "I think you're being a little hard on yourself."

I groan, making him laugh even harder.

"Believe me, Caleb. April does nothing she doesn't want to do. If she's chosen to talk to you, even if she's moved out, then count that as a win."

"Thank you," I say.

"You're good for my friend. If you weren't, billionaire or not, I'd have kicked your ass by now."

It's my turn to chuckle. "I don't doubt it."

I like him. He's straight-talking and has taken care of April.

"So, what do you know about Crawley?" I ask.

There's a pause. "Not much, only what April told me. One of the girls at the club got a little too involved with his son. Apparently, they were going to elope. The girl disappeared. His son didn't, so they didn't elope."

"He could have paid her off," I add.

"Maybe, but I also know he was on the girls' *beware* list."

"Beware list?" It didn't take a rocket scientist to work out what that list was.

"I think you know what I mean. Crawley and his friends are wealthy, didn't like to be told no."

"Didn't management step in?" I ask, my blood running cold. People in power take advantage of those they see beneath them yet again.

"They did. But some girls were willing to add extras off the books. Didn't mind being slapped around. They protected the younger girls."

By the time he's finished, I rub my jaw to release the tension.

"April?"

"She stayed away from him. She's savvy, our girl. Always was streetwise. If he's gone after her now, it's because he considers her forbidden fruit and perceives her as vulnerable or at least did. He may have been all bluster; see how easily she would roll over if at all. Sound like she didn't, so only time will tell. But Caleb, don't think you've got away with it. By being seen with you, Crawley is one of many, who might recognise her. You've placed her in their crosshairs. Don't get me wrong, we are talking about a small number. Most of the patrons were decent guys, or so the girls told me. I may not have worked at the club, but when I wasn't working, I would walk them home. April and I lived with five of them in a bedsit. I heard things."

Shit. Who would have known? How many more of my parents' friends do I need to watch out for?

"It won't happen again," I promise him

I hear a noise in the background.

"April has just turned up," he says.

I'm unsure whether to be elated or worried. He is her best friend, and she needs to talk to him. He understands her better than I ever will.

"Call me," I say before he rings off.

* * *

BY THE TIME I make it into the office, my family is all but blowing up my phone. Funny how April has ingratiated herself into their lives and isn't even aware of the impact she's had. They appear to love her and are in a state of outrage.

When my phone pings again, I'm not surprised to see Gabriel's name flash up.

GABRIEL:
> What the hell's going on?

So typically, Gabriel, straight to the point.

LEAH:
> What he means is, are you both okay?

I smile at Leah's message. We have our own little group chat. Leah, Gabriel and I.

ME:
> I'm hoping we will be.

GABRIEL:
> What's that supposed to mean?

ME:
> April has moved out, but not dumped my sorry ass.

LEAH:
> She's left? Why?

ME:
> It's complicated.

The messages remain silent until my phone rings. Leah's number pinging up.

"Hey," she says, her voice soft.

"Hey, you," I reply.

"What happened? April didn't look like someone who was about to walk out on you. She looked the opposite."

I sink down onto the sofa and stare out of the window. Leah is right, we had gone from special to almost dead in the water in less than twenty-four hours.

I fill Leah in, on what occurred at the party, leaving out none of the details.

"I knew I didn't like that man. I met him once. He gives off serious creeper vibes."

"His particular *Sir* is hereditary, handed down. Old school makes him think he's a cut above the rest of us," I add.

"April's lucky she's got you. And with Elijah on her side—he looked like he was about to tear apart the world last night."

I smile at Leah's words. She and Elijah got off to a rocky start, but that is ancient history now. I think our eldest brother would take a bullet for our sister-in-law.

"She's not alone. She means too much to me. But I'm not sure it will be enough."

There's silence for a moment, and I hear Callum gurgling in the background.

"Tread gently. Be patient. April is smart, but she's had years to build up some major defences. She's been through a lot. She wasn't raised with the security you and I had growing up. That has to leave scars."

"I've told her I want to be there for her."

"Telling and showing are two very different things. April's not going to drop her shields overnight. But if you show her she can trust you, that she can trust us," Leah says.

"When did you become so wise?" I ask her, chuckling.

"I've always been wise, jackass. How do you think I deal with your brother?"

I hear the laughter in her voice, followed by a, "Hey, I heard that!"

I smile even more. My brother did good when he finally opened his eyes and heart, letting Leah into his life.

"Thank you for welcoming April. I know she appreciated it," I say to Leah.

"It's no hardship. She's lovely. And Caleb, it's clear you make each other happy. This is a test. All relationships have them. Gabe and I had our own, as you well know. If you're meant to be together, it will sort itself out."

"I know."

"I've got to go, little man wants feeding. Your nephew is a hungry soul."

"I'll leave you to it," I say, about to disconnect when Leah adds.

"If April wants someone to talk to, tell her to call me."

"Thanks, Leah."

I end the call as my nephew lets rip an angry cry. No one keeps that baby away from his food. Like father, like son.

CHAPTER 58

CALEB

When Elijah walks into my office unannounced and drops into the chair opposite me. I sit up. My brother folding himself into a standard office chair is amusing. His tall, and equally broad frame, makes the chair seem invisible, like he's floating on air.

"Morning," I say brightly.

"Did she leave?" Elijah asks.

He never wastes words on niceties. I suppose years trapped in a marriage to a conniving and lying bitch will do that to a man.

"Yes," I say, leaning back, resting my hands on my desk.

"Not good." He leans back, his giant arms crossed over his chest. "April's good for you. She brings you down to earth. You need someone like her. What are you going to do about it?"

I bite my lip to hide my smile. My brother has never hidden the fact he disapproves of my lifestyle. Even if his life choices have contributed to that path. He's not exactly been the poster boy for marriage or a successful relationship. At six years our senior, Gabriel and I, were impressionable seventeen-year-olds when he and Darra tied the knot, with Lottie arriving on the scene soon after. It wasn't many years in before it became clear their marriage was not a match made in heaven, yet for reasons unknown to us, he's stuck with it. For me, shying away from commitment was the easier choice. I didn't want to find myself trapped in the same unhappy spiral my brother was caught in.

"I'm trying hard to convince her I'm good for her, too. She's not quite as convinced, but I'll get there. I will not throw in the towel."

Elijah graces me with a smile, and I almost fall off my chair.

I stare at him.

Who is this man, and what has he done with my grumpy ass brother?

He shrugs. "You've got the wrong impression of me," he says drily.

"What? Are you trying to tell me you aren't a grumpy bastard? 'Cause you've done a bloody fantastic impression of one for the past few years." I laugh.

Colour darkens his flawless cheekbones, and he drops his gaze. "I'm going to try to—"

I hold up a hand and stop him. "No judgement. I'm pulling your leg. Look, you should have shared your problems, let us help. You aren't an island, Eli. We're all adults. We could have supported you."

He nods, accepting my words. But it's too late to make those changes. I have a suspicion there is more at play here than he is letting on, but it's up to him. All we can hope is that the next time he needs help, he'll trust us to have his back, the same way he has ours.

"Back to April," he says, wanting to change the subject. "I did some more digging."

I groan at his words. April hasn't chewed me up and spat

me out yet after the last *digging* Elijah did. But that doesn't mean it isn't coming.

He ignores me and continues.

"It looks like April's mother didn't give her up easily. There was a catastrophic set of incidents that led to April and her mother being separated."

I run a hand down my face, knowing if I go down this path, take this information, I'm playing with fire.

I sit up. I know April has abandonment issues where her mother is concerned. She remembers love and laughter, then nothing. Confusing as an adult, but for a small child. My heart breaks for her.

"I told you her mother is looking for her."

I tilt my head in acknowledgement. "I don't know whether she's interested in hearing her mother's side of the story. It may give April some closure."

Before I can say anything, he holds out a slip of paper. "Her address and phone number."

I go to take it, but he pulls it back.

"Tread carefully. Her mother is married with two small children, but there isn't a lot else to know. She has a job, got an education, although later than most. I'm an information man. I can't tell you anything else. What you choose to do with that information is up to you." Elijah flicks his wrist forward so the paper is now within my reach before standing up. "If you need me, you know where to find me."

Without waiting for a reply, he makes his way to the door.

"Elijah," I say, as his hand encircles the handle.

He turns to look at me.

"Thank you," I say. "I'll speak to April and see what she wants to do. She needs to have the choice."

He turns and leaves. The room seems so much larger without him in it.

I stare at the piece of paper in my hand. There's a name,

address and telephone number written on it. The address is in Yorkshire. I pick up my phone and start to dial before stopping. I drop my phone back on the desk with a sigh.

Trust.

I need to show April she can trust me.

CHAPTER 59

APRIL

I sit in the nightclub, the music thumping. It is not my usual hangout, but when Caleb's sisters and Penelope Dawson turn up on my doorstep and demand I join them for a night out, the shock alone has me agreeing.

"Welcome to Lilith's. A private members club. No press allowed, but there are still plenty of arseholes present, just so you're aware," Harper says, leading us to our table.

The club is spread over multiple floors, but the girls and I head for the main bar area, a large room filled with booths and tables.

"Wow, this is quite something," I say, taking a seat.

"It certainly is. Come midnight, it's packed," Kat says. "Tonight is about getting out and letting your hair down."

I wonder if Caleb has told them I've been hermitting myself away. I go to work, then straight back to the apartment.

Kat touches my arm and gives it a squeeze. "Tonight is about drinking and dancing. I expect to see you strutting your stuff on the dance floor later."

"Only if you join me," I tell her and when she smiles, I

notice how much like Caleb she is. She really isn't the ice queen people make her out to be.

It's been a week since I left Cal's. We've talked on the phone daily, but he keeps his distance, giving me the space I asked for. I miss him more than I thought possible. The ache that has always been a permanent resident in my chest is back. I had not realised it had subsided while I lived with Caleb, but now it is back with a vengeance. Only this time, the longing is so intense I feel tired all the time and am no longer sleeping. I miss him.

I've heard nothing more from Sir Leonard Crawley. As promised, Cal and his family appear to have taken care of the situation. I'm not naive enough, to think it's over. Men like that don't just give up. He's probably just biding his time until I let my guard down. There is no way I want Caleb, or his family hurt by my past, whatever they say.

The night goes on, and I find myself relaxing. Caleb's sisters and Pen, as she told me to call her are great company. We have spent the night, laughing and dancing. I have very few actual girlfriends, so this is new and novel, and I find myself enjoying it.

"You must have one magic pussy to have tamed my brother." Harper giggles, the alcohol clearly going to her head.

"Harper!" Kat snaps. "Don't be crude."

"What?" Harper answers. "Caleb has never been able to keep it in his pants. He likes sex. What's wrong with that? It's perfectly natural. Not sure why everyone is so hung up on it."

Kat shakes her head at her younger sister, before shooting me a sideways glance. "He's been searching. He wants what Mum and Dad had."

"Don't we all," Harper says.

I can't stop myself, the alcohol clearly having gone to my head too. "What did your mum and dad have?"

It's Harper who smiles, an almost wistful smile. "Love. In bucket loads," she sighs.

Kat continues, "They were the perfect pair. They just got each other. They could read each other's moods. They laughed, talked, and debated. And could they *debate*. Heated, passionate debates." They all laugh at the memory. "But most of all, when they loved. They loved each other and us with a passion, both physically and mentally. That is what my brother has been looking for. What he's found with you."

Her honesty shocks me.

Is this what they think? That Cal loves me?

He told me he's fallen in love with me, but…

A vice clamps around my chest, and a look of pure panic must appear in my expression because all three of the girls laugh.

"Don't worry, when a Frazer man falls, he falls hard. My mother will tell you that. You just need to decide if you want that level of devotion for the rest of your life."

I find the thought almost impossible to comprehend. We hardly know each other. Yes, we're compatible in the bedroom. Caleb is a sex god. Who wouldn't be compatible with such a man? But as for the rest? Yes, we talk, we debate. We argue, and we laugh. My mind wonders to our time together, to the simple things we do and how I no longer feel alone.

Is that love?

I can't be the only one who he's had that with.

"Stop overthinking," Kat says, squeezing my shoulder. "What will be, will be."

I stay silent, not sure what to say. Alcohol has loosened their tongues and I'm not really comfortable discussing this with them. Before I can think on it any further, Harper pipes up.

"Now, Pen, who is this new man I keep hearing about, and does my big brother know?" she asks.

We all turn to face the tall beauty who has been friends with the Frazers for years, happy the attention is diverted from me.

"Ah, Kristophe," she says smiling.

CHAPTER 60

CALEB

Mason pulls up outside Scarlett's apartment building. Another week, and she'll be free to move into the apartment above the dance studio. The builders are completing the finishing touches. I head to the door, bouquet in hand. If I'm doing this, I'm doing it properly. No messing. I need to make April feel safe and cherished.

She buzzes me in, and I make my way up the stairs. My heart beats faster the closer I get to her. It's not like I haven't seen her, but that saying, absence makes the heart grow fonder, is true where April is concerned.

As I pass, one of the downstairs doors opens, and an older lady with snowy white hair and a full face of makeup pops her head out. She scowls at me until she notices the flowers, and her expression softens.

"Taking April somewhere nice?" she asks.

Why am I not surprised April is already on a first-name basis with the other residents? She knew every receptionist, maintenance man, and cleaner in my building by their first name within a fortnight.

I smile. "Mount Crystals," I say.

I'm going for excellent food and privacy. Robin Downsend runs a tight ship, making it the place to go if you're known and want a hassle-free evening. I don't think having her face plastered all over the newspapers is what April needs right now. Elijah has taken care of Crawley's threat, but I'm treading carefully. When you poke the bear, sometimes it has a tendency of biting you and I don't want April in Crawley's sight.

"Fancy... but not too fancy. I think our girl will like that," she says. "Have a lovely evening." Without another word, she shuts the door, leaving me staring. I shrug and make my way up another flight of stairs, knocking on April's door.

The door opens, and April grins, her hand under her hair as she fiddles with her earring. She steps back, letting me enter. She looks stunning. The dress she's wearing is breathtaking.

"You look—" I stumble, looking for the right word.

April turns to face me, her eyes twinkling.

"Caleb Frazer, lost for words. Now that must be a first."

She chuckles, but the flush to her cheeks does not go unnoticed.

"There seem to be a lot of *firsts* with you," I admit, holding out the flowers.

April takes them.

"They're beautiful," she says, burying her nose in the bouquet. "Come in and let me quickly put these in some water."

She disappears into the kitchen, only to return a few moments later with them in a vase. She places it on the side before walking up to me, her hands snaking around my neck.

"Thank you," she says, pulling my mouth to hers, her lips teasing mine. When I wrap my arms around her waist and pull her closer, she pulls back to stare up at me. "I've missed you," she admits, taking my breath away.

I drop my forehead to hers. "Not as much as I've missed you."

She stares up, our eyes locked. "You're just missing the sex," she replies.

"I will not deny missing your delectable body." I pull my head back and drag her hard against me, letting her feel exactly how much I've been missing her. "But I miss you. I miss your presence, chatting about our day. I even miss your singing," I say with a smirk.

She grimaces at the memory of the day I came home early from work to find her singing at the top of her lungs in the shower.

"I just miss your body," she says, pulling back and grinning at me. "As for conversation. We'll see how tonight goes."

I chuckle as April wiggles her brows before walking further into the apartment. She returns a moment later, clutching her bag.

"Ready?" I ask, holding out my hand.

"I think I am."

She interlocks her fingers with mine.

"So what are the plans?" she asks as she turns and locks up. All I've told her is we're going for dinner.

I pull a folded piece of coloured paper out of my pocket, one identical to the ones from our date jar.

April stops, her brows furrowed. "A *jar date*? I don't remember…"

I place a finger over her lips. "I may have added a few of my own to the jar, while you've been gone. We were getting a little low," I lie, making her laugh.

"Low?"

I shrug.

"Lead the way," she says smiling as she links her arm through mine.

We make our way downstairs to where Mason is waiting.

"Evening, Ms April. Lovely to see you again," he says, opening the car door.

"It's lovely to see you too, Mason," April replies.

Mason grins at me as I shake my head. Smooth operator. Another one, April has charmed.

The drive to the restaurant is relaxed. We talk about our day, our fingers still interlinked. We've been messaging and talking on the phone, but this is the first time we've seen each other since she moved out.

The restaurant is busy, as always. Robin greets us at the door, taking us to the table I requested. A table tucked away in the corner. I recognise a couple of other guests, nodding in their direction. Their eyes drift to April with interest.

"Enjoy your meal," Robin says, having settled April in her chair.

"Thank you," April says, smiling up at him. My heart jumps.

I raise a brow and shoot it in Robin's direction, earning myself a smirk when April looks down. We've been friends for a long time, and I've been a customer for years. What is it with my friends finding my love life suddenly interesting?

"This is lovely. I've heard great things about the food," April says, picking up her menu.

"Robin knows how to create the perfect customer experience," I say drily.

April chuckles. "You deserve all you get," she says, her eyes sparkling with mischief. "The playboy, dating. Ouch. What will it do to your reputation?"

I growl. "I've given up my playboy ways. There's only one woman I'm interested in." I lean across the table and take her hand in mine. "I mean it."

I rub circles on the back of her hand with my thumb. Her eyes drop to the movement.

"I need time," she says, her eyes meeting mine.

"And I'll give it to you. Just don't shut me out. I know we've been intense, and it's all happened so quickly. But when I tell you I love you, I mean it. I just need you to believe it."

Our waitress arrives before April can reply, taking our drinks order. I decide against pushing any further. April needs to find her own way back to me. Although I'll do everything in my power to prove to her, she's the only woman I want from now on.

* * *

"Well, if it isn't Caleb Frazer. Long time, no see."

I freeze as I'm enveloped in a floral scent that almost steals my breath.

"Patsy," I say, looking up to see a past date appear next to our table. "It's been a while."

"Too long." She pouts, annoying me as she continues to ignore the fact I'm with someone.

"Patsy, this is my girlfriend, April," I say, feeling a little agitated by her brazen disregard for the woman who is sitting opposite me.

Patsy turns and gives April a dismissive nod. April bites her lip, although her eyes sharpen when Patsy's hand comes to rest on my shoulder.

"You haven't returned my calls," she says, brushing the material of my shirt as if removing a piece of flint.

I remove her hand, dropping it.

"No," I say. A coldness slips into my tone, her rudeness beginning to grate on my nerves. I look over her shoulder. "I think your date is waiting for you," I say, giving her an empty smile.

She flicks her head.

"He can wait," she says. "I've missed you."

She reaches for me again. This time, I stand up and move away.

"I'm trying not to be rude," I say, working hard to keep my cool. I only ever went on one date with this woman. I didn't even stay the night. She gave stalker vibes even then. How did I end up with her being here of all nights?

She turns and gives April the once over.

"What's she got that I don't?" she asks.

Her over-painted lips pout even more, her eyes fill with tears.

What the hell?

April stands up, matching Patsy in height.

"I think you need to go back to your date. Show some self-respect." April's eyes don't leave hers. They stand, their eyes locked until Patsy flicks her professional blow out and walks away.

"That would be... everything," I say as we take our seats.

April turns to me, her brows raised.

"She asked what you have that she doesn't? It sounds corny, but everything." I shrug.

April can't keep the smile from her lips. "That really is corny. But I'll go with it."

I return her smile.

"So, is this what it will be like every time we go out for dinner? Your exes invading our space?" she asks, biting her cheek as she straightens her knife and then fork.

"Heaven forbid," I say, cringing.

Damn, this is not how I wanted this evening to go. I don't need reminders of my playboy past being brought up at every move.

April's hand comes across the table to rest on mine.

"Hey, it's okay. We both have a past. We just need to work out how we can navigate a future without it blowing up in our faces." Her expression is serious. "If it's not Sir Leonard, it will be some other creep. If we come out as a couple, then it won't matter. The press will do all the digging. I can just see the headlines now. *The City's Most Eligible Playboy Falls For Merryfellows Stripper.*"

She's not wrong. The press are a law unto themselves.

"I'm not going to lie to you," I say. "Sir Leonard has been quiet, but that does not mean he'll remain that way, even with the threat of exposure Elijah has hanging over him. It's also true that a lot of the men who frequent Merryfellows are old and entitled pricks. But they don't scare me. Most would want their association with that place kept quiet. It's why you had to sign the NDA when you worked there." I squeeze her hand. "As for the press—I love you, and I'm proud of you."

Her breath hitches, and my heart begins to race. Her eyes fill and I clamp down on the emotions that are racing through my system.

"But—"

A rush of fear sets in.

I take her hand, stroking my thumb over the back of her fingers. "I've lived my whole life in the public eye. The good, the bad and the ugly. When you're ready, and if it's what you want. Quentin can help us release the narrative we want. It's better to get in there first. Owning your past will be better than hiding it."

"But what about your family?" The quiver in her voice breaks my heart.

I smile. "My family love you. What part of my sisters taking you out, did you miss? You make me happy. They'll support you whatever you decide."

April withdraws her hand and places it in her lap. I watch as her shoulders sag and a heavy feeling settles in my chest.

When she looks up, I'm shocked to see the lost look in her eyes.

"I'm going to be honest. I can't simply take a leap of faith. Every time I've let myself feel safe, believe life has taken a turn for the better, something has happened to destroy that. From the age of three, I have lived each day not knowing what is going to happen next. I'm sorry, Cal. I can't—"

Her voice catches and she bites down on her bottom lip. I hold my hand out on top of the table, relieved when she takes it, interlocking our fingers. "I'm not ready. Please, I beg you. Don't give up on me." When her voice catches for the second time, I raise her hand to my lips. My heart clenches, but I know if we have any chance, I need to do as she asks.

Her words are like a punch to the stomach. I want to take away all the pain she's ever experienced, but I know I can't.

"I'll wait for as long as you need me to. Show how life without me is mundane and boring," I tell her truthfully. I will prove to April Wilson she cannot live without me.

The smile she shoots my way steals my breath. My heart stalls when she says. "It already is."

* * *

I TALK April into accepting a dessert to share.

My stomach churns with my next question.

"April?"

She looks up, taking the mouthful I have just offered her from the spoon.

"Yes, Cal," she says, smirking. My eyes lock on her mouth, and she licks the crème brûlée that has stuck to her lip.

I groan and run a hand down my face. "You'll be the death of me," I say, shifting uncomfortably in my seat.

When we used to eat dinner at home, we often had our own course in the middle. In public, that's not possible. My cock, however, has not got the memo. "In all seriousness, I have to ask you something."

April sits up. "Okay," she says.

Maybe I should wait.

"It's your mum," I say

She sits back in her chair and stares at me. "What have you done?" she asks, her tone accusatory. "Cal?"

I hold up my hands. "Nothing. I swear."

"Then why bring up my mum?"

She takes an angry mouthful of dessert. Stabbing at the plate as if she wishes it is my head.

Shit, I should have left it.

"Elijah."

She shoots me a look.

"I'm grateful for what your brother did at the party. How he stood up for me, but he doesn't have any right. He's out of line. He needs to stay out of my business."

"He is, was." I pause, running a hand down my face. "Look, I'm not handling this very well." I look around and am pleased to see no one is watching us.

"No, you're not." April sits back in her chair.

I smile, unable to help myself. I love the fact April calls me on my bullshit.

"Don't smile," she says, glaring at me.

"I love you calling me out," I say.

"Shame more women haven't," she huffs, shaking her head. "You need reining in. Training."

"I'm sorry," I say, reaching over for her hand, but she pulls it away. "I'm all for being trained. Especially if it's by you." I waggle my brows and receive another eye roll.

"This has to stop," she says. "It's smothering. And wrong on *so* many levels. It worries me you can't see that. Your brother sniffing around in my life." She growls, and my body hardens. Her anger has a way of turning me on as no one else ever has.

"It is," I agree. "It's just something flagged up. Eli thought you might want to know." I inhale before continuing. "Should I keep that information from you? I can. Or I can tell you and let you make up your own mind what you want to do with it."

April sits forward, her forearms resting on the table. Her face passive. "You fight dirty."

I exhale slowly.

"Well?" she says, lifting a hand and waving at me. "Now you have to tell me."

"Your birth mother is looking for you," I say. "She's registered with every lost family website."

"I'd like to leave now."

"April," I say, but she holds up her hand.

"I can't do this right now," she says, and I kick myself for ruining what's been an amazing night. Now, her memories will be tarnished by me and my interfering family.

April gets up and excuses herself. I watch as she makes her way to the bathroom.

Way to go, Caleb!

I call over the waitress and settle the bill, calling Mason to let him know we're leaving and to bring the car around.

When April returns, she's in control. She smiles at the waitress and thanks her for a lovely evening. Repeating the process when Robin approaches. Only I know she wants to be as far away from this place and me as possible.

We get into the car in silence.

"Thank you for a lovely evening," April says, her face turned towards the window.

"Don't thank me. I've ruined it."

She turns to face me. Her expression lost.

"I don't know how to do this," she says. "I want to be

furious at you, but I can't. You confuse me, Caleb Frazer, more than anyone, and that scares me."

"I'll never do anything to hurt you," I say, my thumb stroking her cheek.

She gives me a weak smile. "Not intentionally, but I suspect you will. I'm not sure I can survive you."

She tilts her head into my hand, and I pull her into my chest, resting her head above my heart, wanting her to hear it beat for her.

"You don't need to do anything about your mum," I say, my hand smoothing her hair.

April burrows in deeper against me. "I do," she says. "I've wondered for too long. You know that." Her mind clearly returned to the same conversation mine had when Eli first told me.

"You aren't alone." I drop a kiss onto her hair. "I can be with you every step of the way."

April pulls back and looks up at me. "You'll come with me?"

"Little dancer, of course, I'll come with you. I'll do whatever you need. You only need to ask."

She reaches up, her lips touching mine.

"Can I think about it?"

"Take as long as you need," I say, pulling her closer and into my lap.

My body cannot hide the effect she has on it.

Mason pulls up outside April's apartment.

April drops her gaze, moving back, as Mason jumps out and opens the door for us.

I get out and walk her up to her apartment.

She opens the door before turning to face me. "Are you coming in?"

I take her head in my hands and draw her lips towards mine. "No. You have things to think about."

April nods, her bottom lip disappearing behind her teeth.

"But if you need me, call. I'll be here in a heartbeat, or we can talk. I'm here for you. You're not alone."

"Thank you for an amazing evening," she says, her arms coming up and around my neck.

I pull her flush against me and lower my head, my tongue begging for entrance as I nibble and tease.

When I pull away, we're both breathless.

"Good night, April," I say, stepping away and adjusting myself.

April smirks when she catches the movement.

"Do you need help with that?" she asks, and I like the fact my cheeky April is back.

"I'd not be proving everything I want to prove, if I say yes." I say through gritted teeth.

"I appreciate your sacrifice. Goodnight." She steps inside her door, her face deadpan apart from the twinkle in her eyes.

"Goodnight," I say, waiting until she closes the door and engages the lock. I make my way back down to the car and a solemn Mason.

I know as we drive away, I'm in for a long night and an ice-cold shower.

CHAPTER 61

APRIL

I toss and turn for most of the night. Dinner with Caleb was something else.

The way he squirmed when his ex appeared. How much I miss him, and not just his magic dick. I know in my heart I'm done for. All I can do now is damage limitation.

He reassures me he can control the fall out of my past. But I don't know what to believe. I can't see how we can spin it without it coming back to haunt us.

Then there was his final bombshell. My mother. Is she really looking for me? Do I want to meet her? I'm twenty-five. She left me when I was three. Do I have hangups? - hell yes. Does my past bother me? I know it does. The unknowing is painful. Why did she leave me? Why did she never come back for me? I know deep down I was too young for it to have been my fault, but there's always a nagging doubt in my mind that I wasn't good enough, loveable enough.

The phone pings next to the bed, and I see a message from Caleb. He sent me a pleasant dreams message last night, as he always does, and I've been waiting for this morning's one. I smile.

CAL:
> How did you sleep?

I pick up the phone and dial his number. He answers almost immediately.

"I didn't," I say.

"I'm sorry, beautiful." He sighs. "I shouldn't have said anything."

I smile at his contrite tone. Only Cal would blame himself for giving me that kind of news.

"I'm glad you told me." Not wanting him to feel any worse than he already does. "I've spent a lot of the night thinking about it."

He remains silent.

I inhale deeply.

"I want to meet her. I realised at about three AM that I need to put the past to bed. Stop wondering what happened. Get some closure."

The silence remains, and I wonder if we've been disconnected.

"Cal?"

"I'll speak to Eli, see what he can find out."

I take another deep breath.

"No," I say. "I want to do this, just you and me. If you're up for it."

It's Cal's turn to exhale loudly. "I'll always be there for you. Whatever you need."

Butterflies dance around my stomach. He really has no idea how special he is. This side of him has me falling harder and faster every day.

"Can *you* get me the details?" I ask, my breath catching.

My mind is filled with countless what-ifs, making it difficult to know where to begin untangling them.

My heart is telling my head this needs to happen, or I will always wonder. If it's a disaster, then I'll have to learn to live with it, but I can begin moving forward.

I have trust and abandonment issues. It doesn't take a rocket scientist to work out why. This could be the answer.

"I already have them," he admits. "I'll send them across. And April. Whatever you choose. I want to be by your side."

I swallow the lump blocking my throat.

"Thank you. It means more than you can know," I choke out.

"Whatever happens."

I smile at his words.

"Whatever happens," I repeat back at him.

* * *

As promised, Cal forwards me Sarah's details. I ask Scarlett if I can borrow her office. I need to make this call before I run for the hills and use one of the thousands of excuses that have been swirling around my head all morning.

Punching in the numbers, I wait.

"Sarah speaking?"

"Hi," I say.

The sound of her voice steals my breath. Not something I was expecting.

"Hello?" Sarah says.

Words fail me. The silence deepens, and my heart rate picks up as I wonder if she'll put the phone down thinking this is a crank call. What if she's changed her mind and doesn't want to contact me at all?

"April?" Her voice catches. The desperation in her tone is clear.

My name shocks me back into the present. "Yes," I croak out.

"My goodness… I can't believe… Is it really you?"

The words come out stuttering as if she's overcome with emotion.

"Hi," I say, closing my eyes and focusing on the words.

"It's been so long. I assumed you… sorry," she says, stopping herself.

"I only just found out you were looking for me," I say. Not wanting her to say anything else. Not yet.

"I can't believe it's you."

When her voice catches, the words rush out. "Can we meet?" I ask.

A sob resounds down the phone, and I brace myself at the surprise flood of emotion that hits me. There's silence for a moment before Sarah speaks again.

"I would love that," she says softly. "You have no idea how much."

The details Cal sent me said Sarah lives in Yorkshire with her husband and two children.

"I can come to you," I say. "We can meet up in a hotel, neutral ground."

"A hotel is fine, although my husband, Tim knows all about you. He's been helping me to find you. He'll be so excited," she says, her voice picking up pace, as if she too is excited.

The news shocks me. I don't know what I was expecting. Part of me wondered if I was going to be her dirty little secret.

We spend some time going backwards and forwards. I tell her I can come up in a couple of weekends' time. I just hope that's okay with Cal.

When we finally end the call, it's as if someone has lifted a heavy weight off my chest. I pick up my phone and dial Cal's number.

"Hi," I say. I hear muttering in the background. "Sorry, are you in a meeting?"

"I am, but don't worry. Give me a second." I hear him moving and a door close.

"I could have called you back," I say.

I should have thought about how busy he is.

"No, I'd rather listen to you than that bunch of boring old farts," he says, making me giggle.

"Seeing the average age of your company is about thirty-five, I'm not sure boring, or old, fits the bill. Remember, I've been around them."

He chuckles, and my heart soars.

"What do I owe the honour of this mid-lunchtime call?" he asks, and I remember I called him. This man sends my hormones racing, and I lose all rational thought.

"Yes. Sorry." I stumble over my words.

"April, breathe," he says, but I can hear the smile in his tone.

"Sorry." I inhale. "I called her."

"Who? Your mother?" he asks cautiously.

"I did. She wants to meet me. The weekend after next." I say, hoping he's not going to tell me he has other plans and can't make it.

"I'm proud of you," he says. "I'll book us a room. There's a Frazer Hotel nearby. We can meet her there."

A flood of warmth takes over my body, and I sink back into the chair.

"Thank you. Thank you for encouraging me to do this."

"It's all you, little dancer. I'm along for the ride. I want you to have your dreams. Help make them happen, anyway I can."

The words *I love you* stick to my tongue. I want to say

them to him, know I mean them, but I can't. Not yet. I have a few more things to do. Meeting my birth mother is one of them.

"Will I see you tonight? I can come over and cook dinner," I say. Wanting, no, needing to be close to him.

There's a pause. "I'd love that," he says, his tone lighter.

I can't keep the smile off my face. "I'll see you later," I say before ending the call.

I have a skip in my step as I head back to the dance studio for my next class. Only a few more weeks here, and then I'll be moving back to my studio. I'll miss the banter and the companionship of those I've met here. Although I know it's not over.

"Wow, you look happy," Scarlett says, stepping into the studio.

I tilt my head. "I am," I admit, a grin spreading over my face.

Scarlett steps forward. "You and Cal? Have you sorted out your differences?" she asks.

I know she's been concerned since I moved into her apartment.

"We're getting there," I admit.

I take a deep breath. I'm not sure if I should tell her what's going on, but I'm not sure I can keep it to myself. The bubbling in my chest wants to explode.

"I just spoke to my birth mother," I say, opening my eyes wide and waiting. Not sure what reaction I'm expecting.

It's Scarlett's turn to look shocked, but she grabs my hands and squeezes. "I'm taking it, it went well. You're practically vibrating."

I screw up my face. "I don't know. Cal and I are going to meet her a week on Saturday. I'm confused." I shrug my shoulders. "I'm not sure how to feel or what to say. She abandoned me when I was three. I haven't seen her since."

Scarlett pulls me into her arms.

"All you need to do is listen. See what she has to say. There are no hard and fast rules. Whatever happens next, you can draw a line under the past." She gives me another squeeze before releasing me.

"Thank you," I say, my throat tight. She does not know how much her words resonate.

"You're welcome. I'm going to miss you when you leave," she says.

The door to the studio opens, and the next class enters. I see Lottie in the back, so I wave over. Eli never brings his daughter, it's usually his wife, ex-wife.

"I'll leave you to it," Scarlett says, heading for the door. Before she reaches it, she turns back. "Can you come and see me before you leave? I have a proposition for you. There is a certain rock-star who needs choreography for his new video. I think your style will fit. I want to know if you're interested." Scarlett grins, and I scowl at her. How can I turn down an offer like that?

"That's cruel," I call after her.

"I know, speak to you later." She leaves the room laughing, and I shake my head.

"Afternoon, class."

"Afternoon, Ms April." They chorus. My focus moves from Scarlett and my evening planned with Cal to the teenagers in front of me.

CHAPTER 62

CALEB

Kat has come through. Everything is organised. Our accommodation, our travel. April is sitting next to me, clutching my hand as if it's a lifeline, and I'm happy to let her.

"You've not heard a word I've said, have you?" I say, turning my body to face hers.

"Huh?"

"My point exactly," I chuckle, gaining her attention. "Do you want to talk about it?"

She scrunches up her nose.

I take her face in my hands and drop a kiss on the offending wrinkle. "April, you've been staring into space for the past hour, have grunted answers to every question I've asked. It's not surprising, you've got a lot on your mind. You're about to meet the woman who gave birth to you, a woman you haven't seen in twenty-two years."

"Sorry," she says, pulling absentmindedly at her lips.

"Don't be sorry," I say, rubbing my thumb over her lips. "I just want you to know. You're not alone. I'm here for you if you'll let me."

She tilts her head into one of my hands, as she looks at me, her eyes clearing.

She sighs.

"I don't know what to think, or what to say. My mind is like the inside of a washing machine on a fast spin cycle. Everything is going around and around in my head. Rolling over itself. Every sentence, question, sounds wrong. Suppose she hates me? What if I despise her? What do I do? What if I can't get past all this? We end up hurting each other more than we already have. What then? And then, of course… what if we get on? How do I shut away all the hurt I've got bottled up inside and move forward?"

I pull her into my arms, and I'm amazed when she comes willingly. She rests her head above my heart, and I draw her closer, rubbing circles on her back. When she closes her eyes, I kiss the top of her head.

"What will be, will be."

I smooth her hair back from her face. "This meeting is just a point in time. How you navigate it, after tomorrow, will depend on so many factors. Try not to second guess. Just be yourself. I'm here with you."

Whether she appreciates my lack of platitudes I don't know, but I have a feeling telling April. *She's going to love you. You're going to love her,* won't help matters. Guarantees do not exist, and we are both aware of that.

She wraps an arm around my waist and squeezes, "Thank you for being here with me," she whispers.

"I wouldn't be anywhere else," I tell her honestly.

We stay like that for the rest of the journey.

* * *

April's jaw drops when we pull up outside the hotel. Unlike

New York, this is one of our boutique hotels. A style more reminiscent of our family home.

"Cal, this is stunning," she whispers as Mason pulls up on the gravel driveway. The bellboy collects our cases, and I take April's hand in mine as he leads us through the large double doorway and into reception.

"Welcome Mr Frazer, Ms Wilson. We hope you enjoy your stay. If there's anything I can do. Please ask."

"Thank you, Miriam," I say, greeting the manageress. "Can I confirm you have reserved the private sitting room for our meeting tomorrow?"

She smiles warmly. "Of course. We've set it aside for the day, as requested. Someone will take tea and coffee orders when your guest arrives, and we'll serve lunch when you indicate. Your sister was very clear in her instructions."

"That sounds perfect," I say. Kat likes April and will want everything to be perfect. That thought alone eases my mind, and hopefully Aprils. "Are we in the family suite?"

"You are," Miriam holds out a key card embossed with the Frazer family logo. "Your bags have already been taken up. Mason wanted me to let you know he's in Room 42, should you need him. Can I book you a table in the restaurant for this evening, or would you prefer room service?"

I look at April, taking note of the dark rings around her eyes. "Room service," I say without a second thought.

After the two-and-a-half-hour drive and an early start at the studio, I get the feeling April will want to put her feet up and chill out. If she needs a distraction, then I'm sure we can find something to do.

"There is a menu in the room. Just make a call, and the chef will have your dinner brought up to you," Miriam says, smiling over at April.

"Thank you," April says before I lead her to the elevator.

"Do you have family suites in all the hotels?" April asks as soon as the doors close.

"We do. It was something my grandfather insisted upon. When my father and his siblings were younger, he would often take them with him. He felt it was safer if he knew the environment was somewhere they knew."

"Your father took over the hotel chain?" April asks.

"Dad followed his father into the hotel business, like Kat. The rest of his siblings followed their own paths, like the rest of my family. My aunt oversees Frazer Jewellery, and my uncle runs Frazer Entertainment. My cousins are all in business with them. It was a stipulation of my grandfather and father's wills, all family members are free to use the family suites."

"Wow, there are a lot of successful Frazer's out there," April laughs.

"What can I say, we're a pushy bunch." When April rolls her eyes, I pull her into my arms, dropping a kiss on her lips.

I let us into the family suite, and April freezes in the doorway, her jaw slack, making me smile. I grab her hand and pull her into the room, closing the door behind her.

"Through there is a small kitchen. It will be stocked with snacks and drinks. Help yourself."

Like a child in a toy shop she wanders off into the *small* kitchen. I hear the fridge door open. "Holy—" she mutters, making me smile and I know she has found it fully stocked with everything she might want, from yoghurts, to fresh fruit platters, and a ready-made salad. As well as a selection of cheeses and cold meats.

I sit down as I listen to her move around. The sound of the cupboard doors opening and closing.

Her face appears in the doorway. "Is this you?" She holds up her favourite brand of coffee.

I stand up and walk towards her, wrapping my arms

around her waist. "I didn't think you should be without your favourite beverage this weekend. I called Kat and she made sure they ordered it in."

"Oh gosh, what will Kat think. She'll think I'm one of those high maintenance women."

That has me laughing. "High maintenance women?" I ask, knowing she has no idea. She would struggle to be *high maintenance* if she tried.

"Yes," she says pulling out of my arms and putting her hands on her hips.

I pull her back towards me and drop a kiss on her nose. "Kat would never think that, and like me, she wants you to feel comfortable this weekend."

"Well, I shall make sure I thank her. This is amazing." April says, gesturing to the room and kitchen. "Let me put this coffee back," she says turning away quickly.

I watch her go, knowing something is wrong.

I walk up behind her when she places her hands on the kitchen sideboard and drops her head. Wrapping my arms around her waist, I envelop her in my embrace.

"What's wrong?" I ask.

She turns her head, her eyes bleak. "I'm just a little overwhelmed, I guess."

I rest my forehead against the side of her head and draw her closer. "That's to be expected. It's a big weekend. Just remember I'm here. I'm not going anywhere."

She spins in my arms, her arms going around my neck. "I couldn't do this without you." Her words make my heart sing.

I drop a quick kiss on her lips. "Let me run you a bath and then we can order some dinner."

She moans at my words and my cock hardens instantly. It's been too long since I've had her in my arms. "That sounds like heaven," she says, pressing herself against me.

I lead her into the master en suite and April chuckles.

"Your family understand luxury," she says appreciatively, as I lean over the extra-large bath and start the water going. I pass her a basket filled with oils and bath salts. She places them on the side and begins to smell them. "This one," she grins.

When the bath is ready, I turn around, pulling April to her feet. My eyes catch hers as I draw her towards me. I begin to unbutton her shirt, sliding it off her shoulders, before following with the rest of her clothes.

"Get into the bath, and relax," I say, keeping my eyes on hers and my hands on her shoulders and not on her naked body. "Would you like a glass of wine?"

Her lips twitch as she looks at me, her arms snaking up and around my neck.

"What I'd like, is you, in the bath with me. Helping me to relax." She draws my head down to hers, her tongue tracing the seam of my lips.

CHAPTER 63

APRIL

I tease his lips with mine, slowly as I begin to undress him with the same gentleness he showed me.

He moans against my mouth, sending a lance of desire straight to my already throbbing pussy. I need him with a desperation I didn't think possible. He's done as I asked, given me space to breathe but now. What I really want to do, is rip his clothes off and have him sink into me, but I also want more. Instead, we allow our hands and mouths to explore.

"April, what are you doing to me?" he moans against my mouth as I take his cock in my hand, teasing the weeping head and slit with my thumb.

He trails his hand, lightly down my stomach, with the back of his fingers. My muscles contract, and my head falls back when it reaches the top of my mound.

"Cal," I whisper into the air. His fingers trailing lower, finding my dripping and swollen lips. "Please," I beg as his fingers glide through the evidence of my desire, teasing and tormenting my clit, before heading lower and pressing into my entrance.

"Yes," I moan as he sinks two fingers into me, my muscles contracting around the invasion. "I need you."

He withdraws, his lips tilting, letting me know he's grinning. "Your bath is getting cold," he says, pulling away and taking my hand, leading me to the bath.

He steps in first, my hand still clasped in his. When I said this was a large bath. I wasn't joking.

We sink down into the blissful water and I let out a groan.

"Come here," he says, resting his back against the side of the bath. He turns me so I'm facing away from him before pulling me back between his legs, his hard cock pressed between us. I rest my back against his chest, my head resting against his shoulder, my hands gripping his thighs.

"Cal?" I question. I want the man with a desperation I can't explain.

"All good things," he says, his mouth beginning its exploration of my ear and neck. "Just relax." I squirm when his fingers trail once more down my front. He cups my breasts in his large palms. His fingers and thumb beginning to play with my nipples, gently twisting and pulling them beneath the surface of the water.

I moan and press back against him as one hand snakes lower. Finding my clit once more, carrying out the same torment it has just wrecked on my nipple but now on a more sensitive bud of nerves.

Cal lifts me slightly, spreading my legs to either side of his, opening me to his exploration. His hand travels down and begins its torment of my entrance. A place that is pulsing with need. My muscles contract, making me suck in a breath as Cal's fingers do magical things to my pussy.

When I can't take it anymore, I spin in his arms, grabbing

his throbbing cock in my hand and sliding myself down onto him with one swift movement.

Cal's eyes go wide as his head drops back.

"No more," I say, my body loving the feel of him deep inside me. "I want you. It's been too long," I tell him, beginning to move up and down, my movements slow and controlled.

He wraps his hands around the back of my head and draws my mouth to his. "It has. I love you April Wilson. I'm yours. Take what you need."

I continue our slow and drawn-out love making. Rising and falling, rocking and tilting. Cal's cock finding my magic place, driving my desire higher and higher.

"Cal, I…" the pressure begins to build, as his hand snakes between us.

"Come for me," he says, his tone shooting me over the edge and into one of the most powerful orgasms. This man does magical things to my body.

I continue to ride him, my body loving the sensation of him deep inside as it contracts around his cock.

I feel him grow larger and know he's close. His kiss becomes more frantic, more desperate. So I slow my speed, taking him slower and deeper.

He throws back his head and lets out a yell as his cock jerks, the warmth of his orgasm coating my insides. His muscles tense as he rides his release.

He opens his eyes and looks at me, love glaring back. He pulls me down before I can say anything, his mouth sealing mine in a kiss to end all kisses. When we finally break apart, he pulls me down against his chest.

"Are you feeling more relaxed?" he asks

"Most definitely. You're the perfect tonic," I sigh, my muscles relaxing another notch against him, making him chuckle.

"I aim to please," he says, his hands rubbing circles over my back, his semi hard cock still buried inside me. And that's how we stay, enjoying the feel of being back in each other's arms.

CHAPTER 64

CALEB

We eventually drag ourselves out of the bath and wrap ourselves in the large fluffy bathrobes the hotel provides.

I hand April the menu and ring down our order while she explores the rest of the suite.

"Dinner will be about thirty minutes," I say, standing in the doorway of the second bedroom and holding out a glass of wine for her.

When she turns, I open my arms. She walks into them, snuggling against my chest.

"What do you think?" I ask, against her hair.

"It's beautiful, thank you. I'll send Kat a thank-you message for organising it all."

"She'll love that. She's going to want to know how everything goes tomorrow. You know that. They all will."

She pulls back as if surprised. I look down at the face of the most beautiful woman I've ever known, both inside and out, amazed she is as unaware of the impact she has on those around her.

When she realises, I'm serious she smiles. "And I'll be

happy to tell her. I like Kat. I like all your family. They've made me feel so welcome."

"They like you too. You've tamed their playboy brother and son. That gives you serious kudos in their eyes."

"Tamed? We shall see." She takes a sip of her wine before resting her head back against my chest.

I lead us back into the main area and sit us down on the sofa. I pull her into my arms as we both sit comfortably in silence, drinking our wine and enjoying the peace and quiet. The suite is on the top floor, views of the countryside, clear for miles through the window.

"I didn't realise how much I needed a green fix," she says after a while.

"I know. It's one of the reasons I keep my cars at Mother's. It gives me the perfect excuse to escape and return to nature."

"I like that," she says. "And I'm sure your mother does too."

I chuckle. My mother always loves to see her children. However old we get, she still wants to know we're okay.

"You are welcome to join me anytime," I tell her, keeping my fingers crossed she says yes. I have given her the space she has asked for, but I now need to work on winning her back.

There is a knock on the door.

"Room service," the voice says.

April looks down at us and gasps. Our robes, not hiding what we have clearly been up to.

I smirk before untangling myself from her arms and getting up. I make my way to the door before opening it.

"I can take it from here," I tell the waiter, handing him a generous tip.

He nods his thanks before walking away.

I wheel our dinner into the room. "Problem solved," I tell

THE PLAYBOY BILLIONAIRE

April, who is pursing her lips on the sofa, trying not to giggle.

"You..." she says.

"Are starving. Let's eat, because after that. I'm having you for dessert all over this room."

"I think I can be on board with that," April says, the twinkle returning to her eyes as she stands and drops her robe. "How about naked dining?"

CHAPTER 65

APRIL

I hear voices coming from the sitting room area. I realise it's morning, and Caleb has ordered breakfast for us, the smell of which has my stomach grumbling. As if summoned, he appears at the door, coffee in hand.

"Morning, beautiful," he says, bringing me a cup and placing it by the side of the bed. He drops a chaste kiss on my lips. "Did you sleep well?" he asks, his face filled with concern.

"I slept like someone who had multiple orgasms and needed to recharge," I say honestly, earning myself a smile that melts my panties.

"Glad to hear it. I'd go for another round, but breakfast is getting cold, and we only have an hour before your mother turns up."

His words register, and I squeak. "Why did you let me sleep so long?" I say, throwing the covers back and standing up. I'm naked as the day I was born. I love sleeping skin-to-skin with Caleb. His eyes darken in appreciation, and he takes a step towards me, but I hold up a hand.

"Oh, no, you don't," I say. "I need to get ready."

Caleb holds his palms up in surrender and takes a step back. "Until later, my love. Grab a shower. Breakfast will be waiting."

He leaves the room, ensuring he gives my body the once over with his eyes before he closes the door. I head to the bathroom to assess the damage.

I get in the shower and allow the evidence of our night to disappear down the drain. I wash my hair and wrap it in a towel before grabbing one of the fluffiest dressing gowns and encasing myself in it.

Caleb is sitting at the table, another feast spread out in front of him. He's on his phone, typing frantically when I take a seat.

"Everything okay?" I ask, grabbing a croissant and taking a bite. Stifling the moan that threatens as it melts on my tongue.

He puts his phone down and smiles. "Just answering some of yesterday evening's emails. I was distracted," he says, waggling his eyebrows.

This man is a workaholic. He never has a moment off. He plays hard, but he works doubly hard. Anyone who says he hasn't earned his wealth is deluding themselves. All the Frazer family have the strongest work ethic. Something that surprised me, especially being raised in such a wealthy environment.

"How are you feeling?" he asks, helping himself to the fruit platter.

"Equal parts excited and apprehensive," I tell him honestly. "Last night, however, helped. You're the best distraction." I tell him. I move towards him and drop myself onto his lap, wrapping my arms around his neck. Loving the way his arms come around me and his eyes twinkle with delight. I want him to know I'm not oblivious to his thoughtfulness and needs, that I appreciate him more than words can say.

"I aim to be of service," he says before offering me a strawberry.

I bite it off his fork, closing my eyes as the sweet taste explodes on my tongue.

We continue to feed each other morsels of food until I feel like I'm ready to explode. The food is too good to waste. I will need to dance extra hard this coming week, but then again, what the hell—you only live once, and this is a treat weekend.

I look at the time. Twenty minutes until my mother arrives. My stomach sinks, and the food I've just devoured threatens to reappear.

Caleb walks up behind me and wraps his arms around my waist, dropping a kiss on my shoulder.

"Stop thinking and start doing. Dry your hair, do your makeup, and get dressed. Baby steps, little dancer, baby steps."

I rest my head back against his shoulder. "How do you always know?"

He presses a kiss into the side of my head. "I just do," he says, pushing me forward towards the vanity unit. "Now get ready."

I don't want to think about what the girls said about how in-tune his parents were. It's true he can read me, and I'm getting better at reading him. It's how I know he's not as cocky-confident as he makes out. Why I've taken to being honest with him. Well, as honest as I can be, but I'm learning. He's helping me to see there is another way.

I shake myself off and do what I'm told, listening as Caleb starts up the shower.

CHAPTER 66

APRIL

The room is perfect.

I'll be sending Kat an enormous bouquet. She's been messaging, hoping everything goes well, and trying to arrange another girls' night.

I walk up to the large windows that overlook manicured gardens. The large sofas are positioned opposite each other, and plumped-up cushions offer a homely vibe. My stomach churns as the moments tick by.

What the hell was I thinking? Why am I doing this?

I turn to face Cal, who is standing quietly near the door. My heart stutters as it always does when I see him. I can't believe he is here with me, is supporting me. That he loves me.

I take a step towards him, as a knock resounds on the door. We both freeze, our eyes darting towards the sound.

"Come in," Cal calls.

Miriam, the hotel manager, pops her head into the room. "Your guests have arrived. Would you like me to show them in?"

His eyes move to mine, as do Miriam's. I straighten my shoulders and raise my chin.

"Yes, please," I say, my fingers plucking at the material of my dress.

Cal walks towards me, holding out his hand. I intertwine our fingers and appreciate when he gives them a gentle squeeze.

"You've got this," he whispers, moving to my side as the door opens.

A woman enters, followed by a tall, slender man. The woman stops in her tracks, her eyes locking on mine, her mouth twisting, before a hand comes up to cover it.

It's my turn to gasp, my other hand coming around my front to grip Cal's arm.

"I know you," I whisper, earning a sideways glance from Cal, his expression confused.

"April," the woman who gave birth to me whispers, stepping forward. When I make no move towards her, she pulls up short. The man steps up to her, placing an arm around her shoulder.

"I know you, Sarah. How is that possible?" I say, my brain whirling with hurt and confusion. How and why? Understanding dawns in her eyes.

She nods, her bottom lip disappearing beneath her top teeth.

"You used to come to dance recitals," I say. "You were there."

I can sense Cal's confusion next to me, but the squeeze of my fingers lets me know I am not alone. He has already told me that if I want to leave, I can. I'm in control.

Tim's arm tightens around Sarah's shoulders.

"I did," she says, her chin dropping, but her eyes never leaving mine.

"Did Di know?" I ask, hoping and praying she says no.

"She did. It was Di who suggested it." Her words shoot a lance of pain through my chest. Di knew my birth mother was there and never told me. Cal's arm comes up around me and I realise I must have swayed into him.

"It's not what you think," Sarah's voice pleads. "I contacted her through the agency. Asked to meet you. You told them you didn't want to see me." Her tone is desperate, and she holds up her hands towards me. "Please, April. You were twelve, and you'd just moved in with Di and Julian. I didn't blame you; your life was in turmoil. I just wanted--"

Her voice catches and I find myself frozen to the spot. My thoughts racing... too many questions.

"I'm sorry, I can't do this." I pull out of Cal's arms and make my way past Sarah and Tim, neither tries to stop me, but I can't miss the look of devastation on Sarah's face.

I turn the handle and step out into the corridor, pleased we are away from the reception area and the prying eyes of other guests.

I lean back against the wall and close my eyes. Sucking in some shuddering breaths.

Shit what was I thinking?

I can't do this.

I hear the low murmur, of Cal's voice through the door, although I can't make out the words. I bend double as a wave of nausea hits, the churning in my stomach now on double speed.

I straighten as I hear footsteps approach. Looking up, I see Miriam rounding the corner. She stops when she sees me and smiles.

"Can I get you anything?" she asks, clearly trying to ignore the fact I'm standing against the wall and having a panic attack.

"Can I order some tea and coffee?" I say, as it's the first

thing that comes into my head, although I think I'd rather order a double whiskey or brandy.

"Most certainly. I'll get it sent straight in." She turns and leaves and I push myself off the wall. I straighten my shoulders and turn back towards the door.

I've come to listen to what she has to say to allow for closure. I can't get that if I hide in the corridor. I place my hand on the handle and turn, letting myself back in. I need, no, I deserve answers and I'm going to get them.

"Why? Why did you give me up?"

The words are out of my mouth before I've even re-entered the room fully. The hurt obvious in my voice. My eyes clash with Cal's as I make my way back over to him. He inclines his head, his eyes shining with pride. I stand next to him, taking his hand in mine as I absorb his strength.

Sarah stands and moves towards me. She holds out a hand, and I stare at it. It's only when I look in her eyes, I find myself raising my hand to hers and letting her clasp it. A warmth shoots up my arm and into my chest, my heart stuttering.

"I will not give you platitudes or excuses. I can tell you the truth. What you choose to do with that is up to you," she says, gently squeezing my hand before letting it go.

There's a clatter of a trolley outside, that has everyone turning to the door.

"I ordered some tea and coffee," I say, stepping around my mother and moving towards one of the sofas. "Maybe we can all take a seat."

I need to sit down, unsure how much longer my legs will hold me. My body is shaking, it's all I can do to stop my teeth from chattering.

Miriam brings the trolley in, and Cal acknowledges her with a smile. I'm sure it's not her job as hotel manager to act as tea person, but I suspect she wants to ensure what goes on within this room stays within the room. No newspaper stories or gossip.

"Thank you. We can serve ourselves," Cal says, before she turns and leaves, closing the door behind her.

Cal's serves everyone drinks before making his way to sit next to me, his thigh touching mine. Tim and Sarah taking a seat opposite.

Sarah takes a sip of her tea before placing the cup back on its saucer, the slight clatter as they connect, highlighting the tremor in her fingers.

"I was sixteen when I had you," she begins. "I'd been on holiday with my parents. We were about to move house. We had already packed up the old house and were having renovations done on the new one. Dad decided a nice holiday in the sun was just what we needed."

She smiles as if her words bring back fond memories.

I remain silent, although tension curls through my body. Cal rests a hand on my leg and I find myself clasping it in both of mine, a lifeline, as Sarah continues.

"Jeffrey was a year older. He was on holiday with his family too. We hit it off right away. Were inseparable. One thing led to another and —" She pauses. "The holiday ended. We were moving, and I didn't know our new address. Jeffrey gave me his, and I hid it in the inside pocket of my suitcase. We promised to stay in touch. First love."

She smiles again, but her eyes radiate a level of sadness when she looks at me. "You have his eyes," she says suddenly, her gaze shifting to Tim's. I watch as he takes her hand in his. He is sat as close as Cal is to me. Protecting, supporting.

Sarah's eyes return to mine as she continues. "My case went missing on the flight home. Some might say it was fate. I didn't really think much about it until a few months later, when my clothes started getting tighter. I was five months along before I knew I was pregnant."

"Five months?" I say. You hear stories of people going full term, but Sarah is slight. How on earth did she not know she was carrying me? As if sensing my question, she shrugs and lets out a self-deprecating chuckle.

"We'd been safe, or so I thought. I was young and naïve. My periods were never particularly regular, and I was in my exam year. There was always an excuse."

"Why didn't you just give me up for adoption?" I blurt out. She clearly hadn't wanted me. I was an accident through and through.

Sarah stares at me wide eyed, as if my words are a shock. I watch as she blinks back the tears that threaten. "Never," she whispers. "I loved you with all my heart," she says, wiping a tear that's escaped and making its way down her cheek.

I shake my head, my thoughts spiralling. "I don't understand." *If she loved me, then why are we here?*

Sarah takes another sip of her tea, the cup shaking so much I watch as liquid almost breaches the top. Tim takes it off her and returns it to the table. She takes in a breath, before exhaling it slowly.

"My parents offered to help me raise you. We were doing great. I went back to school after you were born to finish my studies. Mum looked after you during the day. Dad went out to work."

She pauses and I watch Tim clasp her hand, bringing it to his lips. She turns to him and gives him a small smile.

"Then Dad got sick, and our world changed. Mum had to go out to work, and Dad was too sick to look after you. I dropped out of college again, and in the beginning we managed." She clasps her hands in her lap and stares at them. "Foster care was only supposed to be a short-term solution. I got to see you every week. Mum and I would come and take you out to the park. We'd go shopping."

I gasp. "I remember. The blue swings, and yellow…"

"Roundabout." Sarah smiles. "You loved that roundabout. Faster mummy, you would say, faster." Her smile drops. "The problem was we all had too much fun. When we took you back, you'd get distraught, crying and screaming. Dad was getting sicker, and it was not possible to have you at home, so your social worker suggested we stop the visits. That they were too traumatic for you… and your foster parents were struggling."

A suffocating vice clamps itself around my chest as I take in her words. Someone stopped me seeing my mother because I cried. Pain like I've never felt before shoots through me.

As if sensing my pain, Sarah looks up and shakes her head. "It was the last thing I wanted, but I was nineteen, and they convinced me it was best for you. I left you with Mr Ted."

My eyes fill. "I still have him," I tell her, my voice strained.

Sarah looks up and stares at me, her own eyes glistening. "You loved that teddy. I bought it for you before you were born. It went everywhere with you."

Cal squeezes my hand again, and I rest my head on his shoulder.

Sarah gives herself a shake before continuing.

"Dad died, and Mum went into a decline. Dad's pension wasn't enough to pay the bills. The social worker recommended that I return to school to complete my education. That I should try to make something of my life before I brought you back to live with me. Only when I got my education, they told me I'd need a job and a salary to support you. You'd just been moved to your second foster family." She pauses and runs a hand through her hair, holding her head. "The problem was by the time I had all those things, you were no longer three. You were twelve. You just moved in with Di and Julian."

I let out a sob, as I know what is about to come. "Di asked me if I wanted to see my birth mother," I whisper, not wanting to say the words aloud. "I told her. I told her…"

"Stop!" Sarah says her eyes coming up and clashing with mine. "You don't do that. Don't you dare beat yourself up." She moves, coming to squat in front of me. She looks into my eyes as she takes both my hands in hers.

"That's why you were there. To see me?" I whisper, suddenly understanding.

"I was, and it was the best time. I loved watching you dance. You were so graceful." Her smile is filled with warmth when she looks up into my face. "Di would let me know how things were going, exams, competitions. I think she felt sorry for me." She drops her head. "Then my job took me away. I went to see Di, and she promised to keep in touch, which she did. She's a wonderful woman."

"Why the websites?" I ask. "Why did Di not just tell me herself when I reached eighteen?"

"I wouldn't let her. If you ever asked about me, she would have told you, but when you didn't… the lost and found websites were my best option. Tim is the one who suggested I put my details on there." She looks over her shoulder at the man, staring at her with the same look Cal gives me. "Then, if you ever wanted to track me down…"

I sink against Cal, my hands still clasped in Sarah's.

"I'm so sorry, April. I wish I'd been older… that things were different. I know it sounds weak and feeble, but I did what I thought was best for you. I loved you so much. I only ever wanted the best for you."

I lift my gaze to Tim's, and he smiles the most genuine smile. His love for Sarah shining through.

"When your mother told me she had a child and lost her, my aim has always been to help you find your way back to one another. This can't be easy for you. I think we both appreciate that, but we would love for you to be part of our lives." He returns to gaze at his wife. "Build a relationship. If you want to." He looks down at his hands, before raising his gaze to mine once more. "There is no pressure. But you have two younger siblings, who I know would be thrilled to meet their big sister."

I let out a sob and the tears I've been trying to hold in, break free. My chest swells and I find myself being encased in Cal's arms as the floodgates open. He rocks me in his hold, kissing my temple and murmuring sweet nothings. But as the tears fall I realise it's not despair I feel, but hope. Hope for my future.

Cal wipes my tears with his thumbs and cups my face, Sarah still clutching my hands.

"April, I'm so sorry," Tim says sounding devastated, his face white.

I look across to him and shake my head. "No, please don't apologise. You have no idea what your words mean to me. What today has meant to me."

I turn my head back to Cal. "The choice is yours, little dancer," he says. "It will always be yours."

I give him a brief nod. I let go of one of my mother's hands and raise one of his to my lips, before dropping a kiss on his palm.

When I finally gather myself together. I turn to Tim and my mother and say, "I'd love to meet them." Sarah lets out a sob and I lean forward, pulling her into my arms. There's been too much pain. We hold each other tight, my mum rocking me in her arms for the first time in twenty-two years.

CHAPTER 67

APRIL

The weekend has become so much more than I could imagine. Caleb hasn't left my side, for which I'm grateful. I'm not sure what I would have done without him. He's my rock, my champion. He's listened as I've talked, held me while I've cried, most importantly, he's been a comforting presence, making sure I'm not alone with my thoughts.

After our initial meeting, I talked to Di on the phone, and she confirmed Sarah's story. She cried tears of joy when I told her where I was, telling me I needed to update her after the weekend and how proud she was of me. That had me crying, too. Cue more Cal cuddles.

Today, we are heading home. But first, we've arranged to visit Sarah and Tim at home.

We've talked a lot about the past, and she's helped clarify what memories are real and what are the figments of a little girl's imagination. Today, I'm meeting my half-siblings.

"April, do you want to come and see my dolls?" Lois says, coming to stand next to me.

"Lois, leave April alone," Sarah says, shooting me a look of apology.

Lois is seven, and Nick is five. Their childhood is the opposite of mine. They're being raised in a loving and stable home, but the resentment I thought I'd feel isn't there.

"It's fine," I say, smiling at the younger girl who's been eyeing me up since our arrival.

I stand up only to have my hand grabbed by a much smaller one as I'm pulled from the room. As I leave, Nick distracts Caleb with a multitude of toy cars. Looks like we both have our hands full.

Lois leads me into her bedroom. I take in the pink decor and smile.

"Is pink your favourite colour?" I ask, taking a seat on the beanbag Lois points to. Hundreds of stuffed toys and a large wooden doll's house fill the space.

"It is," she says, handing me a doll. "She's my favourite, but you can play with her."

I look up in surprise to find little eyes shining at me.

"Thank you," I say, my chest suddenly feeling a little tighter than usual.

"My Granny, mummy's mum, says she used to play dolls with you. *Play for hours.*" Lois's words steal my breath.

Does my grandmother talk about me?

"She always gets a sad look on her face. I think she's going to be very pleased to see you again," Lois says, handing me a set of dolls clothes.

The innocence of the child in front of me surprises me. It's clear I've not been the dirty little secret I assumed I'd be. Instead, it looks like they've been waiting for me to come home.

Surely not.

I sit on the floor and play dolls with my little sister for the next hour. She chats non-stop, telling me about her best friend, how she started dance lessons, even about a boy at school, who is a real pain. When I tell her I teach dance classes, that's it. She gets changed into her ballet clothes and shows me what she's been learning.

We practise some steps, and I teach her the dance I've been teaching the children her age. That's how Sarah finds us.

"Ah," Sarah says, smiling from the doorway.

"Mummy, April is a ballet teacher. She runs her own dance school. She's been teaching me a dance she teaches her children."

Sarah looks at me, her eyes shining with an apology, as if Lois has somehow put me out.

"She's got all the hallmarks of being a great little dancer. Taking after her big sister," I say, ruffling Lois's hair, letting Sarah know everything is fine.

Sarah's eyes well up as she looks between me and her youngest daughter.

Whatever this is between us, is going to take time. I think we both know that. There will be plenty of tiptoeing around one another. But I hope one day, we'll be able to have some sort of relationship. I get the feeling Sarah desperately wants to make everything okay. But I can't rush it. I can't open myself up—it's not who I am.

"Can we show Daddy and Caleb?" Lois says, jumping up and down. "You can dance with me. Big sister, little sister." She grabs my hand once more and pulls me towards the door.

"I think Caleb is playing cars with your brother and Dad," Sarah says as I'm pulled past her and out of the door.

We find Caleb and Tim with Nick on the floor of the living room. Caleb appears to have built a car park out of old boxes. There's even a ramp leading to the upper levels. When I look more closely, I see that there's also a road system.

"What have we here?" I say, standing in the doorway, Lois still clutching my hand.

Caleb looks up, his eyes sparkling, as he catches our joined hands. "I told Nick I build buildings, so we built a garage to house his toy cars."

"Impressive," I say, my heart melting a little more as I watch my billionaire lover play with a stranger's child on the floor of their living room.

"It's sturdy, too," Tim says, clearly impressed.

"Daddy, April's been teaching me a dance," Lois says, stepping into the room. "Do you want to see it?"

Tim turns his attention to his daughter. "I'd love to."

Lois scowls at the mess the boys have made, and I bite my lip to hide my smile. Tim looks at his daughter. "Although I think you might have to show me somewhere else."

Lois's scrunched-up face smooths. "I could dance it on the lawn. It's dry and not too cold," she says.

"I want to learn a dance," Nick says, his little bottom lip sticking out.

It's my turn to step into the room. I crouch down next to my little brother.

"Boys don't dance," Lois says, clearly not wanting to share this moment with her brother.

I turn and smile at her. "They do. I have lots of boys who attend my dance school."

Lois tilts her head and stares at me wide-eyed. "Really? We don't have any boys in our class."

"They don't all do ballet," I tell her. "There are lots of different types of dancing."

"So, can I do a dance?" Nick asks.

"You can," I say, touching his hair before I can stop myself.

There's a small noise behind me, and I look to find Sarah in the doorway. Her hand over her mouth, her eyes full.

"Sorry," she says before turning and leaving the room.

Tim goes to stand, but I put a hand on his arm. "Let me go," I hear myself say. Knowing somehow, it's me she needs to speak to.

Lois reaches for me. "Stay with your daddy a moment. I want to talk to Mummy."

Lois nods her head, her eyes falling on the structure Caleb has made for her brother.

I leave the room, finding Sarah in the kitchen bent over the sink, her head bowed. She senses me enter, and turns to face me, her eyes puffy and bloodshot.

"Sorry," she says, giving me a weak smile.

I move into the room and lean against the counter opposite her.

She wipes her face with her hands. "I'm just being silly," she says.

"Why silly?" I ask, not sure I understand. She invited me here.

Is this not what she wanted?

"Maybe silly is the wrong word. Seeing you on the floor with your brother and sister. Hearing them talk to you… it's a dream come true." Her voice catches, but she shakes herself. "They've always known about you. That one day you might come home, and they would get to meet you."

I stare at her, not sure what to make of her statement. I picked up on Lois's comment earlier, but this is different.

"Why?" I ask, unable to keep the surprise from my tone.

Sarah's eyes fill with more tears. "Because it's always been my dream. To have my baby back." The sob she lets out breaks something inside me, and I take the woman who gave birth to me into my arms and rock her while the years of despair come flooding out. I'm not sure when we're joined by the others, but I find myself enveloped in a group hug. Lois and Nick hugging our legs.

"It's okay, Mummy," Lois says. "April's home now."

I bend down and take her face in my hands. "I am," I say, looking up at my mother and knowing the words are true. I've come home, and I will try my hardest to create a future where they are.

Tim and Caleb are standing by the door. Tim's expression does little to hide the emotion he's feeling, and Caleb looks at me, his eyes glowing with—love.

The rest of the day flies by. I teach Nick a dance, and Lois shows her dance. By the end of the day, everyone is exhausted.

"Do you really have to go?" Lois says, clinging onto me, tears streaming down her cheeks. "We've only just found you."

I pull her into my arms. "I promise I'll be back to see you soon," I say, stroking her hair back and wiping her tears, only to have Nick throw himself at me too, nearly knocking me off my feet. He buries his head in my shoulder, and I scoop him up, standing with him wrapped in my arms.

"Don't go," he howls, following his sister's lead.

"Hey guys, April has to work. She's a big sister. So, like Mummy and Daddy, she must go out to earn money," Tim says, stepping forward.

I give Nick one last squeeze before handing him to his dad.

"I will be back, or maybe once I move into my new apartment, you could come and visit me. Maybe you could come to one of my dance classes."

Both children's heads fly up, their eyes going to their parents. "Can we?" they both chime, making me laugh.

"We can discuss it," Sarah says firmly. "April needs to have time to settle into her new apartment."

"Awww, but that will be ages," they chime, making me laugh. Looking at them both, I don't think this is something they'll let drop.

"Or you can stay at mine. I have plenty of room and a pool," Caleb says, all eyes spinning to him. My mouth drops open.

"What?" he says, smirking at me as if my surprise is unfounded.

"You only let the boys stay," I say in my defence.

"I'm a boy, so is Daddy," Nick chirps up.

"That you are," Caleb says, ruffling his hair.

"I want to be a boy," Lois says, her bottom lip wobbling as if she's afraid she's going to be excluded.

"I also let my sisters stay sometimes," Caleb says, smiling down at her. She returns his smile with a watery one of her own. "And I let your sister stay, so I think I can stretch to letting you and your mummy stay."

Lois steps forward, only to have Caleb swing her up and into his arms. "How does that sound?"

"Perfect," Lois says, wrapping her arms around his neck and planting a kiss on his cheek.

"That's sorted then. We just need to arrange a date."

Sarah steps in. "We'll let you get home, and we can put our diaries together," she says, allowing everyone a breather, an out.

I step forward and take her hands in mine.

"I want that," I say, letting her know I want to see them again. "Thank you for a wonderful weekend. It's been more —" My voice catches.

Sarah's hand comes up and cups my cheek.

"It has," she agrees. "I have your number. Is it okay to call?"

I can't keep the smile from my face, knowing that is what I want. I want this. I didn't realise how much I needed it.

"Most definitely," I reply.

Mason is waiting for us by the kerb. More hugs and a few more tears and we make it back on the road.

Caleb takes my hand in his.

"How are you feeling?"

"Like I've been run over by a lorry—several times. But I'm on the mend," I tell him honestly. I'm emotionally drained but in a good way. "Thank you for being here. For having my back," I say, leaning up and pressing my lips to his.

"I would not have been anywhere else," he says.

"You surprise me every day," I tell him honestly.

"Good. That way, you'll never get bored with me," he says, pulling me into his arms and deepening our kiss.

CHAPTER 68

APRIL

Moving day.

Samuel, Dan, Caleb, Gabriel, Scarlett, and Seb, with Leah and baby Callum, directing proceedings from the corner. Harper turns up with a moving-in hamper filled with delicious treats and a couple of bottles of champagne.

"What?" she says, looking at her brother. "There are eight of us. One bottle will never be enough."

Caleb shakes his head, and I laugh at the siblings.

"We're supposed to be working," he says, grabbing another box of something and thrusting it into his sister's arms.

I look around, realising there are a lot of boxes being brought in. Especially seeing I lost everything I owned in the fire.

"Where have all these boxes come from?" I ask, grabbing the scissors and opening the latest one Seb has placed on the side.

Caleb looks at me, his gaze not quite meeting mine. "Caleb?" I say.

"When we went shopping, I made a note of all the things

you liked—throws, pillows. And all the things you'd need. Pots, pans, coffee machine."

I pull open the box and recognise the beautiful faux fur throw I saw when we were shopping. It feels more like a weighted blanket. I did not realise he saw me eyeing it up. Cal had been on his phone.

I drag the blanket out of the box and hug it to me. "It's…" I stare at the thoughtful man in front of me. "Thank you."

I've learned over the weeks and months to accept his gifts. It's something he loves to do. I reach up and place a kiss on his lips. "I love it."

His grin says it all. Twenty more boxes appear, each with their own surprise. Pillows for the sofa, another throw for the enormous bed, Caleb insisted on buying me as it matches his. His argument being he intends to stay over in comfort.

Plates, glasses, cutlery. The list goes on. Kat has sent an enormous bouquet delivered in a beautiful vase.

> *Enjoy your new home.*
> *I included the vase, as I assumed you wouldn't have one yet.*
> *Looking forward to your housewarming*
> *Kat xx*

WHEN I FIRST MET KAT, she was distant. But now. I may be ten years younger, but we're becoming firm friends. Not something I'm used to. Girl friends have been few and far between.

Leah places the flowers on the kitchen island, while Gabriel and Caleb hook up the flat screen TV. The builders have incorporated all the cables into the walls, but the boys make themselves useful drilling holes and arguing about where each bracket goes. Watching the twins is hilarious, especially with Leah rolling her eyes every five minutes.

"Are they always like this?" I ask, stepping into the kitchen.

"Yes." Is all she says laughing.

I walk into my bedroom to find the bed made up, my new throws and pillows skilfully arranged. Harper comes out of the en suite, jumping when she catches sight of me.

"Sorry," she says. "I couldn't resist. I love interior design and fashion. I thought I'd make it welcoming. Heaven only knows, you won't want to be making up your bed after everyone finally leaves."

I stare at the woman who's three years younger than me. She and I could not be more different. She's decked out in designer labels, likes to party hard, and lives her life through social media, yet there's something about her.

"Thank you, Harper. I love it. I would never have thought to dress it like this. It looks amazing," I tell her truthfully.

I would have thrown everything on the bed.

Harper grins, and I realise something. Her older siblings treat her like the baby of the family. But I suspect there's a lot more to Harper Frazer than they realise.

"If you want to dress the sofa or anything else, please feel free. I have the flare of a gnat," I admit.

"Really?" Harper says, as though not truly believing me.

"Really. Your brother has spoiled me, but I'm clueless. If you're willing to help."

"Absolutely. If you ever want a shopping companion," she says. "Not that I'm saying there's anything wrong with your clothes." Her cheeks darken and I laugh.

"Harper, that would be great. I've never had a girlfriend to go shopping with." I laugh.

Harper's eyes widen in surprise.

"I spend all my time at the dance studio," I explain. When she nods, a horrible thought crosses my mind. "I won't be able to shop where you shop. My little business doesn't pay that much. But I'd love to go shopping with you."

"Done deal," she says, coming forward and tucking her arm into mine. "It's all about choosing appropriate items."

It's only then I look around and notice the knick-knacks on the sideboard. A photo frame with pictures of me when I was younger. Me dancing with Di. There's even a picture of me with Sarah, from when I was a baby.

I break free from Harper's grip and move to the chest of draws.

"Where?" I say, turning to find Caleb stood in the doorway.

"I wondered where you disappeared to," he says, stepping into the room.

"I'll leave you to it," Harper says, heading for the door, touching her brother's arm as she leaves.

"Where?" I repeat the question, picking up the photo of me as a baby.

"Sarah sent me some photos. She has an album from when you lived with her. I also spoke to Di. She gave me the ones of you dancing."

A lump forms in my throat as I take in the photographs and their frames. My smile spreads when I see one of myself and Caleb. I remember the moment. We are lying on a picnic blanket in the park.

There's another one of us with his family, taken at his mother's birthday.

"You don't have to keep that one," he says, stepping up behind me, wrapping his arms around my waist.

"Why?" I turn my head and stare into his eyes. "I love it. I may have to move these out of my bedroom, however…"

"Excellent plan," Caleb adds, scooping them up, leaving only the pictures of me and him on the chest of draws. "These can go into the living room."

He drops a kiss on my nose, and I spin in his arms, wrapping my own around his neck. "This is wonderful," I say.

"You can show me how wonderful later." He drops a kiss on my lips, just as Gabriel barges in.

"Put her down," he says, covering his eyes and making me laugh. "You have a houseful of people."

We both laugh, Caleb's arms still around my waist.

"The boys have arrived," he says, as Caleb groans.

I look at him, half amused, half surprised.

"They wanted to wish you a happy housewarming," Caleb says, looking apologetic. I step out of his arms and grin.

"Really?" I can't believe how much love everyone is showing me as I make my way back into the main room.

"There's the lady of the hour," Tristan shouts, pointing to the three cases of wine he's placed on the kitchen unit.

"I hope that's the good stuff," Caleb says from behind me, and I shoot him a look.

"Only the best for your girl," Tristan says, winking at me.

I approach him and give him a hug.

"Thank you," I say, trying hard not to let the emotion show in my voice.

He looks down at me and smiles, the warmth in his eyes, letting me know he's here because he's chosen to be.

"Don't forget us," Quentin and Xander say in unison, both holding presents wrapped with enormous bows.

I can't keep the smile off my face as I approach them both, taking their gifts and giving them both a kiss on the cheek.

"She's mine," Caleb says, growling at his friends, while it's my turn to smirk.

"We know," they all say together, holding up their hands and laughing. Caleb's possessiveness sending a warm fuzzy feeling through me. I experienced the same feeling when he was approached at dinner. I never thought I'd have possessive thoughts towards anyone. But where Caleb Frazer is concerned, *he's mine.*

The impromptu housewarming party goes on late into the night. With no-one else living nearby, there's no risk of my neighbours complaining. By the time Caleb and I fall into our new bed, I'm happy Harper had the foresight to make it up. I sink into its comfort and groan in delight.

"You're only supposed to make those sounds when I'm touching you," Caleb says, pulling me into his arms and spooning me from behind.

"And I do, but this mattress."

Caleb chuckles in my ear. "That's okay. You can moan at the mattress and me in the morning, but right now, I think we both need some sleep."

"Deal," I say, snuggling into his arms, my eyes drifting closed. "I love you," I say, before the world goes dark.

CHAPTER 69

CALEB

I walk into Mount Crystals to find my sisters already at the table. I shouldn't be surprised. Despite their age gap, these two are getting closer.

"There he is," Kat says, getting up and dropping a kiss on my cheek.

Harper does the same.

"No, April?" Harper says, sounding disappointed. She seems to have hit it off with April. I see her name popping up on April's phone all the time.

"No, she's got a choreography job in Manchester. Working on a pop video for some rockstar," I say, almost spitting out the final words. Lucas is April's age and gorgeous, with a string of women following him around.

I watch my sister's try to smother their grins, but they fail miserably.

"Don't laugh at me," I say. "I came here for advice. If you're just going to take the piss, then I'll leave."

They both squirm before sitting more upright in their chairs, shooting each other a look.

How did I think this was going to be a good idea?

I need a woman's perspective otherwise I'd be talking to Gabe.

"What kind of advice?" Kat asks.

"April told me she loves me," I say, quickly.

Harper squeals and claps her hands, while Kat sits and stares at me.

"What's the problem?" Kat asks.

I run a hand through my hair before placing both hands on the table. "She was falling asleep when she said it and she hasn't said a word since."

My heart rate had picked up at her words, but then there had been silence followed by her gentle snore. When we woke up the next morning, I made love to her, but nothing. It was like I imagined those three little words.

Both women's faces take on an identical expression, furrows appearing between their brows. Only Kat has dark hair, while Harper is still in her purple phase.

"Have you asked her?" Harper says, clearly confused.

"No. I want her to tell me of her own free will. What if I misheard her? I could scare her off. She's got a lot going on. She's about to head off to choreograph for *bloody* Lucas Sommerfield's music video - the rockstar stud! I don't need her to think I'm some possessive and jealous jerk."

I run a hand over my face before sighing and my sister's chuckle.

"I don't think you have anything to worry about where Lucas is concerned," Kat says, laughing into her drink. "I'm not sure he's April's type."

"Not helping," I huff, unsure who this new Kat is. "Look, I'm trying to be patient. She's moved into her own apartment. I stay over, take her to dinner. With everything going on with her birth mother. Now her grandmother wants to meet her. The grand opening of the studio, her choreography." I pinch the bridge of my nose and tail off, knowing I'm being selfish.

"You don't want to add to the pressure you feel she's already under?" Kat asks.

I nod.

"But Caleb, what about your needs?" she asks softly.

I look at my sister, shocked.

This isn't about me.

"Relationships are two ways. They're not all give. You have to receive something, too. If not—"

Kat doesn't finish her sentence. She's got the wrong end of the stick.

"I do," I say, not wanting to put any negative thoughts towards April.

"Does April make you happy?" Harper asks.

"More than anyone I've ever dated before," I tell them honestly. "I can't imagine life without her."

"Then you need to tell her that," Harper says.

I sigh. "I've told her I love her," I tell them both, causing their eyebrows to raise and a smile to appear on both their lips.

"What did April say when you told her?" Kat asks.

"April's past makes it difficult for her to trust. People she loved have let her down. First her birth mother, then her foster parents. I think she wants to believe me, I get that." I tell them honestly.

"And you, dear brother, until April, have been a commitment phobe," Harper says.

I tilt my head at my sister. "Thanks, sis."

But she's right. I never believed I could find love until now.

"You're welcome," she says with a grin.

I take a sip of the wine the waiter has poured, staring at the liquid.

"How can I make her believe I'm not going to simply walk away when and if the going gets tough? Let her know my playboy days are over. She's the only woman I want. Will ever want."

I look across the table at my older sister.

"Are we doomed?" My heart rate picks up at the thought of losing April.

Kat smiles and shakes her head. "No. Don't be so dramatic! April has spent much of her life emotionally alone. She moved families, grew to trust and feel safe, then she moved again. All you can do, is what you're doing now. Be there for her. Make her laugh. Support her. Love her... be your annoyingly cheerful self. Show her, she's no longer alone, that you have her back. That we all do. But also remember April isn't used to our world," She pauses and leans forward, resting her hand on my arm. "Caleb, you're my brother, and I love you dearly, but that playboy image of yours was always going to bite you in the ass one day. You need to be patient, give her time. There's no rush. She's not going anywhere. If April comes to you, your relationship will be cemented. If you force it, she may always have doubts. But also remember, if you come out to the world, you'll be thrusting her and her past into the limelight. You chose to put yourself in the spotlight, April hasn't. She needs to know you'll have her back whatever happens. This is a big deal for her."

Shit, she's right.

I run a hand down my face, knowing my sister speaks the truth, never one to beat around the bush.

I've invited the press in for years. What until now has worked in my favour, could very well be what destroys my future. My father warned me years ago, when I first opened that door, I'd never be able to shut it again. The press will take the good, the bad and the ugly if you let them. I just pray I can protect April from it.

I lean forward, resting my elbows on the table, cradling my head.

Harper huffs, making me look up. "April isn't a wounded bird in need of rescuing. She's a grown ass woman, who has spent her entire life rescuing herself. She's independent and strong. A survivor. You've said so yourself. April loves you. Anyone with eyes in their head can see that. But you, my dear brother, hold all the cards."

I stare at my little sister, my mouth slightly agape.

"What Harper is trying to say, I think," Kat pipes in. "Is, maybe April doesn't want to mistake love for being indebted to you."

I look between my sisters.

Are they right? Have I swept in?

I've done it from a place of love. I'd do anything for her. Isn't that what you do when you love someone?

"If you want to show her you love her, just be there for her. Show her you've changed. April has been let down all her life, she needs to see you are dependable, you trust her judgement and her feelings. Let her realise she loves you and can't live without you."

My heart stutters in my chest.

What if I have to let her go?

No, that's not an option. I love her. I know she loves me. She shows me every time she lets me into her body, when she laughs at my terrible jokes, when she snuggles into my side. We're connected.

When I think of her leaving, my heart clenches, and pain, unlike anything I've felt before rips through my chest.

"Think about it," Kat says, squeezing my hand. "Talk to her. But be prepared. You may need to let her go so she can find her way back to you."

CHAPTER 70

APRIL

I throw my bag down and pick up my phone. One thing this past two weeks away has told me is, I love Caleb Frazer, and I want to be with him. No more messing. I'm all in.

Caleb answers on the second ring. "April, where are you?"

"Hello to you too," I say laughing.

"No I mean it, where are you? I've arrived at your hotel and they told me you checked out."

"You're in Manchester?" I ask, my jaw dropping.

"I am," he says, and I can just picture his hand running through his hair in frustration.

"I'm at home, in my apartment. We finished early. I came home to surprise you," I say, biting my lip when he growls. "Surprise!" I say.

Cal groans. "I was going to surprise you. I had some business up here. I thought while you were working with your *rock star.* I could keep you company out-of-hours."

His husky tone never fails to send shivers of pleasure south.

"It's the thought that counts," I chuckle, although I would

have liked nothing better than to snuggle up next to Caleb after a day of dealing with Lucas and his asshole brother. "When will you be back?"

"Late tomorrow night," he sighs. "I have some meetings in the morning, then Mason and I will be on the road."

"Until tomorrow night then, I missed you," I tell him honestly.

"Not as much as I missed you."

My week choreographing with Lucas Sommerfield was an eye-opener. His brother/manager/record-producing big brother is a tyrant, but he was pleased with the results, so I made it home in record time.

"I love you, I'll see you tomorrow," I say.

Cal groans loudly, making me pause. "Say it again."

"What? *See you tomorrow*?" I tease.

"No, little dancer." My phone beeps, requesting a switch to video call.

I accept, my breath catching when I see his face.

"Hey," I say softly, losing myself in his dark eyes.

"Hey, you," he says back. "Say it again."

"I love you, Cal Frazer. But I've already told you that."

Cal drops his forehead against the phone. "I thought you were dreaming," he says.

"What, dreaming that I love you?" I ask, loving the vulnerable side he lets me see.

Caleb Frazer, to the rest of the world, is cocky and confident. Sure, of himself. To me, he's Cal, with the same vulnerabilities and insecurities as everyone else.

"But you didn't repeat it in the morning," he says, pulling the phone away and closing his eyes.

"If I remember correctly, I woke up to your mouth on my pussy and then your phone going soon afterwards. You were late meeting your mother. From what I remember, we were laughing too hard trying to find your underwear."

"Point taken," he says, grinning, "but you can say it as many times as you like from now on. Just so you know."

I roll my eyes and chuckle. "Don't worry, you'll be sick of hearing it. I promise."

He pulls back, his face becoming serious.

"I love you, April Wilson. I can't believe I'm here and you're there."

He moans again as if in pain.

"Come home to me as soon as you can," I say.

"You can count on it."

We eventually end the call. I throw myself back on the bed, before picking up my phone.

ME:

What are you doing tonight?

SAMUEL:

Are you back?

ME:

I am

SAMUEL:

Tristan's Bar - the guy promised me some wine!

ME:

Perfect.

I get ready and meet Samuel at Tristan's wine bar. Tristan greets us both with a grin and an open bottle.

"For the tickets," Tristan says, placing the bottle on the table in front of us.

I raise an eyebrow.

"He got me tickets for the show he's in," Tristan admits.

"A lady?" I ask.

Tristan shakes his head, and Samuel laughs.

"His mother wanted to see it. I got her backstage passes to meet the lead," he explains.

Tristan takes a seat and joins us. It's not long before Quentin and Xander are pulling up a chair.

"Heard you two were out and about," Quentin says, ordering another bottle of wine. "Where's your other half?" he directs at me.

"Manchester," I say, a little surprised they don't already know this. "He's due back tomorrow night."

"Don't look so surprised. Since you came on the scene, Caleb doesn't write, he doesn't call," Tristan says, pretending to wipe a tear from his eyes. "He's a changed man, and it's all down to you."

"A Marcus, two-point-zero," Xander adds, laughing.

I know how much the guys rib Marcus about having settled down, although I know they all envy him for his family life. Caleb has explained their aversion to commitment and why.

"When are you putting our buddy out of his misery and moving back in?" Quentin asks, only to be thumped hard by Xander.

"Quentin," he hisses.

"I'm just asking. It's clear they're mad about each other."

I stare at the guys in front of me, and Samuel laughs.

"See, I'm not the only one," he says.

"Don't you start," I tell him.

"Start what?" he asks. "That you need to take a leap of faith. That if you want a guarantee, buy a washing machine."

I roll my eyes. It's not the first time he's used these lines on me.

"Don't roll your eyes, baby girl. Even Caleb's friends are saying he's a changed man. The guy loves you. You love him, whether you've admitted it or not. There are no guarantees in this life. But I get it if you're too scared to take a chance at true happiness in case you get hurt—"

"It's not just that," I say, my eyes moving to Quentin. "This is where you come in. I need your help."

* * *

My phone pings, and I'm surprised to see Caleb's name flash up.

CALEB:
Where are you?

ME:
Out with Samuel

I hit send, missing him more than I thought possible. It's only until tomorrow.

ME:
Where are you?

CALEB:
In your bed

His answer fires back instantly. *What? Is he serious?*

ME:
I thought you had a meeting in the morning.

CALEB:
I do, but that's what early starts and private planes are for.

ME:
We really need to discuss your carbon footprint. However, I will be home in ten minutes.

I look up to find the guys all staring at me.

"She's a goner," Tristan says

"He's a goner. Another one bites the dust," Xander chants.

"Go, baby girl. Go and see your man."

"How?" I ask.

"You get this moony look, and the tension just left your shoulders."

I stand up. "Whatever." I laugh. "Thanks for an eye-opening evening," I say.

"I'm on it," Quentin says as I make to leave.

I turn and smile at him. "Thank you. Enjoy the rest of your evening gents."

"You too."

They catcall after me.

I manage to catch a taxi directly outside, giving him the address of the dance studio. I take the stairs two at a time, pausing outside the door to catch my breath. The door, however, is thrown open, and I'm swept up and into his arms.

Cal kicks the door closed behind us and dives onto the bed, pinning me beneath him. "I love you," he says.

"I love you," I say, lifting up and kissing the tip of his nose.

He rolls onto his back, pulling me with him so I'm sprawled on top of him. He exhales.

"God, how I've missed you this past week," he says, pulling me into his arms and holding me tight as if he never wants to let me go.

I swing a leg over his waist until I'm sitting astride him. His cock grows hard beneath me. The skirt Harper encouraged me to buy spreads out around us.

"I think we need to celebrate," I say, rocking against him, my body readying itself, my desire for this man soaking my panties.

I kneel and push down Caleb's sleep shorts, freeing his

cock. It springs up between us, and we both moan with need. I kick off my panties and climb back astride him, Caleb's hands sliding under my skirt and gripping my thighs. I rub myself up and down his cock, driving us both wild as he glides along my slit. I rise up and lower myself down on him, the swollen head of his cock stretching my opening before pushing in. We both groan as I lower myself slowly onto him.

"God, you feel good," he says, his fingers flexing against my leg muscles.

"So do you," I say, tilting my hips, making him hit that magic spot inside me. I rotate my hips, rising and falling until we are both a panting mess.

We continue until he pulls me forward, his mouth latching onto mine.

"I love you, April. More than I will ever be able to show you."

"The feeling's mutual. More than I ever believed I could," I say.

Our mouths fuse, our bodies taking and giving to each other until we fly over the precipice into the abyss.

When we both come down, we lay locked in each other's arms while our breathing evens out.

"I'm glad you came home," I tell him.

"Always," he says, and that's the last thing I remember.

CHAPTER 71

CALEB

> APRIL
>
> Call me

I end the meeting I'm in and pick up the phone.

"April?" I say the moment she answers.

She sounds breathless. "What's going on?"

"I've been given a Service to the Community Award. I'm going to be presented with it next month," she says, her excitement palpable. "I can't believe it."

"Congratulations, little dancer. You deserve it. The community want to tell you how much they appreciate all you've done for their children and the neighbourhood."

I'd already heard April had been nominated. It doesn't surprise me. She's loved more than she will ever realise, and has had such an impact on the lives she surrounds herself with.

"Will you come with me?" she asks suddenly, taking me by surprise.

"I'll be there. Wild horses wouldn't keep me away," I tell her.

THE PLAYBOY BILLIONAIRE

She goes quiet. "That's not what I asked."

"No, it's not, and I will be there, but I won't be there with you. This is about you, April. We haven't announced our relationship to the world yet. I refuse to take the limelight away from you. This is your special night."

There is silence over the phone.

"I love you," she says.

"And I love you. This has nothing to do with love. I don't want this to distract us from our path just because this has come up. I respect you too much. I will be there, sneak a kiss when no one is looking, and cheer you on from the sidelines. When we get home, I will tell you exactly how proud I am of you, but that is private. When we decide to come out to the world. It will be because you are ready, not because it's been forced upon you."

"Okay," she says, almost too quickly.

"My family and the guys will also be there. I'm sure Sarah and Di would also like to attend. I'm happy to have them stay at the apartment if they want to."

I can almost see her smile. "They'll love that. I'll call them now," she says. "Caleb. I love you. More than I can ever show you or tell you."

"I know. But we are doing this on our timeline, no one else's."

She ends the call, and I can't help but feel disappointed that she didn't fight harder. Will she ever be ready to announce us to the world?

* * *

WATCHING APRIL TAKE THE STAGE. My heart is in my throat. She steals my breath like no other woman. The presenter gives a speech introducing April and all she's done for the community. A cheer goes up, and those in the community who have come to support her get to their feet and cheer. Her table does the same. Sarah, Di, Tim, and Julian, along with Samuel and Dan, are on their feet. April turns to the audience, her eyes glistening. She accepts the award with grace. She's brought a community together, and now they're thanking her.

"She looks stunning," Harper whispers in my ear.

I turn and grin at my sister.

She laughs. "You should see the goofy look on your face. You, my brother, are completely done for."

"I'm not denying it," I admit, returning my gaze to April as she thanks everyone, her eyes locking on mine.

"This means a lot to me. But this award is to the whole community. We've stood together shoulder to shoulder to support one another. They say it takes a village to raise a child. That's what we're doing, supporting one another. You are my family, and as a foster child growing up, family is important."

A loud cheer goes up from the crowd. Many of the community members have come to support April this evening.

She turns to my table, her eyes locking on mine. "I'd also like to thank Francesca Frazer and the Frazer Foundation. What you are doing for our community will make a world of difference, and you're offering children like I was, a way of following their dreams. Finally, Caleb Frazer. He's made this possible. He and Frazer Development have rebuilt my dreams from literal ashes and helped provide a safe space for our current community. Thank you."

I tip my head in acknowledgement. I intend to show her exactly how proud I am of her later after I drop her mother, Tim, Di, and Julian, back at my apartment.

April inclines her head as she looks at me.

"Before I go, and allow you good people time to enjoy the

beautiful food and wine. There's one more thing I want to say. Someone told me recently that I should buy a washing machine if I want a guarantee. That life doesn't come with any. Sometimes, we have to take a leap of faith. Someone threatened to expose something from my past a few months ago." Her eyes lock on mine. "I've decided to own it. No one should have power over another through fear or intimidation. Fear that has nearly held me back from finding true happiness." She shoots me a shy smile. "Those I care about now know the secret I've kept hidden for the past two years, that includes my community, as they are my family. My big secret turned out to be not so big to them." April chuckles.

"We love you, April," someone shouts from the back, making her laugh.

"A press release has gone out this evening, it explains how I raised the initial money to buy my dance school as an exotic dancer at Merryfellows."

A gasp goes up around the room.

What the hell is April doing?

A hand clamps down on my arm, and I realise I've gone to stand.

"Listen," Quentin hisses in my ear.

I sink back into my chair, my eyes never leaving the woman I love who is standing on the stage, sharing her journey.

"I spent four years earning enough money to open my dance studio. Merryfellows was a means to an end and allowed me, an ex-foster kid, to follow my dreams. That path led me to my community, to helping the kids who needed somewhere to go. But still, fate wasn't done with me. She had her own plans." Her eyes lock on mine. "She led me to Caleb Frazer, a man who has not only saved my business, and our community, but showed me my past doesn't need to define me, that I'm a survivor. Caleb, I'm sorry I ever doubted you.

You're one in a million, and you have changed my life and stolen my heart. You said when I was ready. Well, I'm ready now. Tonight, I walked in here without you by my side. I never want to stand anywhere without you next to me."

Quentin lets go of my arm, and I'm on my feet, heading towards the stage. I climb the steps two at a time and sweep April into my arms, burying my head in her neck.

"You told me to own it. I spoke to Quentin, and he told me they can only use my past against me if I let them."

I pull back and cup her face in my hands, dropping my lips to hers.

"I love you, little dancer," I whisper against her lips. "I don't give a rat's ass about your past or what anyone else thinks, but I know you do. You are the kindest, bravest, and most selfless person I have ever met."

"I love you."

"Good, 'cause you're stuck with me now. You just told the world we're together."

Cameras are going off all around us, and a cheer goes up when I kiss her this time.

Loud whoops go up from April's table, where her foster mum and dad, Sarah, and Tim, Samuel and Dan, and a host of April's dance students are all sitting. Our table follows suit. Tristan, Quentin, and Xander make the most noise of all. Seb, Scarlett's husband, is holding her while she sobs into his shoulder. Meanwhile, Kat, Harper, Gabriel, and Leah are grinning like Cheshire Cats.

I smile down at April, pulling her to my side.

We leave the stage, only to be surrounded by our friends and family.

"I've got it covered," Quentin says in my ear. "Control the narrative."

Her fear has always been unfounded, but I know it has

bothered her. I squeeze my friend's shoulder as a sign of my appreciation.

"Darling, I am so happy for you," my mother says pulling me down for a hug, having finally let go of April. "You can celebrate later, however, tonight is still about April." Her face getting serious. "You hold on to that woman, and don't you ever let her go."

"I have no intention," I tell her truthfully.

"You really love her." My mother's knowing tone has me staring down into her face. "It's there for all to see. I remember seeing that same look in your father's eye. It took me a while to recognise it, but when I finally did, I was gone, too."

I reach over and squeeze her hand. I'm not sure how she survived his death. I'm not sure I could if anything happened to April. Their love was monumental.

She smiles and grips my hand.

"I'm glad you've found her," she says, her eyes moving to April, surrounded by those who love her.

Samuel looks over and winks. His grin unmissable.

CHAPTER 72

APRIL

The news of Caleb and my relationship takes on a life of its own, but he is by my side every step of the way.

Before the award ceremony, I took Quentin's advice and spoke to Sarah, as well as my students' parents. Sarah was upset, but more because I was forced to give up on my conservatoire dream. As I told her, it was meant to be. If I hadn't left and worked at Merryfellows, I would never have bought the dance school or met Caleb. I may never have reconnected with her. Things happen for a reason. Not always obvious at the time. Most of the parents had simply shrugged and told me it was none of their business—I was an amazing teacher, and that was all that mattered.

The dance studio is swarmed with press and photographers, so much so Elijah has used one of his contacts to employ a security firm. It's not all been a bed of roses. There are also plenty of hate messages. Caleb Frazer fangirls and boys saying he can do better. We've decided to ignore them. Cal only has eyes for me, something he has shown me time and time again. I'm a survivor, and it will blow over, even if it is unpleasant. I'm staying off social media for the time being, and there is no point in fuelling the fire.

I've moved back into the penthouse. The dance school has become inundated with applications since I received my award. As more and more of the new development goes on the market, the number of people wanting to sign up for classes is increasing. As a result, I've employed a manager. She's moving into the apartment above the studio tomorrow, which is the reason I've been able to take today off.

Today, I packed up all my photos and soft furnishings and moved them *home*.

I hear the door to the penthouse open and step out of the kitchen. "How was your day?" I ask.

"Even better now, I know you're going to be here every night when I get home," he says, pulling me into his arms and dropping a kiss on my lips.

I smile against his mouth, and he takes the opportunity to deepen the kiss, his tongue stealing into my mouth, teasing mine. I groan as he pulls me flush against him, his cock pressed against my stomach, showing me exactly *how* pleased.

We make quick work of our clothes, Cal laying me out on the large rug in his living area. My throws, cushions, and photographs are now strategically placed around the apartment.

"Beautiful," he says, looking down at me. I graze my nails down his chest, teasing his nipples until they are hard pebbles under my fingertips. He draws one of mine into his mouth, teasing it with his tongue while his thumb torments the other.

When we are both panting, he lifts one of my legs, placing it over his shoulder. He leans forward and groans as the tip of his cock grazes my wet entrance. He slides in easily, my body welcoming his. I bite my lip at the sensation, my fingers digging into his forearms.

"That's so deep," he groans, and I move my hands to link them behind his neck, pulling him down towards me. My flexibility means he slides in deeper as I draw his face to mine, letting out an even deeper groan as I split with him deep inside me.

"Fuck me," he says, making me chuckle.

"I thought that was what I was doing?" I say, capturing his bottom lip between my teeth and sucking down, my leg between our shoulders.

He rolls his hips and deepens our kiss, our tongues tangling while he slides in and out of my pussy. I untangle my leg from his shoulder and wrap my legs around his hips. We pick up our pace, and I rotate my hips until he's hitting the magic spot only Caleb can find. I moan into his mouth as his pubic bone connects with my clit.

"I love you," I tell him breathlessly as my orgasm slams into me.

He picks up the pace, his hands sliding under my ass as he buries his head in my neck, pulling me onto him, my quivering pussy milking him until he finally lets out a yell and empties himself into me.

"I love you too, little dancer," he says, rolling onto his back and pulling me with him, our bodies still joined.

I love the feeling of him buried between my legs almost as much as I love the way he's found his way into my heart.

"So now we've come out of hiding, and the world knows about Capril, or is that Apleb," he says, making me chuckle. "How long do you think it will take for me to convince you to marry me?"

"A month," I tell him, dropping a kiss on his lips. His mouth curls up in a smile.

"Why a month?"

"Because if I say yes now, it's too desperate, and I want you to surprise me."

Cal's hands slide into my hair, and he pulls me down for another breath-stealing kiss.

"I can work with that," he says, and he promptly shows me once again how much he loves me.

EPILOGUE

ELIJAH

My phone rings, and I drop my head.
What the fuck does she want?
I answer with a grunt.
"Is that any way to answer the phone to your ex-wife?"
She laughs, and my skin crawls.
"What the fuck do you want, Darra? I'm busy."
"I just thought I'd give you a congratulatory call. My solicitor just called. Our divorce is finalised. You're free."
I sink back into my chair. I knew it was going through today. Our final divorce order. My sham of a marriage is finally over.
"I wanted to thank you for the villa in Tuscany and the apartment in London. Shame about the cottage on the estate, but as your mother pointed out, that's in trust. Lottie will get that eventually, so I class that as a win."
"Why are you calling? Is it to gloat? As I told the solicitor, you're welcome to it. I got what I wanted. Lottie and my company."
Darra sighs. "I'll never understand you."

"Why?"

"Because you didn't need to marry me. You never loved me."

It's my turn to sigh. "No, but I thought I got you pregnant. That was on me. I'm not someone who shirks their responsibilities."

That was a dig at Lottie's real dad.

Silence.

"And that is why you hate me so much," she says, a certain sadness in her voice.

Does she wish things had been different?

"Darra, you lied about the pregnancy. You duped me into marrying you. Have spent years using Lottie as a bargaining chip to blackmail me. Lottie may not be my blood, Darra, but she'll always be my daughter. That's not something you have ever understood. What I don't understand is—why me?"

There's more silence. "I couldn't let *her* have you."

I stare at the phone in my hand. "What the hell are you talking about?"

"Don't play dumb, Eli. I used to see how you looked at her, how the two of you were, with your in-jokes and nerdy, geeky computer talk. She was so madly in love with you. Even your bloody family has always preferred her and wanted her. I've never been able to compete."

"What are you talking about?"

"Penelope Dawson," she hisses.

"There was never any competition. Pen was my friend. She was *our* friend." I say, but knowing that is not entirely true.

"She was never *my* friend," Darra mocks.

"Fine. But she was mine," I say honestly.

I've never admitted, not in years, what I lost when Darra announced she was pregnant.

That day, I lost my best friend, the only person who truly saw me, and not just the Frazer heir. I'll never forget the look on her face or the pain in her eyes.

"Even your family sided with her," she continues.

"What are you talking about? There were no sides. You were my wife."

"They loved her, made me feel like an outsider."

"That's not true."

Although maybe it is. After our marriage, Darra quickly took on the role of Lady-of-the-Manor, ordering staff around and demanding more and more of me. My parents were not fans. It was not the way my family worked. My mother tried. She took her pregnant daughter-in-law under her wing and tried to incorporate her into our way of life. But her endgame became clear as her parents began wrangling invites to every social event and party using our name.

"Ironic that you're finally single, and she's now engaged to be married. She got tired of waiting and caught herself a billionaire."

My blood runs cold at her words, but I refuse to let her poison taint me anymore.

"Goodbye, Darra."

I end the call and run a hand over my short hair.

I pull up the news feed.

American Billionaire Kristophe Lansdown announces his engagement to tech titan Penelope Dawson

Below the headline is a picture of the happy couple. Pen is in her usual black, while Kristophe stands awkwardly beside her.

My mind wanders back to my first meeting with Penelope Dawson. A smile forms as I think back to how that first meeting changed the course of my life.

***

Read Elijah and Pen's story in The Broken Billionaire.

For additional scenes and to stay up-to-date with new releases, sign up to my Newsletter at www.zoedod.com

ABOUT THE AUTHOR

Zoe Dod writes emotionally intense billionaire fiction, with complex characters, swoon-worthy romance and a host of plot twists that will leave you guessing until the end. Her books are written in British English.

Prior to becoming a writer, Zoe began her working life as a software development manager in The City of London. In her mid-thirties she retrained as a primary school teacher, and loved teaching children to write and tell stories. She left teaching to spend more time with her family, and it was then she uncovered her love for writing romance.

Zoe lives in The New Forest, Hampshire, England with her husband, two adult children (when they're back from uni) and her four rescue fur babies.

She loves reading and writing. When she's not doing either of those, she's on long walks in The New Forest or attending Zumba classes

Sign up for her monthly Newsletter www.zoedod.com
    You can follow Zoe on
    Instagram: @zoedod_author
    Facebook: Zoe Dod - Author
    Tik Tok: @zoedod_author

ALSO BY ZOE DOD

<u>Forgive Me Series</u>

Always You

Only You

Until You

<u>The Frazer Billionaires</u>

The Donor Billionaire* (Gabriel's story)

The Playboy Billionaire* (Caleb's story)

The Broken Billionaire^ (Elijah's story)

The Ice Queen Billionaire^ (Kat's story)

The Rebel Billionaire^ (Harper's story)

* * *

* Coming 2024

^Coming 2025

Printed in Dunstable, United Kingdom